Sun Ascendant

BOOK 2
THE TARNISHED CROWN SERIES

C.F. DUNN

ISBN 978-1-915981-01-1

Published by Resolute Books
www.resolutebooks.co.uk

For my moma

List of Characters

The Langton family:

The old Earl – died in battle
Duarte Langton – his eldest son – died in battle
The Earl – his second son
Robert Langton – his youngest son
Felice – wife and countess to the Earl
Elizabeth (Bess) – their eldest daughter, married to Lord Dalton
Margaret (Meg) – their second daughter
Duarte – the Earl's son
Cecily – their youngest daughter

Langton retainers and servants

Nicolas Sawcliffe – Master Secretary to the Earl
Hyde – the Earl's steward
Louys – the Earl's esquire
Alun – groom to the Earl
Godfrey – Sawcliffe's clerk
Miles – Robert's esquire
Edgar – groom to Robert
Master Clay – Master of the Kennels
Lady de la Roche – Mistress of the Nursery and aunt to Felice Langton
Joan – chief nursery maid
Alice – nursery maid and maid to Isobel
Kat – nursery servant

The Fenton family:

Sir Geoffrey Fenton
Lady Isobella Wray – his wife
Isobel Fenton – their daughter
Buena – her servant
Arthur Moynes – their steward
Jack – kitchen lad
George – sergeant-at-arms
Adam – sergeant-at-arms
Oliver – the reeve
John – head gardener

The Lacey family:

Thomas Lacey – betrothed to Isobel
Henry Lacey – his father
Lord Ralph Lacey – Thomas's uncle
The Plantagenets:
Edward IV – Edward Plantagenet, King of England and eldest son of Richard, Duke of York
George Plantagenet – Duke of Clarence and younger brother of the king
Richard Plantagenet – Duke of Gloucester and youngest brother of the king
Elizabeth Woodville (formerly Grey) – wife and queen to Edward IV
Henry Plantagenet – Henry VI, King of England
Margaret of Anjou – wife and queen to Henry VI
Edward, Prince of Wales – their son

The Neville family:

Richard Neville, Earl of Warwick – cousin to Edward IV
Isabel Neville, his elder daughter and Duchess of Clarence – wife of George
Anne Neville, his younger daughter and wife of Edward, Prince of Wales (son of Henry VI)
John, Marquis of Montagu – his brother

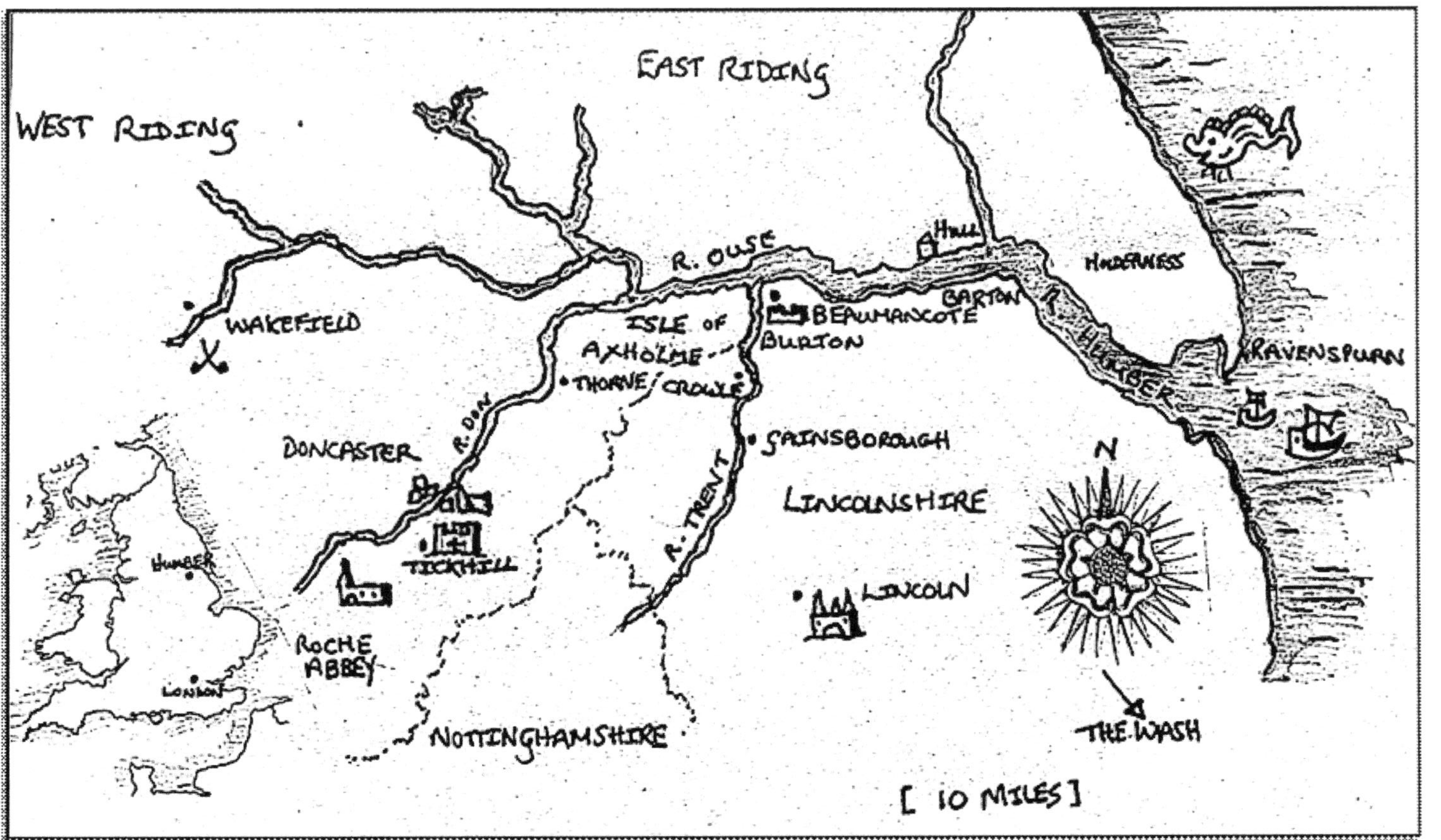
EAST RIDING
WEST RIDING
R. OUSE
HULL
HOLDERNESS
WAKEFIELD
ISLE OF AXHOLME
BEAUMANCOTE
BARTON
BURTON
RAVENSPURN
R. HUMBER
THORNE
CROWLE
DONCASTER
R. DON
GAINSBOROUGH
N
LINCOLNSHIRE
R. TRENT
TICKHILL
HUMBER
LINCOLN
ROCHE ABBEY
LONDON
NOTTINGHAMSHIRE
THE WASH
[10 MILES]

APPROX ROUTE OF THE GREAT NORTH ROAD AND SELECTED BATTLES TO 1471

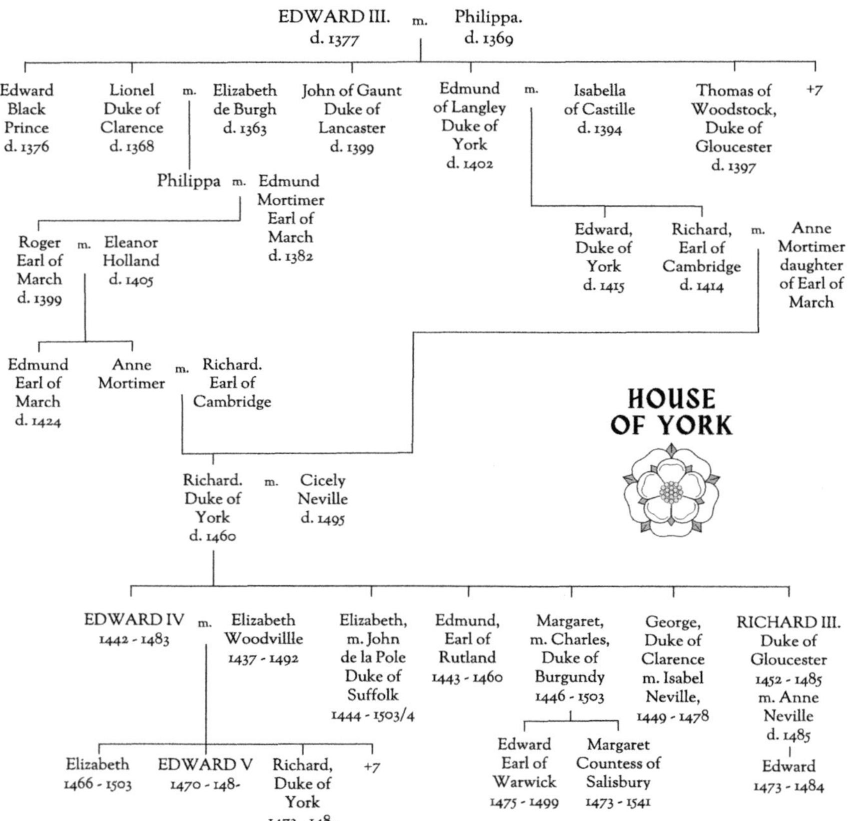
EDWARD III. d. 1377
m.
Philippa. d. 1369
Edward Black Prince d. 1376
Lionel Duke of Clarence d. 1368
m.
Elizabeth de Burgh d. 1363
John of Gaunt Duke of Lancaster d. 1399
Edmund of Langley Duke of York d. 1402
m.
Isabella of Castille d. 1394
Thomas of Woodstock, Duke of Gloucester d. 1397
+7
Philippa
m.
Edmund Mortimer Earl of March d. 1382
Roger Earl of March d. 1399
m.
Eleanor Holland d. 1405
Edward, Duke of York d. 1415
Richard, Earl of Cambridge d. 1414
m.
Anne Mortimer daughter of Earl of March
Edmund Earl of March d. 1424
Anne Mortimer
m.
Richard. Earl of Cambridge
HOUSE OF YORK
Richard. Duke of York d. 1460
m.
Cicely Neville d. 1495
EDWARD IV 1442 - 1483
m.
Elizabeth Woodvillle 1437 - 1492
Elizabeth, m. John de la Pole Duke of Suffolk 1444 - 1503/4
Edmund, Earl of Rutland 1443 - 1460
Margaret, m. Charles, Duke of Burgundy 1446 - 1503
George, Duke of Clarence m. Isabel Neville, 1449 - 1478
RICHARD III. Duke of Gloucester 1452 - 1485 m. Anne Neville d. 1485
Elizabeth 1466 - 1503
EDWARD V 1470 - 148-
Richard, Duke of York 1473 - 148-
+7
Edward Earl of Warwick 1475 - 1499
Margaret Countess of Salisbury 1473 - 1541
Edward 1473 - 1484

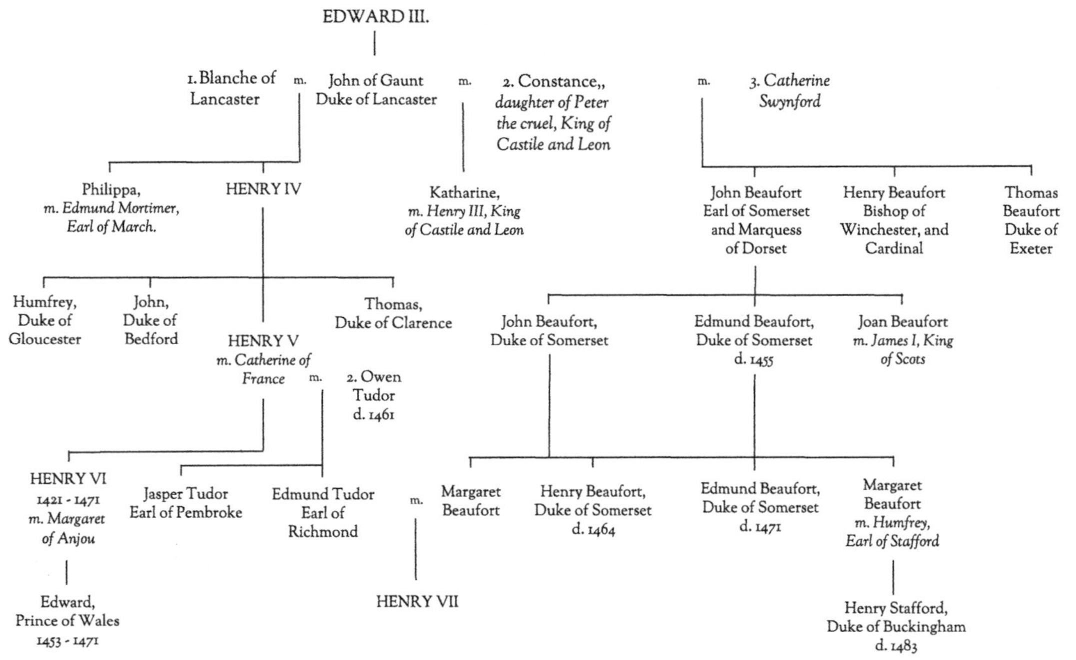

EDWARD III.

1. Blanche of Lancaster m. John of Gaunt Duke of Lancaster m. 2. *Constance,, daughter of Peter the cruel, King of Castile and Leon* m. 3. *Catherine Swynford*

Philippa, *m. Edmund Mortimer, Earl of March.*

HENRY IV

Katharine, *m. Henry III, King of Castile and Leon*

John Beaufort Earl of Somerset and Marquess of Dorset

Henry Beaufort Bishop of Winchester, and Cardinal

Thomas Beaufort Duke of Exeter

Humfrey, Duke of Gloucester

John, Duke of Bedford

HENRY V *m. Catherine of France* m. 2. Owen Tudor d. 1461

Thomas, Duke of Clarence

John Beaufort, Duke of Somerset

Edmund Beaufort, Duke of Somerset d. 1455

Joan Beaufort *m. James I, King of Scots*

HENRY VI 1421 - 1471 *m. Margaret of Anjou*

Jasper Tudor Earl of Pembroke

Edmund Tudor Earl of Richmond m. Margaret Beaufort

Henry Beaufort, Duke of Somerset d. 1464

Edmund Beaufort, Duke of Somerset d. 1471

Margaret Beaufort *m. Humfrey, Earl of Stafford*

Edward, Prince of Wales 1453 - 1471

HENRY VII

Henry Stafford, Duke of Buckingham d. 1483

HOUSE OF LANCASTER

Previously in Wheel of Fortune…

STRONG-WILLED AND single-minded, heiress Isobel Fenton is determined that nothing will separate her from her beloved manor of Beaumancote – even if she does have to marry to stay there. But as unseen witness to a summary execution, she is propelled into the world of personal feud and national politics, and her life will never be the same. Only child of respected knight Geoffrey Fenton, Isobel is left in the protection of the formidable Earl on her father's sudden death. She soon discovers that her former status means nothing in the Earl's household, especially to his bitter Countess; but to the emotionally detached Earl, Isobel is much more than the daughter of his loyal retainer: she holds the key to the power base in a troubled region, and she is about to be married to Thomas Lacey – heir of his enemy for whose peremptory execution he had been responsible.

The country is in turmoil. The Earl of Warwick and the Duke of Clarence foment rebellion. For almost ten years, Edward IV – a physically attractive and charismatic man – has ruled with Warwick's support, but this is about to end. With the Midlands in uproar, King Edward wants peace in the shires, and the last thing he needs is potential trouble in the form of an unwed heiress.

The Earl is unwilling to let Isobel go. He prevents her marrying Thomas Lacey and instead takes her as his mistress. Thwarted in his ambition, and with a deep resentment towards the Earl, Lacey looks for an alternative master and turns to Warwick and Clarence to further his aspirations.

To appease the Countess, Isobel is sent back to her manor only to learn she is in imminent danger from Thomas Lacey. Crossing the frozen moors with Robert Langton, the Earl's younger brother, to evade capture, she returns to the castle and the Earl's iron control. As *Wheel of Fortune* closes, despairing of ever being free, Isobel's frustration erupts into a last, violent bid to end her confinement. With the tip of her blade poised over the Earl's heart, she makes ready to strike.

Prologue

In his haste he had wrenched Isobel's smock, and it now lay twisted around her shoulders, exposing her breast to the nip of the air. Clearly defined by the stronger light of day, the painted figures above her smirked, and she had a sudden urge to punch them, to wipe them out. Their cavorting was meaningless – this was no marriage bed and she no bride. The Earl lay beside her, one arm above his head, oblivious to the world and her ferment. Sudden fury, dormant and smouldering, erupted. Snatching her girdle from the table by the bed, she unravelled the layers and removed the hidden dagger, whispering from its sheath as she withdrew it. Careless of her movements, she kneeled above him with the dagger ready to plunge, her heavy hair almost obscuring the point of penetration. She raised her arm. His eyes flicked open, met hers, and his hand whipped around and grabbed her wrist. She struggled to free it from the vice of his grip as, slowly, he pulled her arm until the point of the dagger lay over his heart. He held her eyes with his. "Kill me." She gritted her teeth, willing herself to strike. "Kill me, Isobel," and he let go of her wrist. Needle-sharp, the dagger dented his skin, the fine black hair of his chest curling around the tip of the blade. Furious, despairing, she pressed harder, drawing from him a sharp breath as the point pierced his skin, releasing a bead of blood. Fascinated, she froze under the watchful grey eyes that willed her on. "Kill me. Release me," and he closed his eyes, the lines between them smoothing as if already in death.

She gasped and sat back, dropping the knife as pity blunted her desire for blood. Covering her face with her hands, she crumpled inside, searing frustration and contrition drowning out revenge as hot tears forced from behind her lashes. The bed creaked as he moved. She felt her hands taken and, keeping her eyes tight shut, waited for his anger to engulf her.

"Do you hate me so much?" he asked, regret seeping softly. "What have I done to you?" She ventured to look at him and found eyes darkened by remorse as he brushed hair dampened with tears from her face. "Where is my Isobel? What have I done to her?" And he leaned forward and very gently kissed her eyelids in turn. She gulped back the emotion lodged in her throat, feeling the heat of his body and a new, unexplained fire in her limbs at this sudden tenderness. Liberating her hands, he captured her face and, sensing the change, his mouth lifted in response. "There she is," he murmured, "my Bel."

"I HAVE FAILED to woo you as a lover should." Leaning on one elbow, the Earl caressed the ankle nearest to him poking from the tumbled covers. "I had… expectations… demands…" he trailed off, gathering his thoughts, and kissed her toes still reddened and itching from freezing the day before.

"When you sent me back home, you did not do it for me, did you?" she asked. "You wanted to use me to trap Thomas."

His hand hesitated on her ankle. "It is not all as it seems—"

"And to get me out of the way." Her lips compressed, unwilling to let go of her resentment and still angry with him for undermining her potent hate. She pulled her leg back under the covers.

"Not all is as it seems," he said again, leaning back against the pillow. A thread of the intricate embroidery decorating the border in scrolls had loosened, tickling his neck. He scratched absent-mindedly. "Sometimes we make decisions that go against the desires of our heart." He turned his head and found her looking at him, more puzzled now than angry, and broadening his accent he declared, "Ee culd eat ket off a midden," throwing the covers back as she pulled a face. "Wait there," he told her when she began to rise, and she flopped back, nonplussed.

Taut-thighed and incongruous in his nakedness, he returned balancing in one hand a large plate with a selection of foods arranged on it in heaps, holding the beaker in the other hand and the gilt wine ewer suspended from two of his fingers, slopping wine. She couldn't help herself; she smiled.

"You might help me rather than laugh at my discomfort? I could not carry the hand-water as well." She took the ewer from him, then, draping his robe around her, she tiptoed to fetch the silver basin with its now cold scented water. She carried it awkwardly, her sore toes catching the edge of his robe and making her wince as she tried to maintain a degree of modesty.

He let her settle back on the bed and disguise herself in the sheet before presenting her with the bowl of water. He watched her wash her hands. "Isobel, you do not need to cover yourself in front of me."

She held the bowl for him without meeting his eyes. "I do, my lord."

He picked up a thin wedge of pie and offered it to her. She went to take it from him, but he held onto it, obliging her to bite off the end. She ate with greater relish than he expected. He smiled at her hunger. "It is hardly *ket*, is it?"

She shook her head, finishing her mouthful. "I do not think your kitchens would dare serve you rank meat, my lord."

He consumed the rest. "No, they would not," he said with an undercurrent of threat. Selecting discs of sausage with segments of preserved pear, he thought he saw her flick a quick look in his direction. "What is it?"

"Will you not punish me?"

His mouth curled. "Do you want me to?" A flash of alarm told him she didn't understand his jest. He fingered his chest where a small patch of blood matted the tangle of hair. "Would you have killed me, Isobel?"

She glanced sideways at his chest, then down at her hands. "I wanted to."

"And do you now?"

He watched the colour of her face ebb and flow before she finally answered. She shook her head. "No."

"Then you have my answer, also."

Chapter 1

Winter 1470

Robert Langton hadn't intended saying goodbye before he left several days later to join the Duke of Gloucester. He thought the timing apt because he felt turned inside out every time he remembered Isobel Fenton, and upside down when he thought of his brother. He had left Martin behind with instructions to join him when healed enough to ride, and taken his few men with him. The Earl had cast a reproving eye over the scant gathering in the bailey.

Robert pulled on his gloves in short, terse tugs. "I have no need to maintain a large retinue at present."

"It would be wise to be seen with more than you have here. A knight on twenty pounds a year could do better. You are able to support a greater retinue than you display."

"As you do?" He straightened the stirrup, but the Earl reached out and stopped him from mounting.

"Yes, I do. I have a position to maintain, and you are my heir. You need to be seen, Rob, not hiding away like some Marcher lord in his barmkin, stealing sheep and robbing his neighbours. Now you are bound to Gloucester you are in a position to build your affinity and to find yourself a wife—" As Robert yanked his arm from his grip and mounted, the Earl said more urgently, "Brother, war is coming. In the name of God give me something to fight for."

Isobel leaned against the cold stone, watching the brothers in the courtyard below, willing Robert to look up just once before he left. She couldn't hear what they said but, once Rob had ridden through the inner gatehouse and out of sight, the Earl spun on one foot and came with angry strides back inside. She retreated to her room.

"Would the priest hear my lady's confession?" Ursula asked.

"He was busy," she evaded, not wanting to admit she couldn't face the man's patronising patience and the shame she felt every time she thought of confessing. And partial confession seemed worse than none at all, like trying to deceive God.

Sitting by the fire, Ursula had taken up Isobel's smock and was mending it with tiny stitches. She hadn't asked how it had come to be torn, nor did Isobel enlighten her, but she thought that she had probably already guessed. Isobel sat opposite her, twiddling her thumbs and thinking about Rob's sudden departure.

"Ursula, what are mistresses supposed to do?"

"Do, my lady?" Ursula blinked. "Give their lord what a wife cannot – or won't."

"What is that?"

Ursula went quiet as she stitched, her mangled hands surprisingly agile. "Respite from the cares of his life, the court, his travail. Give him a little of the life he might have had if he could have chosen it for himself. Love, perhaps."

"How can you say that? He has everything that Lord Robert lacks."

"Does he?" She continued working on the linen, drawing the rent seam together, making the tear invisible. Isobel wished she could do the same for her hurt, for Rob's, then found herself reflecting on the Earl, and an eel-like slither of compassion found its way under her skin for this man who had told her to kill him, begged her to *release* him. He hadn't seemed invincible then, nor so very cruel.

"He has no heart," she said finally, almost to herself.

"Doesn't he?" Ursula said again. "My lady is very young—"

"Do not keep saying that!" Isobel snapped, irritated, or was it because it felt as if her determination to hate this man was being systematically undermined, and what would she have left to fight against then?

"My lady is hungry, perhaps? Or tired?" Ursula said, putting the smock down and rising. "My lord is demanding and forgets you need rest."

Isobel frowned and blushed. "Why are you so patient and forgiving? I never hear you complain even though I know your hands hurt you, and Jesu knows I make your life no easier stuck here like this."

Ursula sat again and held out her hands in front of her, the scars accentuated in the light of the fire like rumpled cloth. "I have nothing to complain about. My good lord lets me live here; I have enough to eat and my lady to serve, and when my boy comes…" She smiled vacantly, letting the words drift with her thoughts.

"Your hands," Isobel ventured tentatively. "Did you fall in the fire?"

"The fire? No, not the fire."

Isobel waited. "Not the fire?" she prompted when it appeared that the pause might stretch into eternity.

Ursula ran a length of thread through the wax of an unlit candle. "This will help make the seam stronger," she said, and began to hum quietly. "Not fire… the Countess… no, no, shhh, not a word, not a word…" She wobbled her head, beginning to rock, and Isobel feared she would lose Ursula's train of thought to a nether world only she and her son occupied.

"The Countess burned your hands?" she pressed. "Why?" Ursula's humming became a thin song, and her eyes rolled. Isobel wanted to shake her but bit back her impatience. "Did you do something to anger her?"

Ursula stopped crooning, grabbing both of Isobel's hands between hers. "Do not make her angry. I merely wanted to please my lord, make him happy; he was so unhappy…" She released Isobel's hands and held out her own before her again. "We were boiling water for her bath, her ladies and I, and someone must have told her about my lord, for she came into her chamber, took hold of my hair and dragged me to where the water heated in a cauldron. I begged for mercy, but she thrust my hands in the water. Not for long. It didn't take long." She smiled sadly. "I didn't see my lord again. He sent me away and found me a husband, and now I have my son and he will come and fetch me. Did I tell you about my son? He is a good boy, dutiful."

Isobel snorted. "The Earl discarded you like… like…" She ground to a halt, aware that this was exactly what she had desired. She pursed her mouth. No, not to be *discarded*, but released, let go – on *her* terms, not his. And why would he do that? Ursula ceased rocking, and now her owl-like face peered at Isobel from the confines of her coif. "Why do you look at me in that way?"

"My lady does not understand. My lord did not forsake me, he saved me. He made me invisible."

Isobel's ire deflated like a popped blister, feeling suddenly very stupid and very young. "Did you love him?" she asked eventually.

"Yes, of course. He is so very fair-featured and noble-hearted. People say the King is handsome, but he knows it too well, although he has a way about him. But my lord was never vain in that way; he would rather be hunting with his dogs than dancing. I did love him. He was kind to me."

"Then… he did not force you?"

Ursula surprised her by clapping her hands and laughing. "Why would he do that?"

Taken aback, Isobel said the first thing that came to mind. "Because he has no heart."

"It is true he did not love me, but he had a heart once, before *she* stole it. But you are here again, and now you can give it back."

"I do not have his heart," Isobel said, a little crossly. "And where else would I be since I cannot be at my manor?"

Ursula might have answered, but a knock at the door forestalled her, and she went to open it. She came back with a fardel of coarse wool, secured with a strip of linen. "There!" Ursula exclaimed, placing it on Isobel's knees. "My lord has sent you a gift."

Mollified to a degree, Isobel unwound the cloth wrapping, revealing a red and white striped piece of fabric with a bell swinging from the end. She held it up, brow screwed in a frown. "Why would I want a hood?"

Ursula gasped and plucked the head-covering from Isobel's hand.

"What are you doing? Give that to me!"

Ursula held it out of reach. "This is not for my lady; there has been a mistake. Perhaps it was meant for me? What will my son say? What will he say?" She began rocking again, clutching the hood to her bony breast.

Isobel retrieved it from her. "For goodness' sake stop that, it is only a hood, although why my lord should send it to me I do not know; this is what servants might wear. Or a jester." She removed her own headdress and replaced it with the new one, laughing as she jangled the bell.

Moaning in horror, Ursula snatched it from Isobel's head. "No, my lady, not servants—" she lowered her voice to a whisper, "—*fille de joie*. In Leicester, it is decreed that all harlots wear them as a mark of their… trade."

In the scant moment it took Isobel to translate the French and the expression on Ursula's face, her mouth fell open in dismay. "Why would he insult me with this?" She shook the hood like a dog with a rat, making the brass bell sing. For a horrible moment, the thought crossed her mind that Robert might have sent it. "Who delivered it?"

"A boy from the kitchens, my lady." Adding insult to injury but leaving her none the wiser. "My lord would not send such a thing to you." For once Isobel had to agree. "My lady must tell him—"

"No," Isobel said quickly, then, "I shall not bother him with this; it is best ignored. Whoever sent it will gain no pleasure from the slander." Re-wrapping it, she hid it in the bottom of her chest beneath her clothes, but it left an ugly taint and every time she looked at the chest she imagined the hood shouting to be released, waiting for recognition.

Chapter 2

"OPEN IT – IT is a gift."

Cautiously, given her last experience of an unexpected gift, Isobel lifted the lid of the padded box only to find another inside: a chequered board in alternating squares of brown wood and white bone. "Oh!" She extricated the folding games box with care, putting it on the table in front of her to examine it more closely. Her finger outlined the carved ivory frieze framing the board with scenes of hunting and music, dancing and courting couples.

"Look inside," the Earl suggested, and she did so, gingerly unlocking it and hearing the rattle of gaming pieces. The interior, as exquisite as the outside, had a pattern of green and white intersecting darts contained within panels of ivory. Isobel selected a pawn with one hand and a carved counter in the shape of a white rose in the other.

"Well?" the Earl asked, perching on the edge of the table, swinging one leg and smiling at her childlike awe. "I cannot have you complaining of being bored when I am away."

"Thank you, my lord," Isobel said quietly. "It is very beautiful."

"Set up a game of tables for us; I have not played it for a while." He slid to his feet and hooked his chair towards him before his page could dash forward to help. "Some wine, I think, and wafers." He ruffled Chouchou's head. "These long evenings are made for entertainment, are they not?"

Isobel removed the chess pieces and selected the discs of green and white bone. "Will you be away long, my lord?"

"Ah, is that why you are quiet?" Taking the green counters, he began laying them on his side of the board. "I must see to the affairs of my estates, and I will be paying a visit to your own manors to ensure their security. His Grace will also expect me at Court. But I should be back for Margaret's wedding, and that is nigh on six weeks from now." He mistook her silence for regret. "I would take you with me, but the days in the saddle are long and I ride hard. Estate business makes for a poor companion, Isobel; you must remember when it took your father from home."

She nodded, but she had had her servant Buena and Alfred her dog, and her garden and own things around her. And no Countess to avoid. Talking of whom… "My lord, might I be permitted to see Lady Margaret before she weds?"

He finished setting up his counters and sat back with his fingers interlaced over his stomach, watching her place her last piece. "You know that is not possible."

"I know that I am not permitted, but that is not the same."

"Nonetheless." His fingers jerked restlessly. "Why is it so important that you see her?"

"I would like to know whether she has kept up with her Latin studies…" He raised a brow, so obviously wasn't taken in by *that*. She tried again. "She is so young. She is not ready for marriage."

"She is prepared; she knows her duty as a wife and will be obedient. More so than you," he added, in an attempt to lighten her mood. She responded with a barely constrained huff. Why did men have to be so blind? Or was it that they knew, but chose not to see?

"My lord, I am not speaking of saying '*yea*' or '*nay*' to her husband, but of those other… duties men expect. She is still a girl in a child's body, and he is such an old cog… I mean," she amended hastily, "Lady Margaret is delicate in her manner, and he is… not."

"I see, so my choice of husband for my daughter is to be determined by her delicacy of feeling, is that it? Perhaps you consider a boy her age a better match than this lord you liken to a bull-bottomed ship? This is not a matter of personal happiness – she is not some girl from a town who can marry where she fancies – this match secures an alliance with a family whose estates will extend our influence beyond our own."

"He is so old—"

"He is over forty winters, but he is established and loyal and he has no surviving male heirs to dispute his estates on his death. Please God she has a son first, but Margaret will make a very wealthy widow, and then she will be able to marry where she wishes. But, until then, she is a daughter of this family, and she will do her duty as do we all."

"As must I?"

He suddenly leaned forward, lowering his voice. "We must all do our duty, Isobel. If we are free to follow our hearts it leads to nothing but ruin, as this realm now suffers. Would Warwick and Clarence be so disaffected if the King had done his duty instead of marrying his desire? Look where wedding Grey's widow has brought us – to the brink of misrule – elevating Elizabeth Woodville and her family above their station and causing a rift I fear cannot be healed. The King should have made a match with a royal princess abroad as Warwick had brokered for him. He should…" The Earl severed his remark. Isobel had never heard him speak out about the King like this before. He resumed in a more moderate tone, "If my brother had married our father's choice he would be better placed than he now finds himself – without great estate, lacking affinity, and with neither the wife he married for love nor a child to remember him. Those of us who have responsibilities beyond ourselves must bear the burden of them in return for the riches and honours we earn."

"But why can happiness not be found in a suitable match?" she pressed, accepting the wine his page offered and selecting a pink and green marbled wafer from the gilded dish.

"What is happiness?" He held up a wafer and his own goblet. "The freedom to starve? To watch your neighbour take your land, your animals? To whom do my tenants turn to settle disputes? Who will defend you and your inheritance from Thomas Lacey's ambition, Isobel? I will do these things because it is my duty to serve the King and protect my affinity, and to do so I must make a sacrifice of my happiness. I will do my duty, but in return I expect absolute loyalty and obedience and that includes deciding my daughter's marriage."

Maybe Isobel was feeling particularly contrary, or perhaps she no longer felt the fear of the Earl she once did, softened by their intimacy. "My parents married for love."

He sat back. "Did they. Is that what you were told?" He regretted his comment as her face fell. "I do not say that affection might not grow between a couple, Isobel, especially if there are children, but sometimes there are greater considerations than love, and comfort has to be found elsewhere."

"For a man, perhaps, but a woman cannot."

"You are testy today! Women have the consolation of the children they bear, denied to men because of Man's warlike nature as determined by God." She tutted. "Do you doubt this?"

"Do *you* believe it, my lord?" she enjoined. "What if a woman has no child? What if she is destined to live out her life lonely and without love or the hope of it?" She paused, then said, "Ursula was your mistress, was she not?"

"She was," he affirmed, cautiously.

"Have you seen her, my lord? Spoken with her? Her life is one of memories and false hope that her thankless son will one day remember he has a mother and come for her. In the meantime, she waits out her days in service to *me*. Was she not like me once? Before her hands were spoiled and you had her married to the first man who would take her?"

"Is that what she told you?"

"She… did not use that form of words."

Against the gold of the beaker, his finger tapped out the moments before he answered. "Isobel, she was my mistress in the months before I married. She was willing and I looked for – needed – a diversion." He smiled briefly. "But my wife is vengeful. When she burned Ursula's hands, I could not be sure she would not take revenge on her again, and yes, I did find her a husband, a good man, who would treat her kindly and protect her in a way I had not. I ensured she had bride's money of her own, and when he died and she had no kin with whom she could live, I brought her back here where she would have some sort of life and my protection."

"But she has a son."

"No, she *had* a son; he died years ago, and it turned her mind. She could leave if she wished, live out her time in peace and security in a convent, but she chooses to stay and she is safe enough—"

Isobel's mouth turned down. "Now that she is old."

He raised his brows. "Yes, partly. And because she has a reason to stay."

"What is that?"

He dipped a wafer into his wine and held it, translucent as glass, to the light of the fire. "So she can serve you." He bit the wafer, looking at her.

"She deserves more than *that*!"

"Does she? Do any of us?" Isobel couldn't find an answer for that, so she asked the one thing that had dogged her since receiving it.

"My lord, did you send me a hood of striped blanchet?"

He picked out another wafer. "A hood? Why should I make you a gift of a rough wool hood?"

Chouchou rested her muzzle on Isobel's knee, looking plaintive. She gave the dog the last part of her wafer and stroked its satin head. "I must be mistaken."

"Mm, you must," he echoed with a curve of his mouth. "I would not give you such poor fare. Here," he called the dog. "Sit," he commanded, and she did so, looking adoringly at him. "Do not feed her; she is in whelp and it will spoil the pups."

"How do you know?" Isobel asked, canting her head at the animal. Chou looked the same as she always did – soft and ridiculously loyal.

He clicked his fingers and swirled his forefinger, and the dog sank to the floor between them, rolling over onto its back, tongue lolling, legs paddling expectantly. "Look," the Earl bent down, waiting for Isobel to do the same. "See her teats, here, and here? They are more pronounced than normal, and she is quieter and more affectionate." He gave the bitch's belly a rub, then snapped his fingers again and she leaped up. "I put her to my best dog; she is perhaps two weeks gone."

Isobel tickled the dog behind her ears where she liked it. "We only had Alfred in the house; my mother would allow no other." Chou licked her and she smiled.

"He was a good hunting dog in his day," he said, and Isobel was surprised he remembered. "Now, let us play or she will be whelping before we have finished a single game."

THEY HAD PLAYED three games when, thoughtfully, the Earl remarked, "Perhaps Margaret would like one of the pups as a wedding gift. It would be good company for her. What do you think?" Isobel coughed on a fragment of wafer, and he gave her the wine glass and waited until she had sipped the irritation away. "Well?"

She thought about Meg being far from home among strangers, with the demands of womanhood she would not at first understand, and a household in which she was expected to lead and yet had no authority except that of her husband. And she considered that had she been allowed to bring Alfred, perhaps he might have represented a little of the life she had once known, and she would have felt happier for it. So, eventually, Isobel said, "Yes, my lord, I think she would like that," and he looked relieved, as if it had been playing on his mind. He pushed his chair back from the table and held out his hand to her.

"Come over here." She went and stood before him, and he pulled her onto his knees. She sat stiffly and he wrapped his arms around her. Nuzzling her neck, he kissed the lobe of ear peeking from her headdress. "All this talk of bedding and whelping," he murmured, "puts me in mind of our own pleasures." He ran his ringed hand over the flat of her stomach. "I wonder what your belly would look like full of child?"

"My lord…!" she exclaimed, sliding to her feet, but he recaptured her, holding her fast, his chin rough against her neck.

"Here…" he said, pressing one hand firmly into the folds of her robe, the other finding its way to her breast, "… and here." She squeaked in protest, and he laughed. He looked over his shoulder. "Out," he said to his page waiting in the shadows.

She tried to control his exploring hands. "You have children, my lord, why would you want another?"

"I wish to plant my seed in the garden of your womb and watch it grow." He bent to kiss her stomach through the cloth. "Or else enjoy the trying." His hand moved up to bring her chin around to face him, making her look into his eyes. "Will you become quieter and more affectionate, my Bel, with my son growing in you?" His thumb caressing her cheek, he touched her lips softly with his own.

The door to the chamber opened. "My lord."

"What is it?" he barked, and then looked around when his groom didn't answer. He uttered an oath and, releasing Isobel, she jumped up, skin flaring. She curtsied. He rose more slowly.

"Madam, how can I serve you?" he asked with exaggerated courtesy as his wife froze the air between them. Felice averted her head, and the Earl sucked his teeth. "Isobel, leave us; I will call for you later."

Ursula nodded awake from her chair. "My lady, I did not mean to sleep. I did not expect you." She peered at Isobel. "My lady looks pale."

"It matters not. Warm me some ale with hyssop, my stomach aches. And take some for yourself if you wish; it is cold tonight. Have you supped?" She sat down, but the cramp that had niggled became insistent and she detected a familiar warmth between her legs. "Leave the ale for now. Bring my casket, and then heat bathing water and warm stones for me."

From the casket, she drew the rough linen wads the size of her hand and stuffed with wool that she had made for Meg not so very long ago. She had shown her how to secure them between her legs with a strap of linen suspended on a girdle beneath her smock. She hoped the girl would cope with her courses, and that Alice would remember to heat stones to ease her pain. Then she recalled the Earl's words to her moments before the Countess had interrupted him. At least he would not touch her tonight, nor for the days in which her blood flowed in case it poisoned him and made him impotent. She gave a wry smile. Women might be unable to stop the flow of blood each month, but at least in this one thing they exercised some control over the demands men placed on them. Isobel found a part of herself wishing that Meg's bullish husband would find out the hard way, then regretted it as she visualised the encounter and what it would do to the girl.

"My lady?" Ursula touched her shoulder. "The water is ready, the ale also."

As she lay in bed hugging the rocks to her stomach, Isobel felt certain she could celebrate one other fact: she wasn't with child, and for that she offered up a silent prayer of thanks to the Virgin.

THE NEWS SPREAD through the castle like locusts through Egypt, although Isobel didn't hear until Ursula came hurrying into the room the following morning.

"The Countess is with child?" Isobel said, sitting up and shaking sleep from her head. "How?" She rephrased the question when it looked as if Ursula might explain the act in detail. "I mean, *when*?"

"Not a month gone, my lady." Ursula straightened her shoulders and her mouth. "In my day, we said nothing until past the third month for fear of frightening the child from the womb." She crossed herself. "Prayers are to be said hourly until her delivery, although my lady never had a moment's difficulty, unlike many. *Blessed*, some say, or a *witc*..." Her eyes slid across to Isobel, who ignored the comment as she calculated the weeks. "Waste of incense," Ursula grumbled, arranging Isobel's clothes and pouring freshly heated water into her basin. "She had better avoid rue in the mornings, that is all I can say." She continued muttering to herself as Isobel bathed and dressed behind the makeshift screen, still numb from the revelation. She had understood that the Earl and Countess no longer shared a bed, and everything she had seen or heard bore witness to his dislike of his wife. What the Countess thought of him she could not hazard a guess, but her demeanour could freeze walnuts off a tree. After the initial shock came relief – he would no longer expect her company – followed swiftly by anxiety. Her servant's incessant jabbering rattled her nerves.

"Ursula, shh! I cannot think." She sat on the cross-framed stool while Ursula unbraided and began to comb out her heavy honey-coloured hair. Would he let her go back to Beaumancote *now*? Surely with a few more men she would be safe enough. And if he didn't? She doubted the Countess would forgive and forget, but if the Earl had no more use for her, would he feel obligated to find her a husband, and if so, who? Her heart scuttled erratically – his brother? No sooner than she thought it, she dismissed the idea as fantasy. But it lingered, that tiny hope that had wriggled under her skin during those days spent with him and that lay between the warmth of her heart and cold reality.

By the time the Earl summoned her, Isobel had already made up her mind to ask him directly to let her go home. She would refuse to marry someone of his choosing, and she couldn't stay in the castle. It would leave him with little choice, but she felt certain that, given his own changed circumstances, he could find nothing to which he might object. Buoyed by the thought, she held herself erect as she approached his privy chamber, and even managed to look his groom directly in the eye when he let her in.

Arrangements for the Earl's departure were obviously well advanced, and the room had been stripped of arrases, the carpets rolled, and plate, ewers, and his beaker packed. It felt strangely foreign, vacant, robbed of its identity as she herself had felt once on entering it. Now, she almost missed what she had grown accustomed to, and it unsettled her.

On the other side of the room the Earl was speaking with his chamberlain and chief gentlemen. Papers scattered the naked table before them. Too impatient to wait to be buckled into his riding cote, he tugged at the straps without looking as he talked. Rings shadowed his eyes and he looked tired, and Isobel suspected he had spent the night celebrating. He glanced up and saw her and, in that instant, she knew something had changed. He dismissed his gentlemen.

"You left this," he said, handing her the gaming box. "I expect you have heard the news by now?"

"Yes, my lord. My words are worthless, I know, but I wish you joy and felicitations."

"I do not think them deserved." A swift, awkward smile, so unlike him. He gave up fiddling with the buckles and left them dangling half-done and mismatched. "I missed your company last night. I fear I will be adrift without you these next weeks to remind me of my mortality." A little of the sardonic lift to his mouth she was used to reappeared. "I have left instruction for your maintenance. You will receive all that you require. Anything else and you have funds accrued from your manors, although some will be needed for enhancing the garrison I will leave there, small though it might be."

"My lord—"

"And another thing," he continued, "for your own weal, keep away from my wife. She has other matters to distract her now, but it is as well to be cautious. Do you have ready coin?"

"Yes, a little, but—"

He unhooked his own purse from the belt draped over the back of the chair. "Take this; it will procure anything you might need – unless it be a gown of ermine." Again, that transient smile, as if he needed to fill every moment with words. "And, Isobel…"

"My lord?"

"I meant what I said last night. When I return, if God wills it, I will not neglect you." It was now or never; she opened her mouth to speak, but he placed his finger over her lips. "I will make you the mother of my child."

The untidy buckles dangled, and she stared at them stupidly, her mind corkscrewing. "You… you do not wish me to leave?"

"Have I not said as much? I would not abandon you, Isobel. There is much I could say, but it will keep for now." The moment had passed in which she could make her plea for freedom. She undid his misaligned straps and started to re-buckle them. "Such a thing a wife might do," he observed, as she finished the last buckle. She let her hands drop to her sides. "Now," he said briskly, reaching for his belt, "do you have a message for your steward?"

She could think of many trivial items to impart to Arthur, things she wanted to confide in Buena, but nothing suitable she could pass via a great lord, so she just said, "May it please you, my lord, tell them I wish them well and that they are constantly in my prayers," and left it at that.

"And do you wish me the same, Isobel?"

She would not lie, but then she found she could not wish him ill either, so she ended up saying nothing at all. After a moment's uncomfortable silence, which said more than she could, he lifted his brow in a show of regret. "Then I shall entreat God to keep you safe from harm." He surprised himself by the vehemence of his statement, reflecting, even if briefly as he kissed her, that it was the closest he had come to a conversation with God for a long while.

Chapter 3

SOMETIMES, SHE REFLECTED days later, you take yourself by surprise and all that you hoped or dreamed or wished for becomes less relevant when it is achieved. It is true she had wanted him gone from the castle, freeing herself of his attention and expectations of affection she would not, could not, reciprocate, but she discovered that there had been benefits to his presence not anticipated. The first of these became evident within days of his departure.

The castle became strangely quiet and the Earl's absence conspicuous. People she had become accustomed to seeing in his service, even if ambivalent or curious towards her, had left with him, leaving the Countess's household more prominently displayed, like boils. Isobel avoided them at every opportunity.

Sullen rain fell steadily into the beginning of March, and moisture oozed from the walls. Everything seemed to be in a permanent state of damp, and Isobel's clothes clung to her legs with the smell of wet wool and lank fur accompanying each step. With her hood drawn over her head against the rain, she did not see the huddle of women sheltering in the chapel porch until she almost ran into them. "Excuse me," she said, trying to inch into the dry. They looked over their shoulders at her but didn't move. "Might I enter?" she said, drawing her hood back enough to see and wiping rain from the tip of her nose with her hand. She recognised several ladies from the Countess's chamber. She had little enough to do with them before and had no quarrel with them now, but they barred her way and made no shift to move. "Please, let me pass," she said, "I am getting soaked."

One moved enough to let her by. As she squeezed through the narrow gap they made, she thought she heard a muttered *"Bold hussy!"* followed by shushing noises from the others and subdued laughter. She didn't look back, but remained in confused isolation throughout mass, and was the first to the door by its end.

Clouds had weakened and Isobel returned to her chamber in a fine drizzle, not caring now if she looked like one of Alfred's less savoury finds. Ursula fussed around, one moment scolding her for getting wet, the next drawing her to the fire and chafing her hands between her own to warm them.

"Ursula, what are they saying about me?"

"Wet through as if you'd fallen in the river. It will be the death of you, and my lord will have me sent from here, and how will my boy find me then?"

"The Earl will not send you away. Tell me, what do they say about me?" Ursula stopped rubbing but didn't meet her gaze. "You have heard something, haven't you?"

"People say things. People always say things, but it doesn't make it thus for saying them. You are my lord's true lady, not a…" She broke off and fumbled a dry pink kirtle over a stool to warm it. Isobel peeled her wet gown from her shoulders and started to pull her soggy kirtle over her head. She emerged the other side.

"What was that?"

"My lady?"

There it was again: a sound of metal clashing, becoming footsteps, and then a terse thump on the door. It opened abruptly, and Isobel recognised the sergeant from the gatehouse as she scrambled to cover herself.

Ursula shrieked her protest, standing in front of Isobel with one hand extended as if to shield her from view, while she flapped the other in the direction of the men crowding the door. "Be gone, be gone!"

"Your pardon, mistress," the sergeant held his men back, "but t'constable wants men on't tower parapet right away."

"Why?" Isobel asked, regaining her voice and pulling Ursula out of the way as soldiers from the garrison pushed past and began arming themselves with crossbows from the wall racks. As swiftly, the room emptied as they ducked under the low doorway onto the narrow parapet walkway, sending doves scattering into the sky.

The sergeant looked over his shoulder as he followed them. "There's a force beyond the gate. In these times, we can't take any chances," and he was gone from view. Moments later he was back.

"Who are they?" Isobel pounced as soon as he reappeared.

"I don't rightly know, mistress, but you're best stayin' here out o' sight."

She hopped from one foot to the other, pulling on damp shoes. "Is there no banner displayed? Do they come armed? What do they want?" she asked, but he continued down the stairs without pausing to answer. Huffing in frustration, Isobel swung her cloak around her shoulders and followed him. "Sergeant, wait!"

Deployed men ranged along the castle walls by the time Isobel found a place near the sergeant from which she could watch the scene below. By the gates the steward listened intently as the constable gesticulated, then spoke. The constable began to argue, but the steward indicated the Countess's apartments with a hand and a raised brow, and the younger man stood back, mouth rigid, then jerked his head in acknowledgement. He swung away, shouted an order, and the great chains announced the grinding ascent of the portcullis as it ratcheted up beyond the gates. Murmured dissent flowed along the parapet as across the bridge hollow hooves rang.

Isobel did not recognise the men in glittering half-armour as they rode at the head of the small company that entered the bailey, but she knew their standards and the insignia upon them: the Earl of Warwick's bear and ragged staff, and beside it, the black bull of the King's brother, the Duke of Clarence.

Dark hair badgered with grey, the older man leaned down from his horse and clapped the constable on his shoulder. Next to him, a full-faced youth – not much older than Isobel – hard-eyed the defences without any pretence to humour. He must be the Duke of Clarence; he certainly dressed the part, but he bore little resemblance to his younger brother, and made scant effort to take part in the conversation.

Warwick, though, seemed in no hurry to make a move and appeared to be sharing some anecdote involving flapping his arms like a chicken then breaking its neck. He roared with laughter, and the constable visibly relaxed. Clarence looked away without smiling, and his horse shook its head against the tautly held reins, making the enamelled gilded discs decorating the harness jingle thinly.

"Now, what'll they be wanting?" the sergeant muttered under his breath. "They've a lively enough company mustered beyond our walls to make a pile o' trouble."

"But the Earl's from home," Isobel whispered.

The sergeant scratched his chin. "Aye, and they'll know that right enough."

Isobel watched the easy conversation between the earl and the steward. The tension had dissolved, and the dozen or so men still on horseback chatted as if on a day out hunting. The watchers along the walls had lowered their arms. Clarence, in his close examination of the tower, passed a lowered remark to Warwick, and in that one look, Isobel saw no sign of leniency. This prince was made in a different mould, a brittle brightness, like eggshells. She saw it clearly but, if true, it passed undetected because the steward slapped Warwick's horse on the flank and signalled to the guards to let them pass. As the group moved forward, Isobel registered a familiar profile. She hid behind the sergeant before she could be spotted. "And thus Troy was taken," she murmured to herself, thankful for his broad back. What would Thomas Lacey make of her current plight except to crow? More to the point, what was he doing *here*?

The gatehouse had all but emptied into the bailey. Guards remained alert along the walls and the battlements of the tower, and the portcullis blocked entry or exit across the bridge, but it was all that stood between the castle's defences and the soldiers gathered on the farther bank of the river.

Flashing a glance around the court, the sergeant took her by the elbow. "You'd best be away inside, mistress."

She blinked, stuttered, "You must get a message to the Earl."

"*Must* I? And why be that?"

He didn't know about the Earl's suspicions relating to Thomas, and he couldn't know; she'd been sworn to keep it secret.

"Surely he would wish to be informed if His Grace of Clarence and the earl had business at the castle with such a company as this outside the walls?"

"Aye, he might sure enough. But it's not for me to tell 'im. Besides, it'll take three days to put a rider that far—"

"Send to Lord Robert, then; is he not with the Duke of Gloucester?"

He scrutinised her face and must have read something of the urgency there because, instead of questioning her persistence, he nodded slowly, like a head of reedmace in the wind. He ran his sleeve over his nose; sniffed. "He is, aye."

Chapter 4

In the gathering dusk, Felice watched Clarence and Warwick mount their horses and ride from the bailey and out of sight. Courtesy demanded she provide the hospitality of a warm chamber for the night, but the earl had declined as graciously as she had offered so that neither were bound to continue the charade they had adopted for longer than necessary.

But the message had been delivered as he intended, and now left with it, she had a decision to make.

Warwick had settled in the chair and warmed his hands by the fire. "I am sorry to have missed my old friend. In these uncertain times I would value his counsel were he inclined to give it."

"My lord will be grieved to learn of his loss. What little service I can extend to you is poor in comparison." She inclined her head, and he acknowledged it with a slight smile.

"You honour us, my lady. His Grace and I are cognisant of the love you bear us."

Felice cast sideways at the young duke. He coughed and continued his morose contemplation of the fire, occasionally flicking the gold strap end of his sword belt against his open hand.

Warwick frowned. "Forgive His Grace his lack of conversation; he awaits the birth of his first child – his heir, and my grandchild – and is much taken up with the thought."

"I will offer masses for the safe delivery of the duchess and the child. May it please Almighty God, the Virgin, and all the Saints of Heaven it is a son." She unwound her beads from her belt and touched her lips to the reliquary cross suspended there.

Warwick's brow rose. "Amen to that. A son is all we desire, is that not so, Your Grace? A son and heir would solve many of our problems."

Clarence shifted away from the fire and grunted assent. He sneezed and, standing abruptly, went to the window. Felice wondered whether Warwick was aware of her own news and waited without further comment for him to get down to business.

"You have heard of the unrest in the eastern counties, perhaps?" If she had, Felice made no move to acknowledge it. "Knowing we cleave to the King in all matters—" Clarence let out a barely contained snort, and Warwick winced and sucked his teeth before continuing, "—and how the King's Grace looks to the Earl to maintain peace in the region, we come out of friendship in this time of unrest and offer what assistance might be required to maintain the security of the realm."

"Security, my lord? I was not aware that there was such a need at present. We have seen no disturbance in these counties."

Clarence pushed away from the wall and came back to the fire. He swore under his breath as he stumbled, and Felice, taking in his raised colour, wondered if he had been drinking.

"Have you not, madam?" Clarence addressed her for the first time. "If so, your eyes must have been closed or else you choose not to see. Perhaps—"

Warwick interrupted as Felice's expression froze. "I wrote to the Earl, madam, a letter between friends, seeking his counsel on some matters regarding the weal of the realm." Her face remained unchanged, but he noted the tightening of her mouth. So, the Earl had not told her about the letter. He continued. "These disturbances, these… grievances, reflect the disease that threatens the King's peace and those wishing to protect the King from any who would subvert his governance and restore the natural order of our fathers." He clenched his hands in front of him. "His Grace's good nature has led him to be deceived by those who justify their influence by the rewards heaped upon them, and yet they are not earned, and the King is deaf to the honest counsel of those who love him most – his closest affinity, his kin – who have to watch while this great realm is brought into disrepute by those not best placed to govern it."

Clarence sniffed. "The Queen's pack bay for our blood—"

"And for the blood of those who, like your husband, seek to serve. Madam…" Lowering his voice, Warwick obliged her to come closer than comfortable, and he sensed the restless stirring proximity to her always brought. She averted her eyes. "Felice, the time is near when we must all make choices." She sat back, her calm demeanour at last exposed as a fiction and vulnerable to his blunt decree. "You have been the victim of false counsel as much as I. Your eldest daughter—"

"Is married, my lord."

"But is denied favour at Court because of the Queen's jealousy. Of course I know of it," he said as her look sharpened. "All England knows it, and the Queen's kin laugh openly at the remembrance of it. How many insults to the honour of this family can you bear? You have other daughters; will they be denied union with husbands worthy of this name? I have an unwed daughter – Anne – and please God I find a husband for her before all are swallowed by that Gorgon that sits by our King and usurps his manhood."

Felice managed, "You speak *treason*!"

"I speak the *truth*. The King has lost his way, and the true heir of York is the man who will restore the natural order to this realm."

"My husband will not countenance disloyalty."

"Your husband's loyalty is to the House of York, and *this* is its true heir." With a flourish, he presented his son-in-law, whose marked lack of regality was all too apparent as he blew his nose on a silk square he had drawn from his sleeve. "He is the fulfilment of his father's destiny, blessed with the virtues of a true king and not bound by a woman's girdle to her kin. There can be only one king of this realm, and God did not endow Eve with the wit and strength to rule. It is a hard physic, but order must be restored or we will all live to rue it."

"My lord, what is it you want of us?" *Us?* Hardly, but of her husband, perhaps.

"Want of you? Madam, you misunderstand." He laid a hand on his son-in-law's decorated sleeve. "His Grace will reward loyalty beyond expectation: a place at Court, a noble husband for your daughter – Cecily, is it not? And for the Earl… well, let's just say that the Queen's kin and their affinity will no longer be needing the honours they have been hoarding."

"Do you think she'll tell him?" Clarence said when they left the Countess's apartments for the waiting horses below.

Warwick pulled gloves over his fingers and rotated his seal ring through the leather. "That will depend on whether her ambition outweighs her malice, and how far her influence has waned since the death of their boy. Not as far as I thought, it seems. She is with child again, have you not heard?"

"It might not be his."

"It will be; I've tested those waters before and found them… chilly."

Clarence answered with a cocky grin. "Perhaps what you were offering was not to her liking."

Warwick took a second to scan the boy's face: good-looking to a degree, he could see the familial likeness to his older brother, but without his charm and with a tendency to sneer, which he was doing at this moment. He resisted the temptation to crush him, and instead replied, "I did not say I was wholly unsuccessful." He mounted his horse and took the reins in one hand. He envied his son-in-law's agility, if not his wit, as Clarence followed suit. "It augurs well. If the Earl has taken to his wife's bed again rather than that of his mistress, Felice Langton might yet be useful to us. She can be very persuasive." He pulled his horse around, looked over his shoulder, and saw Felice still watching from the window. "It is in our interests to help her in any way we can, George. We need this cock with his hen, or we will end up having to pluck his feathers and then we'll have lost him."

"And if that fails?"

"Let's hope we can woo him with offices and promise of reward. Perhaps by then he will have a son to leave it all to; that is an incentive, trust me."

"There is always the office of Constable of England," Clarence slid in.

"I believe Your Grace jests. Your brother Gloucester would be sure to miss it, and I still have hopes he will join with us."

Clarence snorted. "Do you think so, when he has already benefited from your misfortune? Ed has been very generous with your offices."

"You forget it will be within your power when *you* are king to be equally benevolent."

"Then you do not know Richard as I do;" Clarence sneered. "Loyalty *binds* him."

"Then ensure he is bound to *you*," Warwick snapped. Then more evenly, "Remember, you are his brother also; give him reason to love you." He spurred his horse. "Come, George, you look feverish; let us quench it with a little ale and see what comes of this encounter. We sow a little, perhaps we'll reap a lot, eh?" He leaned towards him and thumped the young man's back. He had been as a father to the younger York boys, and they had been the sons he never had. They owed filial duty, and he would demand it.

FROM HER VANTAGE point in her chamber, Felice could see over the castle walls to the smoke rising from the winter fires of the sprawling town below. She imagined the little lives of the commons for whom their hearth represented their world and, for an instant, envied the simplicity of their uncomplicated existence. But she had responsibilities far beyond anything they could imagine, to uphold her family honour and the dignity of her blood. Which way to proceed? Warwick's attendance had reminded her of the pleasures she had forgone in the pursuit of her husband's interests, his attraction still potent despite the intervening years thickening his waist and thinning his greying dark hair. It galled that her brief flirtation had failed to rouse her husband's jealousy, and all the effort made in pleasing him had been wasted. Had she a mind to, if her pride allowed, would she let Warwick rekindle that flame? And would her husband notice? Would he care?

She imagined a sensation deep in her womb to be the first marking of the life that grew there. Her husband might give little heed to his wife, but this child represented their future together, and she would let nothing come between them and his potential heir – not Warwick, not his slut. The presence of the whore rankled, an unclean feeling she wanted to see washed away. She was still considering her options when she heard a small, thin voice at her side.

"Madam ma mère?"

Felice opened her eyes and found her daughter's pallid face peering into her own, appeasing, vapid. She looked away. "What do you want, Margaret?"

"Y… you wanted me to attend you, madam."

Warwick wouldn't have been so eager to offer a husband if he had met the girls. Felice might not like Raseby – she found his manner akin to a burgher and had heard English spoken better by a Burgundian cog master – but he was willing to overlook the girl's shortcomings and brought an allegiance her father valued. However, Margaret might be betrothed, but Cecily was not. With her position restored at Court and the Queen's kin no longer stealing the most eligible matches, who knows what husband she might contract for her youngest child? A change in allegiance could work in their favour. Would the gamble be worth it? Should she send word to her husband, or wait until his return when she could exert what influence she had remaining?

"Madam?"

"Do not whine, Margaret, and stop fidgeting. All that hand twisting makes me nauseous. You are not wringing a bird's neck – be still. Lord Raseby has returned from Flanders and has sent you a gift. You must write at once and acknowledge it."

Her thin face lit. "What is it?"

Such pathetic eagerness. Irritated, Felice whipped, "I have greater concerns to occupy me. His servant is below; do not keep him waiting."

"I shall write prettily in French," Margaret declared, "so he will be pleased with me."

Felice barely hid her scorn. "Do as you wish; his clerk will have to read it to him whatever language you choose. And Margaret," she said as her daughter made to go, and the girl turned back hopefully, "have Master Sawcliffe wait on me."

Had she been facing Margaret as she spoke, Felice would have noticed the pall of disappointment; as it was, she had other things on her mind.

Robert Langton mapped the small room until he knew the face of every tile making up the red and cream chequered floor. The murmur of voices in the adjoining room finally ceased, and he looked up as the door to the King's chamber opened and Gloucester appeared. He beckoned Robert to follow him.

Gloucester said nothing until in his own rooms, then he motioned to the chair near the table and installed himself in another. The remnants of a meal lay to one side where it had been abandoned in haste. Close by, the Duke's greyhound, now full-grown and all skinny-limbed like its master, bounced up bright-eyed and begging. Tearing off a chunk of bread, Gloucester cautioned it to gentleness and let the dog take it from his fingers.

"Dogs," he remarked, watching the animal wolf and then lick fragments from the rugged floor. "All he thinks about is food. If it came to it, whose hand would he follow – mine or that of the man casting bread upon rough waters?" He smiled briefly, catching the impatient shift in the man before him. "His Grace thanks you for your diligence, my lord Langton, and will act upon the intelligence."

Robert released the breath he had been holding. He rubbed his thumb over his forehead. "And the castle, Your Grace? Will you grant me leave to go?"

The Duke straightened the skewed quill hastily cast aside when Langton had first told him the news earlier that day. "Is there any reason to suspect it will come under attack?"

Langton frowned. "No, Your Grace, but…"

"But…?"

In the short period of time in which he had been in the service of the King's youngest brother, Robert had quickly come to realise there was little point in keeping anything from him. What the Duke didn't learn directly, he would work out for himself, and the conclusions he reached could be uncompromising. Rob gestured to the creased paper, roughly folded into a square on the table.

"The message speaks of danger. If Your Grace will allow me to—"

The Duke held up a hand to stop him. "Danger to what – or whom?" The greyhound gave up snuffling for lost crumbs and looked for attention from its master instead.

"Isobel Fenton."

Gloucester sat back and contemplated Langton. "And why should the Earl's mistress be in peril, my lord?"

Did the whole Court know his brother's business? The news seemed to have spread as fast as the French fever plaguing the east coast and now finding its way up the Thames. "It is she who sent the message."

"Is she aware of what we have discussed previously regarding Thomas Lacey? Can she be trusted?"

Langton answered without hesitation. "On my life, without question."

"On *your* life, my lord? I hope not." His smile quickly became serious again. "Loyalty deserves its reward and she her safety, but I cannot spare you. Send one of your men to ensure her protection and another to warn the Earl. With the unrest, we must call to arms as many as can be mustered. The King has issued letters to Warwick and my brother Clarence, urging them to raise men in his name. But with this new intelligence, he is cautioned to mind them as well as he would a dog that's inclined to bite." The Duke's own animal nuzzled his hand and was rewarded with a pat. "The castle is well-defended, and Mistress Fenton will be safe enough until the Earl returns."

Robert compressed his lips. "Your Grace, for Isobel Fenton the danger lies within the walls, not outside."

"How so?" The dog placed an elegant paw on the Duke's arm. "Enough, Hector," he admonished, but instead fingered its ear absent-mindedly as he contemplated Robert through appraising eyes. "Faith, my lord, if your loyalty to your brother's mistress is a measure of your fealty to me, I will fear no evil." Unfolding the message again, he read, *"'Atque Troiam venerunt Danai ferentes dona.' 'And to Troy came Greeks bearing gifts.'"* He stroked Hector's ears, and the dog tried to chew his sleeve. He sighed and disengaged its jaws. "Mistress Fenton seems to have launched a few ships, my lord; will she be the ruin of Troy?"

"Or the saving of it, Your Grace?"

Gloucester suddenly grinned, looking his seventeen years, and Langton was reminded that this boy he called "lord" had yet to be tried in battle. Strip-thin, but strong and quick-witted in the practice yards, the Duke proved fearless. Only time would tell whether he could face his enemy with equal determination. For all of that, Gloucester fenced with words readily enough, and his needle wit was more than a match for many a man. Now he canted his head as he looked at Langton.

"Perhaps *Penelope* rather than *Helen.* She was a woman worth protecting."

They eyed each other, and then Robert inclined his head. "Thank you, Your Grace."

"But I wish you to return within the week. If what this indicates is true—" he flicked the message with a finger, "—then Warwick is seeking support and, although His Grace bids them muster troops, there is no guarantee that Warwick does so for the King."

BY THE ENTRANCE to the arbour where Isobel waited hooded and cloaked against the persistent damp and prying eyes, clumps of Candlemas Bells pierced the snow, nodding humility in their drooping heads of white. Despite the lengthening days, the sun fed little warmth into her bones, and she rose from the stone bench and crouched to pick the short-stemmed flowers. It was the only place where she could be certain no one would go at this time of year. No one else except the one person she wanted to see. She didn't have to wait long. Pricking her ears, the Earl's dog ran to meet Cecily moments before Isobel heard her song of greeting to the Lady Snake tree. She had run ahead as usual, her poppet in her hand.

"My lady," Isobel called softly. "Cecily."

The child looked up from patting the dog. "Is'bel!" she squealed and, running, threw herself into Isobel's arms. Such simple love, such absolute acceptance. Isobel held the girl tightly then, careless of the damp ground as she kneeled, looked into the child's face.

"I swear you have grown. You will be almost as tall as me by summer. Are you eating well?"

"Nan eats lots and lots and I like meat chewits and I can do this – look," and she wobbled a tooth with her finger.

"A new tooth! You are growing so well. Do you clean your teeth every day as I told you?"

Cecily's eyes wandered and she hopped from one foot to the other. "Yeeees," she said doubtfully. "But I pee all by myself," she declared.

Isobel hugged her and then looked up as Chou ran towards the linden allées from where new voices chimed. "I must go," she said, straightening and preparing to leave before being seen.

"No!" Cecily clung to her, and Isobel tried to gently prise her fingers from her skirts. She held on, and by that time it was too late anyway.

Isobel didn't recognise the young woman at first. Face cowled in a thickly furred hood and dressed in a magnificent garnet-coloured Burgundian gown, she and Alice approached the tree.

Cecily called out, "Meg, it's Is'bel. Is'bel is here!"

Margaret stalled and stopped some distance away. Taking Isobel by the hand, Cecily urged her towards her sister. Meg's cheeks showed flashes of high colour, but her pale eyes were dark underneath and her skin looked tacky. She licked her lips and, for an instant, it seemed as if she might address Isobel, but she held out her hand to Cecily instead.

"Come away; you are not to speak to her."

"But it's Is'bel, Meg. Look, she likes Nan's tooth," and she bounced up to her and waved the poppet in her sister's face. "Nan has a new gown like yours." Margaret touched the doll and gave a pinched smile.

"Bring Nan; we must go."

"But, Meg—"

"*Now*, Cecily. Madam ma mère forbids us to talk to her. Alice, bring Cecily." She swung around in waves of brocaded silk that almost swamped her, too fine for a walk in a garden, too old for a girl of nearly fifteen.

"My lady, wait!" Isobel called.

"I cannot speak with you."

"But you can hear me, my lady." Isobel moved a step closer, compelling her to stay. "Margaret—"

"You will address me with due courtesy, Mistress Fenton." She would not turn around, nor did she look at Isobel, but she had stopped at least.

"My lady, when you are wed – when you are a wife – if you need someone, if… if you send for me, I will come." And Isobel pressed the small posy of flowers into the girl's hand. "The Earl will let me attend you, I am sure of it." Meg said nothing, but gripped the stems tightly, then with what might have been a nod of her head, she turned and walked away.

"Look after her," Isobel said quietly to Alice as the girl picked Cecily up and bobbed an awkward curtsy. "Look after them both."

Ursula hovered near the door where Isobel had left her. She ushered Isobel in, securing the door behind her. Chouchou nudged between them, nosing her hand for attention.

"Did you see Lady Cecily, my lady?"

Isobel undid her cloak and Ursula took it from her. "I did, and she has grown and seems happy enough. Meg was there, but she did not look well." Isobel held her hands to the inadequate fire; in her haste to reach the garden without being seen, she had forgotten her gloves and her fingers itched with cold.

Ursula added a skimpy faggot of wood to the fire. "Lady Margaret has been given a great gift; everyone is talking about it. Lord Raseby had it made for her from silk bought in Bruges. The finest cloth from the Duke of Burgundy's own mercer. They say she will attend Court when she is wed."

"Yes," Isobel said softly, "she is wearing it today."

Ursula gave the fire one last prod. "And were you seen, my lady?"

"I think not. I cannot bear being caged in here. I almost wish…" She shook her head at her own inconsistency. "I almost wish the Earl were here, then I could go where I please and no one would dare cross me." Chou rolled onto her back, exposing her rounding belly. "And we have an extra mouth to feed, do we not, Chouchou?" The dog had turned up a few days earlier and seemed reluctant to leave except when the bell rang for feeding time in the kennels. Her appetite was insatiable, and her diet – as strictly prescribed by the Earl – was considerably better than their own at present. Isobel gently stroked the little bumps already evident beneath the tautened skin, and the dog paddled the air and tried to lick her hand. She hadn't the heart to send her away. "I hope no one comes looking for you. We can be invisible here together." She smiled again, but this time touched with irony; it was not so long ago she had bemoaned the fact to the Earl. Now, it might just save her skin.

Chapter 5

Chou's whining woke Isobel from a troubled sleep. She put out a hand in the dark and found the silken head raised and tensed, listening. Isobel heard it this time: a softened knock, but urgent. And again. A growl threatened to break into barking.

"Quiet, wait," she said, adjusting to the charcoal night. The knock repeated, followed by a voice she recognised. Scrambling over the dog, Isobel made for the door. "Alice? What is it?" The girl tumbled into the room, unkempt, unslept.

"I had to come even though they said I shouldn't," she panted, throwing a look over her shoulder into the passage as the door closed on the darkness. "But the physicians have tried everything, and she is no better—"

"Better? Who? Is Cecily ill?"

"No, Lady *Margaret.* She took a fever the day we saw you in the garden, and we thought it was but ague because she seemed better this noon and took nuncheon. But she waked in the night crying, and hasn't stopped, and sickens every time she moves her head. Please come. She's been bled and physic given according to her charts, but nothing helps. Lady Margaret keeps calling for you; I didn't know what to do." She rattled out of breath as Isobel hurriedly dressed, dragging on hose and shoes even as Ursula handed her casket to her.

"Stay here," she told her, and then to Alice, "Where's Joan?"

"I've not seen her since all-night was called."

DAWN BRUISED THE sky, bleeding into the passage to the nursery through narrow windows, and a thin sound – unearthly and wounded like an animal – met them long before Alice opened the door to the apartments and the stench of sickness and burning herbs filled Isobel's nose. Bent over a basin, Meg's shoulders heaved, ending in a cough as she fell back against the bed's bolster, and the high-pitched wail resumed, cutting through the heavy pallor of the chamber, trailing into a moan, then silence. Kat heated cloths in water by the fire and, tucked to one side, Cecily huddled, frightened.

Isobel choked, swallowed. "How long has she been like this?"

"She seemed better this morning, only her head still ached; but when she woke she sickened, and now I can't rouse her except when the sickness comes." Alice licked her lips, looking sideways towards the door. "There's talk of poison—"

"Shh," Isobel hushed, moving to the bedside and placing the casket by the posy of flowers, touched to see them there. She placed the backs of her fingers against the girl's bloodless cheek, being careful not to wake her. "It'll be no such thing as poison unless the French have a new weapon in this ague." Meg's skin felt cold and dry but raised in discoloured dimples like plucked chicken flesh. Isobel straightened, puzzled. "And you say she has been bled?"

Alice nodded. "Twice; look," and she held the light a little closer and drew back the cover to reveal Margaret's arm lacerated near the crook of her elbow, still stained red. Meg whined in the stronger light but didn't open her eyes.

"But she is cool to touch," Isobel murmured. "The letting must have rebalanced her humours, yet she shows no sign of recovery." She leaned closer, smelling blood and bile. "What is this?" She pointed to a mottled patch of skin illuminated by the candle. It looked as if a series of dots had spread and joined like drops of rain on red marble. "And this?" She pressed a finger gently against a livid mark. It neither rubbed nor faded. "Did the physician do this?"

Alice craned to look. "I don't think so. That wasn't there earlier."

Carefully peeling back the damp neck of Meg's smock, Isobel saw similar blots on her throat like bramble juice stains on the fingers of a child. "And here, also."

Margaret stirred, her eyes flicking open and shut. "Is'bel," she murmured, barely audible.

"I'm here, my lady."

"My head… eyes… hurt."

Soothing limp strands of hair from the girl's face, Isobel said, "I know. I'll make something to take the pain away." Then, to Alice, "It is her headache that causes the sickness. Has she taken dwale or any substance to quell the pain?"

Alice pulled a face. "Joan said to give her valerian to quieten her, but I made a decoction of camomile and honey as you showed me, so it didn't taste so bad."

It explained the reek of dank dog. "You will find opium and henbane in the casket. Take them and mix with rosemary and honey, then slake with strong wine so it runs freely. Heat it well and strain it. Can you get the wine? Good. Go. Be quick."

Kat was gingerly folding a heated cloth, letting the steam rise to cool it a little. She lifted it and was about to place it on Margaret's forehead, but Isobel stopped her. "No, she needs a cold cloth to her head. Bathe her hands and feet instead."

"Joan said make the head-cloths as hot as Lady Margaret can bear."

"Joan is wrong. Here, leave them, I'll do it. Take care of Cecily. Has she shown any signs of fever?" The girl shook her head. "Good, then take her from here, wash and dress her, and find her something to eat away from this foul air." She turned back to Meg, whose eyes peered glassily from half-shut lids, and softened her voice. "And let's make you more comfortable, my lady, and find you a clean nightshift." Isobel smiled, but inside drifts of hopelessness piled up as her eyes, becoming accustomed to the weak light, made out further irregular daubs of dark red rising under Meg's chin, below her ears, down her neck. She had never met with anything like this. She had seen worse: lesions and ulcers, the itch, burns, boils, and rashes – things she understood, things she could treat – but not this. In Margaret the humours warred against each other. If one was treated it would be to the detriment of another, and where there was conflict within the body, it would almost certainly lead to death. Isobel bustled the thought away and took the cooling cloths. "Let's get you washed while these cloths are warm," she said, lifting the heavy winter covers from the girl's legs. She halted, speechless, gagging.

"What is it?" Alice asked as she returned, then saw the blue-black discolouration and smelled the unmistakable odour of dead flesh. Her hand flew to her mouth. Isobel gave her a warning look. "Alice, is the dwale ready?" she asked brightly. "This will help you sleep, my lady." Holding the beaker to Meg's lips, Isobel dripped dwale into her mouth.

Meg licked her dry, colourless lips. "Will you stay with me?"

"Yes, of course, my lady, I will not leave—"

"No, I mean when I'm wed. I would hav'you with me." Her words slurred.

"Yes, of course." From beside the fire, Alice cast a furtive glance at the bed, then at Isobel. Patches of early light now squeezed in lines between the closed shutters, like life – thwarted but insistent. Isobel wanted to believe the girl could somehow survive, wanted to imagine a different future for them both. Marriage for Meg now appeared preferable to what seemed inevitable. Clutching her beads through the fabric of her purse, she formed a prayer in the absence of conviction. Opening her eyes, Isobel found Meg watching and, even in the restricted light, her pupils looked small and tight.

"Why d'you pray for me?"

"I pray Our Lord will make you well—"

"No…" She tried to move her head, but even the slight rocking movement made her whimper. A faint sheen varnished her brow, and her breathing quickened and shallowed, but she managed, "Why do you pray for *me*, when I treated you s'cruelly?"

"It matters not; you believed you had cause enough. Sleep, my lady." Isobel dipped a sponge in vinegar water and bathed her forehead, but Meg clasped her arm with surprising strength.

"Tell me," she insisted.

"My lady, you believed only what you were told. You cannot be blamed—"

Her brow creased. "But I *knew* they were wrong. I knew and I said nothing. Joan, the others… they said things that… that…"

"*I* do not hold you to account for the misdeeds of others," Isobel said fiercely. Then, more gently, "I never thought you were to blame. Please, rest now."

"Then I'll ask my father to let you come to me. When I am well. When I'm wed…" she trailed off in a murmur as sleep took her.

"When you are well," Isobel repeated softly.

A grunt of surprise came from across the room. "What are you doing here?" Joan stood slack-jawed and chewing. She had Isobel's ribbon wound into her hair, and her dress gathered lopsided on her waist as if carelessly donned. Wearily, Isobel pushed away from the bed as she came towards Joan's wagging finger.

"The Countess'll have something to say with you here with her daughters, corrupting them with your filth, Lady Margaret being wed soon and all. You mark my words, she'll have you whipped and no mistake, and there'll be no stopping it this time." She jabbed a finger smelling of sweat and sex in Isobel's face, and an indescribable loathing rose in Isobel's gullet for Joan's hypocrisy, her contempt, and her absolute disregard for the girl lying on the edge of life next to them at whom she had barely glanced. Isobel wanted to grab that stabbing finger and snap it. She wanted to vent all the stored fury and frustration of the last months and pour them into the woman's ugly mouth and watch her choke on the bile of her choler. But she didn't. Instead, reaching out, she grabbed the loosened end of the ribbon and wrenched it from Joan's hair. Joan's hand rushed to the back of her head, her face dissolving into venom. "Kat, fetch the guard! Go on, do it; what are you waiting for? You saw her attack me and tear hair from my head!"

Kat started from her daze and scuttled from the room. Folding the ribbon in on itself until it formed a silky parcel, Isobel turned her back on Joan and, tucking the ribbon into Meg's open hand, closed her fingers around it and kissed the sleeping girl's forehead. "Do not try to take it from her," she warned, lifting the sheets from Margaret's legs far enough to release the smell of death. Joan recoiled.

"What have you done to her? She weren't like that when I left."

"And how would you know? When were you here to see? Did you look? Do you even *care*?"

Covering her nose with her sleeve, Joan backed away. "You've poisoned her, that's what you've done. You and your *cunning* box."

"What is this talk of poison?" The Countess stood in the open doorway. A guard flanked her, and Kat bobbed up and down behind them like flotsam on the river. "Why was a guard summoned to this chamber?" Stepping into the room, she spotted Isobel behind the part-drawn bed hanging, and her expression froze.

Joan formed a rapid curtsy. "My lady, I sent for the sergeant when I found Lady Margaret ailing and Mistress Fenton where she had no right to be." Replicating Isobel's action of moments before, Joan swept the bedcovers to one side. If the Countess had been in any doubt of the gravity of her daughter's illness, she wasn't now. Her nostrils flared, but she controlled the urge to cover her nose.

"What with the herbs she'd been given—" Joan's eyes slid to the beaker by the bed and then towards Isobel, "—I thought *she* might be up to mischief."

The Countess's gaze fell on the beaker with the distinctive casket next to it, and beside them, the posy of flowers. Her face hardened; she crooked her finger. "Bring it here."

Pushing past Isobel, Joan retrieved the empty beaker and gave it to the Countess. She sniffed it and then handed it to Sawcliffe, who had appeared like an apparition behind her.

"It is but dwale of my own devising," Isobel said, seeing the look that passed between them. Sawcliffe whispered something barely audible, and the Countess gave a curt nod and he motioned to the guard.

"This will stand further investigation. If I might suggest Mistress Fenton spends a little time answering a few questions, my lady?" He gestured with his hand for Isobel to follow him, but the guard's grim expression left her in little doubt what lay behind Sawcliffe's invitation, and she clutched the bed hanging like a guilty man.

"My lady, I've done nothing to harm Lady Margaret. She was like this when I found her."

"She was nothing like *this*," Joan interposed.

Sawcliffe's head swivelled like a hawk's. "You'll have your say; until then, keep quiet. Mistress Fenton…?" Again, the exaggerated courtesy which gave her no choice but to follow him. She reached for her casket, but he tutted, shaking his head slowly. "I think not, Mistress; let it remain."

WITH THE IMAGE of the Countess tossing the delicate posy of flowers into the heartless fire burned in her mind, Isobel was led from the family apartments across the bailey towards the tower. She ventured to ask, "Where are you taking me?" but received no answer.

On entering, instead of ascending the stairs to the Earl's council chamber, Sawcliffe opened a low door set in the thick stone wall. The gloom intensified as day faded behind them, the only source of illumination coming from a lantern, now being lit, set in an alcove in the single vaulted chamber. Light pooled on the glistening walls. With her feet slithering on damp stone, she put out a hand to steady herself, and it came away greened and wet. From the other side of the room wafted air fouled with rat urine. She wanted to retch.

Sawcliffe indicated an upturned barrel as if it were a throne. "Mistress Fenton?"

She drew back towards the door. "I should not be treated like this. I cannot stay here. I want to see the steward. I must see him, I can explain—"

The guard gave her a shove towards the barrel, and she stumbled past Sawcliffe, turning in desperation. "Do not leave me! Please—"

"I am a patient man, mistress, and I find that time spent in contemplation and without distraction often helps a person recall their crimes without needing further... persuasion."

"I've done nothing wrong!"

He smiled, "So you say," and took the single lantern from its niche.

"The Earl will not allow this," she threw at him in a last attempt. "I am the daughter of a knight. I am the Earl's mistress."

Sawcliffe halted and cocked his head to one side. "Indeed, you are. And Lady Margaret is his daughter and the Countess his noble wife. Where, do you think, do *you* stand?"

He closed the door, leaving Isobel stranded and bewildered and with nothing but the stump end of a candle to light the chamber. "Master Sawcliffe, *please*..." she called out to the retreating footsteps, but they neither hesitated nor turned back, and she strained to hear the last of them until they faded altogether. Only then did Isobel notice the cold.

So hastily had she dressed when Alice came to fetch her that she wore only her night smock and a kirtle – no outer gown and nothing for her shoulders – and the lightest pair of shoes that were already letting the chill through. On brief inspection, there was nothing in the chamber to make it any better. Low-ceilinged, a tall man would have to duck as the vaults fell sharply to either side. A thin slime covered the stone floor in narrow rivers of green where water had spilled from the well head set to one side. She pulled a face; at least she could survive by licking the floor until starvation set in or the rats consumed her. A bucket of sorts lay in one corner, and a plank pallet without blanket or mattress on the other. A hermit might survive here, but the walls crowded in until she felt herself gasping for air, and sweat stood on her brow. Closing her eyes, Isobel sought her garden and its warmth, and gradually her breathing eased. Now shivering, gingerly she pulled her skirts free of the floor, sat on the pallet and, balancing the tallow candle on the top of the barrel, held her hands around the flame. Crouched down, the room appeared bigger, or was it that she was already disappearing from the world?

In such deafening solitude the reality of her situation became apparent, and the initial numbness that had enfolded her dissolved, leaving her raw. In the family apartments of the Earl and his Countess, their daughter lay dying. Would it matter whether the accusation had been fabricated when the Countess herself found truth in it? Would the Earl believe her? Would he believe Isobel?

Isobel had done the one thing she had sworn to herself she would never do: invoked his name to save herself. She had used that tenuous link between them to barter her way out of this place, and the knowledge of it stung as if she had betrayed that part of herself that held true to all that she had been, should be, and hoped for. As if it were possible to feel any filthier than her surroundings already made her, Isobel felt ragged inside and torn.

And in all of this there was Margaret. If Isobel cried, it was more in anticipation of her loss, at the shock of seeing Margaret's young flesh corrupted by whatever it was that ate at her life, and at her own inability to help her or offer what comfort she could. The candle guttered feebly as it consumed itself. Soon it would fail, and Isobel would have to resign herself to darkness. Here in the depths of the castle she was no one. She might not exist at all.

It may have been hours later – or days, judging by the biting hunger that devoured her – when Isobel heard breathing outside the door and grunts as the bar grated from its socket. Light from a lantern shed multiple points into the dark, momentarily blinding her.

"Ursula!" Her servant hurried in, dragging the door closed behind her. "What are you doing here? How did you get in?"

Holding a finger to her lips, Ursula whispered, "Invisible," her voice vibrating Isobel's ears. She deposited a large bundle on the pallet and, holding the lantern close to Isobel's face, examined her. "I have brought you some clothes, my lady. And these," she added, fumbling the bundle open and pressing something into Isobel's hands. Candles. She could smell the beeswax in them; they would burn for hours. Isobel lit one from the lantern's stub, immediately welcoming its distracting scent. "From the Countess's oratory," Ursula added with a note of satisfaction.

"What's happening? How long have I been here? How is Lady Margaret?" Ursula looked bemused, her owl features emphasised in the eerie light. Isobel counted to ten, then tried again. "What day is it?"

"Why, it is today." She bent and fished in the bundle, bringing out a cloak. She blinked as if trying to recall, then burrowed again. "This is all I could find. A mere morsel."

Almost snatching the napkin-wrapped bread from her hands, Isobel sank her teeth into the rough pulp: maslin – and more rye and grit than anything else by the taste of it. Hunger made it the finest manchet but a villain of her manners. "Thank you," she remembered to mumble. "What news of Lady Margaret?" she asked again.

"She ails—"

Isobel huffed, "I know."

"—but she lives yet," Ursula finished. "The Countess is having masses said for her, and there are rumours…" She turned doubtful eyes on her.

"I know," Isobel said again, glum this time.

"I do not believe them," Ursula insisted, "and when my Earl returns he'll have you released, be certain of it."

"With his daughter mortally ill and the Countess out for my blood?" Isobel sucked her cheeks. "Bonds of kinship are stronger than the heart. Hearts can be broken, but the blood ties we are born with endure whatever happens to us."

Ursula spent moments studying her before she answered. "There is *nothing* that love will not overcome. You will understand one day when you love. There is no bond in this realm greater than that of love. I have seen it. It destroys all peace; it is merciless. I have felt it." Her voice dropped as if she spoke to herself, but every word struck as clearly as the reverberation of a bass bell, because whatever Isobel had, it did not – could not – ignite her soul or consume her as Ursula described.

Ursula snapped out of whatever place she had been in and became herself again. She held out the cloak. "It is so cold in here and damp. My lady must ward off evil humours, for a terrible sickness lies in these walls. Men weaken before long, and their teeth loosen and their gums bleed." She helped pull the cloak around Isobel's shoulders. "When Master Holt was kept here beforetime, he was so afflicted he had to be carried out by two men. You should have seen his legs! Pitted like an old apple skin. Blue-black dots. All over. It mattered not, though," she said.

"Why?" Isobel asked, taking the cords of the cloak and securing it. "Did he recover?"

"He might have done," she said, "but he did not live to find out. When my Earl returned from the royal court and heard the charge, Master Holt was hanged within the hour. Had not even killed the huntsman, only cut off his ear, but my Earl wouldn't have brawling and it wasn't the first time Master Holt had stirred the peace." She prattled on, handing over a flask with something bitter mixed with ale "to ward off ill humours". Isobel ceased to listen. She had witnessed the Earl's justice first-hand and was unlikely to forget.

"Shh!" Distant voices saved her from having to hear the gory details of the execution. Thrusting the reduced bundle into Ursula's arms, Isobel snuffed the candle in the lantern she carried and ushered her towards the door. "You must not be caught here, or you will be beaten for certain."

She took Isobel by surprise by wordlessly embracing her, then whispered, *"Invisible!"* and with her skirts hardly stirring the air, she slid from the room, barred the door, and vanished. Isobel waited, but no sound of discovery came, and she remembered to push the candles out of sight just as the door opened.

Sawcliffe entered the room as if he expected to see someone else there and stood for a moment eyeing Isobel as she shuffled beneath his smile, wondering whether he remembered her former apparel. His gaze slid around the chamber, resting on the candle, then on her cloak, before rising to meet her eyes. She resisted the urge to look away and met his gaze.

"I should not be kept here," she began more fearlessly than she felt. "As a knight's daughter, I should be shown respect." Sawcliffe picked up the beeswax candle and sniffed it. Isobel clenched her hands in front of her to stop them shaking. "I wish to see the steward. He alone has the authority to decide what should happen to me and w… where I should be held." She dug nails into her palms.

Sawcliffe's clerk had accompanied him, a big man and silent, and the two of them made the cramped room shrink. Isobel found herself retreating and felt the uneven wall at her back. The clerk placed two stools at the rough table. Putting the lantern he carried on the planks, he settled himself on a third stool to one side. From a leather case slung over his shoulder, he withdrew paper, a quill, and a pot of ink, all of which he aligned with precision in front of him. Sawcliffe nodded to one of the stools, sitting himself on the other and arranging his gown in neat folds over each arm. "Be seated, mistress."

She remained standing. "What authority do you have to question me?"

He raised a neatly arched brow. "The lord steward is engaged on the Earl's business, and I am responsible for such matters as this until his return. When that shall be is in the hands of Almighty God, amen, amen, amen, for the ways are treacherous, are they not, Mistress Fenton?"

What ways? What did he mean – the half-drowned paths that served as roads in winter, or something else?

"Be seated," he said pleasantly. "There is no need for further discomfort. If you answer truthfully, all this—" he waved his hand at the darkened room, "—can be ended. I expect you are hungry, no?" His teeth gleamed in the lamplight. At the click of his fingers, his clerk handed him a small basket from which rose a rich, savoury aroma, making Isobel's mouth water. Sawcliffe put the basket on the table between them and removed the napkin, releasing a heavenly scent. Beneath, a pie – crust golden and flaking and gilded with saffron – heaved with meat and gravy.

"Here, take it," he held it out. "Eat, whilst it is still hot from the oven."

Saliva gathered. Isobel swallowed and averted her head. "It is a day of fast."

"Hmm, so it is. This was made for Lady Margaret. Ailing, she does not have to abstain from eating flesh. But, alas, she is too ill to eat. What a pity. Still, it is a sin to waste good food," and he bit into the side of the pie, sending fragments tumbling and juices glistening at the corners of his mouth. Isobel's stomach growled, and she clasped it to smother its protest.

He replaced the pie with an iota of regret and pushed the basket to one side, where it continued to taunt. "But, as you say, it is a fast day." Dabbing delicately at his mouth with a finely embroidered hand-coverchief, so at odds with his plain-clothed austerity, and brushing crumbs from his wool gown, he resumed seamlessly. "Who paid you to poison Lady Margaret?"

Isobel wrenched her eyes from the basket, her mouth falling open. "What? *What!*"

"In your possession is a purse of coin. Who gave it to you?"

Gathering her wits, she closed her mouth. He must have had her room searched. "Th… the Earl."

He dismissed the suggestion with a sneer. "Why would the Earl give *you* his purse?"

"Before he went away. He gave me money in case I… I needed… it."

"There is no record of it. Who paid you?"

"No one… I didn't… I wouldn't. She's ill—"

"Lady Margaret's attendants say she had recovered, yet she sickened when you went to her rooms. Why were you in her apartments? What were you doing? Who sent you?"

"I tell you the truth. No one sent me. I went because… because she wanted to see me and—"

"You lie. Lady Margaret could not have asked for you because she was unconscious. *Why* did you go to her rooms? *Who* sent you?"

"She *did* send for me," Isobel protested. "Ask Alice."

"Alice is unable to tell us anything. She sickened shortly after you left. She has a fever."

"Wh… when she recovers, she will tell you, Meg… Lady Margaret was conscious when I arrived. We talked. Sh… she spoke to me."

"She *spoke* to you?" he asked softly.

Isobel faltered at the change. "Yes, when I got there she was awake, and she said she wanted me to… to…" She stuttered to a halt as Sawcliffe's eyes narrowed.

"You claim she spoke to you, yet now she cannot be roused, and she weakens and her flesh putrefies."

"I gave her a potion to help her sleep, that is why you cannot wake her."

"You admit," he said slowly, enunciating each syllable with precision, "that you gave Lady Margaret a potion?"

"It was but dwale!"

"From which she is unlikely to wake, God have everlasting mercy on her soul, amen, amen, amen." He crossed himself. "The facts stand for themselves. You can make it easier on yourself and confess now or face further inquiry. Who paid you to poison Lady Margaret Langton?"

"I did *not* poison her. I would not hurt her."

"Oh? She snubbed you, did she not?"

"Yes, but only because she had been told lies about me."

"She snubbed you, and you sought revenge. Taking advantage of her sickness, you gained admittance to her apartment and, feigning compassion, fed her a potion, draining the cup and cleansing it of any trace of poison. Who told you to kill Lady Margaret?"

"I did *not* want to hurt her!"

"So," Sawcliffe said, "who did?"

The clerk's quill scratched across the paper, loud in the pause that followed. He stopped. Waited. By now, the shaking in Isobel's hands had travelled to her shoulders and beyond control, and no amount of warmth could have driven it away. The clerk waited patiently, quill poised. Sawcliffe folded his hands before him on the table.

"I believe you to be an honest girl, mistress, and, until recently, your lack of worldliness and your father's death – God rest his soul – have made you vulnerable to the deceits of men. You were to marry Thomas Lacey, were you not?"

Isobel wanted to wipe a dribble from her nose and searched in her purse for a handkerchief but found none. She sniffed instead. "Yes," she murmured.

"And you were disappointed in that ambition?" She nodded.

"But you continued to correspond." Not trusting her voice, she shook her head. He leaned towards her. "When did you last see Thomas Lacey, Mistress Fenton?"

See him? What could she say? That she last saw him in the company of the Earl of Warwick a matter of days ago? Or in the hall of Beaumancote at Yule? She had been told by the Earl to say nothing, sworn to remain silent. But Sawcliffe acted for the Earl; would he not already know, should she not tell? Or would any admission merely justify Sawcliffe's suspicions?

He saw her hesitation. "Let me make myself plain. I believe you have maintained a connection to this young man. Did you let him have knowledge of you? Did you entrap the Earl and even now plot his death? Did Thomas Lacey persuade you? Has he made promises to you? Speak, confess, and your punishment will be swift. I have no wish to force it from you."

Isobel trembled from head to tail and couldn't have formed a word, let alone a confession. All she could do was shake her head in a show of resistance.

"You disappoint me. I had hoped to spare you further torment, but you leave me no choice." He reached into the leather bag resting on the table and withdrew a folded paper. Isobel instantly recognised the broken seal of Lord Lacey and the letter Thomas had sent her oh, so long ago it hurt to remember. "I have no need of your confession; this is evidence enough of your communication. Do not think that my lord will hesitate to punish you. Treachery is abhorrent. You will be tried for petty treason."

Words stumbled from her mouth. *"Treason?"*

"You conspire with Thomas Lacey to cause harm to the daughter of the Earl, *ipso facto* you conspire against his flesh as if it is his own. Be glad it is not counted *high* treason, or you would be drawn before burning."

The stool clattered on the stone floor as Isobel stood. "This is madness! I have no affiliation or... or anything with Thomas Lacey.

Th… the letter is nothing. Thomas only told me of my servant's illness…" It sounded as implausible now as when the Earl's caustic comments about the letter had reduced her willing gullibility to mere stupidity. But he had accepted her innocence nonetheless. "My lord will speak the truth of it when he returns."

"Sit down, Mistress Fenton."

The clerk righted the stool, but Isobel looked wildly about her, seeing the door to freedom, calculating her chances of making it to the gatehouse before being caught. And tried. And burned.

"Sit. Down." She sat.

"The Countess is convinced of your malice. The Earl has favoured you beyond what might be expected, and she suspects you have beguiled him. She calls for your immediate trial… wait—" he raised his hand, cutting short her protest, "—and it would not be difficult to prove the case." Rising from the table, Sawcliffe cracked his knuckles. He moved around the room examining its grim confines, finally coming back towards the table until he stopped behind her. Isobel didn't move, feeling the heat of him on her back, felt the tip of a nail map a delicate line down her neck leaving a trail of gooseflesh. The clerk kept his eyes fixed on the paper in front of him. Sawcliffe breathed out. "It would be a pity to see such youth wither in this place only to be wasted on a pyre. What would your father say if he knew his daughter had let herself be plucked, hmm?" He turned away abruptly, the sudden cold welcome after the stifling scent of clove. "However, there might be something I can do to persuade my lady not to press the case against you." He halted by the clerk, peering over his shoulder at the transcript. "For this I will need something in return." Isobel's head shot up, and Sawcliffe shook his head. "No, *that* is a pleasure my office forbids. I am an obedient man, and there is some flesh of which I will not taste, although I daresay the fruit is sweet enough." He put a hand over the page on which the clerk wrote, and the man ceased writing. "Godfrey, bring me the sealing wax; you know where it is."

Sawcliffe waited until the man's footsteps could no longer be heard upon the stair, then swept onto his stool in a wave of spice, leaning forward across the table with his hands flat against the wood, urgency in his tone. "I will ensure your release and, in return, we will meet on occasion in more pleasant circumstances and resume our conversation—"

"About what?" Isobel interrupted.

He sat back, crossing his hands and resuming his benign smile. "Nothing more than your day-to-day observances: who you see, what passes between servants, idle chatter, tattle."

"But… I am kept apart from the household."

Heavy-lidded eyes regarded her without blinking. "You are kept close to the Earl."

Had she misheard? "*Spy* on him? You would have me compile reports on the *Earl*?"

"Guard your voice," he said, a sharpness returning. "For the sake of my lord I would have you relate such matters as may pass between you so that I may better protect him."

"If it is in the Earl's service then there is no reason why I should not tell him, Master Sawcliffe."

"Great lords do not wish to be concerned with trivial matters. That is why they employ men such as myself. And I employ whatever means necessary to ensure his continuing security. Now," he said, picking up his clerk's transcript in his left hand and Thomas's letter in his right, "you have a simple question to ask yourself: do you undertake this little service for me, in which case there need be no reason to keep a record of what has passed here today, and you will be free to leave." Holding the transcript close to the candle, he tempted the flame. "Or, do you face the consequences of prosecution for petty treason, the outcome of which, you can be assured, will secure your death and, for me, the everlasting gratitude of the Countess." He waved Thomas's letter in front of her, reducing his voice to little more than a whisper as he heard the first echoes of his returning clerk. "Mistress Fenton, the choice is yours." Tucking the two pieces of paper into the leather satchel, he quirked one eyebrow meaningfully and, rubbing his hands together and cracking his joints again, stood. "Ah, Godfrey, I am finished here. I find such close confinement in damp quarters troubling." He crushed the wick of the candle between inked fingers, leaving only the light of the lantern to eerily light his face. Demon shadows danced as he lifted it high. "All fruit withers. All burns in the cleansing fire. And, rest assured, fire *is* coming to rid this land of infestation. Let yours not be the fuel for one of them.

I give you until Vespers." With that, the door shut, leaving her in the dark.

"But I do not know what hour it is!" Isobel called after him, pressing her face to the grill, his echoed reply becoming less distinct as he moved away.

"*'None shall know the hour of His coming,'* Mistress Fenton. Think on it."

Think on it. That was all she *could* do. Shuffling forward in the darkness, Isobel patted the air until her hand came into contact with the barrel, then she fumbled her way onto it. She sat miserably contemplating her options. No bell rang. Only the intermittent drip from deep in the well marked the passing of time. She shifted, and her foot bumped into something on the floor. Hands outlining a basket, she detected the still-warm pie. She shoved it away with a violent kick until it was safely beyond temptation.

What now? Isobel had witnessed the Earl's justice first-hand, knew he gave no quarter to his enemies and expected none in return. His justice was absolute. Would he believe she conspired with Thomas against him, against his daughter? Could he believe that of his mistress? Would he?

What did she owe him but a void marriage contract and an enforced familiarity? For all the freedom being his mistress gained her, she might as well remain in this cell. He had failed in so many ways to fulfil his duties as lord, so why didn't she defend herself and tell Sawcliffe that it was the Earl who had instigated the letters to Thomas? Why didn't she agree to the terms laid before her because, quite frankly, she could save herself by becoming his informant? It'd be simple. Slip Sawcliffe a few words now and again – nothing substantial, no more than gossip – and he would guarantee her safety.

But Isobel had sworn she would tell no one about the letters, and it was not just her oath that bound her, but her father's. And it was not just the Earl who trusted her, but his brother. Robert's regard meant more than she had realised, and the remembrance of him, so close she could feel the rise and fall of his chest as they rode the free fens together, was the spark of hope burning inside. Something else niggled away like a maggot: Sawcliffe didn't know. Sawcliffe didn't know because the Earl hadn't told him, and if he hadn't told him, he didn't trust him.

So why should she?

Isobel could no more act as his spy than she could have harmed Meg. She couldn't confess to something she had not done because it betrayed the only thing she had left – her integrity – and the roots of that integrity went far beyond the day of her birth to the time of her forefathers. Choice was an illusion, something perhaps Sawcliffe could not understand. Isobel would not betray the Earl because the Earl was more than the man, he was what her father had believed in and what she had been brought up to revere: loyalty before all else – before her own life. Whatever he had done to her, no matter how she felt about him, Isobel was as bound to the idea of him as her father before.

Affinity.

The question now would be, how far did the Earl's loyalty extend beyond his own family needs and that of the King? What bound him to *her*?

Nothing.

Pulling her feet off the damp floor, she wrapped her arms about her knees and buried her chin in the wool of the cloak. It felt damp and already smelled musty like an old sheep. Grimy and bedraggled, Isobel hardly thought the Earl would give her any further consideration than he would an alewife if he saw her in that state. At least an alewife had something else to offer him. Without the Earl's protection, her situation became more precarious than ever. What did that mean? Would she find herself in the unthinkable position of *gratitude* towards him? Plead for *clemency*? And even so, would he return in time, or was the Countess even now instructing a pyre to be built in the bailey? She wondered, in a brief, grim moment, whether the sergeant-at-arms might show her mercy and render her senseless with a ligature about her neck before the flames reached her. She had but one real option: to agree to terms with Sawcliffe and buy herself time.

Time.

DEVOID OF LIGHT to mark the passing of time, Isobel must have drifted because she started at the sound of scuffling close by and in a half-waking state saw Sawcliffe, a pie clenched between his teeth, scuttle under the door. Isobel shook her head free of dreams. Rats. Several of them by the hubbub they made, fighting over the remains of the pie, and made bigger and louder by the dark. And another sound – distant voices raised, angry, coming closer. She realised, with a rush of fear, that Vespers must be near, and a decision had to be made.

Smoothing her hair and rubbing her sleeve across her face, she rose, scattering the rats with blind feet, her breathing halting and expectant. The securing bar grated from its socket and, grasping her bidding beads in both hands, Isobel closed her eyes.

A grunt of surprise, then, fiercely, "I did not believe it when told you were being kept down here. In God's name, what has put you in this place?"

Her eyes shot open, wincing in the sudden light. Rob stood there, his thick dark hair curling slightly and sticking to his forehead, his travelling clothes wet-patched and spattered with mud. She stepped towards him and put out a tentative hand. "Is it raining?" she said, feeling stupid.

Handing the lantern to someone behind him, he took her by the elbow and bent to look in her face. "What have they done to you?"

"You came. I… I never thought you would come." She swallowed to regain some semblance of composure. Failed. "I am accused of poisoning Meg," she rushed, words tumbling like a river bursting its banks. "Master Sawcliffe says I've conspired with Thomas against the Earl, and the Countess will see me burned for it. He has the letter – the one from Thomas – and he wants me to… to tell him… to tell…" She ran out of words. "But you know the *truth* of it, you know I would never hurt her. Please, do not let them burn me!"

"*Burn* you? We will see about that," he muttered.

She used her sleeve to wipe her nose and choked out, "H… have you seen Meg?"

His eyes closed briefly, and he nodded. "The priest is with her now, waiting to perform Extreme Unction."

So soon? "Can nothing be done?"

He shook his head. "Nothing." He led her to the door. "I'll have you escorted to your chamber. I am going back to be with her until the end; it will not be long now. My brother… he would want me to be there."

"My lord, please, tell her that… that… I…"

She couldn't continue. He simply nodded again and said, "I will," and turned to swiftly walk away and out of sight.

"Mistress?"

Isobel had forgotten the other man waiting. "Pip!" she gasped.

Philip Taylor's face crumpled into a beam, the light emphasising the folds. "*Pip*, is it now? Aye, I reckon you've earned it right well enough bein' in here." He grimaced at their surroundings. "My lord wants you safe, an' I reckon there's a jug of ale in it if I see you aright. There's nowt that'll come between me and my cup, as you well know. Let's be getting you back, an' I can be getting on."

He lit the way until dull daylight made the need for the lantern redundant, and he snuffed the flame as they reached the first step, giving her a moment to adjust. She hesitated, momentarily disoriented.

"None'll stop you, lass," he said quietly. "Lord Robert near rode his horse into the ground to get here, an' he'll not see ye harmed, mark me, he won't."

Chapter 6

ROBERT RETURNED AFTER nightfall, long after Isobel had bathed and Ursula had washed from her hair the last taint of the cellars. Sitting by the fire, Isobel listened to the tolling of the bell that marked the passing of the Earl's daughter and added prayers of her own to the sombre notes rising from the chapel tower.

Chou raised her head in greeting as, stiff-limbed from hours in the saddle, Rob lowered himself into the chair. He said nothing to begin with, and Isobel didn't ask, and he spent what seemed like ages watching the flames consume wood. Eventually he breathed out.

"Her end was peaceful." He stopped, sucked in his cheeks, then continued. "She slept most of the time, but then she woke and seemed confused; she thought you would be there. I told her you were looking after Cecily, and she found solace in that. She worries – worried – for her sister. Meg said you were going with her to Wales; I… do not think she realised how ill she had become." He turned aside and studied the simple tracery of the window, giving them both time to compose themselves. He cleared his throat. "She was holding this when she died." He extended his hand, and in it lay the crumpled ribbon.

"I wished her to have it," Isobel whispered.

"She knew that, Isobel, and the thought of it brought her much comfort, but the Countess would have taken it if she had seen it." Remembering the fate of the posy of flowers cast into the fire, Isobel nodded.

"I am glad you were there," she said after a while. "It is right someone she loved was with her at the end."

"Yes." He sounded so dejected. Isobel wanted to reach out and comfort him, but there was nothing she could think of to make it any easier for him or for herself. The fire hissed and spat, reminding her of her own mortality – if any such reminder were needed – and of a brief life, so easily extinguished.

As if he read her mind he said, "You will be safe enough now. There will be no summary trial while I am here, and I doubt my brother will see events in the same way as his wife on his return." He smiled but without humour. "The Duke gave me leave to attend matters, but I am bidden to return immediately." He looked exhausted. Although he had bathed and changed, and days in the saddle against raw winds had beaten colour into his skin, beneath he was ghost-pale and his eyes sunken.

She placed an uncertain hand on his arm. "Will you not rest, my lord?"

Covering her hand with his own, calloused from hours in the practice yard, his tired smile became reflective. "When I was a boy, my father used to say that the only rest I could expect would be in my grave. *A lord's duty is never done,* he would say. *Whether it is in governance of your lands and family, or in service to your king and God, you will never be at rest. The only peace you can find is in here,* and he tapped his chest and then his head, *because you'll find none on this earth until you're part of it.*" Rob frowned. "I used to think he exaggerated, that he surely could not include his wife and sons in such a bleak condemnation of life; but later I understood that it wasn't that he bore little regard for us, but that love and loyalty came at a price, and the price he paid for a lifetime spent bound by duty was to feel the hurt more keenly. I understand that now. I wonder whether it is better not to form attachments than to see them severed by death, or by… others." As he removed his hand from hers, she felt its absence. She thought of the grief of loss inflicted unwittingly on her by her parents, and then of Rob's own, caused by the death of his wife and before that the succession of stillbirths they had endured together. And now this.

"Will the Duke not grant you leave of a few days more?"

"He might if he knew the circumstance; he is fair-minded enough. His Grace is also grateful to you for your intelligence. He is exacting in his demands, but rewards fealty equally."

"It sounds as if you like him."

Thoughtfully, he nodded. "I do. I presumed he might be like Clarence, but he could not be more different. It has taken me a while to get to know him, but the greater my acquaintance, the more I see in him. The Earl saw it, but then he had met the Duke beforetimes when he lived in Warwick's household, and he is a good judge of men – or a boy, as His Grace was then." He accepted the spiced ale Ursula offered him, warming his hands around the glazed cup, although sweat gathered at his hairline.

Isobel had been drawing a loose thread from her sleeve as he spoke, picturing the young Duke and his steady, perceptive gaze. "My father said that loyalty was the greatest demand that could be placed on a man, and the greatest gift that could be bestowed."

"Did he?"

"I said that I thought it was love, as Christ taught us, but he laughed and said that loyalty went beyond love, because love issues from feeling, and the heart is a kinder master than the head. He said that loyalty is more than a matter of the heart – it binds men whether they wish it or no, sometimes for generations." She shook her head. "I am not sure whether I understood him then."

"And now?"

Isobel considered her father's absolute loyalty to the Earl and thought it misplaced. "Perhaps less now than I ever did. Anyway, it was always *men's* loyalty of which he spoke. Women have no say in to whom their father gives his allegiance, or their husband, or brothers, or sons."

"It appears you do not agree with your father's choice of lord," he said quietly.

"It is more that his allegiance is expected to be mine, that's all," she dodged. "And that even if my conscience dictated otherwise, I am bound by his choice. When does a woman's loyalty count?"

"When she uses the senses God gave her and warns of potential treachery, that's when. Even now, Gloucester has informed the King, and the King will not let the matter lie. You might be a small fish in a big pond, Isobel, but a small fish might see what others miss… what is it?" he asked at her sudden burst of laughter.

"It is just something my father used to call me."

"And? Why do you smile? Tell me," he insisted, his own mouth curving in response.

She had never told another soul this name, so precious and personal as it was, so she hesitated. Then, "He used to call me 'Minnow'."

When Isobel raised her eyes, she found him looking at her with a softened expression and any regret at spilling her name so wantonly evaporated in the warmth of his smile.

"Minnow," he said, softly. "I like that. Minnow."

And so did she. Isobel liked the way his mouth formed her name and the way the timbre of his voice mellowed it, and saw how close he now leaned so that either of them only need stretch a little and their lips would touch.

A metallic clang sent a shaft of sound between them, and Ursula bent to retrieve a copper bowl still reverberating on the floor. Isobel had forgotten she was there, almost forgotten the events of the last day. So had Robert. He sat back, awkwardly, preparing to rise. "I must go," he said. "The Earl will be returning soon, and preparations must be made."

ROBERT HAD SEEN the flash of disappointment in Isobel's eyes before she masked it, and he had left her with greater reluctance than he liked to admit. Now back in his own chamber, his skin burned, and he longed to rest it against something cold. His head ached, and a skewer of white-hot steel pierced his left eyeball. He closed his eyes only to find hers, pools of cool water, looking back at him. His face flared and with it his temper. He hit the first thing with which his fist came into contact, and the leaded pane collapsed under the impact. Martin appeared at his side.

"My lord—"

"Get out!"

"But my lord, your hand…"

Robert looked down: blood dripped steadily from where the torn lead and shattered glass had lacerated his skin. It meant nothing. He felt nothing. "Leave it." He took the handkerchief with which Martin attempted to stem the flow and bound it himself, tying an untidy knot and drawing the loose ends tight with his teeth. "Get yourself something to eat. Go!" he insisted when his esquire wavered.

Breathing hard, he collapsed into his chair, leaning on his undamaged hand. He ran a finger around his neck and found it wet with sweat but, despite the heat pulsing in waves, he shivered and his limbs ached. He must be more tired than he had first thought.

Like a shoot beneath the soil, Isobel Fenton had been growing in his mind, pushing towards the surface of his consciousness until, just minutes ago, she had burst forth rendering him speechless and confused. Had it been like this with his wife, Ann? Had he felt this mixture of excitement and fear, a trembling deep inside, burrowing, a thought so insistent that it throbbed? He couldn't remember, and the realisation came as a shock. Isobel Fenton filled him as completely as a well of water until she flowed around him, drowning out all other thoughts, drowning *him*. He had hoped that time spent away from her would have cured him of the sickness he had acknowledged growing in him some months ago, cauterising it with absence before it grew too large. Too late.

The bell still tolled its mournful message, each beat heavy with loss, and he felt it more keenly because lying beneath the sorrow for his niece was a deeper, more brutal grief: Isobel belonged to his brother. She could not be his, and this new anguish was made more potent by remorse, guilt tinged with envy, fuelled by love. What had she said to him, that loyalty was the greater master? She had a point, but had she ever loved?

Sweat cooled in the steady stream of cold air filtering from the broken window. His chamber felt empty and lifeless. The fire hastily lit on his return was now nothing more than greying ashes. Only the remnants of the once-warm heart still glowed feebly. It would need feeding or it would go out, like his own. Crouching, Robert picked up split sticks and placed them over the embers, waiting until they caught before piling on more. Drops of rain falling down the long shaft of the chimney hissed, but the new fire burned bright and clean. The eager flames failed to warm him, and he dragged the cover from his bed. Wrapping it around his aching shoulders, he settled back into his chair with his feet on the hearth.

MARGARET HAD BEEN prepared for death. Washed and laid out in spectacular mourning, and her thin hair dressed to make it look full, her skin had been delicately powdered back to life. She might have been sleeping except the Earl had never seen her so lovingly cared for in life, and the scented oils and balm failed to disguise her decomposing flesh. Thus she would go to her tomb next to her brother, and there she would lie incorruptible for eternity while the world perished about her. His child, his daughter, whom he had barely known and loved less than she deserved. He shut his eyes and tried to picture her as she had been.

"She has you beguiled." Tight-lipped, Felice stood next to him. "Your wanton has you so deceived you turn a blind eye to the poisoning of your own kin."

The Earl caught a fleeting image of Meg, lit by spring sunlight in the courtyard, dancing after... what were they?

"You are deceived, my lord. Master Sawcliffe has evidence of it."

Dandelion clocks. He smiled at her delight.

"She is a traitor," she insisted. "You have taken her to your bed, and look how she repays you. You are bewitched."

His eyes snapped open. "Enough! Is there not death in abundance that you look for hers as well? Have respect, madam, and let our daughter rest. Your bile will poison the child you carry."

"*Your* child, my lord. Your son—"

"My *son* is dead. Isobel Fenton's death will not change that, and I'll be damned to Hell if I let our daughter's time in purgatory be stained with her blood. I pray her time will be short; she has done nothing to deserve more."

"Pray? You?" Felice almost snorted. "When was the last time you said a Paternoster? Do you even know where you keep your beads, or is it in the same place as your heart?" She genuflected, bowed to the altar, and in a flurry of jasmine-scented silk turned on an elegant heel and left him standing there alone with his daughter and the bewildered faces of the attendants.

THE EARL WOKE sometime during the night and lay listening to Isobel's steady breathing next to him. Hunger for her had not diminished over time and distance, but he found his appetite unsatisfied and a stone of disquiet lodged in his belly. Chouchou snored on the floor next to them, and the Earl gave up trying to fill his mind with sleep and rose without disturbing them.

Padding soft-footed across his privy chamber, he slid across the metal bar securing the shutters and viewed a distorted land barely lit by the vivid sickle of a waxing moon in the cloudless night. He made out the dark line of the river, the swell of land beyond, but the familiar woods were rendered an indistinguishable smudge and clarity eluded him. He tried to recall the scene as he had surveyed it so many times – a mirror of his memory – warped and imperfect. How much of his life had become so, laid bare under the moonlight so that only the bones of what made him a man stood proud of the flesh of ephemera? How would he stand before that last judgment on a day he had pushed out of mind because he could not bear to look at what he had become? History scarred his forearms, marks he had often found Isobel tracing with her eyes as he held her, silent as always; but she had never asked him about them, never showed any curiosity. Did he care if she knew? Did it matter what she thought of him? And he realised, without a shadow of doubt, that it did.

He grew cold by the window. He closed the shutters on the world and retraced his steps to find his gown and a candle. Leaning forward to light the wick in the remains of the fire, the icy key he always kept close swung against his naked chest. He enclosed it in his fist and, drawn by the memories held inside, he unlocked the aumbry to which it belonged. Once, a long, long time ago, he had found himself standing on the riverbank mesmerised by the water. He had heard the shouted warnings, but watery voices drowned out caution, and he had reached to touch the silvery ripples. And so he found himself now and all his willpower impotent against the lure of what lay within the cabinet, waiting to pierce his ironbound heart.

Inside, a proud knight rode his painted horse, the blue and yellow trappings worn almost translucent from hours of play. Taking the toy, the Earl spun the wheels, hearing their rattle. Had his son heard the free voices in the river that morning, had they called to him, soft and alluring? There had been no one there to stop him. He had slipped away from life as easily as he had escaped his nurses during morning devotions – silently and without notice – and it was only when his favourite plaything was discovered on the riverbank that the search switched from the castle to the river. His body had been discovered lodged in the roots of a tree, limbs limp like rags.

The knight's lance had become dislodged and lost. In reaching for it, the Earl's hand nudged something hidden in the back of the aumbry. He withdrew his arm and there, suspended from his open palm, lay a string of paternoster beads, so long obscured they might as well have been lost – a man's beads, heavy with Aves of jet and gauds of coral, the silk-tasselled end an indeterminate colour in the yellow candlelight. He felt his heart swell, and his head swam with memories, and the image of his daughter became tangled with his son until they became one. Crushing the beads against his lips, he attempted to stifle the pain crawling from his chest up his throat and gulped air, but it continued in relentless pursuit, running him down, pinning him with a spear of grief.

Isobel awoke when Chou snorted, the dog's claws clattering against the carved wooden post as she rolled over and sat up. Isobel's exposed shoulder was cold and the bed beside her empty. The dog whimpered. Isobel leaned over and soothed her head, but she remained alert.

"What is it?"

Chou's claws tic-ticked across the floor towards the other side of the chamber where a faint glow hinted at candlelight beyond the thick bed hangings. Curious, Isobel slipped into her smock and followed.

A figure kneeled by the open cabinet, and in the moment he moved as Chou nudged his arm, Isobel recognised the misery on the Earl's face.

"My lord?"

His back stiffened. He almost threw something into the cabinet. "Go back to bed," he said, his voice rough and congested. She took a few steps forward, close enough to see his back flinch. He half turned. "Did you not hear what I said?" He held something so tightly his knuckles glowed white. She had never seen him like this before, cowed, almost vulnerable. Kneeling beside him, Isobel eased the object from his grasp before he crushed it. She recognised the little toy horse and its rider she had seen captured in marble and resting in the hand of his stone son.

"What was his name?"

The Earl cleared his throat and rasped, "Duarte. His name was Duarte – Edward."

"After the King?"

"After my brother and grandfather. But… for the King, also." He took the knight from her, brushing dust from the crevices of the wood until the gilded rider shone in his glittering armour. "They did not deserve death, Isobel, neither of them. She should not have died." He faltered and tried again. "My daughter – Margaret – Meg, knew nothing of sin."

"She was blameless," Isobel said quietly.

"But *I* am *not*." He accused his own chest with his forefinger. "God forgive the rest of us if He exacts vengeance on the innocent for the sin of others. How long do they have to suffer for my iniquity? How long will He make *me* suffer?"

"I… I know not – no one knows. We all sin by our very nature; but Margaret had no rooted sins, merely venial, and she desired nothing more than to find peace with God. He is merciful; her time in purgatory will be short and lenient."

"Unlike mine." He paused as if considering whether to continue. "When my son died, I asked learned men how long he would have to suffer, but they could not tell me. They did say, in great detail, *why* he should suffer and what I should do to lessen his suffering through the saying of costly masses, yet not one was able to tell me how *long* he would remain in that state, separated from God by *my* sin."

"What sin?" Isobel asked. "God sees all and forgives those who seek it. Nothing is beyond Him."

"There are sins of the flesh and of man's weakness, and God knows I am as guilty of those as any; but there are mortal sins, Isobel."

"Nothing is beyond God," she repeated earnestly, "as long as confession is made and penance sought. And you have confessed, haven't you, my lord?"

Isobel couldn't see his face, but his hands screwed shut. "How – how can I repent? How can I right the wrong I did? I thought that in doing my father's will... by obeying him..." He faltered, sounding more confused than anything. "Even now, after all this time, I am punished through the suffering of my children." He looked at her then, and Isobel's heart crumbled.

"My lord, you must make confession."

"How? I do not know how anymore. I believed my son's death was my punishment, that if I kept away from my daughters they would be safe. But my Meg... my girl... I have wronged her." At the mention of her name his voice gave out, and she felt her resolve against him weaken in the face of such abject misery.

"My lord..." She touched the crown of his head, unsure how to comfort him. He reached for her, pulling her to him and burying his face in her neck, holding himself to her until the shaking in his body eased and his tortuous breathing subsided. Isobel kneeled there, stroking his thick hair as he gradually regained control.

Eventually, he sat back on his heels without meeting her eyes. He still held the toy. As he released it, indentations marked his palms where the wheels had bitten his flesh. He looked at it for a moment more, then placed the knight on the shelf in the cupboard. "So shall I bury my daughter," he said, and closed the door.

Isobel started to shiver, partly because of the stream of cold air filtering under the door and creeping like mist across the floor, but also because the man before her, who had always represented invulnerable authority, had revealed a part of him she had never imagined existed. She had always believed his indifference to his daughters stemmed from a lack of feeling, a lack of feeling because of the corrupted nature of the man. It was easy to hate him for it, to pile one iniquity upon another until it became an unassailable obstacle. Any kindness he demonstrated towards her she had warped until it became something else, something dark and self-serving. If Isobel trembled now, it was because her resolve to hate him had been undermined like snow on the riverbank at the onset of spring, and she could not face that, not now, not after everything he had done to her.

He led her back to bed and had her lie by him, covering her in the linen and heavy velvets until she stopped shaking, and all the while he watched without touching.

"My lord, let me attend the funeral tomorrow," Isobel said before she became too sleepy to ask.

"It is better you are not seen."

"I will stay hidden at the back; I want to pray for her," she insisted.

"I know you do, but you can add your prayers in private devotion. I have masses being said in every church in each of my domains. I will ensure she... Margaret, will not go unsung." He had regained his composure, drawing over himself the mantle of authority he usually assumed, and Isobel wondered whether she had dreamed his vulnerability. "I know you held her in your heart and keep her there still."

"I will pray for her, my lord." *And for you*, she wanted to say, because she couldn't hate him enough – not in her confused state – to wish him eternal damnation. But she didn't, because the time when she could have said that, and he might have been prepared to listen, had now passed.

Chapter 7

"HOW LONG HAS he been like this?"

Martin shifted uneasily. "Lord Robert dismissed me yestereve, my lord. I found him this morning."

With a sense of foreboding the Earl leaned against the post of his brother's bed and silently counted to ten as he gathered the rising panic and quelled it. Rob lay in a tangled mass of bedclothes, glassy-eyed with fever, skin glazed. The Earl swore under his breath; he had seen this too many times before. "Call my physician."

The steward gave a shallow bow. "He also has the French ague, my lord. Shall I have his apprentice fetched?"

"What? Oh, yes. Make it quick."

"Yes, my lord. And your chaplain?"

"God's teeth, would you have me bury my brother alongside my daughter!" Hyde's expression remained unchanged and as phlegmatic as ever. The Earl moderated his tone. "No, he has other duties to attend. Let us pray Lord Robert is not one of them."

"Amen, my lord," his steward said, with an unnerving degree of sincerity, and the Earl found himself wishing, not for the first time in the last months, that he could summon the same depth of piety, then perhaps all this would stop, and he could find some peace. He refocused on his brother to find him awake and struggling to speak. He placed a hand on his shoulder, feeling the sweat in the clammy cloth of his shirt, and found little resistance as he pressed him back onto the pillow.

"Robert, I must away. The King bids me ride immediately to meet him with what men I can muster. Welles has roused a rabble in Lincolnshire, and the King will not allow it to pass unchallenged, not after last year."

His brother struggled to sit upright again but collapsed back against the bolster. "I'll join you as soon as I can. In a few days, God willing. As soon as I can ride." He licked his lips, his throat rough and parched from fever. "Tell the Duke… I will not fail him…" He lifted his hand, but it fell feebly against the covers.

"I will tell His Grace the French have bested you, shall I?" the Earl jested, then frowned as Robert, in attempting to speak again, failed. "Be still, you are in no fit state to ride, let alone fight. Besides, I need you here. I cannot leave the castle undefended. This insurrection…" he shook his head, suddenly pensive, "… this *rebellion* might be nothing more than minor discontent stirred up by Welles, but should it go ill for us – should there be no other way – see my wife and daughters… daughter," he corrected himself, "safe to our estates in Portugal, and stay there until the way is clear for your return. Bess will have Dalton to fend for her."

"And Isobel?"

The Earl pursed his lips in thought. "Let her go home to her manor; it is all she has ever wanted, and that is something at least I can give her. I have left enough men to defend it unless an assault is sustained."

"Lacey will not give up."

"If it comes to battle, believe me, I have no intention of him leaving the field alive, little brother – no matter whose side he is on," he added wryly. "And if by some chance he survives and I do not—"

"I'll protect her," Rob promised weakly.

The Earl raised a sardonic eyebrow. "I was going to make you swear on our father's tomb to kill Thomas Lacey yourself, but I appreciate your loyalty to my mistress." The Earl frowned as Robert closed his eyes and grew visibly wan despite the fever forcing colour in distinct slashes across his cheeks. He squeezed Rob's arm, noting the burning flesh beneath his hand. "I am depending on you to make a full recovery. You are my heir; I need to know that this—" and he described the room and all that lay unseen beyond it with a sweep of his hand, "—will continue even if I do not."

Robert managed a half-smile in response. "The only way you'll know is to come back."

ON LEAVING HIS brother fitfully sleeping, the Earl turned left at the stair. In bidding goodbye to his wife in her solar, he outlined what was to happen in the event he should be killed or captured, much as he had always done before departing on an unknown road. But this time he amended his usual instructions. "Whatever injury you believe I have done you, no matter what happens to me, I place the welfare of Isobel Fenton in your hands. Should any mishap befall her, whatever the cause, I will hold you, and you alone, responsible. I have left instructions to that effect."

Felice lifted her chin and stared down her pinched nose. "You admonish *me*, but let *her* go unprosecuted? Margaret is dead." She brought her beads to her lips and genuflected. "Yet her attendant said that she had been recovering well. The Fenton girl knew Margaret had been bled but a short while before, so for what reason other than harm did she give our daughter dwale, if not to ensure she would not wake from it?" The Earl continued to look dispassionately upon her, and a small twitch set up in the Countess's left eyelid. She stilled it with a self-conscious movement. "The wench gave Margaret a posy of Maids of the Snow the very hour she sickened—" The Earl snorted, and Felice gritted her teeth, stabbing a finger in the direction of the chapel. "You may mock, my lord, but the evidence of ill intent lies *there*, where we buried her. Master Secretary has proof that the Fenton girl has been in communication with Thomas Lacey – *Lacey*, my lord, against whom you have sworn vengeance. Why do you hesitate to send the harlot to trial?"

"That you so readily seek it. Your concern for my weal is touching. This loyalty—"

"Do you doubt it?" she challenged. "Have I ever been anything but dutiful towards you?"

"Well, have you, madam?"

Stung, she floundered. "Why do you say that?"

"Warwick paid you a visit and had privy words with you."

She flushed. "Not privily; the Duke of Clarence was there also. I make no secret of it."

"But nor did you send word to me. Why?"

"There was nothing to impart. They stayed but a short while. I did not think it of any import to tell you—"

"The Earl of *Warwick* and the Duke of *Clarence* come visiting with armed men outside my gate, and you think it of no *import*? What has to happen for you to deem it to be of enough importance to tell me? Instead, I have to rely on someone else to convey what my own wife should have informed me the moment they left."

"Sawcliffe told you?"

"Should he not have done?" It confirmed his suspicion: Sawcliffe worked both sides of the bed equally, but to whose advantage? He would let her misapprehension fester; it might make her more circumspect in her dealings with his secretary in future. "Loyalty is priceless, is it not, madam? Thomas Lacey made up part of the entourage. Were you aware of *that*?" By the look on her face he doubted it, but he could use it to his advantage anyway. "You ask me why I do not prosecute those intent on my destruction, and I say to you, beware they who plot against my family and my king. None is safe who betrays my trust, Felice. They who lie with the enemy beget bastards."

"I did not betray your bed!"

"So you say."

"I have borne you four children—"

"And how many were mine?"

She clutched at his arm, "—and I carry the fifth. It is a boy, my lord – I swear to it – a boy, an heir of your own body."

He removed her hand. "We shall see whom he favours. What did Warwick want, Felice?"

"I told you, he wished to be remembered to his old friend."

"And to see into whose camp I would fall should I be forced to make a choice? Has there ever been any doubt, or did he think you might be able to persuade me?" He circled his wife as if gauging her resistance, until he stopped behind her and she could feel his closeness. "How did he persuade you, Felice? What did he offer – offices and titles for me, a favourable place at court for you and Bess, perhaps? Or a good marriage for Cecily?" Running his hands down her arms, he noted she shivered at his touch. "Or something else?"

She pulled free. "You do me much dishonour!"

He knew it; he knew he pushed her away at every opportunity as if it had been all her fault, but he couldn't stop himself. Her desperate attempts to win him back had been pitiable before they became spiteful, and now all he could see when he looked at her was years of division they had failed to overcome.

"Perhaps before long you will no longer be grieved by my presence. You will make a wealthy widow, Felice; no doubt you will marry someone more deserving of your devotion." He looked away so that he did not have to see the shock on her face, nor examine himself in case he was obliged to acknowledge that some small part of him welcomed the less complicated prospect of death, and add it to the already insurmountable sum of his sins.

ISOBEL HAD NOT expected to see the Earl again before he left, and her hair dripped over her shoulders, soaking the back of the hastily donned wool gown and making it smell of Alfred on a damp day. Ursula fussed with a linen towel until Isobel grew impatient, and the woman retreated to the back of the room, leaving Isobel to drape the cloth as best she could. The Earl took it from her and began to squeeze water from the ends. Despite the hum of activity around the castle as men prepared to march, he appeared distracted and subdued.

"If I do not return," he began, "I have instructed you are to go to Beaumancote if it is safe for you to do so. Until that time, while I am away – and if God grants him life – my brother will ensure your safety." Taking a handful of her hair, he examined it as it lay curled in his palm, strands lightening as it dried, and she let him, neither drawing nearer nor pulling away, but staying passive and mute. His voice remained low. "Do you wish me harm, Isobel?"

She lurched away from him. "N… no!"

"You gave Margaret a potion so she slept. You must have known she might not wake from it."

"She was suffering. I gave her a little dwale to ease her pain and help her rest. I did not hurt her – I couldn't, I *wouldn't.*"

"Would you do the same for me if I needed such comfort?"

She hesitated for no longer than a wingbeat. "Yes, of course."

"And will you mourn me should I die?"

She did not answer immediately; she had no answer that he would believe, but as his brows drew together in resigned hurt, Isobel relented. Standing on the tips of her toes, she kissed him swiftly on his cheek. "I will pray for your safe return, my lord."

Surprised, he touched his hand to his cheek, then leaning down, lifted her towards him in a single movement that took her from her feet, and kissed her, softly at first and then with increasing intensity until his intention became plain. Isobel managed to disengage his mouth long enough to gasp out, "My lord – Ursula..."

"Leave us," he motioned without raising his face to see the woman did so. As she passed, Isobel thought she heard a whispered *"invisible"* leaving a note of sadness in the air behind her as Ursula closed the door.

As Isobel kneeled to help buckle his belt of elaborate gold and enamelled medallions of Christ and the saints, she felt the lightest touch on her head, like an anointing, and looked up. As if caught with a stolen thought, the Earl blinked. "Your hair is still wet." He cleared his throat, becoming suddenly stern. "You will take a fever. You must ensure you keep well."

She stood, less irritated by his commands than might previously have been the case because there was concern behind it, and that touched her more than she wanted to admit.

"Will you do something for me, Isobel? Will you see that my brother makes his recovery? Attend him until he is strong again? He is all I have left."

"And the Countess and your daughters," Isobel added. "Especially Cecily. She misses her sister."

"Elizabeth is now another man's concern; but Cecily, yes – she too. As for my wife, I think you know she is so only in name. I doubt she would grieve for me. So, will you remedy my brother?"

"Gladly, my lord," Isobel said with feeling, "and he will be well on your return."

Chapter 8

THE PHYSICIAN'S APPRENTICE eyed the beaker with suspicion. "What is that you give?" he asked, prodding her arm and spilling drops of the hot liquid on her hand. Blowing her cheeks, Isobel managed to restrain her temper but not her tongue.

"The wings of ground beetle steeped in cowbane and bitter almond," she snapped, not for the first time that afternoon. "Slaked with dragon's blood and mixed with arsenic. Here, try some." She thrust it under his nose, and the man recoiled. He had poked about her casket, questioned anything she had and everything she did, criticised the preparation of herbs, and scolded her attempts to air the room. Now the absurd man, with his blunt nose lifting his top lip giving him a permanent sneer, stood there weighing whether he should call a guard or a priest. "For goodness' sake!" Isobel raised the beaker and took a swig. He still wavered, no doubt waiting for her to collapse in agony or grow horns. "It is nothing more than camomile and honey, a little ginger, and sage. My lord's throat keeps him wakeful, and he is thirsty."

"You have not prepared the waters properly. Did you consult Lord Langton's charts?" That was particularly irritating because he was well aware that Isobel's knowledge of astrology was minimal. Her mother had rarely consulted charts when treating them at home, and her father thought it best left to the experts. However, Isobel had enough knowledge to be able to predict Blunt-nose's future if he continued dancing about in front of her like a scrawny hare, so she declined to comment and stepped around him.

"This will ease your throat, my lord," she said, holding the beaker to Robert's lips. He took a few sips, coughed, and then a few more.

"I did not know poison could taste so good," he croaked, "or that the poisoner would be so fair."

Isobel blushed and concentrated on removing the small bag of barley from around his throat. "This needs reheating, my lord."

"It helps ease the pain," he rasped. "*You* help, Isobel."

She turned away. "You are feverish again. Perhaps a little more letting—"

The physician's apprentice jigged across the room in a state of anxiety. "My lord requires letting?"

Robert stopped his advance. "No more knives; what ails me cannot be alleviated with a fleam. This is no ill humour that needs balancing. You can go; your own master needs you more than I."

Isobel had spent the past few days beside him, bathing the heat from his raging skin, listening to his mumbled fears, imagining she caught her whispered name, watching him sleep. As his fever diminished, so the clarity of his mind returned, and with it the direction of his thoughts.

"You look tired—" he swallowed carefully, "—and you seem troubled. Is there news?"

Isobel shook her head and laid his newly-washed hand back carefully on the quilted cover. He lifted the other. A bigger hand than his brother's, it felt hot and heavy in hers. "Would you tell me if there was, or do you consider my state too delicate?" She met dark eyes, no longer glazed with fever, but the colour of a mere reflecting the sky, and clear. Turning his hand over and washing his palm, she smiled and shook her head again. "Then I must rely on Martin for tidings; he has no such tenderness of feeling." His fingers closed over hers and any notion that she could put aside her feelings for him evaporated in the warmth of his smile. "Will you read to me?" he rasped. "I have not the strength and it will help pass the time. Unless you have something better to do?"

"My time is yours, my lord, as the Earl instructed me to care for you."

"And do you?"

Disengaging her hand, Isobel dropped the sponge in the basin and rose from the stool. "What would you like me to read?"

"Let it be of your choosing. Surprise me. Martin will show you where my books are kept."

Where other men might keep their precious plate, Robert kept his books. Isobel recognised the Latin work Margaret had striven to read, a Book of Hours, and a small book in the shape of a heart, each page decorated with tiny pictures of fruit and flowers around French lays d'amor. For a man who had little, in this cupboard he stored great wealth. "What did you choose?" he asked as she returned to his bedside, but she held the book out of sight behind her back. He grunted, "I sicken, and you tease me."

"You said you wish to be surprised, my lord."

"And now you accuse me of being fickle."

Without replying, she began to read. After some time, she paused when he seemed to be asleep, but he spoke. "Why that tale?"

"Do you wish me to read something else, my lord?"

"No," he said shortly, "that is enough."

Closing it, Isobel saw a different script decorating a page near the front, and deciphering the uneven hand read: *Ann Milton - her booke*, and beside it a few curved lines making a tiny bird.

"It is a martlet. The book belonged to my wife." Rob was watching her, expressionless.

"I am sorry," Isobel said, shutting the book guiltily as if she had somehow intruded on a private grief.

He exhaled. "Do not be; it is past. It already seems so long ago." He frowned, contemplating the painted coffers of the tester above his head, depicting intertwined roses and leaves on stems that snaked about one another like limbs. Isobel imagined his wife looking at them when she lay in this bed, and then Rob lying with her as his brother lay with Isobel, and then what it might be like if she lay with Rob instead.

Jumping up to put the book away, she almost tripped over the edge of the prie-dieu in her haste, but not before he must have seen the heat creeping up her neck and scalding her face. But if he had, he did not comment, and by the time she put the book back where it belonged, Isobel had collected her thoughts and bustled them back where they would be hidden, secret, and confined. Gathering the contents of the casket, she closed the lid. "You must wish to rest, my lord. I will let your gentlemen attend you."

He lifted his head from his pillow and tried to sit up. "And you will return later?" Isobel hesitated, then nodded, and he flopped back, the effort too much. "Then I will let you go. But only for now, little dove, only for now."

Isobel ran all the way to the neglected wild garden where no one could question the turbulent thoughts that crowded until she felt they might tumble in an incoherent mass from her mouth like a gargoyle spewing water. Her head ached, her legs felt heavy, and the clouded sky pressed down until the weight of it subdued the castle and the land around it. But anything was better than the confines of her room and Ursula's silent interrogation, because she would see what Isobel believed must be clearly branded on her face.

With her stomach cramping a little, she left the paths and headed for the river. Recent rain had fed it, and it ran deep and free. Roots of felled trees clawed at the bank as the high water dragged from between their fingers the protecting soil, leaving them naked and exposed. The water was brown with it, churning last year's leaves and snippets of branches from further upstream, a mass as confused as the thoughts in her mind, mired with confliction. Had these thoughts been hers, and hers alone, she might have kept them hidden and in time they would wither from want of attention and she could pretend they had never occupied her mind at all. But every word, every look Rob gave her fed her imagination until it bled into her heart, making it swell when she saw him and shrink when she did not. There could be nothing in it. His brother possessed her as fully as if they were bound in law, and only his death or his command would sever a bond that increasingly suffocated. Rob felt it – she was sure of it. Had he been indifferent, Isobel might have managed to smother the flame burning inside her, but she saw it in him too, the light in his eyes when he looked at her, the same brightness that inflamed his brother.

A branch had been caught in the torrent, and it bobbed desperately until the end became snarled in roots, clinging as the water ripped it away from her sight. Is that how the child had died – alone, desperate, terrified? Isobel remembered his father's haunted face in the thin moonlight and felt crushed by it. And somehow the father and the son became entangled until it was the Earl's face she saw submerged in the water and Isobel the roots he clung to.

She heard fleet paws behind her, and Chouchou nudged her leg and thrust her neat head into her skirts. "How did you find me, my little shadow? Are you hungry again, hey?" A crow's caustic comment from the apple tree broke her thoughts. There was no peace here. How could she find peace when conflict waged war in her head? Isobel made her way over the rough ground until her feet found a firmer path that took her back to the castle to face her battles alone.

Isobel's stomach twinged, and she tried stretching to ease the cramps, but neither her belly nor her mind would let her rest and eventually she gave up trying to sleep and rose to place the ewer by the fire. She added a bag of fragrant herbs, and chewed willow bark while the water heated, wishing she had some of the Earl's wine to numb the pain and dumb her thoughts. She held her breath as a spasm hit her, releasing it slowly as it passed. Eve had much to answer for.

Rising early had the added benefit of being able to pass unremarked through the family apartments. At one point Isobel thought she heard Cecily call her name but, on straining to catch the slightest sound, she heard nothing more than Joan's fat snores from deep inside the room.

Robert still slept when his servant, blinking awake and rubbing his eyes free of sleep, let her into his chamber. A pallet had been pulled to one side of Robert's bed and the dishevelled linen piled at one end. A night candle still burned on the table by the prie-dieu, but that was the only light; day had not yet broken the solitude of night. Isobel waved the man back to his bed but, yawning, he took his bundle of clothes and, after he had made up the fire, took his leave.

Isobel had nothing better to do but watch and wait and listen to Rob's even sleep. She felt safe there and, for the time being, content. His covers askew and his sheets untucked, one arm was flung behind his head, exposing his chest and shoulder to the early morning air. Isobel drew the sheet to his neck and straightened the counterpoint to keep out the chill. He stirred, turning his head towards her, but did not wake. His dark brown hair flopped over his eyes, and she parted it carefully before it woke him. The flash of a scar ran from his lower lip to his jaw through the stubble masking his chin. Isobel could feel the heat radiating from his skin, saw how his gullet rose and fell as he swallowed carefully in his sleep. She wanted to reach out and touch him, to have him respond to her in a way that echoed the desire lodged in her belly. How many times over the last months had she studied the Earl as he slept? Yet not once had he kindled this warmth she felt for his younger brother, and the thought frightened her. In the time Isobel had known Thomas, before she knew what to expect in a marriage bed, she neither understood nor anticipated feeling anything other than a fondness for him as his wife. And in the months she had been the Earl's mistress, even that delusion had been shattered, leaving her cold and heartless. Yet, in the presence of this man, Isobel found herself yearning for him to wake, to open his eyes and smile at her, to speak her name. She felt breathless at the thought of it, reckless, and she needed to know if he felt the same way, too. But she couldn't, she mustn't, because she was not his nor he hers, and fledgling love – such as it was – must be snuffed out and denied. Isobel belonged to his brother, and Robert's own bonds of loyalty could not be breached for something as unimportant, as insubstantial, as love. He would marry someone worthy of him, who would increase his estate and give him an heir. She would be unsullied and chaste, and he would love her. And Isobel? What would become of her? She almost laughed. She would become Ursula as soon as the Earl tired of her or the Countess gave him a son, whichever was the sooner – obsolete and not even as desirable as the excrement that gong farmers fought to collect to spread over their fields, and with far less respect. That being so, Isobel might as well forget harbouring any desire for this man sleeping in front of her, because he had a different future mapped out for him, and she wasn't part of it.

The bell rang from the chapel, and Robert's Book of Hours still lay on the prie-dieu, waiting for his private devotion. Isobel took her beads and kneeled on the velvet cushion, resting her elbows on the padded top, where dents in the worn pile marked the time he had spent there. She recited her Aves and Paternoster dutifully but, no matter how she tried to discipline it, her mind kept wandering. "Sweet Mother of God, *hear* me, make me obedient."

"For whom do you pray, Isobel?"

Opening her eyes at the sound of Robert's voice, she could not answer until she had silenced those in her head. How long had he been watching her?

"I did not mean to wake you, my lord."

"Why do you pray?" he repeated, his tone softening.

"I make my devotions." She held up the beads as evidence, because why should he believe her if she didn't believe it herself?

"Come here." He held out his hand, and she wanted to yell at him to stop being kind, to bark a command, berate her for her lassitude, anything but look at her as if she mattered to him because she shouldn't, she couldn't.

"Isobel?"

She heard him move and then an oath sworn under his breath. He had managed to sit half-upright against the bank of pillows but had slumped back with his hand over his eyes, his chest pumping short, shallow breaths. He laughed weakly, ending in a cough. "I should not have tried to sit so quickly. My spirit is willing, but my body weaker than a newborn foal." He took his arm from his eyes. "Have you any potion for me this morning? Or perhaps what I need is a purgative. Can you purge this from my flesh?"

"What ails you?"

"You do. You lie beneath my skin like a hair shirt."

"And irritate you beyond words until you cannot wait to be rid of me like fleas!"

"No," he said evenly. "As a constant reminder of my weakness and what I cannot have."

"My lord—"

"Robert. My name is Robert – or Rob, if you prefer."

She dropped her gaze and snapped her beads around her wrist. "You must be hungry, my lord; I will call your servant."

"Isobel, wait!" he called, and she stopped by the door. "I am hungry, more so than I realised, more than food can satisfy. But before you go, let me see you close to."

It was darker by the door, and almost reluctantly, because it took her back within the arc of light in which she could not hide, Isobel went to him. He studied her face, her mouth, and, reaching out, touched her lashes with immeasurable gentleness, removing the last tear that clung to them.

"What violence have you done yourself?" he asked softly, his fingers briefly caressing her cheek, leaving her skin yearning for his touch.

Aware of the irony, and her voice shaking a little, Isobel held up her hand, making her beads rattle. "Mea culpa."

"Ten Aves would be penance enough, and that nine too many." Squinting, he drew her hand towards him. "Let me see those." He fingered the jet gauds and the tassel of tiny coral beads, his brows pulled into a frown. "This seems familiar."

"It was my mother's; she willed it to me."

"Ah."

"My fader wished me to have another, but I wanted this one to keep her close. I was too young to understand it must have hurt him to see me use it. Perhaps you saw her with it when you brought my father home from battle? She often had it with her."

"Yes, perhaps." His frown smoothed. "That must be it." His hand still lay on hers and she made no effort to move it. He cleared his throat. Rubbing his hand across his rough chin, he gave a rueful smile. "I must look like a Scots borderer. If you send for my servant, I'll have him shave me. Martin has not enough hair on his face to know how to shave, and my brother has taken the only decent barber with him. If you find me with my throat cut, you need look no further for an assassin." He pulled such a comical face that Isobel couldn't help but laugh, and his eyes lit with amusement.

"I think you are feeling better this morning, my lord."

"I think I must be, but not so well that I can do without your care. You had better go before I find a reason to keep you here, but return later, if you will."

Perhaps it was because her courses ran freely, releasing the ill humours that had dogged her mood for days, or because he had *asked* her to return, not bidden it, that Isobel felt light-headed and fleet of foot as she almost danced her way back to her chamber, disregarding the glances she earned from those she passed – until, that is, she bumped into Joan.

"Watch where you're going!" she said before she recognised Isobel, and then her lip curled. "Oh, it's you. Thought you'd be long gone if you had any wits about you. What are you looking so pleased about?"

"Because I have the pleasure of seeing your radiant countenance." Isobel skipped past her without stopping.

"Eh?" Joan called after her, and Isobel pictured her downturned mouth like a trout but not as pretty. "And don't you go thinking you got away with it. The Countess will have you; she's not forgotten, she won't forgive..." But Isobel passed beyond hearing and beyond care, buoyed by love.

Ursula was not so easily avoided, however. "My lady left early this morning," she all but accused, her arms folded on her flat chest.

"What of it? I can go where I please, Ursula, you are not my keeper."

"My lord said you were to keep close to your chamber."

"That was before Ro... Lord Robert returned, and anyway, the Earl bid me tend him. I do my lord's bidding. Obediently."

"Lord Langton is beyond danger—"

"And I am almost out of patience."

Ursula blinked, and Isobel instantly regretted her irritation. "Forgive me, but the Earl made me promise to care for Lord Langton until his return. Do you understand?" Her hands twisting in front of her, Ursula nodded. "Good, now bring me breakfast and some water to wash. I wish to eat then change. I need fresh hose, and is my blue gown to hand?" She didn't move. "My blue gown, Ursula, is it mended? And the matching shoes?"

"Your *fine* gown, my lady?"

"Yes," Isobel said firmly, rummaging for her comb with her back to Ursula so that she didn't have to look at the doubt drilling through her shoulder blades. "I feel so drab. It will cheer me to wear it." Isobel heard her move towards the chest without answering, and she breathed out, wondering why it was so difficult to lie and whether she would ever get used to it.

Isobel was finding it difficult not to laugh. Rob must indeed have been feeling better because, pale as he might be, he sat in his chair in front of the window while his servant struggled with a blade against days of stubble. The man approached him again, and Rob flinched as the blade nicked his skin. "God's wit! I could do better myself blindfolded. And drunk." He put his finger to his face, and it came away bloody. Spots of blood decorated the edge of his shirt, and from where she was standing Isobel counted at least two other nicks on his neck.

"My lord, this knife—"

"Is the one I keep for the purpose. It is not the knife, Edgar, but the one who wields it. Enough, I would rather suffer Hell's flagellation than continue under your ministrations. No wonder His Grace recommended your services to me; he could not abide his skin flayed every morning." Edgar's face fell, and Robert raised an eyebrow at Isobel. She could tell when he was joking even if the poor man, new to his service, couldn't. She failed to suppress a giggle. "There, even Mistress Fenton could make a better job of it."

"I could, my lord, but then I used to shave my father every morning, and he also had the bristles of a boar. Or so he claimed."

Edgar's mouth fell open, and this time Rob laughed before he lapsed into a cough, from which it took a full minute and honeyed wine for him to recover enough to speak again. "Edgar, shall we test Mistress Fenton's skills or risk Martin's attempts? Can they be any worse than yours?" Edgar saw the jest this time but still measured the interplay carefully. Martin, however, leaning against the window embrasure and used to his lord's dry banter, felt his smooth chin and grinned. "If my lord will indemnify me against a suit for malpractice, I am willing to give it a go."

"That, I could not tell you," Robert said. "You need the advice of one practised in law; Sir Geoffrey Fenton would have been the best man for the task." He aimed a smile in Isobel's direction, and she returned it. "Failing that, I would place a bet on my lord of Gloucester knowing the answer."

"But he's the same age as I am!" Martin protested, a touch indignant.

Rob cocked his head on one side and eyed his esquire with the same sort of look a buzzard gave its prey. "Mmm, I also made the mistake of underestimating him once. His Grace has a keen mind, and he exercises it in the direction of the law. I made a wager with him recently; I'll make sure I check my facts before I do *that* again." He turned to face Isobel. "So, Mistress Fenton, you say that you can shave this hog? Is it worth a gamble, gentlemen?" In reply, Isobel held out her hand to Edgar and he darted a look at Rob, then gave her the blade. With a basin of clear hot water and another of cold, and a clean cloth at her elbow, she moistened the scented olive oil soap. Testing the curved blade with her thumb with a purposeful air, she said, "Ready, my lord?" and with her fingers pushed his head to one side, exposing his neck. He winced as the cold blade rested against his skin at an angle. "Keep still," she ordered and in one smooth movement removed a swathe of stubble, making a sound like hail on a stone roof. She repeated the action – softening the hair with warm water, soaping the area, and running the blade across the surface – until his neck stood clean. Edgar and Martin craned to look as Rob ran his hand over the area. "I have not finished," Isobel said, bringing his head level with hers, and started working on his jawline, across his upper lip, and finally his chin. His eyes followed hers, the shape her mouth made when she concentrated on not cutting him, her smile when he almost sneezed, and in all that neither of them spoke. They didn't need to, for everything that needed to be said passed between them in waves. Isobel was sorry when at last his face stood free of stubble and she was obliged to move away before their proximity, and his hand resting against her hip so that she could feel the pressure of it through her dress, raised comments from the two watching men. She barely registered their murmured approval, nor noticed the new voices at the door until they became raised and intruded on her world, and then she swung around to see where the distraction came from.

Martin ceased his good-natured jibing and Rob's face straightened when the steward and constable approached with a mud-dashed messenger. Sawcliffe ghosted in behind.

"Well?"

The steward inclined his head. "The Earl has reached London safely, my lord. The King has met with the Duke of Clarence at Baynards Castle and seems reconciled to him taking the west road to his duchess. Lord Welles and Lord Dymmock have sought pardon from His Grace for their transgression against Lord Burgh, and it is granted, but…"

Robert narrowed his eyes. "But?"

"The King has taken the great guns from the Tower and makes ready to march north, and the men are well-equipped and numbered."

Rob sat back. "His Highness will not be caught out again, not for a second time. And nor shall we," he said, addressing the constable. "Warwick's still raising troops for the King?"

"Aye, it would seem so, my lord."

"Looks can be deceiving."

"Indeed they can, my lord."

Standing to one side, the messenger licked his lips as if to speak. Rob motioned to him. "You have something else to report?"

The liveried youth removed his felt hat with the Earl's silver griffin badge. "My lord, the Earl bid me tell you to look to the castle defences inside *and* out."

"Did he say why?"

"No, my lord, just that 'beware the hand of friendship extended in times of need.'"

"And that is all? Sawcliffe, have you any further intelligence?"

The secretary stepped out from behind the steward, the scent of clove oil all-pervading. "My informants tell me that the disturbance in Lincolnshire extends beyond the current concerns, my lord."

"Meaning?"

Sawcliffe directed a glance at Isobel. Rob frowned. "Speak. There is none in this room I would not trust."

"There is rumour that the King is not content to let matters lie from last summer. They see His Grace's coming to the north as evidence that he means to exact revenge on the commons for Conyer's part in the rebellion. They are fearful, my lord, and fear spreads like fire when it is not quenched."

Rob smiled grimly. "And the King means to extinguish it."

"Whereupon it is no longer rumour, my lord, but fact," Sawcliffe said.

"The King's muster will outnumber rebel forces," Rob said. "He will be swift in dealing with them and act decisively. The question is whether this remains an isolated problem."

"It is my belief the rot extends further, my lord."

The steward and constable murmured their agreement, and Rob asked, "Your evidence, Master Secretary?"

"I have reports from across the county – from Stamford to Lincoln, from the Wash to Barton—"

Isobel bristled. "Not Beaumancote. My manors are loyal to the King."

"Of course, mistress," Sawcliffe soothed, but she remembered all too clearly his unbridled threats so recently made and was not deceived.

"There is no doubt of your loyalty, Mistress Fenton, nor that of your manors," Rob interjected before she could speak, "but we have our own lands in Lincolnshire, and we wish neither to get drawn into rebellion nor be the victim of it. Sawcliffe, send word to our manors in the north.

They must increase their guard and any information must be brought directly to me." Robert watched him go. He had become increasingly drawn over the course of the exchange and now slumped back into his chair.

"Your orders, my lord?" the constable asked.

"Extend the watch and alert the town guard to any sign of trouble. Martin—" he beckoned the young man, "—you wanted to taste battle; now is your opportunity. Make ready my horse and harness—"

"You cannot go!" Isobel shot out, irrespective of how it might appear.

"It is not a question of can or cannot," he said, rising unsteadily, "but that I must." He stood, tried a few steps, and all colour left his face. He put out a hand to balance himself, then sat heavily in his chair, shaking.

Hyde frowned. "Forgive me, my lord, but if the castle is threatened, we have need of your lordship here to defend it. The Earl left specific instruction."

Rob breathed carefully to prevent a coughing fit. "And that included me overseeing the defence, is that it?" The steward bowed, leaving his answer open to interpretation, and Rob said, "Well, it seems that my body defeats me. In the meantime, we will make what preparations we may in the hope we need none. Be not disappointed," he said to his esquire, "the time will come when you shall be tested in battle, and then you'll pray that it is your enemy's blood you taste and not your own, and that your enemy is your enemy and not your friend. God knows it is hard enough to tell sometimes." He leaned his forehead against his hand, the last of his energy spent.

Once Edgar and Martin had helped him back to bed and the room had emptied, he and Isobel were left alone. "Is this what you wanted?" he asked her. "For me to linger here in safety while my brother risks his life to defend ours? Did you implore *him* to stay?"

"I am sorry I spoke out, my lord; I did not mean to."

"You have not answered my question."

She shook her head, and he gave a restrained smile. "Do I gather then that my welfare means something to you?" He had lost the frustration that had dogged his tone moments before, and Isobel met his eyes without answering. He held her gaze. "Give me a reason to get up in the morning, Isobel," he said softly. "Give me a reason to stay."

Chapter 9

OVER THE NEXT few days the weather wavered on the verge of spring, and the mood of the castle – responding to infrequent news from beyond the walls – echoed its ambivalence. Isobel reflected its temperament: hopeful after she had been in Rob's company, becoming less so as he recovered and spent more time in counsel. It wasn't that she doubted their growing attraction, only that his developing strength negated the need for her care, and without that excuse, they had none to be in each other's company without causing comment.

And as soon as he was well enough, he would leave.

She became confined to her room again, not so much because Felice might attempt retribution while Rob was in residence, but because every time Isobel saw him, or heard his voice, or his name was mentioned, her heart expanded until it squeezed from every pore and she felt sure it could be read in her face. She felt sick with it and, when finally she slept, fitfully and without respite, she woke more tired than when she had laid her head down. Isobel wanted to cry, to shout, to laugh, and she struggled to maintain her composure, giving up when at last Ursula went out, and she sat locked in her chamber wracked with fear that he might not love her as she did him, and terrified that he did because there was an immovable wall between them that was his brother.

On the fourth day since the arrival of the messenger, Rob sought her in her room. "There is news?" Isobel asked, reading the tension in his face.

"You have not heard?"

She grimaced a look around the boundary of her chamber.

"No, well, I am sorry not to have seen you these last few days." He kept his voice even, but he meant so much more than he dared reveal in front of Ursula, who had risen when he entered and now watched them without blinking. "Welles has issued proclamations throughout Lincolnshire. He is claiming the King is intent on destroying it and calling on the commons to repel His Grace's army. He is issuing a muster of the people at Ranby Hawe, near Lincoln—"

"But that's out-and-out treason!"

"And not the worst of it. This is hardly a petty local disturbance by several disaffected gentlemen – it is spreading. Welles's rebels are being reinforced by men from the north."

"Whose men?"

"I think you can guess, although there is no proof – not yet." He took on a note of urgency as he bent closer. "Isobel, this is bigger than anyone expected, and if…" He stopped, conscious of Ursula's straining ears. Isobel looked over her shoulder.

"Ursula, fetch me nuncheons."

"My lady has only just broken her fast."

"Do not argue. I'm hungry. Go."

Robert waited until Ursula, grumbling to herself, left, and Isobel had secured the door against further intrusion, before he resumed. "If this spreads, Jesu alone knows where it will stop, and there will be no quarter this time. If Warwick and Clarence take the King, they cannot let him live."

"The King's own *brother* is set against him? I thought them reconciled?"

"Clarence has ridden to meet Warwick; I doubt the King believes the story that they raise troops for his banner any more than I or my brother are deceived by it."

"Will they attack the castle?"

"They will have no option if they defeat the King. Even if he is offered peace by Warwick, my brother will not negotiate with a traitor. He will stand or fall for King Edward, you know that."

"And you with him," Isobel said, cold chilling her blood.

"I would have it no other way," he said flatly. "Besides, I am Gloucester's man and he the King's, and so far, the Duke has resisted every attempt to be courted, although Warwick can be *very* persuasive." He must have seen the fear sitting on her shoulders like a crow, because his voice lowered and softened. "Not all is lost, Isobel. The King is well-prepared this time – forewarned *and* forearmed – and he's no fool. Even if Warwick has yet to declare himself, he will have to reveal his hand soon if he is to take advantage of this uprising, and then there will be no going back until one or the other is defeated. We will have either King Edward in his own right or Clarence will be King George dancing to Warwick's tune – although God alone knows how long *that* would continue until they come to blows. Clarence sways with whatever wind favours him, but if he were king, I believe Warwick would quickly find the air cooling. And with the old king still rattling about like a pea in a pot, there will be no peace until we have one king, and one king alone."

"And old accounts settled?" Isobel asked, remembering the look of grim triumph on the Earl's face as Ralph Lacey's head rolled across Beaumancote's damp stone. And Thomas, no more than a boy, whey-faced and trembling, watching and sowing the seeds of vengeance. But Rob had not been there, he didn't know.

But he must have guessed, because he said, "Isobel, even if we lose, peace in the shires will still have to be maintained. As long as Beaumancote can be defended the rule of law will apply, and if you make your allegiance to the new king, Lacey will have no grounds on which to base his claim. Felice will have her own hide to save and no time to think about taking yours. In that situation, there is little reason why you could not return to your lands to make a new life for yourself. And, if we win," his mouth distorted, briefly, "my brother will continue to protect you."

Isobel hadn't been thinking of her own skin but, now that he mentioned it, she felt a flash of annoyance that somehow her loyalty would be seen as negotiable when his was not. "Why would I seek reconciliation with a new king?"

"What do you mean?"

"Why do you assume I could simply change my allegiance any more than you could, or the Earl, or my father?"

"Because you have no quarrel with Clarence, or King Henry, or with Warwick for that matter."

"Why, because I am a woman?"

"Isobel—"

"Or of no importance? I am both, but how could I be reconciled to a new king if all I have ever believed in, all that I care for, is lost?" She remembered, in a recollection so faint it might have been little more than her imagining, her mother kneeling in concentrated prayer when her father was away. She must have made a noise because her mother had looked around, and Isobel had seen the look of utter desolation before she had covered it with a smile and put her hand out to her daughter, her coral chaplet gently swaying. The Earl had brought her broken father home only days afterwards. Her mother had never let her see her so vulnerable again, not until she lay dying with her defences in rags. Isobel's throat tightened at the memory. "You men – you make your wars while women sit and wait for your return. And if you do not, we are expected to heal our own wounds, bend to a new lord, and carry on. Why, because we have no voice other than that of our fathers or husbands while they live and, once they are dead, we are empty vessels until some other man fills us with his own thoughts? I choose my allegiances not just because they were my father's but because I believe them to be *right*. I owe allegiance to King Edward because I was brought up to, but my *loyalty* has yet to be earned."

"Careful," he cautioned. "I understand what you say but others might not."

"Sawcliffe?"

"Among others." He took her hand in his as if wishing to impress upon her the importance of what he was about to say. "Guard your thoughts, Isobel. They are safe with me, but I cannot protect you if I am not here. Even then, there might be some from whom I cannot protect you at all."

"Who?"

"Great lords like Warwick or Clarence, or those who seek to serve them and rise in their esteem. Men like that will not hesitate to step upon your back – men like Thomas Lacey. None will cross my brother lightly – he is close to the King, and his affinity makes him worth wooing; but me?" He shrugged, letting her fill in the space his words left. "My brother is in a better position to protect you than I will ever be." There was a finality in what he said, as if there was little point in either of them harbouring any hope of a different fate, and with it, her heart shrank a little. Neither had made any declaration to the other, nor spoken of the future, nor made promises they knew they could not keep, but what was left unsaid made the absence of it all the greater and Isobel wanted to say something – now – before it was too late. She wanted him to know, but what could she say that wasn't out of place, or that would presume something as yet unvoiced, and that trod upon untried ground? She withdrew her hand and fumbled about straightening the lining of her cuffs. The moment passed.

"Isobel, look at me." A seam wouldn't sit true; she yanked it back into place, avoiding his eyes. "Isobel, I do not want to leave without saying… without telling you—"

Her head jerked up. "Leave? You cannot leave. You have been so ill. You must not, you cannot… what about the castle? You said you must stay to protect it. You said…" Her voice broke on a rising note. "Please… you cannot…"

Rob put his hands around Isobel's flaming cheeks and brought his face close to hers. "Shh, no, Isobel, my dove, stop. I must and I will. It is my duty; it is what I have to do to preserve what we have – what we fought for – what my father *died* for."

Dread billowing from her like a sail, Isobel tried to pull away from him. "H… how can I rest if I know… I might never see you… again?"

He silenced her with his mouth, warm and soft at first, becoming determined as he felt her yielding response, her fears melting under his touch, evaporating in the heat of desire.

Chou's whining at the door roused her. She lay for a few moments more, gathering herself and adjusting to the gloaming. Rob's hand rested against her stomach, and she pushed back against him, feeling his solidity down the length of her body. His breathing quickened as he woke, and his arm tightened about her waist. He felt so real, so warm, so *alive*, and her womb wakened to his exploring touch. She had felt nothing like this before. Lifting his head, he kissed her neck slowly, gently – once, twice – pumping blood to the surface of her skin, making it quiver at his touch. His breath warmed her ear. "Let the dog be, just a little longer."

"Ursula must be outside."

His hand found the curve of her breast, his lips the corner of hers. "Then Ursula must also wait," he murmured, leaning over Isobel and easing her face around to his.

"She will guess," Isobel insisted half-heartedly as her mouth found his.

"Then let her *guess* and wait."

In the dying light of the fire, Isobel marked out his features with the tips of her fingers, finding the height of his cheekbones, the narrow bridge of his nose and where it flared slightly at the tip before falling to his full lips above the measured chin, and all the while he watched her, his eyes darkened in the half-light, his breathing steady. Stroking his jaw where rough bristles threatened to push through, Isobel smiled. "I see Edgar has managed to shave you without mishap."

"Except for here." He touched a place on his throat, and her fingers joined his to feel the scabbed skin. She stretched to kiss it and felt the vibration in his neck as he spoke. "I cannot tell you how I wished for it to be you wielding the knife this morning, nor begin to explain how much I have longed to be with you like this."

The dog whined again, jamming her nose to the gap between door and floor. "Chouchou," Isobel called her, but she lay down, giving reproachful glances now and again, and would not budge.

"She is her master's dog," Robert said quietly. "Heart and soul."

Cold reality imposed itself. Isobel struggled with the voice screaming inside her head, *"I am not his!"* and instead said, "What have we done? What do we do?" The dog's whining was growing louder. In a moment, she would break into barking and then someone might feel it their duty to investigate the disturbance and find Ursula on the stair, and what might she say then in the absence of her mind? "Rob…"

He kissed her gently. "I know," and reluctantly rose from the bed. Without speaking, he helped straighten her disarranged skirts and twisted bodice, and Isobel retied his loosened points and picked his quilted doublet free of strands of fair hair. Then he lit the candles on the pricket stand with a taper from the fire while she straightened the sheets on the bed and hid the evidence of their betrayal with the covers. If only that were enough.

"Will Ursula say anything?" he asked as they devised a fable out of her game board and set the pieces on it as if they had been in a state of play.

Isobel hauled the stool in front of the table. "It is not that she would knowingly say something—"

"But that she might when her wits are slack?" he finished, and she nodded.

Isobel picked up the cushion that had slid to the floor. "She loves him."

"Do you, Isobel?" Pressing her lips together, Isobel shook her head. Resting his hands on the back of the chair facing her, he bowed his head in thought, then said, "On his return I will speak with him."

"No! Rob, you mustn't! He will not forgive the betrayal, and it would drive a wedge between you."

"And I cannot live with the deception. I have never lied to him, and I will not start now. If Felice gives him the son he needs he might be reconciled to her, and you will be free."

Chouchou started her whimpering again. Isobel glanced nervously at the door. "*If* she has a boy he might, but right now he loathes her, Rob, and he will not be crossed, you know that, not even by you." The dog gave a single yip, then another, deeper and rounding into a bark. "At least wait until the child is born, or until he tires of me. Please, do not risk his displeasure."

"You sound frightened of him."

Isobel shoved the image of the severed head to one side. "I… could not live knowing I caused a rift between you. Robert, please…"

He drew a deep breath and exhaled slowly. "As you wish. I will say nothing for the time being, but it does not sit easy with me – not for your sake, or my brother's. Nor mine," he added as an afterthought. He frowned as Chou started tearing at the bottom of the door with her claws. "We had better let Ursula in and Chou out. What has it come to that a master has need to deceive a servant and a dog; who is lord here?"

"The Earl," she said, and he gave a grim laugh.

Ursula entered the room with her face averted and gave due deference to Robert; but with Isobel she remained oblique, her eyes sliding to the bed and then to her face and then to the man sitting with a game piece in one hand studying the board. All evening, once Robert had left and long past the call for all-night, Isobel thought Ursula might say something, but her silence became obstinate, and eventually Isobel gave up trying to elicit a response.

She lay in bed that night listening to the wind picking at the shutters, trying to hold on to the image of his face, the touch of his hands, recreating the sensations once only imagined and which they had made reality. But try as she might, she failed to capture that which remained as transient as mist and as illusory.

"When can we be together again?" Isobel had whispered to him as he made his goodnight. Brought up short, he opened his mouth to answer, but found he had none. Subduing the swell of foreboding, Isobel nodded, and pain passed across his face.

Not so very long ago, she had lain in the same bed with the Earl before he had bidden her farewell, and not once had she thought to ask after him or enquire whether he even lived, and she remembered something Ursula had said in a passing moment Isobel had all but forgotten. Ursula had been embroidering a border of columbine in tiny stitches onto a coverchief, singing to herself and intermittently rocking, when suddenly she looked up with a blank expression and, shaking her head, had said, "You will break his heart," before returning to her task. Isobel had thought then that it was part of her madness but, as she lay in the stillness of the room with nothing but her thoughts to occupy her, she had to ask herself whether Ursula had seen something in her that foretold a bleaker future: whose heart did she think Isobel would break?

Chapter 10

SMOKE FROM THE last round of cannon fire still hung over the field as the Earl hacked his way through pockets of enemy, focus concentrated through the narrow field of vision afforded by his helm as he searched the weaving thickets of men. Sweat ran in rivulets, catching on his eyelashes, gathering on his top lip where he tasted salt. His horse had been cut from under him by a stray arrow that had pierced its flank, and its scream still rang in his ears. He had refused another mount and, oblivious to the cautious ring thrown around him by his retainers, outpaced them. He found himself amongst a mean straggle of black-and-yellow-striped foot soldiers, angry wasps jabbing with polearms and trying to find a hole in his defences. But he had one purpose and one alone.

From the corner of his eye, he glimpsed a raised axe as it fell, dodging it and bringing his sword around. Catching him at an angle, he neatly sliced the back of the man's thigh, severing the tendon through flesh and fabric, sending him face first and flaying to the ground. The Earl delivered the fatal wound, thrusting the blade of his misericorde into the man's exposed throat. Instinct had him spinning around and ducking as a flanged mace sailed perilously close to his steeled head. He raised his sword to fend off the full force of the blow, and the mace glanced off his pauldron, leaving his shoulder numb and the sword spinning from his grasp. Slipping in the mud and wedging his foot against the hulk of the slain man, the Earl threw the full weight of his armoured body against the soldier, metal buckling as he bore them both down. The man-at-arms grappled, the mud embracing his back sucking him close, and brought the mace against the Earl's helmet in a clumsy blow. It was enough to knock him sideways. The Earl gasped for breath, hauled himself around and, clenching his mailed fist, brought it down on the open helmet of the man, feeling flesh and bone give way. It took a matter of heartbeats to extinguish his life with his dagger.

Reclaiming his sword from the torn soil and with his head still ringing, he scrambled to his feet in readiness, but a call went up, echoing through the joggled ranks of men. The Earl, straining to hear through his own breathing, looked around. The fight had moved away. He spotted a number of his men in blue and yellow working their way through stragglers with a will, but his own blood was less inflamed than it had been. Pushing up his visor and dropping the bevor covering his mouth, he bent to catch his breath and to still the resounding rushing in his ears that deafened him. "My lord!" a voice called. The Earl tasted blood and spat it at a clump of mangled grass. "My lord Earl?" A touch on his shoulder had him wheeling around, his dagger glinting in the weak sun as it ripped the blue and red surcoat covering the decorated breastplate of a much taller man. A movement and an oath had the Earl staggering back into a rough kneel. "Your Grace, forgive me!"

The King inspected the remains of the royal surcoat and, with a sharp jerk, tore it from himself. He tossed it to the ground. "God's teeth, my lord, you had me wondering whose side you take! This battle's done – if you could call it such. Get to your feet for the love of saints before someone takes you for a traitor and presents me with your head. There's enough around here without adding yours."

The Earl rose unsteadily, blinking sweat from his eyes, and the King regarded him through long lashes. "You are injured, my lord." The Earl rotated his numb shoulder, feeling for damage. The King gestured. "No, your head," and the Earl put his fingers to his exposed skin; they came away red, the blood already congealing on the metal tips of his gauntlet.

"I did not feel it," he murmured, surprised to find his vision blurring, and he looked up to see the faces around him distorting and sliding from view.

"Help him!" the King barked as the Earl buckled at the knees, barely aware of the hands supporting him and the shouts for a surgeon as he disappeared into darkness and beyond relentless day.

He regained consciousness sometime later and lay with his eyes closed while he orientated himself. From outside, the clatter of polearms, thump of carts, and the moaning of the wounded told him the clear-up was well underway. The lining of his tent kept out the brightest of the sun, but the golden orb still penetrated his eyelids, and he moved his head out of its glare. It hurt. He groaned.

"My lord?" He heard Louys from somewhere close. Not lifting his head, the Earl peered through weighted lids and saw his esquire standing above him, dressed in clean linen.

"What day is it?" His parched throat stung.

"The same day – the twelfth of March, my lord."

"How many men have we lost?"

"Four, my lord; our losses are few compared with the rebels. The day is ours."

The Earl was tempted to point out that the fact of his lying there and not in chains somewhere made their victory obvious, but the lad didn't need his enthusiasm curbing; that would come soon enough when the nightmares set in. The Earl rolled onto an elbow, sat up, and felt the bandages around his temple. He would live. He accepted the wine held out to him. "You did well; your father will be proud of you."

"Thank you, my lord. I took down one of Welles's own men. He was wearing livery. And a man with a billhook – I know not whom he served…" Louys's voice trailed off, and he shrugged and then remembered he shouldn't, so grinned instead, making his curls bob. The Earl had seen the soldier with the bill, if *soldier* could be a term applied to the scrawny scrap of a boy, roughly clothed in little more than a gambeson and no match for his esquire's axe and armour. He had seen the look on the boy's face before Louys had hacked at it. Louys would remember it too in the years to come; he wouldn't be able to forget it. His squire had fallen silent. It didn't take much imagination to guess why.

Without meeting the youth's eyes, the Earl swung his legs to the floor. His head thumped, but it didn't reel as before. "You conducted yourself like a knight and survived, and that's all that matters. The rest is nothing; it happens to us all."

"All?"

"Most."

Louys dared ask, "Even the King?"

"Yes, His Grace also shat himself when first tested on the field." His mouth lifted into a half smile. "And even your lord, although I'll thank you not to speak of it. Here," he stood, testing his balance and the strength in his shoulder, "help me get clean and dressed, there is work to be done."

"YOUR GRACE, THE day is yours."

Inside the royal tent, the stench of fear and blood that had clung to the inside of the Earl's nose like a privy chute as he crossed the ground to the King was replaced by the jasmine smouldering in clay dishes over open coals. It reminded him of his wife. He nodded to the other men in the crowded pavilion and accepted the cup of ale and the offer of a chair with equal gratitude.

"It is, my lord, but tomorrow must be ours as well, and the day after. Are you fit to ride?"

"I am, Your Grace. On the morrow…?"

"Mm." The King threw back the remains of his ale and wiped his mouth with thumb and forefinger. "You have not heard. My loving brother has been careless." He tossed a stained piece of paper in the Earl's direction. "That was found on the body of a messenger wearing Clarence's livery beneath his gambeson. Can't ask a dead man now, but it's clear enough without interrogation confirming it."

The Earl scanned the scrawl, finding the words blurring at the edges. He blinked to clear his vision and read on. "It was intended for Welles?"

"Arranging to rendezvous. God's teats, Warwick wouldn't have made the mistake. Trust George to be caught like a whore with raised skirts." He rattled his fingers on his leg, then, addressing the small group of men nearby, "My lords, I thank you for your service this day. Lynes, wait upon my orders." He waited until they had bowed and left before continuing. "I had hoped this business would have been otherwise. Parr vows he heard cries of *'a Clarence, a Warwick.'* Did you?"

"I cannot say, Your Grace. Can anything be heard clearly when you are gutting a man?" He waved the letter. "If further evidence is needed of their complicity, this states it."

Gnawing at loose skin on his thumb, the King stared at the stained parchment, wrestling with his thoughts. He grunted and, jumping up from his chair, plucked the letter from the Earl's hand. "That settles it: there can be no more doubt. We ride north. No quarter, my lord: your predictions were correct, your intelligence proven." He looked at the Earl. "Are you troubled by this? Like my brother, you were in my cousin Warwick's household for a time, were you not? How does it feel, my lord, knowing that the man you've trusted as a friend for this long has deceived you?"

The Earl held his gaze. "Your Grace knows I am true."

The King assessed him for moments longer then broke into a grin. "Jesu knows I've seen the evidence of it time enough. Like father, like son – the old Earl could always be relied upon in our need. There is some truth in the saying, *blood will out*, as can be attested by Welles and his idiot son. I would have honoured the clemency if I could. As it is…" He raised his hands and let them fall.

"The point was well made, Your Grace. Richard Welles and Thomas Dymmock knew what they were doing when they sought to betray you, and their heads serve as a reminder to those who might neglect to remember it."

"Did you see Lacey?"

"If he was there, I did not find him, although a number of his men were on the field."

"And there are now fewer than before?"

The Earl acquiesced with a brief hint of upward movement to his mouth, but not enough to be called a smile. The King rubbed his thumb slowly against his cheek. "I know the quarrel you have with Lacey, and Christ and all His saints know we have reason enough to avenge the deaths of those we love, but this discord in the shires breeds strife, and – wait—" he held up a warning hand, and the Earl clamped his mouth shut, "—I will not hold you to account if you make amends on the field of battle for the injustice done to your family, my lord, but we need to make peace where we can and from what you say about him, Lacey's loyalty can be secured—"

"For a *price*, Your Grace."

The fair-haired younger man raised his brow. "Granted, at a price. All men have their price, eh my lord?"

The Earl's look hardened. "Not all, Your Grace, and some men have gone beyond being bought with promises of clemency, or anything else."

The King declined to comment, in which time he picked up his eating knife from beside the dish, turning it over in his hands and examining the elaborate handle of ivory lovers in an eternal embrace. "The Queen made me a gift of this on the birth of our daughter. Our daughters..." He turned towards the Earl, leaning against the edge of the trestle. "Until I have a son, George is... was, my heir. If he fails to submit to my authority, what alternative do I have? He has to." He pinned the parchment with the knife. "What it is to be betrayed by a brother, eh?" He let the knife fall, and as quickly his mood changed. He nodded towards his attendant gentlemen. "I'll send this lot of vagabonds about their business, and we'll share cups as we used to and see what entertainment can be mustered from among the wenches here." For all that the King was on his third cup, he looked sober enough as he sat back down. There were evident advantages to his height other than being able to crush men's skulls and dominate a room and most of the women in it. "I saw a redhead yestereve, young wife of one of the merchants from Stamford supplying us – hair the colour of a strawberry roan – burnished copper, if her brows were anything to go by. She had an easy eye, and I doubt her old husband would complain if she spent the evening comforting his king. He can always claim the bastard to be his own, and men would think the better of him for it." He eased his hips in the chair, resting one foot on the knee of the other leg and draping his large hand over it. "I'll invite her to sup with us and see if there's not a friend she can bring with her to keep you company. Battle always gets my blood up."

The Earl examined his fingers, now free of the blood of dead men that had soaked his glove, except for a brown-black line lodged beneath one nail. His hand shook a little. He frowned at it and clenched his fist to make it stop. He felt unaccountably weary, and his skull throbbed incessantly. The King might make a favourable impression on the girl with his fair hair, broad shoulders, and easy manner – not to say a full purse – but he doubted he presented so attractive a picture with his head bound and his mood grim. Loneliness swamped him and, for a second, Isobel looked up at him from his mind's eye. He lifted his beaker in salute. "I am happy to partake of the ale, Your Grace."

Raising his own cup, the King laughed. "I'll take the pair of them if you'll have none. I've missed your company, my lord. I could always rely on your fidelity in all matters to remind me of the virtue of it, so I need not abide by it myself."

"It is an honour to serve Your Highness," the Earl replied wryly.

"I mean it," the King said, sobering. "I regret the… misunderstanding between the Queen and your daughter. Sweet girl – most comely; how is she?"

"Married. How fares Her Grace?"

Grinning again, the King shook his head. "Keeping my bed warm until my return, I hope. I hear your Countess is with child again?"

"She is, Your Grace."

"Then may St Margaret of Antioch speed her to the safe confinement of a son. God knows I've planted enough seed to breed an heir, but all I get are girls, not that they're not delightful little chicks – Elizabeth sings very prettily. At least their dam breeds like a mare and has sons from her first husband to prove it." He winced and sucked his teeth. "I had forgot your loss, my lord. It is hard to lose a boy." He gulped the contents of his cup and looked around for more.

"My son? Yes, Your Grace, and my daughter, also, not long past." As he said it, he felt a twist in his gut he recognised as grief. He had barely thought of Meg until now.

"God's blood, a maid, too?" Crossing himself, the King looked momentarily downcast. "Still, you have a living daughter."

"Two, Your Grace. My youngest, Cecily, is the same age as the Princess Elizabeth."

The King clapped his hands on his thighs. "Well, then, there is comfort in that. Talking of comfort, I hear you've taken a mistress."

"Your Highness is well-informed. It can be of little interest to any but myself."

"Are you telling me to mind my own business? It *is* my business when it involves Fenton's estates and his heiress. You have made arrangements for her marriage?"

"Not yet."

"You'd better see to it, or I will; there'll be plenty of takers. I wish the region around the Humber and Trent secured. Come, my lord, why so glum? She cannot be the only pretty face to amuse you and, if memory serves, the Lady Felice was thought the fairest woman south of the Humber, although even the prettiest face can prove wearisome in time." The Earl drank rather than answer and the King changed tack. "My brother, Gloucester, speaks highly of Lord Robert. He has proven himself a reliable man. He is free to marry again, is he not?"

"He is, Your Grace, and it is time he made a more suitable match than the one he chose for himself." The Earl cursed himself for his blunt-headed stupidity as the younger man's face froze long enough for his error to register.

Moments passed and then, "Ah, well, when it comes to *affaires de cœur,*" the King remarked, mildly, "Reason plays no part, as I know too well. However, I might be able to help in this respect." The Earl looked up. "Widow, about twenty-three years, no children as yet – but she was not married long – and with no one to dispute a very sizable estate. Violante De Bray—" he pursed his lips, staring at nothing in particular, "—and as sweet as her name suggests."

"And well-plucked, Your Grace?"

The King grinned, shrugged. "Possibly, but all the better for it."

The Earl doubted his brother would think so. "I know the family. I will think on it."

"But not too long, my lord; she will not remain unwed. Oh—" he added, rubbing the toe of his boot against his calf, "—and I neglect to mention her brother is gravely ill, may St Christopher preserve him, and his estates are entailed to his sister on his death."

"I thought him Warwick's man?"

"He was, but all men come at a price, my lord; their sisters also."

THE DAY HAD been dry and unseasonably warm, but dusk and clear skies brought chill wrapping around his ankles as he walked, a little unsteadily, back to his own encampment. Carts were already laden and ready to move on, and his men, restless after the skirmish which had hardly tested them, waited for orders.

Winter damp rose though the fragrant reed matting and into the soles of his boots, but his pavilion was warmer than the air outside. Sitting in his own chair, he waved the food away and settled instead on warming his feet by the brazier making steady inroads on the cold.

The King had presented a workable solution to the problem of finding a suitable wife for Rob, although his brother might need persuading to overlook her infidelities if the King had already ploughed that particular furrow. At least the seed had been royal. She came with land and the promise of more to come, as well as the blessing of the King, the potential of which could not be overlooked. It would also secure estates in the south-west – virgin territory for the Langton family. Becoming reflective, he remembered that Meg would have been there now had she lived. Life was short and unpredictable, and he was not immune. Whether Robert liked it or not, he had a duty to secure the future of the family. Even if Felice produced a boy that survived, his father's life couldn't be guaranteed to continue long enough for him to come of age. Rob would have to be entrusted to protect his nephew's inheritance, and that, too, depended on Robert's continued existence. His brother's bloodless face, his skin clothed in sweat and his mumblings barely coherent, was the last he had seen of him. He knew he lived – he had received messages from him since then – but the image of him had somehow burrowed into his mind like tooth worms and, in taking hold, wouldn't let go. He rested his head against the back of his chair.

And what of Isobel? How long could he keep up the appearance of finding a match for her when he had no intention of letting her go? Perhaps he had always meant to keep her. She had been his from the beginning, from before they had ever met, as if she had been destined to be his by right of birth… but that was another lifetime and one he tried to forget. He became aware of Louys standing close by trying not to fidget. "What is it?"

"My lord, Sir David Musters, Lord Morris, and your other gentlemen are outside. You requested they attend you."

He had? Hell's teeth! He must have drunk too much of the King's ale. He rose too rapidly and regretted it, and waited for the dizziness to subside before allowing anyone to be shown in.

"Grantham?" Morris queried, after the Earl had outlined his instructions to the half-score of men gathered in his pavilion. "My lord, we should be in pursuit of the rebels, not *celebrating* at Grantham." Not long indentured to the Earl, Morris didn't know him as well as David Musters, who was shooting him warning looks the young man missed as he mistook the Earl's intense concentration as interest in his point of view. "Does the King intend to pardon this treachery? What will the rebels make of it if they see the King so weak that they can raise a rebellion and sup with him after it? My lord, I killed a man wearing Clarence's bull. I heard others shouting *'Warwick!'* What clearer treachery is there than that? If the King won't act, if he is more intent on wenching than warring, he is not fit to rule and perhaps Warwick has a point." There was a sharp intake of breath from a number of the lords, but several of the men murmured their agreement, though none dared voice their dissent so vociferously. The Earl let him finish, counted silently to ten, and exhaled. Lowering his voice, he spoke slowly and clearly.

"My lords, gentlemen, for those of you who have come recently to my service, if I have failed to do so before, let me make this clear: I serve King Edward and, while in my service, you will do the same. If any now here disagrees, let him speak." He paused, meeting the eyes of each man in turn, noting those who met his squarely, those who flinched, and those who looked away. "I take it from your silence that you are in agreement. Should any man fail in his duty to fulfil the contract made between us, do not be deceived – you gave your oath freely, and willingly I pledged my good lordship in return. If any choose to betray that trust, I will deem all bonds severed, and I will hunt him down and he will meet his end as surely as Welles and Dymmock lie dead this night with their heads separate from their bodies." He let them retrieve the image, held it in front of their thoughts, then reminded them who was responsible. "If you have any doubts of our lord King's determination to maintain peace in this kingdom, dispute them with His Grace. I am certain he will be all too willing to listen."

Outside, the sun had set and the scent of iron and death from the bloodied field was carried on the smoke of the campfires in the still night air. From a copse, an owl called.

Morris looked as if he might argue the point, but Musters cleared his throat. "My lord, we are all true and loyal men. Morris here hasn't had a gut full of battle as we have, and he has no quarrel with any other than those he picks for himself, do you, lad?" He clapped his hand on the boy's back a little more emphatically than perhaps needed, but the youth took the hint and swallowed his tongue. "That's right, when you've seen as much trouble as we have you don't go looking for it, not if you want a long life, for enough will come looking for you." Again, there was a general murmur of agreement from among the more experienced men, and this time Morris demurred. He bowed, lower than required.

"I have spoken out of turn and ask your forgiveness, my lord." He looked up from under dark lashes to gauge the Earl's reaction and met a measured stare in return.

"Loyalty has its own reward, Morris, but with dishonour comes death. Remember it well."

As they left the pavilion, through the fabric walls came Musters' bass voice. "Learn to pick your battles, lad; Ralph Lacey failed to heed the warning – and *he* didn't live to regret it." A throaty chuckle followed, matched by those within earshot around him.

"Who's Ralph Lacey?" Morris was asking when they passed beyond the Earl's hearing so that he couldn't hear the reply, nor be reminded of it.

Chapter 11

"GRANTHAM?" Richard of Gloucester looked up from the map spread on the trestle in front of him. "And that three days ago?" He scoured the map and placed the white king from his chess set, arrayed ready for battle on its board close by, on the Lincolnshire town.

"Yes, Your Grace. The Duke of Clarence and the Earl of Warwick left Coventry and make for Burton. They were never at Leicester as they indicated." Robert Langton peeled off his riding gloves and took the ale offered to him, drinking thirstily. The Duke exchanged words with an older man with years of experience to offer, then turned back to Langton.

"And the evidence of intent to take the throne is certain?"

"It is. His Highness has Thomas de la Lande and Robert Welles, and they have made full confession. There can be no doubt of the extent of the betrayal. But with Scrope and Conyers still under arms in the north—"

"My brother will have to move quickly to prevent Warwick and George combining forces and unifying the north country against him," the Duke finished without looking up. He picked up a white knight, changed his mind, and selected a red piece instead, putting it down roughly where Burton lay between Coventry and Derby. "When you left Tickhill, what was the mood of the people there?"

"Those in the lands under the Earl's lordship are sound, Your Grace, and intelligence has it that Warwick has not found the encouragement he expected, and the Duke of Clarence even less so. He garners little support." Rob felt uncomfortable speaking about Gloucester's brother in less than charitable terms.

"I am not surprised," the Duke said, "it was ever so. I believe Norfolk has joined the King, and I have word that Worcester and Suffolk will shortly do the same. And what of the manor belonging to a friend of ours? Is the dispute settled? Are the lands safe?"

It took Robert more than a few seconds to realise that the Duke referred to Beaumancote, and at the thought of Isobel he felt his colour deepening and cursed his fortune that Gloucester's quick eyes had seen it. "As far as I am aware, Isobel Fenton's steward has reported no further troubles along that stretch of the Humber, Your Grace, and the Earl reinforced the garrison at Yuletide."

The constable said something Rob didn't hear as yet another messenger was shown into the room in haste. Breaking the royal seal, Gloucester swiftly read the contents of the letter he was handed. With his forefinger, he moved the white king to Newark. "It seems news travels faster than the bearer. My cousin Bedford has been sent north to rout Conyers and Scrope. Hmm, but the King is offering clemency to George and Warwick. Clemency *without* safe conduct – the message cannot be clearer: total submission to the King or pay the price of treason with their lives." He retrieved the red bishop from the map, turning it over and over in his hands, his dark brows drawn in consideration. Without warning, he slammed the piece on the map, making the constable start and look around. "Fetch paper and quill," he said sharply, "and take this message to the King."

Recognising his younger brother's neat script, Edward read the hurriedly written words with finger and thumb squeezing his chin. He grunted a laugh as he read the final words. He turned to the Earl. "You will be comforted to know that Langton reached Wales safely. It appears my brother Gloucester has him raising troops for the Crown."

The Earl felt a surge of relief that Robert was out of imminent danger, followed almost as swiftly by concern that his brother wasn't at the castle to order its defence. Now that the King had brought the army to Doncaster days after reaching Newark, they were within spitting distance of the castle at Tickhill, and war was coming perilously close to his own lands.

"I think it meet to remind my good cousin Warwick and my brother Clarence that time is running short on their offer of clemency and on my patience. We'll have Robert Welles and Richard Warren's heads; their deaths will serve me better than they did in life. As for a general clemency, we'll see whom it brings out of the woodwork, hey, my lord?"

IF THE KING reverted to indolence all too readily, so too could he turn on a coin and act with an alarming degree of rapidity, and a man would be a fool if he thought he could rely on the King's good temper. The Earl had seen the results of trying his patience, and a victim of it lay headless within yards of where he stood now watching the proceedings with grim authority. It was why Edward was king and why the Earl did not regret his own father's choice of lord. Had old King Henry proved himself as able, this grievous situation might have been avoided and order would have been maintained. King Edward would be mere Earl of March and York still alive. And his own father? Perhaps he would have lived and the Earl be standing here in different circumstances. As it was, Welles – like his father barely two weeks before – lay dead before them, and Richard Warren readied himself to follow. Ultimately, this had to be the fate of Clarence and Warwick, because how could such blatant disregard for the King's authority go unpunished? Yet to follow such a course risked galvanising Neville resistance and alienating the family further from Edward. And Clarence? He had none of Warwick's charisma, but he was the brother of the King, and Edward had done everything in his power to undo Warwick's influence and reconcile the duke to him. A restless crowd had gathered to watch the executions. It never ceased to amaze him – people's lust for the blood of strangers – as if death didn't present itself in so many forms already, so that none knew whether he would wake the morning after he laid himself down to sleep. To wish death on another seemed so contemptuous of life. Warren's neck now lay exposed, his face frozen with fear. The Earl looked at the expressions of the watching people: fascination, interest, distaste, horror among some –

none dispassionate except for the few children too young to understand the implication of the blade now cutting the air towards the man's neck. A child of no more than four or five years, curly-haired like Cecily and with her thumb in her mouth, flinched as the blade struck, parting flesh, bone, and sinew, and the head thudded, rolled once. She took her thumb from her mouth and turned and buried her head in her mother's skirts while cheers sprang up from the onlookers as if this had been the culmination of some street amusement. That child had more sense of the value of life than the adults around her. Turning abruptly, the Earl left the crowd to their morbid entertainment and returned to his sparse lodgings, to be greeted by Musters' squat frame warming his backside at the hearth. The older man let his cloak fall and, touching his hand briefly to his breast where the Earl's griffin gleamed, greeted him. "You were right, my lord; Lacey left Rotherham on the Rawmarsh road this morning."

Handing his own fur-lined cloak to his servant, the Earl indicated the stool by the fire, but remained standing. "How large is his retinue?"

Musters thought better of sitting and contented himself by planting his feet solidly apart. Calculating, he rubbed at a stubbly chin too creased to be smooth-shaven. "About two hundred – mostly on foot, some mounted, men-at-arms, a good number of archers – all well-equipped, I'd say, and fresh enough to make trouble if he turns east and heads this way."

The Earl's teeth gleamed in the firelight. "I'll stake my life on it. If he has any sense he will want to keep the river between them and the King's castle at Conisburgh, which means he'll turn east at Mexborough and follow its course to Doncaster and enter at the north gate by the bridge. He must be denied entry to the town. Send word to Dalton, I want him here within the hour. Have you seen Henry Lynes since we arrived?"

"Yes, my lord, he's at the Angel. I'll tell him to attend you equipped and in harness."

"Good, and have prickers sent out; I want to know the exact movements of Lacey and his men." The Earl began to get changed rapidly, and when Musters made no move to leave, he glanced up from removing his shoes. "Is there something else?"

"And the King?" Musters ventured. "What do you wish me to tell His Grace?"

Musters had known the Earl for long enough not to push a point. He waited while the Earl shunted his arms out of his short houppelande and Louys helped him into his arming doublet and began tying buckles and points.

"I will inform His Grace," the Earl replied shortly.

A FORBIDDING WIND from the east brought morose cloud that lay uniform across the heads of the Earl's men, subduing their mood. As he shifted in the saddle to look around him, his lip touched the edge of his bevor rising to protect his mouth and jaw, and he tasted cold metal. He wanted to spit but swallowed instead. From his vantage point he was able to make out the lands through which the Sprotbrough road ran, broken by frequent stubby stands of trees, but not enough to hide two hundred men. To the north and east his own lands lay, inviolable to any but his allies, and God forbid Lacey to place a foot upon it without his permission. The Earl quashed the rising tempo of his heart. A level head and a steady hand would be needed for his plan to work, yet impatience had him searching the horizon once again. By taking the longer route, Lacey's caution would have cost him in the time it would take to work his way upriver – time the Earl had put to good use by placing his men beyond the town gates ready to intercept the rebel. His men, their array of yellow and blue piercing the dull day, were getting restless. He could sense it in the edgy chinking of harness, smell it in the horse sweat on the air. Tired they might be from weeks on the move, but they spoiled for a fight. And he was going to give them one.

Movement from the direction of the town caught his eye. He squinted until the rider came into focus and swore into his bevor as the King's messenger was directed towards him through the ranks of men. He had left sending word to the King warning of Lacey's movements until the last possible moment. He thought he had more time than this.

"My lord!"

"Sir John," he returned, unsmiling, bringing his horse around to face him.

"His Grace greets you well and requests you wait upon his pleasure."

A royal request brooked no argument but might be open to negotiation. The Earl glanced towards the west road: still nothing. How long could he plausibly stall the King?

"I will attend His Grace upon completion of this matter of His Highness's security."

Sir John nudged his horse close to the Earl's and leaned towards him and away from curious ears. "My lord, it is on that matter which His Grace wishes to see you. He desires you to return immediately. Lord Lacey made Doncaster by another road not an hour ago and is yet with the King."

Eyes flashing, the Earl wheeled about and, shouting curt commands to his captains, heeled his horse towards the bridge and the town gate.

LACEY WAS KNEELING in submission before the King when the Earl marched into the great hall with his spurs furiously striking the stone. Just one short step and a single thrust and his blade would finish what Ralph Lacey had started. Alarmed, Lacey looked up as the Earl took a pace forward, his hand already on the pommel of his sword.

"Step back, my lord," the King warned. Breathing heavily through a grill of teeth, for a split moment it looked as if the Earl would push past the King's outstretched arm. The massed lords, brought together to witness Lacey's obeisance, ceased their whispered discourse. The Earl's recent head wound stung him back to the moment, and the time to strike passed. He stepped away, bowed. Was that triumph on Lacey's face? But it was too quickly disguised for him to read, and his hand itched to smash the false servility from the youth. He had a fleeting sensation of teeth and bone collapsing beneath his mailed fist and took his hand from his sword, forcing it to relax.

"Lacey has confessed his error and has sworn loyalty, and brings over two hundred armed men to our standard, with the promise of more should his plea for forgiveness be met with clemency." The King's eyes slid towards the prone man and back to meet the Earl's burning glare. "We understand the weakness of youth, do we not, my lord?" he said pointedly. "Especially when misled by those of greater nobility and years." Head still bent almost to the floor, Lacey's shoulders twitched, and the Earl imagined the bow of his lip sneering. "Moreover," the King continued, looking down from his considerable height on the kneeling figure, "he has information on Warwick's movements and his *intentions*, which he will share with us. I am inclined to be lenient."

Lacey lifted his head and looked to be rising to his feet. "I am your true subject, Highness—"

The Earl slammed his heel down onto the man's back. "Stay down! Your Grace, he will play you false."

"Then he will pay the price. Until that point he has my protection, my lord, as do you – as does *any* loyal subject." He looked around the room, then said quietly, "Let him rise, my lord."

With reluctance, the Earl took his mailed foot from Lacey's back, and the man gathered himself to his feet, cautiously feeling his shoulder blade and throwing the Earl a vicious look, soon covered as the King turned to him. "Count yourself fortunate, Lacey, that my lord Earl did not meet you in the field, or you would not be here now. Serve me loyally, and you will be rewarded. Fail in that duty, and you will have no safe conduct in this realm, and the Earl will hunt you down with my blessing. Understand?"

When Lacey was dismissed, still cringing like a whipped cur, the Earl marked his progress from the great hall, scarcely containing his contempt. The King, placing a restraining hand on his metal forearm, reduced his voice. "I meant what I said: Thomas Lacey is not to be harmed whilst he remains loyal. Do not think you can act freely irrespective of my orders because of the blood feud between you, my lord, nor that the love I bear you gives you immunity from my wrath should you test it. I am aware of what you planned outside the town—"

"Your Grace, he is not to be trusted!"

"And you are?"

"I will never betray you."

"Isn't that *exactly* what you were doing in laying an ambush for Lacey despite my warning to you?"

"In the *field*, Your Grace, in battle..." The Earl stopped rash words spilling from his mouth and started again, more slowly this time and measuring his remarks with care. "Men like Lacey will run to the first hand that feeds them. My intention is... was, to ensure he never runs to another master again. There are those you can trust with your life, Your Grace, and then there are men like Thomas Lacey."

"If you are right, the time will come when he forgets his place and you will be free to exact the revenge you long for, and that eats you from inside like canker, but it will be in *my* time, my lord, and at *my* command." He drew back to his full height, smiling genially to those waiting for his instructions as if they had been exchanging nothing more than gossip. "How now, my good lords, make ready; we move on Rotherham without delay, the better to catch a bear and his cub."

THE SUN HAD set on a cloudless day spent – almost entirely, it seemed to Robert Langton – in observing captains raking through lines of robust, dark Welshmen and fair-haired Marchmen in the pursuit of skilled, healthy individuals willing and able to serve the call to arms. While most of the Welsh needed an interpreter, what they lacked in ease of communication was more than made up for with their skill with arms and a sturdy respect for the coin promised for their service. What might have proved a tedious exercise was sharpened by Gloucester's dry observations, his meticulous attention to detail, and his apparently boundless energy. Langton sat next to him now, the youth marking the stance and attitude of each man presented to him with a rigour that belied his age, tapping out the urgency of the task in the rapid thrumming of his fingers on the board. A narrow-chested captain with a sharp eye presented another list of names, and another line of men snaked across the room and beyond the door, and not even Gloucester's wit could shake the waves of fatigue Rob felt rolling through him or stifle a yawn. The list of names, rank, and rate of pay scrawled on the paper in front of him blurred, the captain said something incomprehensible, and Rob fought to keep his eyes open.

"Are we keeping you from your rest, my lord?" the Duke enquired without taking his eyes from the men. "Do you not relish the prospect of overseeing the retention of another hundred bowmen? And another hundred spear after that?"

Langton coughed and blinked himself alert. "It would make the process easier and more interesting if they were not all called 'Griffith', Your Grace, and if one did not look so like the other that I swear we have counted the same man twice over and are paying him thrice what he's worth. We should consider branding them like cattle."

"If he does the service of two men, I would say he is worth it. *Griffith* must have been a busy man; we have much to thank him and all his offspring for. Ah, here is another one."

A swarthy, slightly taller than average man, bow-legged and with an archer's back, removed his cap and gave a cumbersome bow. He said something unintelligible in response to the captain's enquiry.

"*Gruffydd*, Your Grace," the captain interpreted. "Master bowman."

"They all say that," Rob muttered.

The Duke's mouth twitched. "Occupation?"

The captain shot a handful of words at the man, whose twisted draw-hand, fumbling the leather cap he held, bore testament to years of use with a longbow.

"Forester and huntsman, Your Grace, sound of body and mind an' keen to serve the King, he says."

Gloucester nodded to the man. "Your service is well-met, Gruffydd, and your loyalty will be rewarded."

Rob glanced at the Duke; he was deadly earnest, and what levity he had employed to make the day spin faster, he now abandoned. As the bowman bent over the paper and scratched his signature in the form of an arrow – the line no straighter than a crude twig – and moved down the long trestle to receive his initial payment, the Duke remarked quietly, "It is simple men like Gruffydd the Forester who could teach many a lord the value of fealty. We forget the simple man at our peril."

IT HAD SEEMED an old thing for a young man not yet eighteen to say, and in the quiet setting of the day when he found himself alone at last, Rob turned the thought over in his mind. He had never questioned his loyalty to his brother, not even when he had married Ann against his express wishes. The truth was that his deceit in marrying the youngest daughter of an impoverished lord, with his four sons, two older daughters, and a second wife – all of whom required suitable allowances – harmed no one but himself. For all that his brother had condemned his blatant disregard for pecuniary advancement and family connections, he had swiftly forgiven him and even grown to like his shy and spindly sister-in-law. What test of duty can it be when no test presents itself? What had his brother ever demanded of him that he would not have willingly given? Until now, with a bolt straight through his heart that pierced every waking moment with a barb more deadly than iron and formed out of soft limbs, gentle words, and eyes of sky and water in which he wanted to drown.

Lifting his booted feet onto a stool and crossing them at the ankles, he rested his forehead in his hand, listening to the last song of the blackbird in the trees beyond the moat. It was at times like this when he missed Isobel most, when he was alone with nothing but her face to occupy his mind.

He shunted awake at the sound of the door opening and stumbled to his feet, reaching blindly for his dagger.

"It is as dark as the abyss in here."

At Gloucester's voice, Rob hastily re-sheathed his dagger. "I'll find a light, Your Grace." He bumped around the unfamiliar room until he located the pricket stand and lit the wick in the dying embers.

Standing in the doorway alone, with what looked like a box tucked under one arm, the Duke appeared insubstantial in the light of the single flame, and as uncertain. Gloucester smiled – a little apologetically, Rob thought. "I have disturbed you…"

"Your Grace, forgive me." Rob invited the Duke to enter the sparsely furnished chamber, made not much more hospitable by the light. "How might I serve you?"

In answer, Gloucester proffered the box of chequered squares he carried, the contents of which rattled as he took it from under his arm. "I find myself poor society this evening and in want of an opponent. Will you play chess, my lord?" At Rob's slight hesitation, his face fell. "No matter. Perhaps it is not your game of choice." He turned to leave. Rob wasn't in the Duke's close circle of friends on whom he normally drew for company and, having known him for only a short time, was taken aback.

"Your Grace, I am afraid you will find my hospitality poorly provisioned."

"I did not come seeking hospitality, and as for provisioning, I have all I require. But I am in want of distraction and an honest adversary who will not flatter me into winning." Gloucester, perhaps reading Langton's mind as he calculated how much money he could afford to lose, added, "And I will wager a pint of ale."

"A pint, Your Grace?" Rob rubbed his chin. "Make it a Scots pint, and I will gladly accept."

"A joug it is. I have a great thirst about me, and three pints will quench it."

"Your Grace will need to win the wager first."

Grinning, the Duke pulled the stool to the roughly hewn trestle before Robert could do it for him and opened his box of pieces. He began laying them out methodically and at speed while Rob found another candle. Lopsided and crammed into a dumpy pottery stick, its tallow flame coughed into life as he set it close by, then he went to make up the fire.

The Duke glanced at the faltering flame, then around the room. "Not quite home, is it? War makes beggars of us all."

Langton squatted by the hearth. "And rich men out of Griffiths." He laid thin strips of wood on the fire, blowing the meagre embers back into life. From the corner of his eye, he thought he saw Gloucester frown at his labour and felt he needed to explain. "My squire missed dinner at noon, and I have sent him to find what supper he can now as he is inclined to be ill-tempered if he does not eat."

Gloucester finished laying the pieces on the board. "Ah, and that would be because we did not stop to dine. You must be in want of sustenance as well. I heed the reprimand."

Wiping his hands free of ash dust, Robert came over and sat opposite his duke. "I intended none, Your Grace. War also makes us hungry. The task needed completing, and Martin needed to learn that his duty includes serving his lord at the expense of his belly. It will have done him no harm, and I have little appetite at present and no need of his service. He has yet to face a man in battle after a long day's march – *then* he'll know the meaning of hardship and will yearn for days like these."

"As indeed will I," the Duke observed.

"I did not mean to imply—"

Looking him straight in the eye, Gloucester held up the two kings. "White or red?"

Rob paused, took stock, and then shook his head, smiling. "I think I must be red to be politic, although your king has already lost a battle, it seems." The Duke fingered the rough edge of the white king sporting his broken crown. The chipped walrus ivory gleamed as he placed it on its square. Langton watched him. "When I was much younger, perhaps nine years ago or so and before he became earl, my brother always used to say that I should know when I was beaten and then would best me at some game or other. He said I should know what defeat was like to make victory all the sweeter. I resented him for it then; it was a hard lesson, but it has served me well. But he let me win sometimes."

Gloucester advanced a pawn. "My brother ensured I *never* won. Being older he always chose the game, and he would always win it – one way or another. The first time it looked like I would beat him at chess he threw the board in the air halfway through the game and declared it to be a dull diversion not worthy of a prince. It was the white king that suffered, as you can see."

Rob raised one eyebrow. "I suppose it is His Highness's prerogative to win."

Gloucester observed the movement of a red knight and followed it with another white pawn. "No, not the King, this was my brother Clarence. He could not bear being second at anything, which was never a problem because his vantage in years gave him an advantage in games like this, at least at first. And then my cousin, Warwick, took me in hand and taught me winning moves, much to my brother's rancour. But George, if he did not have the patience to learn, could always remind me of my youth and inferiority at arms in the practice yards, which he did – frequently." Robert recalled the times he had seen Gloucester practise arms in recent times. He wasn't as heavily built as many of his age, but he was quick-witted, skilled, and determined. Gloucester continued, "I swiftly learned that if I could not defeat him in a fight because he was bigger and stronger than me, I could defeat him at tables, or chess, or in rhetoric or Latin. He was never keen on anything that required sustained effort. We played few games after that. In some ways, I would have sacrificed winning to have kept his friendship for a little longer." He moved a bishop and sat back on the stool, waiting for Robert – who was finding the Duke's candour disarming – to make his next move.

"The Earl has often said that he has had to make sacrifices as the older brother, that the burden of expectation is such that he has never been free to make his own choices."

"Perhaps, but then nor does being the youngest have the privileges of seniority. There must be benefit to both, although there are times when I fail to see what good fewer years might bring."

Rob took advantage of the natural pause to select his next move. Whereas Gloucester manoeuvred with ease around the board, seemingly able to talk while contemplating his line of attack, Langton needed to concentrate. He had guessed what the Duke was planning, but outwitting him was another matter. He took a risk and ran his bishop across the board. The Duke raised his brows, and Robert groaned inwardly.

"I think, Your Grace, that one of the two benefits of youth might be in the underestimation of its ability."

"And that is an advantage?" he asked with an air of disbelief, simultaneously removing the red bishop and replacing it with his advancing queen. Robert used his knuckle to knead the scar at his lip, mourning the loss of the piece.

"So it would seem to me at this moment, Your Grace," he offered with a grimace.

Gloucester broke into one of his rare broad and unguarded grins. "And the second?"

"Well, younger sons can… are… obliged to make their own mark on the world. They have a certain degree of freedom from the responsibility their older brother carries, and they can marry whom they wish, despite…" He stalled, brushing away his brother's blighted marriage with the memory of his own happy union and then with the surge of longing that the thought of Isobel now brought, clouded by the inevitable stab of guilt.

"Despite?" the Duke prompted him.

Rob shook his head at his lapse in concentration. "I am sorry, Your Grace, I am more weary than I thought." He picked up a piece, ready to move it from danger. "Despite what might be expected of them or required by Reason to provide for the future. To make a sensible and politic match, I mean," he added when the Duke looked puzzled.

"Are you saying that you did not?"

Rob held the knight suspended, caught off guard by his duke's directness. "My wife, Ann, had little to bring to our marriage, as my brother reminds me occasionally, and it has left me bereft of means to increase my own affinity, as Your Grace knows."

"Do you regret your choice of wife?"

"Not for one moment, nor the arguments it caused with the Earl, for they passed quickly enough."

Gloucester seemed to have forgotten the game. He played with the redundant red bishop, his mind somewhere but not in that dingy room with its poorly ventilated hearth that belched smoke from time to time, making Rob want to cough. He did so now, and the Duke returned to the room and to the game, playing his next move. "I suppose the choice of wife must be made with care; there are some rifts that are hard to heal."

"Yes," Rob said as Felice's acid features cast a shadow over his memory, then thinking of the present situation made worse by the King's ill match – not that he would dare voice it. He didn't need to; Gloucester was already there.

"This trouble we endure, this rising against the King… my brothers…" Candlelight picked out the tones in the Duke's dark hair as he shook his head, struggling to finish his thoughts as they crowded to the tip of his tongue but failed to breach the dam it made. He spent a moment preparing his words, then looked at Rob sitting across the table from him and, earnest and young, tried again. "My brother did my cousin Warwick great disservice when he chose to marry as he did. Perhaps… perhaps had he taken a royal wife Warwick would not have felt such affront. As it is, I fear it is gone too far." He regarded the chessboard glumly, and Rob wondered whether this was why his company had been sought in the first place.

"It must be difficult to have loyalties divided, Your Grace. I know it is difficult, nay impossible to be so torn."

The Duke nodded, running a long finger along the edge of the rough trestle and back again. "I know where my loyalty lies and have never doubted it, despite the kinship shared with my cousin. But George is my brother also, and we were close once, a long time ago and before he forgot himself and became bloated with his own importance like a bladder." The half-smile that the image had conjured faded, and he looked away. "The trouble with being so puffed up is you can get kicked about. I wonder whether George regrets it now? Where will it all end?"

He stared into the candle flame as if it might hold some clue to the future, but it merely guttered in the draught filtering through the ill-fitting window.

"Your Grace, there comes a time when a man must make his own future and live with whatever decisions he takes."

"But that does not make those decisions right, does it?" the Duke said. "And those choices affect other people – people we are supposed to honour and love – our kin. I understand Warwick feeling slighted by the Queen's family, as we all do to a degree, but we have to put that aside, and George has no reason to resent them except that he chooses to do so. It is his duty to his family and his king, but he spurns it."

"Your Grace is not responsible for the actions of others, only for your own. We are all only responsible for our choices, even if events are such that those decisions seem to have been made for us by the circumstances surrounding them."

Gloucester raised his shoulders briefly. "George would say so, yes; and Warwick."

"There are times when we make the best choice we can, and only time tells whether it was the right one."

The Duke surveyed him sombrely but with a quickened interest. "And have you made decisions you thought were wrong in retrospect, my lord?"

"I have, Your Grace, but I do not necessarily regret them."

It appeared, Langton thought later that evening as he finished the ale the Duke had sent him, that this thoughtful, self-contained young man he called lord had cause to rue the actions of others. This present mess they found themselves in was as much the result of wrong-headed decisions as the thwarted egos of the King's brother and cousin. But the source of the strife they currently faced went back far into the Duke's childhood and even his own. And if choices made years ago by others for now-forgotten reasons affected them all so fundamentally, how could he continue to hide from himself the extent of his own failure to moderate his actions, and what might he have to do as a result of what he had already done?

"WHERE ARE THEY now?" The final days of March, and the sun warmed the King's fair hair but did little to improve his temper.

"The last information had them heading across the Pennines, Your Grace."

The King tore his gloves from his hands and threw them onto the table. "So, they show no intention of accepting clemency and submitting to my authority."

"At least they fled Rotherham. Surely that indicates they know they have lost?" William Hastings offered.

"Lost, but not defeated. If they're heading west into Stanley's territory, they must be hoping to persuade him to throw in his lot with them and swing this rebellion. Stanley's wife is Warwick's sister, after all."

"And Clarence is your brother, Your Grace, but he still holds to Warwick."

"You do not need to remind me about that whelp of a brother, Will," the King spat. He turned abruptly, scattering the handful of nobles surrounding the table on which the unfurled map lay. Leaving the men exchanging glances, he strode to the oriel window, leaned his outstretched arms either side of the central casement, and stared through the lozenges of wrinkled glass where varicoloured movement outside indicated a bustling day in the streets of York.

The Earl watched proceedings from the farther end of the table without offering comment. He was used to the King's swing in mood when he believed himself to be outmanoeuvred. It took time to rile him, but when pressed – as he was now and had been these last weeks – nothing would stop him attaining his quarry but complete submission or a decisive battle to finish this petty pitching back and forth across the landscape. It wore at them all, and the emergence of spring in the hedges and copses lining the way did little to raise spirits but mocked their progress. Moreover, as the days passed and it became increasingly obvious that the rebels wouldn't capitulate, the King had privately voiced his concern that the rebellion would drag on and that the conclusion to it would be either his own head on a pike or those of his opponents. Either way, Micklegate would soon be sporting new Yorkist baubles where once his father, accompanied by his brother and uncle, had been on public display. Surely Warwick would remember *that*? How could he forget his own father's lifeless eyes gazing down at him? The Earl knew the King to be still haunted by the thought of his father mockingly crowned in paper where a gold ducal coronet once sat, and of his brother who died with him.

"I have lost one brother in Edmund; I cannot afford to lose another," the King muttered, after a pause.

"My lord of Clarence may yet be reconciled to Your Grace," Brough ventured, treading delicately but without much hope.

"Clarence?" the King said, brooding in his cups. "It wasn't George I was concerned about. Richard, on the other hand, if captured…" He shook his head and, waving a page away, he helped himself to more wine.

"His Grace of Gloucester is young and has no stake in this discord. Surely he could make his peace with Warwick and his life be spared?"

The King downed a third of the wine. "Warwick might be persuaded towards leniency, but Richard?" He wiped his mouth, shaking his head, and put the glass down on the table. "You do not know my brother. He was only a child when our father and brother were slaughtered, but he felt every slight as if he were there. He would rather cut his own throat than change sides." He raised a heavily ringed finger, pointing it directly at Brough. "Have you any notion how much pressure Warwick will have put Gloucester under to support him when things did not go his way? I know my cousin well and how persuasive he can be. Besides—" he jabbed the heavy table carpet, jarring the glass and spilling wine onto the fine pile where it shone like rubies against the rich colours before sinking into the wool, "—Richard might be untried, but he's no fool, and Sweet Mary knows what Clarence would do with a younger brother rapidly gaining his majority and his authority. He could never handle the competition. I expect Richard'd have an accident." His mouth warped sourly, and he slugged the rest of his wine in one mouthful. "So much for the Sons of York."

Listening to the exchange of comments between the King and his closest advisors, the Earl understood the King's fears for Gloucester almost as well as he comprehended the outcome for himself and his own brother should this fight turn into a losing battle for the oldest of York's sons. But he had been in this situation before and seen it turn in his favour on the spin of the Wheel.

"Your Grace," he said, his measured timbre causing the other men to stop their hushed debate and turn to hear him, "with Warwick's support fading and Conyers and Scrope accepting defeat, Stanley will not risk taking the rebels' part against you."

Leaning against the ornamental stonework of the window, the King crossed his arms on his strongly-built chest. "What makes you think that?"

"Thomas Stanley already controls much of those areas not under Warwick's sway. He will not risk losing what he has if he can possibly stay out of the fight. He is not the sort who lets loyalty stand in the way of personal gain; he is too pragmatic for that."

Hastings grunted a laugh, and the King managed a smile of sorts. "Not like you, then, my lord?"

"Indeed, Your Grace, not like me. But Stanley can be bought; he will be hoping for some of the spoils should Warwick be deprived of his lands. He is ambitious and…" The Earl was going to say "devious" but thought better of it and simply said, "… astute." And left it at that.

"Ambitious he might be," the King mused, "but first we must win this fight, or we'll all be scrabbling for our lives, not our lands." Pushing away from the window, he became resolute. "My lords, it is time we routed this rabble once and for all. Gloucester will need to mobilise his Welsh troops, and we'll make ready our pursuit."

Chapter 12

In the wilderness garden, Chouchou rolled onto her back in a patch of sun, exposing the distinct shapes of the puppies beneath her tautened belly. Running her hand gently over the bumps, Isobel contemplated the simplicity of the dog's life. Chou had little choice in what she did, with what dog she was mated, the name by which she was called, her master – yet she appeared contented enough. Perhaps choice was overrated, perhaps it was a phantasm of the imagination designed to beguile as surely as Eve had once led Adam into sin. Sitting on the low stone bench with its crusty yellow growths, Isobel stroked the dog's silky flanks. "Is that what I am, Chou – Eve? And if I am Eve, who is Adam?" The dog yawned, exposing sharp teeth and pink gums, and, shaking her head, rearranged her ears. "No, I know not, either." Isobel sank her face into the folds of her skirts between her knees until the wave of emotion, the pain and pleasure at the thought of Rob, passed. "I suppose he could not have said much else in his letter, not without making it obvious, just in case anyone saw it." Isobel suspected Sawcliffe monitored all correspondence to and from the castle bound to any but the Earl and Countess themselves, and even their letters might not be immune if he thought he could get away with it. "I wager he has even seen my letters to Beaumancote, even though it is none of his business what I say to my own servants. And he has definitely read my steward's letter to me; the seal would not have broken by itself. At least Buena is safe and the manor secure. I have that to thank your master for." At the thought of the Earl, her stomach turned, and she averted her head from the smell of damp dog until the sensation subsided.

When they had heard of his wound from the battle, rumour ran riot around the castle until firm intelligence from the Earl's own messenger quelled it. Even so, the Countess had her household ready themselves for flight should events turn against them. That was a month ago. An early Easter had come and gone, and Lent and long faces had been put aside for another year. The new year had begun on Lady Day with the turning of the soil, and now at the beginning of May, there was still little more than scant reports – brought occasionally on the lips of merchants, passing clerics, or the Earl's messengers – that were out of date before they arrived.

What was she to feel? In the day or so between learning of the battle near Stamford and then the news that the Earl's wound was already healing, she had struggled to resolve the conflict that tumbled incoherently through every waking moment. She prayed for him, of course, as duty dictated, but every time she held him in her mind's eye, she saw his brother, and the frisson of remorse she experienced in quieter moments became a torrent that refused to still until she wanted to scream. Ursula maintained her adulation of the Earl, and Isobel had no one to turn to other than Chouchou, who would forgive anything.

The Lady Snake curled seductively around the tree not a stone's throw from where they sat, reminding Isobel of her recent transgression and adding vinegar to the wound. Picking herself up, she stopped only long enough to gather the sulphur trumpets breaking through their papery shells. Could it really have been a year since she arranged such flowers in the great hall of her own home – a year and a lifetime away?

She made her way back into the bailey and was still so caught up in thinking about her father and about meeting Rob for the first time in her garden – a memory so remote now she might as well have dreamed it – that she failed to notice the flurry of activity until she was being buffeted from all sides by household retainers and servants in livery, setting Chouchou into a frenzy of barking.

"Quiet, Chou!" Isobel stopped a boy staggering under an armful of hangings. "What's happening? Are we under attack?"

A fold escaped, and he gathered the cloth to him, resting his chin on the top bundle. "Don't you know?" he said in that superior way only an adolescent boy can manage. *Obviously not*, Isobel wanted to say, but he went on regardless of her impatience. "The Earl's on 'is way back."

He returned later that day as the last light of the sun lit the catkins in the ewer perched by the narrow embrasure. Chou pricked her ears and was on her feet and out of the door as Ursula opened it, the rattle of dog claws on the stairs growing fainter as she disappeared. "My lord is here!" Ursula exclaimed, clapping her hands and jumping up and down like a child. She bustled up to Isobel, hands flapping. "My lord will be wanting his lady. A lord always wants his lady when he returns."

Isobel resisted the hands already reaching to unlace her dress. "I am not my lord's *lady*, Ursula, I am his mistress, nothing more. I doubt he will wish to see me." Doubt? Or hope? Escaping Ursula's fingers, Isobel sent her to find supper for them both.

When Ursula returned, Isobel had already washed and changed and made herself ready for bed as a disincentive to Ursula's persistent chattering that rattled around her head like sparrows. Or perhaps she believed it would make her immune to being summoned to his chamber, as if the thin cloth covering her somehow made her invulnerable. It did not.

"I expected you to be waiting for me," the Earl said some time after the order came to attend him, and Isobel had reluctantly allowed herself to be primped and primed like a prize horse clothed in trappings. She heard the disappointment in his voice and hated herself even more for minding. "The King gave me leave to return immediately, and we have ridden three days straight to be here."

"*We*, my lord?" she queried, looking at him properly for the first time to be met by his cool grey eyes, darker in the light of the fire and the multiple candles in their ornate stands.

"Yes, *we* – my brother and I. Where were you?" Isobel's heart jumped, and he must have seen it because he frowned. "What is it? Are you unwell? You are very pale." He took her hand in his and held it, and she was relieved that the light in the room was dim enough to obscure her face, but he must have felt her pulse stammer under his fingers because it hammered away in her heart.

"I think I have taken a chill." And Isobel sniffed and did a little cough, hoping he would take pity on her and send her back to her room.

"I thought you were out of sorts. Come and sit by the fire and tell me what you have been doing since I have been away." He sat in his big chair by the hearth and pulled her onto his knees.

"Chouchou has missed you," Isobel said, for want of anything else to say. He looked down at the dog already ensconced at his feet.

"The *dog* has missed me, Isobel? And have you?" he asked quietly.

"It has been a long time, my lord." She removed her hand from under his and, standing, went to fill his beaker from the wine ewer by the fire, but he rose and caught her around her waist. Removing her hennin, he eased her hair from its confines, let it unfurl over his hand, and lifted it to his lips. "Like honey," he murmured. "The wine can wait. Come to bed."

A NEW SCAR, shiny in the light of dawn, razored his forehead close to his temple where his hair fell back as he slept. About the length of her little finger, it had scabbed and healed, and now the pink of the tender skin was fading, and soon it would silver and be added to the other memorials of his lifetime of war scattered over his body. He moved, kicking the sheets free of his legs in his sleep. He looked well: weeks in the saddle had bronzed his face, the muscles of his shoulders were tensioned and his thighs defined. Isobel could see why the women of his court admired him, why the Countess protected her claim on him with protracted vigour; but his features did not touch her in the way they should, nor did they warm her as his brother had done. She swallowed and rolled over, feeling the hollow weight in the pit of her stomach as she did every day when she thought of Rob, leaving her wanting to retch and rid her gut of misery. If she lay still it would pass, and she tugged the sheets, dislodging the cold morning air. She detected movement behind her, then the heat of his body against her own. Isobel closed her eyes, willing him back to sleep, but his arm folded over her and his hand found her breast and his lips the skin behind her ear. Keeping eyes tight shut, Isobel made him Robert as he pressed against her, and she whispered his name into the solitude of her mind as he parted her legs.

"HAVE YOU BEEN eating?" the Earl asked, washing his hands and face in the basin of water and rubbing them vigorously with the linen towel. He opened the shutters holding back the sun, then, handing her the cloth-wrapped bread and placing the cups beside her on the all-night table, he climbed back onto the bed. Breaking the bread, he handed her the soft inside. She took it but didn't eat. "You are a little thin, Isobel, I wish to see you eat."

"I am not hungry, my lord." She replaced the bread in the fold of the napkin, conscious he watched her closely, and, flushing, pulled the sheets to her chin. "You were telling me about your march south in pursuit of the rebels."

He finished his mouthful, drank, and adjusted his position to sit facing her, robustly naked despite the cold air. "Warwick and Clarence headed south-west, we suspected to gain support from Courtney. The King had issued commissions of array from the south-western counties, but there was little point as Warwick was moving too quickly and, anyway, we were in pursuit. The rebels do not have much support among the lords there, thanks be to God, and Gloucester had raised troops in the Marches, which also served as a warning to some who might have been considering it." He laughed shortly to himself, then saw her puzzled expression and explained. "According to my brother, they met Lord Stanley on the road and Gloucester reminded him to whom he owed fealty. Bet Stanley would have liked *that*." And he laughed again, biting off a chunk of bread and letting his arm rest on his upright knee.

"Did… did Lord Langton have to fight?"

"Rob? No, the troops never engaged with the enemy, more's the pity."

"Why could that *ever* be a pity?"

He stopped laughing. "It is what he is trained to do – what we all train for: we fight to protect ourselves and our people from rebels and the Scots. We fight to maintain peace, you know that." He must have detected the irritability in his voice, because he relented. "Do not be concerned; we will have the opportunity to prove ourselves again. I doubt we have seen the last of Warwick; he will be back."

Isobel didn't want him to prove himself. Most of all, she didn't want Rob drawn into a fight he might not win. She laid her head against the pillow, thinking about him, about what he might be doing, feeling, right now.

"Anyway," he went on, "we reached Exeter on the fourteenth day of April, but Warwick had already fled to the coast where he took ship."

"Where was Ro… were the Duke of Gloucester and Lord Langton?"

"Does it matter? What matters is that Warwick tried to take more ships but was driven off by the Queen's brother, Anthony Woodville – Lord Rivers as he is now. You know he wants revenge for his father's murder last year?" Isobel nodded, half-listening. "Warwick's ships nearly foundered in the recent tempest at sea and made for Calais, but he was refused entry even though he has been Captain there long enough to build a loyal following. It seems that although Lord Wenlock is still Warwick's man, the garrison remembered to whom they owed their ultimate loyalty, and a Seigneur de Duras would not even permit the Countess to land."

"The Countess of Warwick was with them?"

"Have I not said? The Countess and her two daughters – the Duchess of Clarence and the younger, Anne – were on board. No, Duras did not relent, and the duchess was forced to give birth on the ship—"

"She was with child?"

"Obviously," he said dryly, but she ignored his sardonic smile. He continued. "Warwick found himself without port or friend, and—"

"What happened to the duchess and the baby?"

"What?" He looked incredulous. "Isobel, I am trying to tell you something important here."

"I know, but what happened? Did she have the baby?"

Lifting his hands in defeat, he sighed. "She gave birth. The infant died."

"Oh."

"So, now Warwick and Clarence are without friends or port. Calais is closed to them, and Burgundy will not jeopardise our trading treaty, so where do you think Warwick will have to go for help? Louis of France – I stake my life on it. Where else is there to go? King Louis is no fool, and with Margaret of Anjou his sister, he will want to milk this dissension between Edward and his brother to its limits. That way he can keep England turned in on itself and not preparing for an invasion of France. He must think God and all the saints side with him." He halted, peering through the curtain of Isobel's hair. "What is the matter?" When she didn't answer, he parted her tresses. "Isobel, are you crying? Why for? The danger to the King has passed for the moment." He tried to raise her face, but she resisted. "Were you frightened the castle would come under attack, is that it?"

Isobel jerked her head free of his hand and heard the snap of irritation when he said, "Isobel, *speak*."

"The baby," she snuffled, wiping her eyes on the edge of the bed sheet. "The poor duchess."

"Oh. Yes. I see." He seemed at a loss. "It is the way of things. She can have other children."

"But not *that* baby. That baby is *dead*. What kind of stupor are we in that... that the poor girl is forced to give birth on a *ship*? Is childbirth not dangerous enough? And for what? All this... this fighting, all these deaths, taking you and your br... brother into danger, and over what? When will this manoeuvring for position ever stop? Who cares who is king!"

Her rising voice choked to a standstill, and she clamped her hand over her mouth as his expression became stone. "I... I did not mean—"

"One day you will realise that this *manoeuvring*, as you call it, protects your land and puts food in your belly and clothes on your back. It ensures the safety of your tenants and the trade in the ports. The law of the land and the peace in the shires are secured off the backs of men like me who fight for them. You are very young and a woman; I would not expect you to understand."

"All I know is that men make war, and war breeds hate, and hate, vengeance. And it never seems to stop but goes on and on from one generation to the next, and babies die when they don't have to, and where is the right in that?" Isobel expected him to be angry again and to chastise her for her wanton ignorance, but instead he levelled his gaze.

"And do you believe for one moment that by laying down our weapons our enemies will do the same? They will perceive our weakness and take up arms against us – and how many children do you think will die then? Do you really think that your father's loyalty to my family was in vain? That the loss of his leg and eye was pointless?"

"My mother thought so."

He laughed softly. "Did she? Well, it is the place of men to die and women to mourn, and she knew that better than any."

Isobel thought he mocked her and scowled up at him, but instead he was fingering the stag scar on his arm and appeared reflective. "Are you not sorry about the Earl of Warwick?"

He came out of his reverie. "What about him?"

"He was your friend."

"Yes, he was, for a long time. Things change – people change. He made his choice, and he was a fool if he thought I would make it with him; but, yes, I am saddened by it." The sun had crept around the side of the window and shone slanting across Isobel's eyes. She moved her face from the glare. "You look wan; here, eat a little." She shook her head. He frowned and, leaning forward, felt her forehead. Then, taking the edge of the sheet, he peeled it from her. Isobel tried to cover her nakedness, but he secured her hands between his and held them while he inspected her. He felt her breasts, first one and then the other. "When did your courses last run?"

Isobel blinked. "I… do not know; I cannot remember."

"Try."

She thought wildly. When was it? Before he left? After? She had lost count of the days, so jumbled had they become. Her mind stumbled as she worked out the dates. The Earl had left to join the King and she had been tending Rob… *Robert!* Her eyes widened and her hand shot over her mouth as the nagging nausea suddenly intensified. She made it to the garderobe just in time.

Flopping against the privy wall, Isobel waited for her stomach and racing mind to settle before the cold air and stench climbing up the privy chute finally drove her back to the Earl's chamber. What could she do or say now? She avoided his eyes and waited for the accusation, for the denouncement. He had donned a shirt and gown in the intervening time and had opened all the shutters, flooding the room with light and making her feel all the more vulnerable in her nakedness. She carried his brother's child. *Robert's* child. Robert's *child.* Isobel shook. Uncontrollably.

"Isobel." She expected to feel a blow or at least to be cast out of his rooms as he strode towards her, but instead, he draped his furred mantle around her shoulders. "Come and warm yourself. The sickness will pass if you have a little bread and wine." Dazed, Isobel allowed herself to be guided to his chair by the fire, which now danced eagerly with fresh flames. "Sit," he ordered, tucking the edge of the robe around her feet and raising them onto the low footstool. "Eat," he commanded, dipping a piece of bread into the wine and holding it to her lips. She ate, numbly. Pulling up another chair, he sat beside her. His eyes shone, his normally stern features animated.

"I do not understand..." Isobel faltered, not sure how to continue but needing to know whether he realised her guilt and just hadn't registered it himself yet. He looked stunned enough, although he was smiling now. Through her addled wits, Isobel was beginning to piece together the dates. He would not know that her courses last flowed shortly after they had lain together. He didn't know, he *couldn't*. But Ursula did.

"Do you sicken again?"

She wasn't used to this solicitude. Isobel shook her head, thoughts scrambling. Would Ursula feel compelled to say anything? And Rob? Should she tell him? Would he guess when the evidence of this greater sin became too apparent to hide? How would he react if he knew that his brother believed the child she carried was his own? If, if, if – around and around until the words rose up her gullet towards the tip of her tongue and tried to explode from her mouth. Rising, Isobel said, "My lord, you must wish to ready yourself for the day. I will leave you to your gentlemen."

"My gentlemen can wait."

"But I must bathe and dress, my lord, and eat something, as you desired."

He released her reluctantly. "Attend to your toilette but return to break fast with me after devotions; I wish to see you eat."

ISOBEL MUST HAVE run up to her room because she was out of breath by the time she reached it. Clothes had been laid behind the guard by the fire to air, and Ursula had left the basin ready with the water in the ewer still warm. Stripping, Isobel washed in the scented water, scrubbing until her skin glowed. The tiny hairs on her arms rose in a haze of gold down as the air cooled them and, running her hands over her body, she tried to see what the Earl had detected. Her breasts were a little rounder, perhaps, and her nipples tingled and were tender to touch; but her stomach lay flat as always. She didn't feel particularly pregnant, apart from the dragging sensation in her belly that lessened by the hour. No one would guess – not for a while. It gave her the opportunity to decide a course of action: to determine what to tell Rob and to prevent Ursula from inadvertently betraying them. She was the greatest threat, and Isobel would have to confront her – and do so soon.

Isobel dressed, but Ursula had still not returned by the time she had combed her hair and tucked it modestly from sight. Nor had she when Isobel rose from devotions. She could delay no longer and trudged down the narrow stairs expecting at any moment to see Ursula's cowled face coming up around the stout newel. But she didn't. Instead, Isobel heard her distinctive bird-like voice as she neared the Earl's chamber. She stopped in her tracks, straining to hear more than the few words carried by the stone. Ursula sounded nervous and gabbled excitedly, then came the taut resonance of the Earl's voice as he replied, ending on a rising note denoting a question. Ursula began to answer. Rounding the corner, Isobel entered the room. Dressed in a brocaded red silk doublet, heavily pleated, the Earl looked a decade younger. Ursula's mouth opened on seeing her, but she covered it with a fluttering hand while darting glances at the Earl. Isobel sank into a curtsy.

"There you are," he greeted, helping her rise because her knees shook, "I nearly sent one of the servants to find you, but then Ursula wished to speak with me, and I was about to send her instead." He kissed Isobel fully on the mouth, careless that Ursula hopped uncertainly behind him, still flapping her hands in agitation. "Now she will have to bide," he said cheerfully, placing the flat of his hand over Isobel's belly. "This child needs feeding. Come, we must not keep him waiting." And he caressed her gently through the thick folds of the skirts.

"My lord!" Isobel protested his intimacy, her skin blooming with heat at the interest of his gentlemen waiting to serve breakfast.

He laughed off her embarrassment. "All will know of it soon enough; in another two months, you will begin to show."

Ursula had become strangely still, her eyes bulging like a frog. Did she not know? Had she not already guessed? It seemed not. Her hand raised as if for permission to speak. Isobel flashed a warning glare, but the Earl intervened. "Not now, Ursula." And he walked Isobel to the trestle without giving her a chance to reply.

"PERHAPS," ISOBEL ventured when she had been served and his gentlemen stood at a discreet distance from them, "I am not with child at all. I have missed but one month of my courses and even so—"

"You are mistaken; you have missed two. I remember distinctly we did not lie together previously when your courses ran. This is the third month. Besides, you sicken easily, your paps are swollen—"

"I am not one of your dogs," Isobel said crossly.

"… and you are quick to anger," he finished mildly. "It also explains your irrational thoughts on the subject of sovereignty and who should be king," he added, this time with an edge that warned her to keep quiet. "You cannot help it; your brain is softened by your *maternité*, as it should be." He lifted a smoked herring onto the silver dish in front of her and poured a little honeyed verjuice over it. "You must eat; you are too thin, and your blood needs nourishment to grow the child or he will be weak and sicken. Stop pinching your hand."

Isobel let go of her hand and picked at the edge of the fish instead, wondering how little she might get away with eating, but he watched with the interest of a hawk and she ended up nibbling to placate him.

"You will break your fast here each morning with me. You are to eat three times daily – aromatic foods, neither too sweet nor sour, and not so much as to burden you. Too much salt and bitter foods must be avoided. Drink only mild red wine – no ale – and walk a short distance each day, and you must abstain from anything that causes you distress." He missed the lowering glance she cast at him and crooked a finger at one of his servants. The dish was removed and another replaced it, laden with tiny, plump breasts of squab. Picturing the nestlings, vulnerable in their coats of softest down, her stomach turned. She exhaled to control the nausea. "You are to tell me if you desire any unnatural foods—"

"Unnatural?"

"Charcoal, clay, sand – that sort of thing."

"Oh."

"And you are to avert your eyes from monstrous images or deformed creatures lest they provoke imaginings that will damage the child. It is well to gaze upon male children, but ensure they are of good birth and sound of eye and limb."

Children? Isobel sometimes heard children playing across the river, but they were too distant to know whether they were boys or girls, whatever their parentage, and as to the slant of their eyes or the straightness of their legs, she couldn't say. But it gave her a thought. "Might I see Lady Cecily, my lord? She is sound-limbed and quick-witted."

He ran his forefinger over his top lip, regarding her. "She is a girl."

"Yes, but she is of the noblest birth."

He conceded her point with a wave. "But she is not to exert you."

"My lord?" Louys bowed. "Lord Langton is here as you requested."

"Excellent!" The Earl tugged the napkin from his shoulder as he stood to receive his brother. "I had quite forgot."

Isobel rose. She kept her head bowed rather than look at Rob and knew not whether he did the same.

"Well met, brother!" The Earl stepped around the side of the trestle towards him and clasped his shoulder, motioning to the table and a cushioned chair set close by. "Why are you attired like that? Do you plan to hunt this morning? Even so, have you broken your fast? Join us; I have news for you that will not wait."

Robert scanned the table of delicacies. "I never thought to see *you* feast before noon."

"Sit," the Earl insisted, patting the chair. "There is plenty enough even for you." His smile broadened. "Isobel has a need to eat, and I must ensure she does." His look became momentarily stern. "I have told you before, Isobel, leave your hand alone."

Robert remained standing. "I have come to take my leave."

The smile dropped from the Earl's face. "I would have thought that you had seen enough of that nag-end of a rouncey of yours. You have had no time to rest, and we have much work to do here."

"His Grace has duties for me in the West Country, pockets of disorder that need calming. I have had all the rest I need." His eyes slid towards Isobel then back to his brother. He looked as dejected as she felt, and if he had slept at all there was no evidence of it in the shadows beneath his eyes. He leaned his arms on the high back of the chair. "What is this news you are so eager to impart? Pray, tell me Warwick has sued for peace and Clarence has taken Holy Orders." He attempted a smile, but it was clearly an effort, and it slipped almost as soon as it appeared.

"Not that I have heard, although the thought of it pleases almost as much. No, this concerns Isobel."

"No, my lord!" she gasped. "Please…"

Rob looked from his brother to her entreating face. "Isobel?"

"And you should be the first to hear it," the Earl continued.

She clutched his arm. "*Please*, my lord!"

He put his arm around her and a cautionary finger on her lips. "Isobel, remember what I said and do not tax yourself. You must remain calm for the sake of the child."

She thought she heard Rob's sharp intake of breath and, with the faintest movement of her head, shook it; but whether he understood the wordless message Isobel couldn't tell because he stood as if struck dumb, until the weight of it filled the vacant conversation and the Earl, half frowning now, repeated, "Isobel bears my child."

Rob began to breathe again. His lips moved as by themselves. "Yes, I heard you."

"And… that is it? No congratulations? No expression of joy? Sweet Jesu, you wished me as much when my last bitch whelped."

Robert winced, ran his tongue over his lips. "I wish you joy," he said, meeting her eyes, and the pain of it ran between them in a wordless flood. Dropping his gaze, Rob looked at his hands gripping the chair's top rail and, slowly releasing them, flexed his fingers. "If that is all your news, I will take my leave." He bowed shortly, "My lord. Mistress Fenton," and he turned on a curt heel to depart.

The Earl released Isobel from his hold. "Robert, stay." His brother stopped by the door. "We have matters to discuss."

Rob shrugged. "There are none I can think of."

"Family matters. Issues of estate."

He made no move to turn. Isobel touched the Earl's sleeve. "My lord, might I go to my chamber?"

"Hmm? Oh, yes, do so. I will send for you later. Remember what I said earlier."

She nodded, but he was already distracted, waiting for his brother's response. Isobel passed by close enough to have heard Rob whisper her name if he chose, but instead he thumped the door frame, twisting away from her as he yielded to the Earl's request.

Moments later, she heard the sound of boots beating the stone stairs behind her.

"Isobel, wait!" She stopped and let Rob catch up. "Here." He grabbed her elbow and hustled her through the door onto the parapet of the tower where doves took fright in a shimmer of wings. The door banged shut, leaving them alone in the gusting wind on top of the world.

"I thought the Earl wanted to speak with you?"

"He does; I have little time. I wanted to see you before I leave."

"Rob…" She reached out to him, but he flinched away.

"Why did you not want me to know, Isobel?" Male voices travelled up the stairs below them, getting closer.

"I did not want you to leave thinking… believing…" They were almost at the top stair.

"What? Thinking *what*, Isobel?"

"That the child is… his." She watched the blood drain from his face, leaving him hollow-cheeked and ashen. She risked touching his hand, and this time he didn't move but seemed to fold in on himself and wither inside. The latch on the door rattled open, and one of the garrison men pushed through, still talking to someone behind him.

"Get out!" Rob roared into life, shoving the door closed on the man's startled face. He wheeled around, colour rising along his cheekbones in slashes. "Not his?" he queried. "Mine? Are you saying this child is *mine*?" Holding her breath, she nodded. "My child," he said to himself as if testing the validity of it on his tongue. He blinked, a smile warming his eyes, lifting his mouth. "My child – *our* child." He half laughed.

"Yes," she said.

The smile evaporated. "I must go to my brother; he has to know."

"He must *not*!" she said, alarmed. "Rob, you have seen what he is like; he's overjoyed."

"And is his happiness more important than mine?" he shot back.

"Of course not! But he will kill you if he finds out."

"Kill me? No, but he might never speak to me again. This is *our* child, Isobel. We will marry and give him my name – his father's name. Is that not worth my brother's wrath?"

She wanted to yell "yes!" to be free of the Earl, to claim Rob for her own, but instead found herself saying, "He would never forgive the betrayal – and that is how he would see it: betrayal by you, by me – and I do not want to see the love you bear each other destroyed by enmity. Look what it has done to the King and to his brother. If the Earl let you live, he would be your enemy for the rest of your life, and why?"

"So that we can be together."

She pressed her forehead against his. "Yes, and at what cost? Let the Countess be delivered of her child, and if it be a son, the Earl will cleave to her once again and I will be forgotten." She lifted her face, and he took her hands, holding them to his lips, his breath warming her skin.

"Is that what you want? I have never lied to my brother. I would tell him the truth and face the consequences."

"I know you would. It is not what I want, but what has to be – for your sake, Rob, for his."

"Then pray God the Countess has a son."

"And I a daughter."

His face softened. "A daughter for my dove." He kissed her gently and, with reluctance, let her go. "Then we are resolved: this is our secret, our lie."

Caught up in his own thoughts, the Earl didn't register his brother's return until Robert sat opposite him at the trestle.

"You have made your arrangements?" he asked as Robert helped himself to wine. Rob avoided answering with a quirk of his brow as he drank. The Earl took that as a "yes". "I have left the food in case you are hungry. You should not ride on an empty stomach."

"You do." Rob picked at the dish nearest to him without looking and regretted it. He disliked smoked fish.

The Earl smiled. "I am used to it. All this," and he waved his hand over the table, "is to encourage Isobel's appetite. She has become thin with the nausea."

"I had not noticed."

"Had you not?" The Earl retrieved his eating knife of jasper and chased gold and ran his thumb along the blade. "There is scant enough of her to nourish the child's blood, let alone hers. You were very cold with her this morning."

"If I was, I am sorry for it."

"It must be difficult for you knowing she is with child." Robert's head shot up, and his expression became stone. "It was thoughtless of me after the losses you have suffered."

Rob rejected the fish and instead took bread and tore it into pieces, dropping them carelessly into the broth to make sops. "You wanted to talk to me about family matters?" He leaned over and selected a spoon.

The Earl had begun toying with the knife again, letting it slip though his fingers until they reached the weighted pommel, turning it over, and letting it slide back down the blade to the point, a mesmerising movement he followed intensely. "Robert, I am more fond of her than I expected to be."

When he didn't continue, Rob flashed a glance at him. "And?"

"And… I do not know what she thinks of me. She is obedient – most of the time – and this child is evidence enough that she takes pleasure in our coupling; but she is remote, and I cannot read her thoughts. She…" Uncharacteristically, the Earl faltered. "She has never called me by my *name* – not once in all these months. I cannot make her *love* me." And he drove the point of his knife through the cloth, pinning it to the wood underneath.

He covered his eyes with his hand and sat like that while Rob's thoughts churned. After some time when he didn't know what to do or say to his brother, nor how to salve the blade lodged in his own gut, he said, "You wanted to speak with me?"

The Earl removed his hand. "It is the King's notion," he said eventually when Rob thought he had changed his mind after all and had decided not to speak. "He proposes a match that will afford you titles with lands and his blessing."

The spoon sat forgotten in Robert's hand. "You discussed a match for me with His Grace?"

"I know you have been opposed to it, but nearly a year has passed."

"I chose my own wife before, and I will do so again."

"And look where it has left you – without a wife, without a child—"

Robert dropped the spoon into the bowl, sending droplets of clear broth in an arc over the pristine cloth. He shoved back from the table.

"You have hardly enough land to call you a lord, Rob. You must marry. The girl is of good birth and a large fortune. Let me at least tell you her name."

Standing without warning, Rob flung the chair back. "I will find my own wife," he snarled. "Without either the King's help or your own."

Chapter 13

THE EARL WAS quieter than usual when he summoned Isobel that evening. She brought her games box, and the russet-haired groom with matching eyebrows like thickets of dogwood showed her into the chamber as he always did. The Earl sat writing at the table and didn't look up. The fire was lit, wine and delicacies laid out to one side, and the makings of spiced clarry waited on the small table next to the hearth. Chou nosed Isobel's hand, and she slipped her the nugget of gingerbread saved from supper. It fell to the floor, and Chou licked it without enthusiasm. Isobel waited for the Earl's reprimand, but none came. Alun smiled cheerfully enough and invited her to sit by the fire.

The pungent odour of singed wax and the thump of a seal on parchment signalled the end of the Earl's task. Isobel started to rise, but he stopped her with his hand on her shoulder and bent to kiss her instead, his roughened chin scratching. She rubbed at the sore spot, and he murmured an apology. Then, "You have brought your games?"

A table appeared at her elbow, and Isobel opened out the box. "What do you wish to play, my lord?"

"You choose tonight."

She began to place the chessmen on their squares, and he followed her movements with an amused expression. When she finished, he leaned forward and moved several of the pieces around. Isobel frowned at her error. "I have not played for some time."

"Did your father teach you?"

"He tried to, but I was not a diligent student; I would rather have been outside in my garden. He and my mother played often, though."

Chouchou wandered away from the fire, her extended belly bulging pinkly where the skin stretched. The piece of gingerbread lay untouched where she had left it.

"Was supper to your liking – including the gingerbread?" the Earl asked, his mouth twitching.

Chou was now pacing the back of the room, where it was too dimly lit to see her properly.

Isobel gave a sheepish smile. "Yes, I thank you, my lord."

The Earl waited for Isobel to make the first move. She hopped a knight over a pawn's head and turned right. "Why did you do that?"

"Am I not allowed to?"

"You are *allowed* to make the move, but whether it was *wise* to do so is another matter. It was not."

Isobel thought it better not to admit why she had chosen the knight. "Oh."

"Why did you choose to move the knight?"

She wriggled beneath his gaze, trying to find something less asinine than the truth. She gave up. "I like the knights' horses."

Interlocking his fingers over his stomach he regarded her with a look she suspected he reserved for the younger idiot sons of minor lords, but he surprised her by throwing back his head and roaring with laughter.

"It is not *that* amusing, my lord," Isobel said, peeved.

"It is, Isobel, it is. You have breathed life into me again." He cocked his head on one side. "My brother knows not what he misses; he refuses to take a mistress and he has no wife, despite the King's command he take one."

She let her pulse even before murmuring, "The King has commanded he marry?"

"In so much that His Grace commends a widow to him, a young woman of noble birth bringing substantial lands and titles to her new husband. Very fair as well, if the King's taste is anything to go by." Isobel must have looked perplexed because he explained. "She comforted him for a time, I believe. And therein lies a problem." He moved a piece on the board, which Isobel hardly noted.

"Why?"

"Because my brother would not take another man's mistress. I have known him long enough to know he prizes chastity above all other virtues in a woman, even if the lady in question has been bedded by none other than the King. Of course, you might help."

Somewhere nearby, Chouchou whimpered.

"How?"

"Persuade him that it is in his best interests to marry her." He pointed to the board. "Did you note the move I made?"

She almost snorted out, "Why would he listen to *me*? I am hardly a pristine example of chastity."

His mouth straightened. "*You* are different."

Isobel hardly thought so, but that wasn't the point. "Perhaps it is too soon after his wife's death to contemplate taking another." His bishop threatened her pawn. Isobel ignored it and instead fed another forward.

"Better," he said, taking her pawn nonetheless. "He cannot afford to wait. There is a dearth of heiresses who are not either mere infants or already promised. This girl is newly widowed; she will not stay that way for long."

"Why is His Grace so eager to have Lord Langton wed?" she asked, trying, without much success, to keep annoyance from her tone.

"Because he wishes to reward my loyalty and that of my brother with an advantageous match. And to ensure the lands and offices of her Yorkist husband remain just that – loyally Yorkist. The King needs to know he can rely on our continued support. It would be wise of Robert to accept the offer; His Grace will not make it twice."

She had that closed-in feeling, the one she had when trapped in church at Eastertide, surrounded by solemn faces and choking clouds of incense, when all she wanted to do was burst out into the spring sun and feel the heat on her face and the clean air in her lungs and run, and run, and run.

Chouchou made an odd sort of grunt followed by a thin whine. The Earl looked over his shoulder, where ripping noises came from the far side of his bed. Taking one of the candlesticks, he went to investigate. Isobel followed.

Chou had pulled an embroidered red velvet cushion from the high-backed bench on the farthest side of the room, and was proceeding to shred it, leaving strands of gold thread glittering in the moving light of the candle as the Earl kneeled by her. He felt her flanks and abdomen with experienced hands. "She is ready to whelp. Isobel, have Alun send for blankets of rough wool blanchet. And bring me more light, if you will."

Kneeling next to him on her return, she stroked Chou's silky ears as he continued to examine her. "Is something wrong?"

He sat back on his haunches. "Not necessarily, but her contractions are not as strong as I would like, and these pups are big for a maiden bitch to birth. She might struggle."

"Poor Chou." Isobel kissed the top of the dog's head, and she gave a feeble wag of her tail and tried to lick Isobel's hand.

"Leave her, Isobel, and return to your chamber. This could take all night." The groom came in with several blankets smelling of cold air and dog, which Isobel began to arrange on the floor as the Earl stroked Chou's flanks.

Alun hovered close by. "My lord, the Master of Kennels asks if you wish him to attend?"

"Not at present, but bid him be ready."

"Aye, my lord."

"Isobel, I said you might leave."

"Let me stay. Chou has kept me company for many weeks, and now I can return the favour. I would not like to be giving birth alone."

"She will not be alone; I will be here, and you have no experience of whelping dogs. It is better you rest. Go." He bent over the dog then uttered an oath and thrust out an arm. "Quick, hand me the rags." A muddy puddle of greenish-brown fluid gathered on the floor around Chou's hindquarters. "That is not a good sign," he muttered. Chou whimpered, trying to turn to lick herself. The Earl soothed her, and she flopped back against Isobel's skirts. "She is distressed. Hold her head and try to keep her still; I need to see what is going on here."

Stroking gently, Isobel began to hum a lullaby from her childhood. The Earl sat up, easing his shoulders. "The first should be visible by now. Come, *ma petite* Chou, where are these whelps? I have promised Lord Howard the pick of the litter after the King."

"There," Isobel whispered to her, "your babies will be the noblest hounds in the kingdom." She kissed her.

"Isobel, do not fawn over her; you will spoil her, and she will come to expect to be indulged rather than give obedience where it is due."

"She needs to be shown love to give it," Isobel said, ignoring his stricture and resting her cheek on the top of the dog's head. "She is a good girl." Isobel started humming again.

"Keep away. You cannot assume she will not nip. When in this state, any bitch can bite."

Including me, Isobel thought, but she did as she was told anyway and let Chou lie her head in her lap as a substitute.

The Earl reached for another cushion and tossed it to her. "Here, sit on this."

Isobel resumed humming, breaking into song as the simple melody drew the words from her.

When the nightingale sings,
The trees grow green,
Leaf and grass and blossom springs,
In April, I suppose;
And love has to my heart gone
With a spear so keen,
Night and day my blood it drains
My heart to death it aches.

The Earl's back stiffened, and he turned. "Why do you sing that?" he demanded.

Taken aback, she faltered, "I'll… sing something else, my lord."

"That was not what I asked."

"My mother used to sing it to me; it was her favourite song."

He must have spent a whole minute holding her eyes with his until she squirmed, and Chou broke his focus with a small squeal. "Sing something else," he said, and bent again to tend the dog. But all the songs had left her.

"Ah, at last," he murmured, as ripples ran along Chou's flanks and her legs quivered. "Come on, come on – that's it." His brow turned into a series of horizontal creases. "This one is stuck, and she has not the strength to birth it." Chou's panting increased as another spasm ran through her, and she shifted. Isobel could see her rear end and what looked like a black nub of a head. Placing his fingers either side of the pup, the Earl tried to ease it from its mother. He grunted with the effort. "Come on, Chou, I cannot do this for you. We must free this whelp."

"Do you wish to send for the kennel master?"

"It is too late for that." Chou gave another squeal, thin and piercing, and the Earl gave a tug and the puppy slid free. "Good girl," he said, wiping sweat from his brow with the back of his hand and leaving a faint smear. Chou bent double and began licking the whelp clean of the thin caul covering it. "That is a big pup; no wonder she was having difficulty. Here." The Earl lifted it in a piece of cloth and placed it by Chou's head. "Make sure she bites through the cord." He went back to her hindquarters, where another head had already appeared.

Isobel peered at the small, dark creature. "It is not moving. Should it be breathing now?"

"What?" He grabbed a piece of cloth and, picking up the pup in his other hand, began to rub vigorously. A tiny paw waved, then the pup twisted weakly in his hand.

"Praise Almighty God!" Isobel said with relief.

"Here, take him and let Chou lick him, then put him to a teat."

"Clever girl," she whispered to Chou, who was diligently licking her pup back to life. "There you are." Isobel put the pup against a swollen teat, and it blindly snuffled and latched on. Chou nudged it with her nose.

"Isobel, have my groom send for some warm milk for her."

When she returned, a second wriggling sausage was being placed beside its littermate. "How many do you think there will be?"

He cast an experienced eye over her belly. "Six, perhaps eight, in all. They are coming quickly now; here is the next one. Ready?" And, as their eyes met, he smiled, and she saw another man, someone younger, more at ease, almost… happy. Isobel gave him a quick smile in return. "Ah, this one will be the King's," he said, holding it up to examine it and turning it onto its back.

"How can you tell?"

"It is a good weight – solid and strong – straight-limbed and a bitch. She'll breed well. Howard will want a dog of equal quality."

"Poor Chou having to give up her babies."

"She is a breeding bitch, Isobel; it is what I keep her for." He bent away from her so didn't see her roll her eyes behind his back.

Six puppies huddled like dark piglets in a row. Several were asleep, the others still suckled. The Earl pushed his shirt sleeves up as far as they would go, but the edges were mired and kept unfurling like a sail. Isobel shuffled towards him on her knees and inched them up further. "My thanks," he acknowledged. "Here is another; looks like a big pup, a dog perhaps. It'll have Howard's name on it." He brought the candle closer still. "One leg's caught…" Without hesitation, he reached in and rotated the pup with a quick movement, and it popped out in its filmy cocoon with one leg askew. He broke the membrane over its mouth and nose, wiping the residue with the edge of his shirt, and severed the cord. He was about to hand it to Chou to lick but became suddenly still, the pup suspended in his hand as he inspected it.

"What is it? Does it not live?" He didn't answer and, to her horror, reached his other hand to the puppy's neck. *"No!"* Isobel cried, grabbing his arm and trying to yank his hand away. "What are you doing? *Stop*!"

Holding the puppy in her face, his own suffused with fury, his teeth clenched as he hissed, "It's a mongrel, Isobel, a tyke. I will have that drunken sot of a kennel master publicly whipped and flung out for letting Chou run with another dog after she mated with my choice." His fingers closed around the tiny neck. "It is worthless. Worse than worthless – it spoils the entire litter and renders the bitch useless. I might as well have the whole lot drowned." Whining, Chou sat up, dislodging the puppies, and sniffed the whelp and licked her master's hand.

"My lord, please!" Putting her hands around the little tubby body, Isobel managed to insert her thumb between his own so that if he squeezed he would snap her fingers first.

"Isobel—"

She held on. "*Please*, my lord, I beg you – do not hurt it!"

The Earl let go of the puppy, and Isobel hugged it to her in case he changed his mind, watchful as he inspected the rest of the litter. "Just the one," he growled, "one and it spoils the rest."

"How?" she asked. "Why can one being different spoil the rest?"

"She's been mounted by two dogs – one, the best in my pack and the sire of my choice; the other—" he jabbed an accusing finger at the squirming bundle she held to her, "—some mongrel she's run with shortly after like a whore. She should have been kept in, as I instructed." He rolled back on his heels and stood up. Isobel slipped the tyke to Chou, and she began to clean it immediately and then coaxed it towards a teat. It latched on, suckling furiously.

"Surely it does not matter? The other puppies are sighthounds, and Chou can breed more. She is such a good mother."

He gave one of his withering looks. "Once she has run with another dog all her future whelps will be tainted by his blood, no matter what their sire. She was my favourite bitch." Chou was conscientiously nursing her brood, occasionally licking them back into line when they rolled away from her, and oblivious now to the fate hanging over them. Isobel put a protective hand on the dog's head.

"What will you do with her?"

"What do you think I should do with her? How should any wanton be punished?" His eyes had become black glass through which she couldn't read his thoughts and, for a horrible moment, she wondered if he could see hers and the writhing guilt written on her soul in blood.

"She is only a dog, my lord. She knows no better."

"And should she be forgiven her infamy because she is a dog? Women are too soft-natured to determine what is right. It is the wanton nature of women that leads to sin. Should Eve be forgiven her disobedience against God because she was merely a weak-minded woman? That is for men to judge."

"And for women to accept the judgment?"

"Of course."

Isobel lifted her chin. "Will you punish the dog that ran with her?"

"Do not debate with me, Isobel," he warned. "I hold those who are responsible to account; a dog has not the wit to determine its course but for the nature which it is given. As for these," he toed the rumpled blanket on which Chou nestled her young, "I keep none but purebred greyhound whelps. I will decide their fate."

"But these others are purebred. The King will not be able to tell them apart from your other dogs, will he?"

"Are you saying I should deceive the *King*?"

"Of course not, my lord, but they look the same as any other, so how will he know that one had a different sire?"

"He will not, but I shall."

She rose to her feet and softly touched his arm, feeling the matted dark hair coarsened with blood beneath her fingers. "My lord, I know I do not understand these things as you do, and I lack your wisdom, but I cannot bear the thought of Chou or her babies suffering. Please, my good lord, be merciful." The Earl looked at her hand, then at the dogs, but the muscles in his jaw failed to relent. He was about to say something, but a servant appeared with a jug and dog bowl.

The Earl's eyes hardened. "Clear this up," he said brusquely, and then to Isobel, "Take that bastard whelp of a mongrel from my sight. And you," he snapped at the groom, "get Master Clay here – *now*."

Shaken, Isobel bundled the pup, now sleepy with its mother's milk, into a cloth and escaped before the Earl had second thoughts. Ursula woke when Isobel rushed in. As soon as she saw the puppy, she collapsed into fits of fluttering and coos. She warmed water while Isobel made up a nest of course green kendal by the hearth and gently placed the pup in it. Then she stripped her soiled clothes and, while she washed, sent Ursula to the kitchens to search for hog casing and milk.

She sat by the fire, too tired to sleep, watching the newborn pup curled like a pale grub, its ribcage steadily rising and falling. Her hands caressed her belly in a matching rhythmic motion. The Earl's sudden transformation had shaken her. If he had reacted that way to the bastard offspring of one of his most cherished dogs, how could she be certain that the affection he declared to her in private moments would not be similarly transient if faced with a child he realised was not his own? Isobel could only guess at his reaction if he came to understand that its father was the one man in all this world he thought he could trust.

Chapter 14

"It's making a funny noise like this." Cecily imitated the puppy's high-pitched squeaking with remarkable accuracy.

"She is hungry. See how she sucks on the cloth? She needs feeding every few hours because she grows so fast – like you." Isobel tickled Cecily's tummy, and the child giggled.

"I'm this tall," Cecily exaggerated, holding her hand above her head. "Will Moff get as big as me?"

Isobel looked at the insubstantial puppy with its long, gangly limbs and silvery fur and wondered how it had managed to survive this long without Chou's milk and care. She knew the other whelps thrived, but Isobel struggled to get enough milk into this little creature, even though she enriched it with yolk of egg and they took it in turns to feed her day and night. As it was, Ursula bore the brunt of the feeding. The Earl called Isobel to his chambers most evenings, and she spent much of the morning trying not to throw up the breakfast he insisted she ate. But for the last several days, since he had received news from a messenger wearing royal livery, she had not seen him and had kept to her room.

"I do not know how big she will get. We will see," Isobel said, avoiding commitment to something she felt beyond her control.

"*Moth* is a stupid name, if you ask me." Isobel had forgotten Joan had accompanied Cecily at the order of the Countess.

"We didn't ask you," Isobel returned shortly. "It is a fine name."

"I chosed it," Cecily bounced, "because it looks like a moff, moff, moff," she lisped, and held her poppet in front of the puppy. "I want it to see Nan."

Isobel protected the pup from the dancing doll. "Careful, my lady. She will not open her eyes for a few days yet."

Joan peered over her shoulder. "It's an ugly brute. I'm surprised the Earl didn't have it drowned. He won't have little *bastards* running around, not with his purebreds, he won't, in case they contaminate his *bloodline*."

Cecily might not have understood the insinuation, but she saw Isobel flinch and knew enough to know the slight was aimed at her. "You're horrible." She stuck her tongue out at Joan and resolutely turned her back.

"Do not feel you have to stay," Isobel said acidly.

"Don't think that I want to, only my lady says I mustn't leave her." She jabbed her nose towards Cecily's back. "Not for one moment, she said. And that's not all she said, not that I'd be telling."

"Telling *what*?" The sound of the Earl's voice had Joan's mouth fall open as she dropped into a curtsy. Still cradling the puppy, Isobel rose more slowly. "I am waiting, girl."

"Nothing, my lord," Joan oozed.

"If you have nothing of worth to say, in future do not speak to Mistress Fenton unless she first addresses you. Leave." He waited until Joan scurried from the room. "Have you breakfasted?" he asked Isobel, only a tad less grimly than a moment before.

"I have, my lord." She wasn't lying as such, only his idea of a suitable breakfast was her idea of a banquet, and her stomach rebelled at the thought of it. Bread and sops had suited her well enough.

"I have, and so has Nan," Cecily piped up. "And so's Moff," she added, pointing to the puppy snuffling blindly in Isobel's arms. She shielded it from his view with her hand, but he brushed it aside, lifting the folds of cloth that kept the animal warm.

"It is still alive," he said, surprised. "What are you feeding it on?"

Isobel indicated the small bowl on the stool. "Warm milk and egg yolk, my lord."

He let the cloth fall back. "Try the milk of goats. And prevent any getting into its lungs, or it will sicken and die." The Earl looked at his daughter for the first time. With his fingers beneath her chin, he raised her face. "Have you been making your devotions, Cecily?" She nodded solemnly. "Say them." He let go and stood with a hand on his belted hip, waiting for her to begin, but she continued staring at him, hugging Nan and twirling a little back and forth. He frowned. "What's wrong with her?"

"You frighten her, my lord," Isobel said calmly, stroking Cecily's curls. "She knows not what to say to you."

"Does she not know her duty? I am her father."

"Yes, my lord, but she does not know *you*."

"I want Meg," the child whispered, and her thumb found its way to her mouth. The Earl looked from Isobel to his daughter, and she thought she saw something else there – regret, perhaps, a sadness that always seemed to exist just below the surface, occasionally breaching his defences and exposing an unknown hurt to the world before it disappeared again from view. She felt a welter of pity for him and tucked it away before he detected it.

It was only once he had left and Isobel relaxed that she realised she had never asked him why he had visited her that morning, and he had never said.

Chapter 15

THE LAST DAYS of spring floated on warm breezes into the gossamer threads of summer.

Speculation about Warwick's intentions in France continued to circulate, feeding pockets of unrest in the country where the King's hand did not so easily reach, but the promise of a good harvest distracted all but a few. The Earl refused to be lulled into a false sense of security and tirelessly oversaw the strengthening of the castle defences: the dredging of the moat, the reinforcement of the walls, and the completion of the barbican protecting the main gate. He worked long hours on the King's business and on that of the estates, going away for days at a time, leaving before sunrise and returning long after dark. Yet he had a vigour about him that grew with the swelling of Isobel's belly. The sickness passed, and she ate with renewed interest as her child grew within her. It had already assumed an identity, and she caught herself talking to the unborn child as if she were already in her arms. Isobel thought *"she"* because she felt so certain it was a girl that she had named her in her mind. It had slipped out one evening when the lingering heat had the Earl fling open the casements to let the birds' evensong sweeten the air. Isobel felt the unmistakable fluttering like wings in her womb as the child quickened. She smiled to herself dreamily. "Eleanor is restless tonight."

The Earl took a last look from the window, the golden light warming his skin and accentuating carved thighs as he walked to the night table.

Isobel had been thinking about where Rob might be and whether he missed her as she did him, and she switched thoughts before the Earl read them in her eyes. He washed his face and hands and rinsed his mouth before returning to the bed. "*Eleanor* is a strange name for a boy. I would have him named Edward, for our king."

"I thought you would not choose a name because it tempts Fate, my lord?"

He peeled back the sheet, revealing her swelling body, and followed the gentle mound with his hand. Despite herself, Isobel quivered at his touch. He smiled and replaced his hand with his lips, speaking between kisses.

"It is safe enough; your sickness has passed, the child grows and moves. Besides, I cannot have you determine the child's sex by calling him by a maid's name. It is a boy." He grazed the surface of her skin slowly, taking his time and savouring it inch by inch. She tried not to react nor rise to his mouth.

"And I am certain *she* is not," Isobel managed, closing her eyes and imagining Rob's mouth where the Earl's now travelled and hating herself for betraying them both. "What will you name your son?"

He paused in his seduction. "I have just told you."

"Your real son, my lord." Had she really said that? She would have to guard against such careless slips. "The Countess's child," she clarified. "She will enter confinement in a month's time; everyone is talking of it."

He rolled over onto his elbow. "Are they. I have not given it any consideration."

He must have been the only one because it was on everyone else's lips. The Countess's apartments had been freshly painted, the walls prepared to take the great tapestries that normally hung in the rooms of state, and ells of fabric purchased that even now were being sewn into hangings for the ceilings, bed, and windows. She had seen it. Ursula had secreted a fragment to show her: Venetian silk in blue and yellow – the proud colours of her husband's house. Perfumes had been procured to produce washing waters and to burn in clay pots through her confinement, and from the chapel, the great crucifix had been lifted down and now hung like a giant bird with outstretched wings in her private oratory. A statue of the Virgin with Christ on her knee kept perpetual vigil by her bed, and in the chapel masses for her safe delivery joined those for the souls of her dead children - a web of silk and prayers woven to protect her and her child from death during this passage to life. The Earl seemed uninterested in the whole business as if, somehow, her pregnancy was irrelevant.

Isobel still hoped and prayed that the birth of an heir would release her from her bonds, but the more her belly grew, the less inclined he was to let her go, until she thought she would never be free. As if to illustrate her thraldom, the Earl had now resumed his languid attack, working kisses from her navel towards her breasts. His tongue brushed a tender nipple, exquisitely sensitive to the point of agony, and Isobel wanted to push him away. How long would Rob wait until he felt compelled to obey the King's command and fulfil his own needs? Isobel's teeth grated at the thought of him with another woman, and she kicked her legs free of the suffocating sheet.

"I'm hot," she complained.

The Earl sighed, rolled over onto his back, and contemplated the painted canopy of the bed. The winter hangings had been removed, and fine translucent linen, with scrolls of silver and gold thread winding around his embroidered griffins, hung in their stead. Isobel played with an edge, waving it to create a light breeze over her and not entirely indifferent to his state of frustration. Nor was she willing to do anything about it, either. They were both in need of distraction.

"This news from France," he said, balancing the chequered board between them so that it didn't wobble and spill the pieces, "has His Grace looking to Warwick's next move. Now that Warwick has made peace with Anjou—" he interrupted his own narration with a short, harsh laugh, "—that must have been a sight; I almost wish I had been there to see it: Warwick kept on his knees to the Anjou woman, pleading his guilt to every accusation she ventured to make against him. I would never have thought it possible, but he is a desperate man and it makes for desperate measures."

Isobel felt a smattering of sympathy for this great lord humbled by circumstance. But then, as her father would have been quick to point out, he had negotiated his own fate and men must live with the decisions they make. At least they had the freedom to choose, which was more than women did. She plonked her queen on her square, making the pieces either side of it rattle. "Do you think he will try to invade, my lord?"

"Undoubtedly. Anjou wants the throne for her son, although Prince Edward will have to wait until old King Henry dies. The combined force of Anjou – backed by her brother, King Louis – and Warwick's substantial northern affinity will be difficult to break if they get a foothold on these shores. It is imperative they do not."

"Then what does the Earl of Warwick get from it all if King Henry regains his throne?" Isobel moved a pawn and waited for him to mirror her move.

"He wants his younger daughter, Anne, to be queen." He surprised her by jumping his knight. She frowned and countered his move. He nodded. "Good, but do not let your thoughts show. Keep them close, in here." And he touched her heart lightly. She immediately smoothed her forehead and adopted a mask.

"Is her marriage to Prince Edward likely to happen?"

"Likely? Their agreement will seal the rift and make the bond harder to break. The marriage is not likely – it is imperative." It was his turn to frown. "Do not fiddle, Isobel, make your next move."

She did – rashly – and promptly lost the piece. "But what about the Duke of Clarence? Surely there will be no role for him if King Henry returns and, what is worse, will he not be in the way?" She thought back to the young man in his gilded armour, arrogance stamped across his face in the simple lift of his lip and dispassionate eye.

"He will, which is to our advantage. Where else does he have to turn but back to his brother the King?" the Earl agreed, bringing forward his queen with a confidence Isobel found intimidating. She studied the array of pieces, unwilling to lose another, thought she spotted a weakness in his defences, but covered the gleam of hope with a blank look.

"How do you know all this?" she asked, moving a bishop surreptitiously under the guise of the question.

"The King is kept well-informed," was all he would say, noting the bishop's sideways manoeuvre. He reached forward, hesitated, withdrew his hand. "That was a good move, Isobel, you have me in check."

"Do I?" She scanned the board. "Oh, yes, so I do. Check," and she laughed at the exasperation on his face.

"I have taught you guile, it would seem, and you defeat me with it," he glowered. "The game is not yet over, young lady." But his pique was assumed, because he broke into a smile and, leaning over the board, kissed her.

THE EARL WAS right. Like a chill wind, news spread from the north of an insurrection led by Henry Fitzhugh. At first it was thought it involved only the Lancastrian diehard who had fought for King Henry at the second battle of St Albans and had been granted back his lands and titles by King Edward in a subsequent amnesty. But the Earl shook his head when Isobel asked him and said that among Fitzhugh's forces were counted Warwick's own adherents. This was no localised rebellion, he said; it foreshadowed greater misrule and would spread like a sore if nothing was done to cauterise it.

Within days, messengers arrived from the south bringing word that the King was marching north to wipe out the trouble before it gained hold.

"Will you have to go?" Isobel asked, when he had met in council with his lords after the latest rash of messages had sent a thrill of fear through the castle wards. "Can you not send Lord Dalton in your place?"

"He lacks experience, and I will not send someone else to do my part. My place is by my king."

"What if it is a trap? You said so yourself – Warwick will have to make landfall somewhere along the coast, and what if the King is in the north and there is no one to defend the southern counties?"

He glanced at the great map of the country detailing his estates and the towns and cities of the land, spread across the surface of the council table in a patchwork of green and brown, blue and red and yellow. "It is a risk the King will have to take. He cannot let this rising go unpunished. You will be safe enough here. Warwick has not yet stooped so low as to bring war to women."

He might not, but Queen Margaret was another matter, Isobel thought. But it wasn't her own safety of which she was thinking. "And will the Duke of Gloucester stay in the Marches and raise troops as he did before?" she asked, hoping the slight quaver in her voice didn't reveal her true reasons for asking.

The Earl laughed. "I very much doubt it; he will accompany the King."

Isobel wrote to her steward warning him to remain watchful, enclosing a note to Buena, which she entreated Moynes to pass to her privily. Among her instructions reminding John Appleyard to bag the pears against birds as they ripened, and to lift the tender plants before the first frost, Isobel slipped in her own news couched in such terms as she thought Buena might read between the lines. *"I am well,"* she told her, *"and have such care as my lord sees fit to have me safely delivered this Yule."* She left it at that and let Buena's fears for her do all the rest.

"Isobel," the Earl said some weeks later when, one morning, she appeared in his chamber having been summoned, "the King will arrive shortly. I wish you to stay out of sight while he is here."

Annoyed, Isobel bit her tongue and tried not to look disappointed. He selected his armorial ring from the jewel casket and slid it over his finger. Skin tanned by months of sun, his grey eyes gleaming brighter from within their ring of black lashes, he looked at her without blinking. "Do you understand my instruction?" Isobel nodded. "Now, with my wife in confinement, she will be too preoccupied to cause you any difficulty while I am away. I am taking Sawcliffe with me, so there will be no repeat of earlier… misunderstandings. Should you need assistance, the constable is under orders to ensure your safety. Anything else?" He paused to consider. "Ah, yes, you are to have any food you desire, but Ursula will tell me if it is—"

"Unnatural. Yes, my lord, you said."

"Hmm, well, that is all. I doubt I will see you before we leave on the morrow, so let me bid you farewell now." His hand clasped the back of her neck, his rings cold on her skin as he brought her face to his and kissed her. Caught between their legs, Moth wriggled on her lead, rolling on her back and trying to bite it. "And keep that animal out of sight," he growled. "She brings disgrace to my kennels."

Isobel didn't think she could get away with pointing out that she never went near his beloved kennels. He had let her keep Moth as long as she didn't let her stray. That was one concession to his golden rule that Isobel was reluctant to test. She noticed that Chou – now that her puppies were weaned – had inveigled her way back into his private chambers where even now she was probably asleep on his bed, looking not one whit chastened by her former disgrace. Her mongrel daughter, however, was doing her best to annoy the Earl and had started chewing the elongated toe of his court shoe. Isobel picked her up before he decided the puppy had pushed him too far.

Despite his stricture to stay out of sight, Isobel left Moth with Ursula and secreted herself by a crossbow loop overlooking the bailey. Leaning her head against the cool stone, she waited for the arrival of the royal party, hearing – long before seeing – the calls go up from the watch manning the tower roof.

The King was unmistakable, towering resplendent above all other men in his retinue; but Isobel hardly gave him a glance as she searched the pennants and livery of the lords in attendance until she saw those of the Duke of Gloucester and, close by, Rob. *See me*, she implored. *See. Me.* At the last moment before he was lost to view he glanced up, his eyes raking the tower windows. He smiled.

His fleeting look had her heart singing, and she danced back to her room ecstatic, to be met with Ursula's wagging finger. "You must take care on the stairs, or you will slip, my lady."

Isobel felt so buoyed that she thought she could possibly fly. "The King has arrived."

"The King! The King!" Ursula trilled, hands flittering above her head in excitement. "We must make you ready. His Grace cannot see you like this."

"Like what?" Isobel looked down at herself – she seemed all in place, not that it mattered one jot. Ursula had already unpinned her hennin and was about to unlace her gown. Isobel stopped her. "There is no need, Ursula, for the King will not see me at *all*; my lord forbids it. I think he is ashamed of me. There – just like you – I am *invisible*."

"Invisible," Ursula repeated wistfully, and she let her hands drop.

Trapped in the tower with the stone heated on three faces, Isobel felt like dough – pummelled and swollen and popped in the oven to bake. By the afternoon, all she wanted to do was escape.

"Fetch Lady Cecily for me. We will find somewhere cool to sit and practise her letters while Moth has a run. And I want to change; I cannot breathe in this gown."

"My lady is showing nicely," Ursula said, patting Isobel's tummy. "My lord must be so proud."

Isobel washed and changed into the lightest gown of pale blue linen with a dark blue cambric kirtle beneath. Neither was patterned, for anything else would compete with the sky, but she had Ursula braid her ribbon through her hair to keep it from her shoulders and cover it with gauze so light she could barely feel its weight.

Isobel kept an eye out for members of the royal household but, as ever, the wilderness was deserted. She sat beneath the shade of the Lady Snake tree while Cecily skipped about with Moth until both child and dog flopped beside Isobel, panting. Crickets sawed the air with rasping *clicks*, bees hummed low in search of pollen and, defeated by the heat, birds hid their voices from the sun. Everything seemed so far away, and Isobel could almost have been at home within the walls of her own garden with no other cares than those of her hives. When Cecily began to wriggle again, Isobel distracted her by sketching letters in the dust for her to copy with her finger. C-e-c-i-l-y.

"Joan says my name means I will be blind," she said, covering her eyes with dusty hands.

"Your name is beautiful. Do you know who St Cecilia was?" Cecily shook dark curls now bronzed by the sun. "She loved music and sang to God in her heart." The child didn't need to know about her martyrdom; there was time enough in the future to learn the extent of human cruelty, and she had experienced enough of that already. "The dowager Duchess of York – the King's dam – is also so called, so you have a fine and noble name."

Cecily laid her head on Isobel's lap and had letters traced on her back as the sun angled on its downward descent with insects caught bobbing in its rays. Beneath the low-slung canopy of the tree, the late afternoon heat waxed heavy. Isobel closed her eyes.

"I thought I might find you out here." Silhouetted against the sun, she would have known his outline anywhere, even if his voice hadn't given him away.

"Rob!" He reached down and helped her climb to her feet, displacing a sleepy Cecily, and she was in his arms before she remembered to exercise caution. He didn't care but held her to him, his face in her neck until he could speak.

"I had to see you."

"I know," Isobel said, breathing him in.

"We do not have long."

She gave a broken laugh. "We never do." Moth had sniffed his strong legs and now practised her bark, jumping back and forth and squeaking.

Rob held Isobel at arm's length. "How are you? You look well. The child…?"

"She's fine, look," and she held his palm to the telltale distension disguised by the folds of cloth and watched his expression melt. "She moves every day now, and I think she likes music because she dances when I sing. Unless she is trying to escape," she added, and he laughed.

Cecily had been staring up at him; now she tweaked his tunic, raising her arms when he noticed her. "Me," she said plaintively, and he lifted her into his arms, kissing her hair.

"Is he looking after you?" he said to Isobel, still looking at his niece as she showed him Nan's newly-made gown.

"Yes."

He nodded, his lips compressed. "And who is this?" he asked Cecily as Moth continued to bounce around his legs, too excited to make any noise. He set his niece down.

"Moff," Cecily said, holding her fingers in front of her mouth and making them like worms. "I called her that 'cos she looked like a weeny, teeny grub all wiggly in the ground like this…" And she imitated a newborn whelp by flinging herself on the dry, scratchy grass and wriggling. Moth jumped up and down on her.

"Will you ride tomorrow?" Isobel asked.

"I must."

Cecily stopped writhing and leaned up on her elbows, her legs stuck out like her doll's. "You aren't looking," she protested, but Rob had taken

Isobel's face in his hands and kissed her, binding love and loneliness into those few moments they had together.

Cecily sat up and crossed her arms on her chest, pouting, but from the other side of the garden distant voices came.

"It is the King," Rob said, springing away and around to face the direction of the approaching voices.

"There it is! I knew I was not mistaken." The King appeared out of the sunlight towards them. "Ah, someone has beaten me to it. My lord Earl, what have we here? A maid and her lover?"

Isobel could not see the Earl's expression; she was too intent on focusing on the pair of fine hose and extravagant shoes that had come to a halt on the ground on which she now curtsied. She had pulled Cecily down with her, but from the corner of her eye could see the child squinting up at the figure towering over them.

"Rise, my ladies, rise," the King bid them. "It is too hot to be so close to the ground."

Cecily sneezed and rubbed her sleeve across her nose. "You're very tall."

"And you, little maid," he said, bending down to her, "are very small. What is your name?"

"Cecily. C-e-c-i-l-y. Who are you?"

"Cecily!" her father barked, but the King signalled his contentment to let the breach of courtesy go unremarked.

"I am King Edward, and these gentlemen are my lords."

Cecily giggled. "Where is your crown?" The Earl looked mortified, and the small group of men either looked bemused or grinned at the small, now rather dusty little girl who had yet to learn to be in awe of her king. "This is Nan," she said solemnly, and Isobel tried not to laugh.

The King flicked a glance in her direction and lowered his voice to a conspiratorial whisper as he asked Cecily, "Lord Robert I know well enough, but who is this pretty lady?"

"That's Is'bel."

"And what is she doing here under this monstrous tree with Lord Robert?"

"She's *not* here with my nuncle, Is'bel's with *me*." Cecily pointed to her scrumpled chest importantly. "And Nan. And Moff. And it's not a monster tree, it's my Lady Snake tree. I can write my name."

"I am sure you can," the King said, laughing as he straightened to his full height, his flax hair snagging in the lower twigs. "So," he said, turning his attention to her, "this is *Isobel*." He rested one hand on the scaled breast of the Lady Snake, a smile practised in seduction curving his lips. Isobel sensed Rob bristle and, from under the King's raised arm, saw the Earl, standing with the other jay-coloured lords, become rigid. With the tree to her back and the interest of the men like a net, she felt trapped. Her heart struck the anvil of her ribs, and her head swam with the heat. She swayed.

Rob stepped forward, but the King grabbed her arm. "Whoa there!"

"Thank you, Your Grace," Isobel murmured without looking at him. He caressed her skin with a finger through the fine fabric of her gown. He bent closer.

"Such sweet temptation." He raised his voice, calling over his shoulder, "My lords, I fear enchantment. Should I call her *Helen* or *Eve*?"

Middling in height, with hair the colour of a squirrel and a nose that fell away at the tip, the lord standing closest to the Earl laughed and nudged the long-faced man next to him. "If she's Helen, Your Grace, what does that make Your Highness?"

"Paris, of course," the King said without taking his eyes from Isobel's flushed face.

"Not Menelaus, Your Grace? Or Adam, perhaps?"

The King let his gaze wander from Isobel's face down her neck to where the sweat-dampened linen clung to her skin. His lips parted. "What is it to be, sweet lady: fair *Helen* or temptress *Eve*? Will kings go to war for you, or will you bring about the downfall of Man?"

From the corner of her eye, Isobel could see Rob struggling to maintain his composure. "Just *Isobel*, Your Grace," she said quickly, extricating her arm and moving away from him.

"Hmm, just *Isobel*, is it?" He tweaked the nipple of the carved Eve and, plucking a green apple from the nearest bough, bit into it, assessing her. "Well, lady, you have given me a puzzle. I have your first name, but not your second."

"Fenton, Your Grace."

He chewed the apple slowly, then pulled a face. "Sour fruit," he said, tossing it to one side and wiping his hand on his silk doublet. "Ah, I see, now I understand. My lord," he addressed the Earl, "I must take you to task. When I asked, you had me believe Mistress Fenton to be quite plain. This lack of chivalry cannot go unremarked. You must make amends or risk her displeasure."

"Your Grace, it matters not…" Isobel began.

"But I say it does." He laid his big arm across her shoulders, hot and heavy, as if they were friends, and fingered the tail of the ribbon holding back her hair. He turned her towards the small group of men whose faces each told their own story. "What say you, sweet Isobel, what price do you place on your honour? A new gown, a jewel, perhaps?"

Let me go, let me go, she begged silently. Why didn't the Earl say something? Do anything? He looked furious with her, but Isobel would rather risk his anger than endure this play the King put on for his own entertainment with she the fool. Unattended, Moth had run off, but she now returned trailing her lead and resumed her jealous yipping at the King's heels. From where he had been observing, the Duke of Gloucester strode forward and scooped up the puppy, holding her aloft with the sun making a halo of her fluffy coat.

Distracted, the King let his arm drop, raising a brow at the wriggling animal. "What an extraordinary-looking creature. Is it one of yours, my lord Earl?"

"She is mine, Your Grace," Isobel said quickly, accepting her from the Duke and thanking him with a brief curtsy for his timely intercession. "My lord lets me keep her. She is a little lively." Isobel put Moth down and held onto her lead to prevent her from biting the King's ankles.

"He might have given you something less…" he waved a jewelled hand, trying to think of something appropriate to say. He gave up. "… ugly. And what is wrong with it? It's lame."

"Her back leg twisted when she was whelped, Your Grace, but she is perfectly strong." He didn't look convinced.

Gloucester had been watching Moth and he now bent down to stroke her head. "She will be a handsome dog when fully grown," he remarked.

"You should have killed it at birth, my lord," Long-face remarked to the Earl.

Isobel answered before she could think better of it. "Why, my lord, because she is not perfect? Does that make her less worthy of life?"

"Isobel," the Earl warned, and she coloured.

"Well said, mistress," the Duke murmured.

"Look at it." Squirrel-hair pointed at the gangly pup. "There's more leg than body. It's so thin it could slip between the pages of a book."

"Like my brother here." The King slapped Gloucester on the back, earning a grimace from the younger man.

"Mistress Fenton raised it from birth," Rob said quietly. "There are few who would show such devotion."

"Well, well." The King narrowed his eyes. "It would seem, mistress, that you have a champion after all." Then to Rob, "Langton, have you given thought to the match I proposed? The lady awaits your answer."

Robert was saved from concocting an excuse when Squirrel-hair let out a yell as Moth sank her needle teeth through the soft leather of his shoe. He shook her off, clasping his foot and balancing precariously on the other.

"Sweet Mary, Hastings, you make much of it!"

"That tyke has sharp teeth, Your Grace!"

"Well then, pray Fitzhugh hasn't employed a legion of them, or we are all lost. Which puts me in mind – my lord Earl, you promised me a whelp from your best bitch's last mating. To your kennels – lead on."

Chapter 16

"SO, WHAT HAPPENED to Lord Fitzhugh?" Isobel brought the edges of the sheet together corner to corner and folded it. Ursula took the sheet from her, folded it neatly once more, and placed it to one side. "Well?" Isobel urged.

Ursula gave a little cough. "By the time the King reached the north, Lord Fitzhugh had slipped over the border to Scotland without coming to blows. Now the King is in Ripon, though how long he'll be there is anybody's guess, but there's no reason to stay."

Ursula flustered as Isobel kissed her cheek. "You are a fount of information."

"That's not all," Ursula went on, encouraged by Isobel's evident interest. "The Countess's waters broke this morning, and she is showing signs of labour. My lord might have his heir by the time he returns, and there will be much cause for rejoicing. The King will stand godfather if it's a boy."

Isobel wasn't sure how she felt about that. Part of her longed for the Earl to have a son, but a tiny speck of envy surfaced that she had not even realised was there until it materialised in all its green-eyed glory. The Countess had the recognition Isobel lacked, status she could only imagine. Hers was a position in society sanctified by marriage and in law, and Isobel had… what? A bastard growing in her belly whose father could claim neither it nor her for his own. A child who would remain nameless. Invisible. The baby flipped in her womb, and she patted her gently. "Let's take you for a walk," she said, and then to Ursula, "send for Lady Cecily." Isobel picked up Moth's leash. She had grown so much already that her paws looked too big for her spindly legs, and the baby fluff had been replaced by pale silk-like fur making her more like the ethereal winged creatures of the night than their grubs for which she was named. She had yet to learn to be brushed and fought the comb with vigour, reminding Isobel – as she often reminded Cecily – of the girl's eternal loathing of the comb. Isobel attempted to tackle the flossy tangle developing around her ears, but a peal of bells from the chapel made her jump and set Moth yipping. It was past None but well before Vespers; it wasn't the bell for the dead, nor the simple tolling of the hours, but a lively chorus of all bells. Ursula startled with eyes round and was off rattling down the stairs before Isobel could instruct her to find out the cause. Minutes later, she burst into the room. "My lady, it's happened! Praise Holy Mary and all the Saints – my lord has an heir!"

DESPITE THE AUTUMNAL nip in the air, Felice rejected the heavy green figured velvet in favour of the rich blue overgown shot with gold and the contrasting yellow kirtle. She had no wish to add the taint of sweat to that of motherhood. She raised her arms for her smock, felt the tingling in her nipples, and caught the unmistakable odour of milk as it oozed. Internalising her frustration, she clicked her fingers. After five days of breasts bursting with milk, she had expected there to be some reduction by now. She had been tempted to let her son suckle just to relieve the pressure, but that would defeat the purpose. Wives of cottagers suckled their young, like sows, and she was neither. The compress of sage and peppermint, held in place over each breast with a leaf of cabbage and bound with winding cloth, soothed, and with enough oil of jasmine the scent would not be unpleasing as long as her husband did not get too close. And that was unlikely. At least the cabbage leaves would prevent her milk leaking and staining her clothes with the telltale sign of her recent maternity. She raised her arms again, grimacing at the instantaneous flow of milk, and let the smock obscure the ridiculous leaves. Next the yellow kirtle of the finest linen, and then the blue gown, embroidered all over in gold griffins and studded with pearls. She chose the great collar he had given her at the birth of their first child and the ring from their nuptials. Her hair had been dressed in oil of rose, which helped disguise the grey strands creeping along her hairline – what little had been left after a session of plucking that had made her eyes water – and it was now arranged about her shoulders like a cape. She felt regal and fit to be the wife of an earl whose lineage stretched back to the days of William of Normandy and whose succession she had now secured. She heard a flurry of titters by the door and then one of her ladies hurried over. "My lady, the Earl approaches."

Easing herself from the daybed, she sat instead on her great chair beneath its canopy. It had been draped with extravagant cloth, covering the pillows that cushioned her torn vulva that still stung when she moved.

"Here." She crooked her finger, pointing at her cleavage.

The girl bent and sniffed. "It is most pleasant, my lady."

Felice suspected otherwise, but there was no time to do anything more about it. "The child," she ordered. "Has he been cleaned?" she asked her longstanding lady-in-waiting, who had been with her since Margaret's birth. She anticipated the twinge of grief at her daughter's memory and suppressed it before it could grow.

"He is still at the breast with his wet nurse, my lady."

Felice tutted. "Fetch him, and ensure he is unswaddled."

Her son was brought to her wrapped in his father's livery as previously instructed. The yellow and blue were garish against his delicate baby skin, but there could be no doubt whose son he was. Thick dark hair stuck up at all angles, making him look like a wet hedgehog, and he had developed a purplish rash across his cheeks. Felice had seen more attractive babies, but he was a boy. She heard her husband's purposeful steps and took the child from his nurse. By the time the Earl walked towards her, she had adopted a pose of utmost serenity. A hush fell among her gentlewomen.

He bowed. "Madam."

She inclined her head. "My lord." She parted the cloth covering the child, his tiny arm waving in the sudden rush of cool air. "Your son," she said, pride swelling her voice.

He inspected the baby. "So I see," he said, and to her consternation the child produced an arc of pale yellow urine, soaking her hand and her knee. The Earl cocked an eyebrow. "You are to be congratulated, madam; he is a fine boy."

Two days later and unopposed, Warwick landed on the Devon coast with an invasion fleet made up of Lancastrian adherents and French mercenaries and marched with ferocious determination north, forming a bow-wave of speculation that the old queen would wreak revenge on a country she thought had betrayed her. By the time the Earl reached the King in York, the rebel ranks had swelled to include lords who had previously maintained their tacit neutrality. He went straight to the King without stopping to change and entered the chamber as the King let fly a gold cup, narrowly missing the Earl's head as he entered the room. "Bastard sons of incubus!" The cup hit the panelled wall and fell to the ground, where it rolled to the Earl's feet. He bent to pick it up, flicked residual drops of wine from his dusty shoulder, and bowed.

"Your Grace has heard the news?"

Edward stabbed a blunt finger at the messenger, who looked as if he would rather be anywhere else than at the sharp end of the King's wrath. "Warwick's managed to convince Stanley and Shrewsbury to join him."

"Stanley needs little persuasion; he swings with the wind, Your Grace."

"Which means he believes it blows cold for us. I should have stopped Warwick from landing. He planned this all along and marked me for a fool."

The Earl placed the dented cup on the nearest table. "And leave the north to open rebellion? Highness, you took the risk and have secured the northern realm. Draw Warwick to battle before he commands greater numbers from his northern affinity. Deny him success on the field, and Anjou has little support among the nobility and gentry and none among the commons. Without supplies, her army will be starved from the land and broken."

"We should take the battle to him," Gloucester urged. "We are well provisioned, and the people support you."

"My little brother – so eager to fight."

"There is no honour in letting the commons suffer the deprivation of war at the hands of Anjou."

"Honour?" The King stared down at the younger man, seemingly benign except for the edge in his voice. "Time will temper your ideals and reveal this life to be an *im*perfect mirror for princes."

Stubborn-jawed, Gloucester gazed back. "But it is as well to live in the hope of it."

Edward broke the tension with a laugh. "I remember the idealism of youth, and it served me well enough." He spoke over his shoulder. "Send word to my cousin, Northumberland—"

"Montagu, Your Grace?" the Earl queried.

The King grunted at his error. "Yes, Montagu. He's to muster as many of his troops as he can and join us at Pontefract without delay. His brother Warwick will rue the day he set foot upon this land."

A SQUEAL FOLLOWED by a giggle and then a moan issued from the chamber above the enclosed garden, amplified in the small space and reminding the men gathered there why they had decided to take advantage of the vestiges of late September warmth rather than linger inside.

Willian Fiennes grinned. "His Grace takes his pleasure where he may. If he tumbles another one, he'll leave a trail of bastards from Doncaster to York."

Cowper rumbled, "And they'll all be sons, I'll warrant, leaving the Queen to bear him nowt but lasses."

"And part base-born at that," Fiennes added with a gruff laugh, easing his stiff shoulder and making his overly long greying hair ride in a silvered wave on it.

The Earl growled, "Passing fond of your head, are you, my lord Saye, because if the Queen hears such tavern talk you will be finding yourself shorter by it, with a pikestaff up your arse and displayed where all can see it."

Fiennes shrugged. "I'll not tell if you don't. If His Grace had married fit for his estate, we wouldn't be here now with Warwick spoiling for battle and the Earl of Desmond without his head."

"Keep your voice down," the Earl warned. "Rivers is but a step away and within earshot. He will not take kindly to the notion that his sister had anything to do with Desmond's… execution. Be thankful Worcester fights for the King and not against him."

"Aye, that's what Desmond believed until Worcester's blade taught him otherwise. He and his sons." A slow, rhythmic thudding set up. Fiennes winced. "His Grace'll have worn the bed out by morning."

Cowper sniffed and spat onto the cobbles. "You believe Worcester killed Desmond's bairns? It is naught but rumour."

Fiennes raised a sandy brow etched in grey. "What is there to doubt? Look what he did to Warwick's men at Southampton – yeomen and gentlemen of no great estate – impaling. He had no need to exact such punishment. He took too great a pleasure in it."

"They were dead at the time," the Earl pointed out, heeling a loose stone into the border of clipped lavender. "And traitors."

"Perhaps, but he went too far. And I swear the King had no knowledge of Desmond's death until he learned of it. What cause had he to have him killed? None. Worcester either acted of his own accord or at the command of… another."

Cowper conceded the point with a grin. "True enough. What sow doesn't defend her nest, eh?"

"Your intemperate tongue will attract the Queen's attention," the Earl pointed out. "As did Desmond's. None is immune. No matter how close he may be to the King, the Queen is closer."

Cowper glanced around the courtyard and, seemingly satisfied they couldn't be overheard, said, "The King's still freed Worcester."

Fiennes plucked a stray twig. "Well, wouldn't you rather have him fighting for you? The man's so single-minded in his loyalty he'd look God in the eye and tell Him He's wrong, argue it, too, in Latin – and probably win; he's no fool. That's if he didn't barter his way into Heaven with his sword." He snapped the twig and discarded it as the glass in the oriel window began to rattle as it took on the pounding rhythm. "You're quiet on the subject, Langton, have you nothing to say?"

Robert pushed himself away from the wall with his heel. "I think enough has been said on the matter; there is little I can add."

"Come now, there's always something to be said when it comes to the King's bed." Cowper winked again. "Why so glum? Can I fetch you a wench to cheer you?"

"Forgive me, my lords, but I will take my leave."

He left the courtyard to the sound of loud moans and the men's ribald comments. Steps came after him. "Robert, wait!" His brother caught up. "What is the matter with you? These men are our allies." A triumphant yell came from the chamber above and then a blessed silence. "It is as well to court favour among those who might one day be your father-in-law, or a brother to you, or stand between you and a sword. Think on it. We have fewer friends than we thought, so we must keep the ones we have well-disposed towards us. Come back and join us. The King will wish us to attend him shortly." He turned, expecting Robert to follow him, but he made no move.

"I am likely to sour the conversation. Make my excuses; I am no fit company tonight."

"Cowper might have a point; you have been too long without a maid to take your mind off things. Here," he thumbed a coin into the air and Robert caught it without thinking. "That will pay for a clean wench to see you through the night."

He meant it as a joke, but Rob's mouth turned down into an unyielding bow and he span on his heel and was gone before his brother could retrieve the jest.

ROBERT WALKED FAST and hard past men lounging at doorways in the sun and towards his lodgings overlooking Doncaster. The previous day he had noted a lack of respectable women and suspected they were being kept off the streets as the town geared itself for yet more conflict. The few women he had seen eyed his potential, but he had avoided meeting their initiating gaze. He wouldn't be seeking one out tonight, and he grasped the coin in his closed fist. He fervently hoped Martin hadn't succumbed to temptation. The last thing he needed was an esquire struck down with self-pity and gleet.

Nodding to Gloucester's guards standing at the door in their murrey and blue livery, he mounted the stairs to the first-floor chamber. The Duke looked up when he entered, quill suspended over the parchment. His chessboard lay to one side, a game left unfinished. Rob bowed. "His Highness was indisposed, Your Grace, but I left the message." He loosened his sword belt and ran a finger under his collar. "It is warm out there for Michaelmas. I think we might have a storm."

"Very possibly." Gloucester signed the letter and set it by to dry. He pushed himself back from the table. "It is the waiting I find difficult."

Rob gestured to the chessboard. "Who is winning?"

"I am." His mouth lifted into a sardonic smile. "I find myself a poor opponent; the victor is known at the outset and there is no sport in that." His secretary folded the letter, attached its ribbon, and lit the taper. Wax dropped in two neat molten blobs into which the Duke pressed his seal. He stood and stretched. "The air is close in here, and I have been seated too long."

"The streets are little better, Your Grace. They reek of stale piss and tripe. At least the air smells fresher by the river."

"A jug of ale would make it the sweeter."

Robert grinned. "Then if it pleases you, I know the best place to find one not more than a short ride away."

"Your Grace will take an armed escort?"

Gloucester took the reins from a stable groom's hand. "Thank you, but no, Sir John. I am assured that the inn at Balby is but a step from here, and we will make do with our own company." He brought his horse's head around and waited for Rob and their esquires to mount. "If the King wants me, that is where I will be. Otherwise, we will return before curfew."

At last free of the town and heading for an inn where they could be assured of some solitude, Robert was less than happy that, over the sound of their own conversation accompanied by the leisurely music of their horses' harness, came the brisk thud of hooves.

The Duke groaned. "The inn is within sight. We can make a run for it. Freedom and ale await."

Robert put a ready hand on his sword hilt. "I do not think he is a messenger. Martin!" he called, and the youth stopped talking to the Duke's esquire and followed the direction in which his lord pointed. Langton was regretting not taking more men when the horseman bounced into view.

"He's an ungainly assassin," Gloucester commented.

Robert made out rough features, a blunt head. He grunted an oath. Raising his voice, he called, "What in Hades are you doing here?"

Philip Taylor trotted up to them, touching his hand to his forehead in salute to the Duke. "If you'll give me leave, Your Grace, summet's been said about a jug of ale, and I says to myself, 'Well, Pip, that sounds like a jug with your name on it,' so here I be. My lord, you nearly forgot to ask me along," he added with an air of grievance.

"You can turn around and head back and take your brew with the other men."

"Pip?" Gloucester queried, taking in the bulk of the man.

"Aye, Your Grace," he said before Robert could answer. "Philip Taylor and *Pip* to my friends. I'll tell ye a tale that's true enough. I were but a pippen of a lad, though some who's less inclined to my friendship might say I was so named because I were a snotty child—"

"Sergeant!" Robert broke in, exasperated.

"Aye, my lord?"

"Quieten your tongue."

Taylor tapped a knotty finger to his lips and then to his temple. "Not a word. Aye, my lord." He sniffed. "I've brought me own farthing."

"And a sword and buckler," Gloucester remarked when they picked up the pace ahead of the group. "He goes about well-appointed."

"He takes his ale very seriously," Robert answered. "More seriously than his lord's commands," he added under his breath.

They reached the inn as the sun set, throwing the sky into a mass of ghosted stripes of orange and pink, becoming more lurid as the minutes wore on.

"Do not refer to me as *Your Grace*," Gloucester said in low tones as they entered the brewhouse evidenced by the noise coming from within. He'd worn a plain travelling cloak, and his long riding boots were already covered in dust from the road. His gloves were unremarkable, which was a good thing since they hid well-groomed hands fit for a prince of the ruling house. Not much could be done about his bearing, though, nor the command that naturally came with his high estate, but he'd pass as a gentleman if nobody spoke to him.

Taylor inhaled through congested nostrils. "It's a fine evening. I'll stay outside, if you don't mind, my lord, and take the air." He winked and patted his sword. Langton thought it a miracle if the man could smell anything at all, but his hearing was good and his eyesight better, which counted for much, and he might as well do a job now he was here.

Robert's request for a private room was met with a good-natured rebuff, so they settled in the corner furthest away from the noisy centre of the one-roomed space, where the chimney bellied out and offered some privacy. It did little for the flames, and the rapidly cooling evening air offered no chance of an updraft. Smoke belched in puffs from the half-hearted fire.

Rob's eyes watered, and he coughed. "We'll be well-smoked by the time we leave here."

"I have never heard it called that," Gloucester shot back, taking the stool in the dimly-lit corner and facing outwards into the room, where he could observe everything. "For my part I prefer the reek of a fire to the stench of a town. At least with the fire you know what causes it. There is honesty in fire." He leaned back against the wall as beakers of horn were laid out in front of them, filled from a long-necked, green-glazed jug.

Robert sent Martin with a jug of ale for Pip, then sat down at an angle at the table. "You have a good sergeant there," Gloucester said, raising the horn cup to his mouth.

A little of Langton's ire abated as he admitted, "He has served me well, Your—" He stopped himself in time. "It is a hard habit to break. Taylor, yes, and he has a nose for trouble. He is the man who accompanied us from Beaumancote to Crowle and kept Lacey's men off our backs."

Gloucester nodded. "I remember you saying." Did he? Robert had only mentioned it in passing and that some time ago. "Has there been any further trouble from Lacey?"

Robert's mouth turned down. "Not since he was given the Fenton offices, no."

"You do not think he should have been pardoned?"

"Do you reward a dog that betrays its master to follow another man?"

"If it can be brought to heel, surely that is better than losing it altogether?"

"*If* it can be trained, and if in the training other – more faithful – dogs do not feel slighted by the favour shown to the undeserving churl."

"And is that what the Earl feels – slighted?"

"I did not say so—"

"No, but you implied it." Leaning forward, Gloucester lowered his voice. "Look, Langton, deal plainly with me even if you think I will not want to hear it. I know you well enough to understand no treason will be meant by it." Robert thumbed the groat his brother had given him earlier that afternoon. Freshly minted, the King's image glinted as it caught the light. The Duke read his hesitation. "And you can trust me; anything you say I will keep to myself." He raised his beaker. "Do not let my youth mislead you. I am long practised in such matters, especially in recent years."

Rob flipped the coin; it landed face up and beaming. He gave a short laugh and shook his head slowly. "I can well believe that." He took his time to find the right words. "The Earl is not aggrieved, but he thinks the Ki… your brother…" That didn't feel right, but he persisted anyway, "… misplaced his trust, and I agree with him. My brother believes his counsel has been discredited by the King's generosity to a man who did not deserve the confidence placed in him." The ale was doing a good job of slipping loose his tongue. Another beaker or two and he might say anything and probably wouldn't care. It was a short ride back to town, and his horse knew the way. Although still watchful, the Duke had relaxed considerably since their arrival, and Rob found himself telling him things long kept between himself and the Earl. "My brother watched Ralph Lacey slaughter our father as he pleaded for mercy. He has neither forgiven nor forgotten, and time has made the memory all the sharper."

"He thinks Lacey's blood tainted? Do you?"

"I always thought my brother harboured the grief and that somehow it turned his reason against Lacey; but I think I have been mistaken and he is justified in not trusting Thomas Lacey one whit. I heard how Lacey dealt with Isobel Fenton – I was there – the threat was hardly veiled. He makes his intentions towards Beaumancote plain, although my brother will do everything to prevent *that* from happening."

"Which he did quite effectively. How is Mistress Fenton?"

Robert grimaced before he could stop himself, feeling exposed under the Duke's steady gaze. He looked away. "Well, I believe." He took a swig and wiped the residual drop from his lips with his thumb, wondering if the young man could read his thoughts or whether it was merely the effects of the alcohol that made him feel as if his mind were laid bare to be pecked at like a corpse among crows.

"She has a kind heart," Gloucester said, reaching for the small chest he had brought with him now sitting next to them on the table. He opened it and laid the chequered board flat, on which he began to lay the pieces. "Your move, if it please you."

Rob took his hat off and ran his fingers through his hair. "What will it cost me this time?"

Gloucester sat back, lacing his fingers in front of him. "Only your company. And possibly another cup of ale. Should I be the victor." He gave an almost impish smile. "And what is your wager?" he asked in return.

"Only your mercy," Robert said, studying the board, "should I survive this encounter."

Gloucester grinned, reminding Robert that this youth had barely left boyhood and had but eighteen winters or so behind him.

"I hear my brother is impatient for you to make a contract with the widow. She will bring her husband's affinity to the marriage as well as her father's. Yet you did not seem… enthusiastic when it was mentioned in the summer."

Rob's beaker halted before it reached his mouth. "Do you know this lady?"

"Not as well as my brother, by all accounts, but I have met her. She is handsome, as you might expect, and well-endowed—"

"As you would presume. Hmm, so my own brother tells me."

"You are not keen?"

Ah, the wisdom or otherwise of telling the King's brother the truth. "I… am not." The table rocked on the uneven flags as Robert shifted, slopping ale on the rough surface.

"Perhaps you have other ideas?" Gloucester asked.

The pooled pale globules shivered as he put his cup down. "Perhaps."

"It must be difficult taking on another man's mistress."

Langton looked at him sharply, but a rough chorus had broken out from the men dominating the centre of the room as a younger woman of about twenty joined them, bringing a basket of what smelled like meat pies and an eye that roamed, lingering in Gloucester's direction. The Duke cast a lean look towards her. Rob remembered it well. "Are you hungry?"

Gloucester angled an eyebrow, making him more like his brother than usual. "I am, but it can wait. Do not let me stop you if you have an appetite." The girl squeezed onto the bench with her back to them. One of her companions gave her a lingering slap on her well-formed backside, and she responded with a laugh, cuffing him in return. Robert rolled the silver groat between his fingers and stood up.

"I'll fetch more ale."

Gloucester tossed a coin across the table. "This will attract less attention. It is all I brought with me, so we had better make it last."

"Even at the usurious cost of a penny a gallon I think we will be well-set for the night."

IT GAVE HIM time to ease the burden on his bladder and clear his head enough so that he wouldn't inadvertently blunder into revealing the truth. He was tired, not physically, but mentally, from hiding from his brother, from the Duke, from himself – and it ate at him like worms. There were moments when he wanted to confide in someone, to share the burden of his deceit. No more so than now – here in this nondescript place where none knew him but his duke. Had he already guessed? His lack of discretion, his hesitation, spoke louder than anything he had said, and this young man, whose eyes probed, saw through him more clearly than he liked to admit.

By the time he returned to the table, Gloucester was playing chess against the two young esquires. He looked up as Robert sat down. "All quiet?"

Rob nodded. "All quiet."

THERE WAS NO sign of the moon, and they had lost all sense of the hour by the time they reluctantly rose to leave. The remains of the penny had purchased several more jugs of ale and a quantity of pies, which once consumed were enough for them to find their stirrups without Taylor's offers of help.

The star-embellished sky had grown cold. Gloucester pulled his cloak around his insubstantial frame, and Rob marvelled, not for the first time, how the Duke managed to keep warm at all, even if the furnace of Gloucester's appetite had him eat three pies to his two. The night might have been cold, but after the fug of ale and smoke it cut a clean swathe through his jumbled thoughts, and as if his horse read his mind it took a few steps south and shook its head, rattling the harness. Muted sounds still came from the alehouse, but they hardly penetrated the stillness of the night. Robert patted its neck, staring through the darkness towards Tickhill as if he could perceive Isobel in its depths whiling lonely hours in the tower. Gloucester followed Rob's blind line of sight. "Langton, are you ready?"

Robert swallowed and pulled his horse around. "We should have brought lanterns, Your Grace, we have let the hour grow late. It is well beyond curfew."

Gloucester's eyes gleamed in the light from the alehouse door as it opened and closed. "We can find our way back, and it will give the guard something to do when we get there. Besides, the night is dry, and I am in no hurry. I would like to hear about Wakefield, if you have a mind to tell it." Martin nudged the Duke's esquire and stopped talking, and Robert grew conscious of the listening night as they drew past the straggle of houses marking the centre of the village.

"Perhaps Your Grace would rather hear Taylor's rendition of his time serving with Talbot in France?" he suggested, nodding towards the dim form of the sergeant's burly back swaying in ungainly fashion on his equally robust horse twenty paces in front of them.

"Another time, perhaps. I am sure it is entertaining, but I am curious about Wakefield. You were there."

"I was, but there are others who can give you a better report of the battle."

"I have heard the accounts oft times before; but only of the death of my father and brother and of my kin, and that is not what I want to know. I wish to know what it was like… the fighting."

"It was my first battle – if such a rout could be called such—"

"Yes, I am aware, that is why I am asking you."

Robert rode on without answering immediately. Finally, he said, "I thought I was in Hell. I thought Hell had come to England and swallowed us whole. What it spat out, what remained, were ghosts of the past. We all died a little that day. Sometimes I think that it would have been better to have died then than to live with the memories. But that would be to deny God's grace in granting us life, and those of us who survived will have to live with the memory as penance for the rest of our lives. There's no glory in battle, Your Grace, no honour in victory – not after that – and certainly not for me."

"Why not for you?"

Even if Taylor gave no indication he could hear the conversation behind him, Robert was acutely aware that the esquires listened as intently as the Duke. He remembered being as eager for details as they seemed to be. Was it a condition of youth that meant young men yearned for what they didn't know, then spent the rest of their days trying to forget? Or maybe it was just him. It wasn't that he was afraid of being afraid anymore – he accepted that fear was a predictable facet of war – just that the heat he had felt course through his body as he held his horse steady next to his brother had been as potent as lust, and it had shocked him. But it had been nothing compared to the thrill of his own sword slicing through the man's upturned face, before reality had hit him and he had staggered to a twisted tree and vomited the blood from his own bitten lip while all around him had theirs cut from their faces. He could still see his sword in the mirror of the man's eyes as he brought it down, still feel the sheer relief that it was not him, and the guilt at that relief. How many times had he asked forgiveness over the years for it and for his failure that day? He became aware that Gloucester was waiting. "There are things I did that I regret." The road became uncertain as they left the light of the village behind, and they rode on without speaking for a time as their horses picked their way forward. Rob detected questions brimming behind Gloucester's silence. "Fear makes you do things you would not recognise in yourself, Your Grace. I lost sight of myself."

"Were you afraid?"

"Yes, I was afraid. I was terrified I would not be able to fight, that I would bring dishonour on myself and my family. That I would fail to conduct myself in the manner I had been taught and be shamed in front of my father and brother."

"And did you acquit yourself honourably?"

"I fought, yes, and I killed – but honourably? That is a question I have often asked myself."

"I do not know how it will be when I fight."

Langton detected the uncertainty in the young man's voice as well as his words. "No one knows how they will react in their first battle, Your Grace."

"I just do not want to be afraid."

"You will be. You will probably want to turn and run – I did – and you might even soil yourself, but there's no shame in fear or excrement, only in…" He stopped, realising – no, *admitting* – for the first time what had gnawed at him since that day.

"What shame?" Gloucester pushed, when Robert didn't answer.

"… in enjoying the kill," Langton said eventually. "We fight because we must, but we should temper it with mercy. I killed men when I could have shown mercy. There was no mercy that day."

Chapter 17

AN EVENING OF ale and quiet company proved merely a temporary cure for the restlessness that consumed both Rob and the Duke for different reasons. The following eve, without thinking, Robert glanced south and west through the open casement towards Tickhill not so many miles away – a brief ride, if that. He could be there and back before dawn. He exhaled through his teeth, calculating the time.

Straightening every conceivable object in the room, Gloucester paced the confines of the space a number of times before he spoke. "We are required to dine, but I have little appetite. While we feast, Warwick makes his plans, and Christ in Heaven knows who else might join him."

Robert came back to the present. "There is news?"

"Nothing any will heed; but I know what I would do in Warwick's place, and it would not be this." He captured the manor in a curt sweep of his eyes. "We need to be ready to leave, but the King will not hear of it." Frustration tightened his voice and pinched the lines of his face. "We are not prepared for battle. If Edwa… His Highness should be captured again, it will not go so well with him. There will be no quarter given, and there can be no other outcome than his death. I cannot countenance that; I cannot live with it." He closed his eyes as if imagining his greatest fears, swallowed, and opened them again. "I have checked the horses, and they are as ready as they can be should we need them; I can do no more. Come, there is a feast to be had, and I will hold my peace."

Captured. The word echoed in Robert's mind. He must capture the moment. "Will Your Grace give me leave? I must send a message; it cannot wait."

"Oh?" Gloucester quizzed, but when Rob failed to satiate his curiosity, he gave a short nod. "As you wish, but stray neither too far nor too long."

ROB NUDGED HIS horse into a walk, rising to a trot as he left the town with the sun arcing towards the horizon. A bell ringing from distant St Mary's marked the hour. Smoke hung over the scattered encampments, with snatches of bawdy song heard on the still air pierced by the shriek of laughter from camp women. He noted the bored guards on the road, who waved him through without so much as hailing him, and the dearth of sentries on duty. Gloucester was right; there was a lack of direction, as if nobody took Warwick's threat seriously. Complacency. "Sweet Jesu," he muttered under his breath then kicked his horse into a canter.

He hadn't planned it; he had not meant to go. It was against the Duke's command, the King's express invitation, and his own brother's wish, but he had no desire to dine in an atmosphere of negligent jollity. Robert had greater matters to attend and a message to deliver in person. His explanation and expressions of regret would come later.

He took the same road he had travelled with the Duke only a few days before, but he would not tarry at the inn. He approached Balby as the sun began its descent. Rooks circled tall elms, clawing the air with coarse voices, but the village was oddly quiet. The road running past the Rose and Crown was empty, the tavern's doors shut, windows obscured by shutters despite dusk having not yet set in. No dog came out to challenge him and sound his arrival. Robert drew his horse to a halt, listening. A sound. There, the faint conversation of hooves and harness, voices guarded, coughs hushed. His skin prickled. Then a shout, a fluster of rising wings as birds scattered from the trees in alarm, and a horseman came tearing from the copse towards him.

Robert drew his sword, bringing his own horse around to face the oncoming steed, but then saw the man's head turned to look behind him, and there, from between the trunks, other men appeared. "My lord!" the man hailed, and Langton recognised the fleeing soldier as one of their own. In his outstretched hand he grasped a blood-soaked rag, which he thrust at Rob, too breathless to speak.

Langton looked at the cloth, then in the direction from which the man had fled. "Ride!" he said. "Ride hard. Ride to the King," and he wheeled his own mount around and rode back the way he had come.

"MONTAGU'S IN *DONCASTER*?" Gloucester repeated, shock draining his voice of substance, leaving it flat and cold and at odds with the raucous diners in the great hall. "You are sure?" Standing at the screens, he looked between Langton and the scout. In answer, Robert held out the blood-soaked yellow griffin the pricker had taken from the dead man's clothes.

Sweat dripping from his nose and chin, the scout shook his head. "I can't rightly say, Your Grace. There's a great host of Montagu's men on't road, an' by the time I'd reckoned they were a bunch of deceiving warlocks there were nowt I could do bar turn tail and ride for 'ome." He wiped his nose with his sleeve. "If I could've done summet, Your Grace, I would."

"Were you seen?"

"Aye, Your Grace, but he'll not be tellin'." He made a quick gesture of a blade drawn across a throat.

Gloucester grimaced and nodded. "You did well. Keep it to yourself." He waited until the scout had gone beyond hearing then, pinching the bridge of his nose and squeezing his eyes shut, said, "I feared this would happen." He breathed out, opened eyes dark with determination. His jaw clicked. "Langton, come with me."

He walked swiftly towards the dais upon which the King sat recounting some tale William Hastings obviously thought amusing because he had broken into a fit of coughing and spilled wine over his hose. Hastings spotted Gloucester and raised a hand. "Your Grace has missed a fine tale—"

Grim-faced, Gloucester continued past him, bent close to his brother, and waited as Edward's smile melted like wax into a frown, and then congealed in shock. The King stood abruptly, eyes wide, mouth ridged.

He took the scrap from Gloucester's hand and held it up as if it were a severed head. The yellow griffin, blotched with blood, stood out on the black and red background. "Montagu?" he said, looking directly at Langton now. "Is this intelligence to be believed?"

Robert bowed his head. "It is, Your Grace. I heard them myself at Balby. They were heading north and east towards Doncaster. They had no reason to be south of us."

The muscle in Edward's temple worked. "Montagu intends to betray us." Staring over the heads of his retinue towards the screens where musicians still played oblivious, he inhaled, curling his top lip towards his nose as he contemplated this latest turn of events.

"What in God's name does Montagu think he's doing?" Hastings exploded. "We must take up arms and face him—"

"All six thousand well-armed, well-trained men?" Saye intervened. "With more warning, perhaps, but our troops are unprepared for imminent battle—"

"And spread too far to be made so," the Earl added. "Doncaster cannot be defended."

Gloucester spoke at his brother's elbow, low and swift and urgent. "You cannot be captured. The horses are made ready. We must leave, and leave *now*!"

"Highness, His Grace is right," the Earl said. "We have no time to lose."

Edward continued his blank contemplation then shook his head as if shaking it free of an image and came to. "Fetch the maps. We must find a way through."

"WHAT WERE YOU doing on the road to Balby?" With a sharp tug, the Earl tested the girth strap on his horse and gave instruction to Louys to check that the little they could take was secure in the saddlebags. He stepped on the hand of a groom and into the saddle. Robert took the reins and mounted his own animal as his brother waited for an answer.

"I wanted to ensure the security of the road. The watch needed to be kept sharp."

"Gloucester sent *you*? That's a questionable task for someone of your station."

Robert watched the young Duke organising men by the light of the torches, giving short, precise instructions and ensuring their readiness himself. "He saw this coming. He has been concerned about the lack of—" he pursed his mouth, "—readiness."

"So you went. Alone."

"I did," he said, in a manner that suggested any further questions would be unwelcome. "Are you not concerned for your family? If Tickhill falls to Warwick—"

"Do you think I have not already thought of that?" the Earl whipped, catching Robert by surprise. "I have to stay with the King." Hunching his shoulders, he compressed his lips. "It is my duty."

Rob searched out Gloucester from among the mounted horses in the vanguard of the ribbons of men now forming as the King made ready to mount.

"You know these roads well?" Gloucester said as Rob drew alongside. Some of the agitation had gone, to be replaced by an eagerness to be off. He was as restless as his horse.

"Well enough, Your Grace."

"We are to take the vanguard and set the pace and give the King cover if we run into trouble." His eyes darted to the way ahead and then behind, as if sensing imminent danger. Edward was taking his leave of the women, lingering with the wide-eyed beauty in the green dress. "There is no *time*," the Duke muttered.

"Your Grace?"

His eyes on the King, the Duke raised his arm ready to signal the off. "What is it?"

"By your leave, my brother would have me fetch what men are left in the garrison at Tickhill for our cause."

The Duke lowered his arm. "We cannot afford to wait. If we do not cross the Wash before the tide turns we will be trapped in Lincolnshire, and God forbid if that land is not as settled on us as it should be."

"But if I go alone," Langton insisted, "I might go unnoticed and ride the more swiftly. Your Grace, I can gather what intelligence I may before I join you at Lynn – confirm how widespread Warwick's hold is."

Gloucester's eyes flickered, and Robert imagined he was weighing up the odds. His mouth pulled into a grim line. "Go, then. Take someone you can trust to watch your back, and see what men you can find at our disposal." He raised his hand once again and this time motioned the column forward without delay.

Chapter 18

UP AHEAD, THE sturdy form of Taylor's horse came to a halt. "Beggin' my lord's pardon," he whispered, "but I thought I heard movement ahead near that stand o' trees, an' I am thinking to myself, that's not right, that isn't."

"Deer?" Rob asked quietly.

"Not unless it's taken to wearing metal shoes, my lord, so it won't be stalkers neither."

Straining into the darkness, they listened for any sound. A distinct chink, followed by a sneeze and a subdued threat.

"I heard that," Rob confirmed. "Dead ahead. At least three score men and horse by my guess, but not ours – not this way. Warwick must have put them up." He felt for the pommel of his sword. "They are between us and Tickhill. We could head southwest, but it would mean risking being caught with the river at our backs. If we cut east it is longer, but we can find a safer path as long as Warwick has not sent men that way."

"Aye, my lord; there's wisdom in safety and folly in a fight. If we come at Tickhill from about face, we can send out our own troops to take this lot without risking thyself."

They crossed the strips of fields surrounding the village to avoid the cotts. Ploughing had started, and the turned soil proved heavy going until their horses found surer footing on unlit paths trodden firm by a summer of feet and hooves. Hardened wheel ruts led towards the spreading copses where leaves absorbed what light came from the stars. Without speaking, Robert pointed into the blackened depths. They let their horses find the way, the churned stems and damp earth matting the inside of his nostrils until all he could smell was fresh decay. A squeal and a flurry of movement had Robert reining in his horse as pigs – two of them – ran between the legs of the startled horses, sending them snorting against each other, metal clashing like an alarm. Then a shout went up ahead perhaps a hundred yards away, and another to the right, and yet a third, followed by the sound of swords being drawn and hooves quickening towards them.

"Back!" Robert hissed. He wheeled his horse on the narrow path and, urging it forward, broke the cover of the trees just as he spotted a small number of mounted men picked out by the lanterns they carried. Blinded by their own light, the troops didn't spot them until, crashing out of the woods, the pursuers almost ran into them. Shouted challenges were met with curt rebuttals, exchange of news, orders given, but by then they were beyond sight again.

Skimming the copse and heading south, they hunkered down on their horses, waiting every moment to hear the cry of pursuit, until they could be certain they were beyond hearing. They drew up to catch their breath in a damp dip of land giving them temporary cover. Taylor dismounted and scrambled to the crest of the low dyke. Following suit, Robert climbed the bank until he could see over the tattered grasses left from summer. He spoke softly, casting his voice along the slope. "That's Loversall ahead. I can smell the smoke of hearths and make out several lights. The land is rough and mostly thickets and marsh with no clear paths except the one through the wood. If Warwick and Montagu have men sown across this land like pox, we'll have no option but to fight or surrender, and I do not fancy our chances in either circumstance. We must gain Tickhill before that route is also cut off." The distant sound of raised voices crossed the land towards them. "If it has not already been."

Taylor slid back over the top of the dyke, crushing vegetation in his haste. "I reckon so, my lord. There's more of 'em and moving fast. We'd best be going."

They struggled over land broken by ditches and dykes, their horses stumbling, clothes tugged by the briers edging the numerous stands of trees until the village of Wadworth was no more than its church silhouetted on its hill behind them. The last sighting of troops had been some time ago, and they believed the risk of the open road justified in the speed it gave them as the first few lights of Tickhill glimmered on the horizon. The horses picked up their pace as they recognised the road and divined food and a stable, but Robert's prayer of thanks was short-lived as a cry went up from behind them. *"Ride!"* he yelled, as the low rumble became distinct as the first horseman appeared out of the darkness. Not waiting to see how many were in pursuit, Rob kicked his horse into a gallop and made for the town.

HARSH METALLIC CRIES of a bell woke Isobel from troubled dreams. Heart pounding and still half asleep, she rolled upright, blinking sleep from her eyes. From beside the bed, Chou growled low and deep, and Moth – raising her voice in a long-pitched howl – picked up the song from the kennels.

"What in Jesu's name is that bell?"

From her pallet, Ursula covered her ears. "The alarm! They're sounding the alarm!"

Isobel heaved out of bed onto the cold floor. "We are under attack? Get my clothes. Quick!"

She had pulled on her shoes when, pacing by the door, Chou suddenly set up furious barking. Shouts came from outside, and then fists hammered at the door. The dogs went wild. "They'll break it down!" Ursula shrieked, hands over her ears again. Isobel grabbed the ballock dagger. Picking up the fire-iron, she tossed it to Ursula.

"Here, arm yourself. And stop making that noise, I cannot hear!" Isobel took hold of Chou's collar. "Moth, Chou – *quiet*! What do you want?" she addressed the door, sounding braver than she felt.

Thumping resumed and then a sharp rebuke, and a man's gruff voice called her name through the stout planks. Isobel swung it open a notch and found a familiar face grinning back at her. "Master Taylor! What are you doing here?"

"Beggin' your pardon, mistress, but there's a mite of trouble brewing 'yond castle walls, and these churls and scallions will be wanting access to the weapons." He thumbed over his shoulder to a number of men crowded behind him, who would have pushed into the room had it not been for his square body blocking the way. "My lord requests you attend him in't council chamber." Behind him the men were getting impatient. "We best be letting this lot get on wi' their work manning the battlements." He nodded at her hand. "And you'll not be needing that, not wi' me about." Isobel looked stupidly at the dagger clenched in her fist, the point still threatening his stomach. She sheathed the blade and stood back to let the men past. "Careful there!" Taylor barked as a man pushed by with a keg of quarrels and another with sheaves of arrows. "Mistress?" He indicated the now unblocked door.

The bell had ceased the call to arms, but it had been replaced by frenetic activity filling the night with demon faces lit by lanterns, the smell of iron, and the urgency of war. In the dimly-lit council chamber, robed men crowded around the table as a dark-haired figure with his back to Isobel pointed at something laid on it. The figure straightened, and her skin flooded with warmth as Rob gave a command and the bodies in front of her shifted like a moving wall as, one by one, they left the room, leaving the few by the table. Rob looked different somehow, changed by his authority. Isobel hung back, estranged. He looked around as if he sensed her there, and his eyes lit as he saw her and then became worried as he took in her frightened face. Leaving the steward to examine the map with the constable, Rob crossed the broad floor and, taking her by the arm, led her back up the stairs to his brother's privy chamber.

"What is happening?" Isobel burst out. "Why are you here? The alarm—"

"It is a precaution." He glanced at Ursula, but she was rocking and crooning in the corner and seemed oblivious. He lowered his voice. "Montagu's men are between here and Doncaster, and we were pursued. We barely made it to safety; the area is swarming with them."

"Lord Montagu? But I thought he fights for the King. And why were you pursued?"

Rob heeled his forehead with his hand. "Of course, you could not know."

"Know *what*?" The child tumbled and kicked inside her, and Isobel curved over, winded.

Grabbing her elbow, Rob's forehead gathered in concern. "For the love of God, Isobel—"

"I'm all right."

"No, you are not. Sit down." She landed inelegantly on a stool as the baby squirmed, and he held her hand between his. "Montagu has turned traitor. We are in flight, and we must get the King to safety."

Dazed, she said, "The King?"

"He makes for Lynn now with what other lords have fled with us."

"And th… the Earl?"

"He is with the King. Isobel, listen to me. You will be safe here – safer than on the road."

She looked at him dully. "Why should I not be safe?"

"You must understand – Warwick and Clarence outwitted us. They have control now. Our king is in mortal danger – Gloucester too. If we are to have any chance of surviving this, we must go."

"You are l… leaving?" she stammered. "Go where?"

"Anywhere that will give us sanctuary."

A disturbance by the door interrupted him, and he swung round with his hand on his hilt. He let it drop, surprised to see the Countess. Isobel ducked back and sat motionless, hoping to go unnoticed. It was the first time she had seen the Countess since the birth of her son, and recent motherhood had done nothing to soften her.

"My lord, why was I not informed of the alert but so rudely awakened by the bell? None will answer, and I am obliged to come here in person to demand an explanation."

"Madam, I had no wish to alarm you in your recent confinement."

"Yet you do so. Why are you here, and why was the alert sounded? Is there news of my husband?"

"He remains with the King, but we must flee. Montagu has turned against us, and Warwick has forces closer than we thought. I am come to gather what men I can without risking the security of the castle. I will ensure enough are left to defend it."

"Soldiers?" For the first time the Countess wavered. "Might the castle be attacked?"

"It cannot be discounted."

Felice's voice rose and tightened. "We cannot stay here, my lord. I will not wait for the castle to be besieged and fall to the enemy. I wish to be taken to sanctuary."

Rob viewed her coolly. "For all his faults, Warwick does not make war on women."

"But *Anjou* does," she hissed. "She will not observe such niceties. The old queen lusts for revenge, and with my son the Earl's heir, she has more reason than not to deprive him of his inheritance."

"My brother is not dead yet, and these walls will withstand all but a sustained attack. Besides, I need to take as many men as I can. I cannot spare any from the garrison to escort you to a place of safety. Sanctuary will be of dubious benefit if you are caught on the open road before you have reached it."

"It is your duty…" the Countess began, haughty but rattled, then she spotted Isobel and raised an accusing finger. "What is *that* doing here? How dare she be in my presence to bring shame on this family!"

Isobel thought she heard Rob grunt in surprise. Flaming with humiliation, she rose heavily, but Rob stopped her. "Stay where you are, Mistress Fenton." Anger brewing, he met the Countess face on. "Madam, she is under my protection, and while I stand for the Earl, I will place her where I deem fit in accordance with his wishes."

Felice's mouth took on a sour bow. "Is that *so*, my lord? Is that *all*? Must I excuse my brother Langton his lapse of propriety in his excessive sense of *duty* to my husband's *lady*?" Rob took a pace towards her, but Isobel made a slight noise and he stopped himself, muscles flinching in his jaw.

"There is no time to waste on such matters. I must prepare the garrison. I suggest you repair to your chambers and see to your children's comfort."

"When will you leave?" Isobel asked when the Countess's departure left them alone at last.

"As soon as I have seen you well-provisioned with all you need to sustain you should I… my brother be forced into a prolonged absence."

"Is that like to be? Rob, I cannot stay here. The Countess—"

"You will be safer here than anywhere else, Isobel. I cannot protect you beyond these walls."

"And who will protect *you*?" she said, a coil of fear rising unbidden and relentless. He took her shaking hands between his and lifted them to his lips. Savouring the few minutes they had alone together, the world became a distant place, until a sudden rattling of armour on the stairs outside the chamber had Rob reaching for his sword. One of the garrison soldiers burst into the room. No more than sixteen and with sweat sticking untidy hair to his forehead, he fumbled his words.

"My lord… the Countess – she's sayin' she's leavin'. She's takin' plate, her household servants, everything she can. An' she's taking the bairn wi' her. But Montagu's troops have been spotted on the road t'Maltby—"

"Stop babbling and slow down. *Where* is the Countess saying she'll take them?"

The boy gulped air. "Roche Abbey, my lord."

"She thinks she will find sanctuary there." He almost swore; contained himself. "And she'll run straight into the enemy if she takes the Maltby road."

The lanterns and torches made no inroads on the crow-black night above the family apartments. Rob avoided an upturned stool, a scattering of clothing, a trunk gaping and abandoned by the main stair. A wagon already piled with household goods made ready to leave and, in a covered carriage, the Countess shrilly rammed instructions as her harassed servants scurried like ants from encroaching fire.

Robert gritted his teeth. "My lady!" he called. He leaped onto the wagon's footboard. "You cannot leave now; there is danger on the road."

"I will not be thwarted, my lord. I mean to take my son to safety."

"Not with that slowing you down." He jerked his head towards the loaded wagon. "Nor by the Maltby road. If you insist on leaving the safety of the castle, you will be taken to Roche across country, but you go by horse and you go now."

"I will not ride with another, and I have not the horses for my servants—"

"There are horses enough for you and your children's attendants, but no more. There is no time to debate it. Your household servants can follow if it is safe enough, otherwise they stay here." He peered behind her into the hollow depths of the carriage where the baby snuffled in his nurse's arms. "Where is Cecily?" Thrusting a small iron-bound coffer at a servant, the Countess exhorted the nurse to hurry to follow her, and began climbing from the carriage. "Your daughter, madam, where is she?" He jumped down. There was no sign of his niece among the scattered figures heaving boxes.

The Countess clicked her fingers at a boy. "I ride alone. My horse, and quickly!" She gathered her skirts. "Cecily was sent for along with the servants, my lord. You there!" She beckoned to a man whose arms were laden with what looked in the dim light like arras. "Leave that. Fetch the plate from the wagon and find packhorses to carry it."

Robert growled with frustration. Wrenching bags from a startled woman, he threw them to one side. "Take two maids with you, and find Lady Cecily, and bring her here *now*!" On the turn of his foot Rob caught another lad by the arm. "In the Earl's privy chamber – fetch Mistress Fenton and her servant. Go!"

"Cecily? Is that you under there?" Moth was investigating something under the Earl's great bed, and Isobel bent down as far as her stomach allowed and saw a pair of round eyes peering out from beneath. "What are you doing? Your lady mother has been looking for you." Cecily inched back, and Isobel recognised the signs of refusal. She held out her hand. "Nan must be chilly; does she want to come and sit by the fire with me?" That did the trick. Cecily wriggled out, Nan clutched in one hand, her parti-coloured ball in the other, dust gathered in lines on her dark blue travelling cloak.

"I don't want to go. I don't want to leave Meg."

Brushing her down, Isobel said, "Cecily, we must hurry. You are going on a ride, and the horses are waiting. You do not want to miss the horses, do you?" From somewhere in the bailey she could just make out the girl's name being called, increasingly desperately and hedged with annoyance. "Let us see if we can find Alice. Do you think you will be riding Pansy today?" Isobel took Cecily's sticky fingers in her own and led the way down the stairs. "There they are," she said as cheerfully as she could as they reached the bottom of the steps to the bailey. "I can see Pansy waiting for you."

Cecily took one look at the small party of horses and her mother on her startlingly white mount and buried her face in Isobel's neck. Even from there they could hear the Countess's cutting tones, and Cecily tightened her grip. "Look, there's your uncle," Isobel said brightly over the child's head, trying not to slip as she hastened towards Rob.

"You found her," he said, clearly relieved. "We must leave immediately." He kept looking behind him at the gate as if he anticipated trouble. He raised a hand to the stable boy waiting to one side with a speckled palfrey glowing palely in the false light of the lanterns.

"You are going with them?" she asked, unlocking Cecily's hands from around her neck. The child clung harder.

"I must. I will return when I can." He tried to take Cecily. "Come, sweetheart," he encouraged, with barely disguised urgency.

"I want Is'bel to come."

"I cannot ride, poppet. Go with your uncle; he'll look after you." Cecily's fingers wound into the fabric of Isobel's dress, anchoring her.

"Cecily!" Her mother's voice knifed the air. "Get here now, or you will have a beating. Go and fetch her," she barked at Joan, whose rancid maw was visible in the half-light.

Cecily spotted her. "No!" she moaned, beginning to panic.

Isobel attempted to maintain her balance with the battling child as Rob tried to unlock stubborn little fingers without hurting her. Unhooking her at last, he held her securely in his arms and almost sprinted to the horses and handed her up to Alice. "Do not let go," he warned. "Open the gate!" he ordered, stepping on a groom's hand and into the saddle in a single movement. The Countess had already ridden to the arch of the gatehouse, followed by a groom with the nurse and baby seated behind him when, without warning, Cecily slid from Alice's arms, landed on her feet and, dodging between the horses' legs, made a run for it.

"My lady!" Alice shrieked. The Countess reined in her horse, glaring as her small daughter evaded the clutching hands of servants as they tried to catch her.

"Leave her! She has caused enough delay as it is." Without further comment or instruction, she kicked her horse into a brisk trot and rode beneath the arch, leaving the child panting and alone.

From his saddle, Rob scooped up the dishevelled girl, swung his horse around, and lowered her to the ground in front of Isobel. "Go back to my brother's privy chamber with Cecily and stay there," he said. "The tower is the safest place to be." And he left, leaving them both bewildered as he rode after the Countess and out of sight.

Chapter 19

ISOBEL SAT WITH Cecily until she fell asleep on her father's bed with one arm around Moth and the other hugging Nan. Her own child kicked occasionally, and she stroked her stomach, wondering where Rob might be on the road to Roche Abbey and what he might encounter. And those thoughts chased away any peace she might have found, and fear writhed inside her until she felt sick with it and couldn't sit any longer. The chapel bell rang regardless of war or earls and kings, and Isobel slumped to her knees, feeding prayers Ave by Ave for Rob's safe deliverance, suffocated by fear for him, for Cecily, for herself.

THEY DIDN'T HAVE to wait long for Rob's return. Grey with exhaustion, he dropped into a chair, accepting the ale she offered him. "Felice and the babe are delivered to safety. I must leave immediately. The King is making for the coast to take ship."

Isobel froze. "Where to? Not France. Ireland?"

Rob drank in long, steady draughts, drowning thirst. "Burgundy, perhaps, if he makes Lynn, or north. There is no certainty either way."

"If he sails from the east coast he must cross the Wash, but you will not make it before the tide turns, and even if you did, the King might have set sail by then. And how can you be certain whither he will go?

Can you not stay here?" Dismissing a servant, Isobel kneeled and sponged Rob's free hand clean of another man's blood.

Their heads almost touched as he leaned close to her, speaking softly and with urgency. "Isobel, I would if it were my decision, but this is a greater matter than my happiness. I must join Gloucester with haste. It is my guess they will head for Flanders. The King's sister – Duchess Margaret – will plead our cause with Duke Charles; it is in Burgundy's interest to support us since Louis of France has openly shown his hand by sanctioning Anjou and Warwick."

"But Rob, if he has been able to cross the Wash, the King might already have left port."

"That would depend on the state of the tide. If I leave now, there is a chance I might still meet with him and offer what service I can." Water ran down Rob's wrist and soaked into the cuffed edge of his sleeve. "Even if Lincolnshire is safer since Welles's rebellion, Montagu will certainly have learned of the King's route and will be in pursuit."

Capturing Rob's arm again, Isobel dried his hand and wrist and motioned him to swap so she could cleanse the other of blood. "The roads to Lynn might be closed to you, and what service can you do your king if you are captured or… dead?" She turned away, dipping the cloth and screwing water from it with undue violence, until he put his hand over hers.

"It cannot be helped, Isobel. I must find a way to join them. Do not forget, my brother is with the King."

She pulled her hand free. "I have not forgotten." She dried his hands, giving herself time to think, then said, "What if you could find another way? My people at Beaumancote can be trusted – you have been there, they know you."

"I have and they can, it is true; but even if I could reach it in safety there is less protection behind those walls than we have here. I would be as trapped, and the only way out would be by roads guarded by the enemy. I have no intention of hiding."

"Not to *hide* at Beaumancote; it is but a place of safety until you can make your escape."

"Isobel, there is no safe way to or from Beaumancote."

She deposited the cloth by the basin. "But there is if you travel the moors of Axholme and cross the Trent as we did before. And when you escape, use the river. My father held offices on the Humber and the Trent, and he maintained them to the great benefit of the people who work the river. My steward will know whom to contact, and the tide will take you faster and more safely than any horse past Hull. With our contacts, surely a ship can be found to take you where you want to go?"

"If we are caught between here and Beaumancote I have not enough men to defend ourselves," Rob pointed out. "And it was only by God's good grace I managed to make it back here at all." He held his blood-soaked sleeve aloft as evidence.

"Then travel with only a few men as servants, as we did at Yuletide, and you might pass unnoticed." Lifting her father's seal on the ribbon from around her neck, Isobel pressed it, warmed by her skin and smooth, into Rob's hand. "Take this to Arthur. I will write my instructions to him, but this will convey more than any words." Rob ached to touch her, she could see it in his eyes, but all he could do was briefly fold his fingers around hers, her heart's pulse beating against his skin as he took the ring.

"Isobel, come with me."

"You must travel the quickest route and the safest. I cannot ride, being so far gone with child, and I would slow the pace. Is the castle not safer if it is believed that there is no one of any worth left? And, as you said, Warwick does not make war on women and children. Lady Cecily will be safer without you here and, anyway, I could not leave her, could I?" She tapped impatiently. "Rob, you must leave swiftly if you are to draw as little attention as possible and take advantage of the general disturbance in the land." She held his gaze while war raged behind his eyes, until her argument held sway and he capitulated.

"I will leave within the hour."

HE ATE HASTILY and mostly in silence while what arrangements necessary for travel were made, and he discussed the defence of the castle and its provisioning with the constable should it come under attack, leaving explicit instructions for the protection of his niece and his brother's mistress. But worry bit him like fleas.

"I am leaving Taylor here with you."

"No," Isobel protested. "You need him."

"I do not intend allowing any harm to come to me, but I must secure your safety."

"I am safe enough in the tower, and I will stay in the privy chamber as you told me, although I could just as well bide in the nursery…" His mouth set in an unbroken line. "No, all right, the tower it is, I promise; just take Philip Taylor with you – please."

"I'll take him until I reach the King, but then I am sending him back. Do not debate it – that is *final*, Isobel," he added when she made to object, his eyes darkening until he looked like the Earl and she ceased arguing.

Taylor had been sent to ready the horses and then returned, marking time in the vestibule until his master joined him. In the brief moments in which they were alone, Isobel handed Rob his riding gloves and small, plain leather belt-bag without comment. Rob spoke softly. "I know not when I will be able to return, and I have to be certain that you and our child are safe. You understand that, don't you?" Isobel nodded, not trusting her voice. He caressed her cheek and kissed her, gently at first and then with an urgency, as if making it the last memory of her he would take with him. Voices came from the stairwell. Laying the flat of his hand against her swollen stomach, he murmured, "I love you," standing back as Taylor entered the chamber, bringing a rush of cold night air with him.

"There's no sign of movement at present, my lord, may it please God, and it's not raining," he said, surprisingly cheerful in the circumstances. Rob retrieved his sword from where he had left it and began buckling his belt. He stood back for her to see.

"Do you think we will pass muster, Mistress Fenton? We travel light enough; all our possessions will now be in the hands of some sergeant in Doncaster, no doubt, or a petty knight. Gloucester will be mourning the loss of his chess box he had to leave behind. Are you ready, Taylor?"

"I am that, my lord."

"Then we will take our leave."

They had reached the stair when Isobel thought of something. "Wait!" Picking up the box of games, she went after them. "Take this for His Grace," she said, thrusting it into Rob's hands. "It is for the day of his nativity; you cannot go without a gift."

For a moment he looked as if he would say something else, but instead he whispered, "May the Blessed Virgin protect and keep you," and kissed her lightly before once again turning to go.

Isobel listened until she could no longer hear their feet upon the stairs, nor the *tink* as their swords hit stone as they passed. "God speed," she whispered, knowing that none but the Almighty heard her.

IT WASN'T UNTIL they had slipped over the Trent and, having made their way finally to the gates of Beaumancote and found themselves sitting at Sir Geoffrey's table with Arthur Moynes, that Rob opened his belt-bag to retrieve the seal.

"What is it, my lord?" Moynes asked, seeing colour rise and flee from Langton's face in quick succession.

"It is of no importance," he replied, handing the steward the Fenton seal. And it wasn't, except that for Robert Langton the strand of coral and black beads with the pilgrim's token and the boxwood acorn nestling concealed in the bottom of the bag represented his world, and he had left her behind.

Chapter 20

RICHARD NEVILLE, EARL of Warwick, was not a patient man, and he fought the impulse to walk out of the Abbot's guest chamber and leave the Countess to rot. But that would not suit his purpose; a man of his position found patience when required, and it was needed now. Besides, it pissed down outside, and he was conscious his clothes already smelled of damp wool and horses. He heard movement beyond the door, a woman's voice, and he resumed his expression of magnanimous cordiality as she entered the room. Behind her, the spectre of a man in clerical clothes hovered, smiling and watchful.

The door closed. Warwick bowed, although he didn't need to, and she returned the courtesy with restrained civility. Unlike their previous meeting, he had no need to dance to any other tune than the one he wished to play.

"Madam, you are well?"

"I am as you see me, my lord. I keep good health, may it please God."

"It grieves me to find you in such altered circumstances."

Her mouth tightened. "As it is with you, my lord. I believe much has changed in your own situation in the last months. You seem, unlike those whom you once loved, to have prospered by it."

He had expected as much and ignored the measured jibe. She had kept him waiting, and he wanted to get to the heart of the matter. "God, in His wisdom, has seen fit to bestow these gifts upon me. Whatever's passed, you have your future to consider, and it does not have to be…

this." He indicated the whitewashed room with its thin fire and meagre furnishings, fit for the abbey but little else. She said nothing. Her face had become pinched since he had seen her last, and the straps of her neck stood proud as she moved her head. She was still handsome, though, and he felt a surge of pity he quickly quashed. "Write to the Earl. Persuade him to return and be reconciled to King Henry, and you can be restored to your life of comfort and honour as befits your station. The King is quick to forgive those who swear allegiance to him and accept Prince Edward as heir."

"As you have been so swift to do, my lord? Why should my husband believe that there is any future in this reign when Queen Margaret still lingers in France with her son, and Queen Elizabeth has finally secured the succession for King Edward by giving birth to an heir in Westminster?"

"You are remarkably well-informed."

"I have means." She declined to say what they were and continued to observe him as if he were something vaguely distasteful and malodorous. "Well, my lord?"

He clenched his teeth, feeling his temper spiralling. "For the very reason you state: that the Lady Elizabeth is in sanctuary in Westminster and has no more chance of making anything of her infant than her husband does in Burgundy. Edward of York lacks the support of his brother-in-law, Duke Charles, and secures no more than *debts*." He thumped the wall, his hand coming away chalked, and regretted it as the Countess noted his failure to maintain self-control in the gleam of satisfaction as her lips parted over neat teeth. It hadn't always been so; once she would have smiled in welcome, but those days were over and now he had to appeal to less base instincts.

Felice concentrated on removing a flake of paint from her skirt, a subtle movement designed to disarm. She spoke slowly, as if in possession of the conversation. "What assurances of his safety and prospects can I offer my husband?"

Assurances! A month in this place had failed to make a dint in her sense of superiority, as if she were in any position to debate with him. Yet she did so, and had reason: it was in his interests – and those of the impotent and decrepit king he had restored to his throne – that the Earl and men like him be wooed away from Edward because the York pup had become a wolf now that he had a cub to succeed him. A golden wolf with mannered charm that rarely failed to please and with which he assuredly courted Duke Charles of Burgundy, encouraged by Edward's own sister, Duchess Margaret. It might be only a matter of time before the duke's indifference melted beneath the warmth of the York sun, and then there would be the might of Burgundy to assist Edward in regaining the throne. Time mattered.

"I offer him assurances of my enduring friendship. Although we have been estranged these recent years, the Earl cannot be in doubt that my affection for him has ever waned. I give my word, my protection, my influence with King Henry to intercede on his behalf and promote his interests at Court. I have never before been in such a position to help those who help me."

"Your modesty is humbling, my lord, as you have two daughters, each you would see married to a royal son. That is playing a safe game, is it not? And where *is* the Duke of Clarence? You could barely be parted before; how does he feel now that the infant Prince Edward is his father's heir?" Her lips drew back over bared teeth. "What surety lies in your words, my *lord*, when your loyalty turns on a *groat*?"

"You go beyond your station, madam!"

She stood abruptly. "I do not go far enough. My husband will not betray his oath to his king."

Leaning forward, Warwick sneered, "*Which* king? We all did. Henry was our anointed lord to whom we all pledged our fealty."

"And you should remember why that oath was forfeit and where it has led us. What has changed, my lord? Same king, different ruler! Who is next on the throne, I wonder: Edward of Westminster? George of Clarence? Or shall it be Warwick – Broker of Kings?"

Warwick curled and then straightened his fingers; this was going nowhere. "Write to the Earl, Felice. You should be aware that Parliament sits the week after St Andrew's Day, when it will decide the attainder against your husband. Make him see what course lies in his best interests – and those of your son. It is damp here, and the air carries with it… death." He gave a curt bow and left her visibly shaken but defiant in the dreary hole she called sanctuary. Impatient he may be, but let winter take its toll and see which of them broke first.

ROBERT SPOKE TO his brother's back. "You had no other choice."

It had rained on and off all morning, and the unfamiliar grey streets were slick with it. Noxious fumes from the streaming central gutter slid between buildings and through the open window. It would be worse in summer's heat, and the prospect of remaining in Burgundy indefinitely filled the Earl with despondency – if staying were even an option. Duke Charles's welcome had been less than warm, despite his wife's tireless diplomacy on her brother's behalf, but King Edward remained buoyant in the hope that Margaret would eventually persuade her husband that Burgundy's best hopes still lay in a Yorkist alliance. Duke Charles had remained deaf to her persuasion thus far, and Edward had found it necessary to distract himself with the dubious pleasures afforded a king in exile, while contenting himself that at last he had an heir, albeit in sanctuary in Westminster with his queen.

The Earl raised his eyes above the steep tiled roofs of Bruges, beyond the thinning cloud to where patches of blue offered some hope of later sun. Was this it? Would he ever see it shine on his own lands again, or was this all he had to look forward to for the rest of his life? His head ached where the mace had made contact. How could so small an injury leave such a lasting reminder of that insignificant day? Hardly a battle at all. But ache it did. He rested it against the cool surface of the wall and closed his eyes. News of his attainder had reached him at Edward's makeshift court at the Bruges home of Louis Gruuthuse, and came only days after Felice's letter relaying the terms by which he could return home in safety. He detected Warwick's hand, although Felice mentioned only the old king, family honour, and the need for their son to have a father.

His son. The Earl rolled the word about his head, but it left little impression, evaporating no sooner than he thought it. His actions denied his son his inheritance. That should mean something, mean more than it did. And now this: Thomas Lacey had been granted the Fenton estates in return for his devotion to the Crown, leaving Isobel with her mother's single dower manor and an income so low as to be hardly worth counting. When he had read the letter, the Earl thought Isobel must be dead and the lands reverted to Lacey through the entailment. For that split moment the world had blackened, and

Edward had steadied him. "Ill news, my lord?" The conversations around him rumbled to a standstill, and from where he stood with Gloucester, Rob's eyes glimmered darkly from a face made ashen in the harsh winter light, his expression immobile.

"Your Highness, Geoffrey Fenton's lands have been granted to Thomas Lacey."

"That ungrateful little tick? I thought I'd rewarded him well enough with Fenton's offices to keep him sweet. I should have had his head."

"Yes, Your Grace," the Earl all but growled.

"A pity for the girl. I would hate to see those pretty eyes dulled. Still—" he raised his empty glass to a servant and watched while wine as dark as garnets filled it, "—you might take your revenge if we make England's shores again, and save me the trouble. I'll have enough to be getting on with, hey, my lord?"

The Earl flicked the edge of the letter against his thumb, thinking. "Indeed, Your Grace."

"You had no choice," he heard Robert repeat behind him.

"No," the Earl agreed, squinting at the brightening sky. "I did not. Nor had you."

"I had less at stake. I know what this means to you. Without your lands and titles, you have nothing to sustain your affinity, and without affinity you are nothing, and our family will be less than the dust on Warwick's feet. Everything you have believed in, fought for, gone. And if you step one foot on English shores your life will be forfeit—"

"As will yours."

Fresh logs cracked in the heat of the fire. Robert ground out a stray spark with his heel. "So, we all face a life in exile with our king on sufferance at Duke Charles's court for as long as he is willing to let his brother-in-law stay, which might not be long if Louis of France has his way. Or, we risk everything and return to England in the hope Edward can rally enough support to defeat Warwick and reclaim the throne. Beyond credible, is it not?"

"It is," the Earl concurred, "and will remain so unless Charles supports Edward, which is less and less likely with Louis wooing Charles like a whore. Charles is hardly one to turn down the best offer, whether he is married to the King's sister or not, and our cause is looking thin. And Warwick and Clarence are making sure Charles knows it."

One final attempt, then, to take back that which had been taken from him, knowing that failure meant inevitable death, as it did for them all. Part of him yearned for a life uncomplicated by faction, loyalty, and deceit, and that feeling had been growing recently, as if distance from all that he had known made him an observer rather than a participant. The Earl leaned against the windowsill, facing his brother. "What will you do, Robert?"

"You ask me that? Not long ago you would be *telling* me what I should do. Do I have a choice? Do you?" The Earl didn't respond. Something in the street outside had caught his attention. Robert joined him by the window. A young woman had stopped to chat with a servant in the doorway of a house to shelter from a sudden shower. "Are you considering the offer of a pardon?"

The Earl watched the girl laugh, shake her head, and move on, dodging the drips from the overhanging jetties. He closed the casement. "Since loyalty and honour brought us here, we can hardly squander what we, and our father, bought so dearly."

Unhooking the purses on his belt, Rob tossed them on the table and slumped in the chair by the fire, stretching out his legs before it to dry the soles of his boots. "Then you have answered your own question." He began toying with a coin that had fallen free of its pouch. "I have pledged my oath to Gloucester, and nothing but our circumstances have changed. Would you have me do otherwise?"

"Break your oath? Never. But what if we cannot return home?"

"Remain in exile, you mean?" Rob said, considering the implication. "I... would have to find a way back, somehow."

"Why?" the Earl pressed. "You have nothing left to go back to – no wife, no land..." Robert cut him dead with a look, and the Earl cursed his own stupidity. "Forgive me, I did not mean to pour salt on open wounds. So, you will not let your bones rest in foreign soil?"

"It is not so much that, but I value the little honour I have left, and it lies in England."

The Earl thought he detected something else in his brother's voice and waited for him to elaborate, but he failed to continue. "Meaning?"

Robert avoided his gaze and continued flipping the silver groat between his fingers without answering. The Earl considered pursuing the point, but Rob had been more terse lately and he could do without an argument. Instead, he said, "We might be in need of that groat before winter's through."

"Are you that short of coin?" Rob tucked the groat away in the smaller of the two purses. It tinged flatly against another object partly visible as he opened the flap.

The Earl frowned, peered harder. "What is that you have there?"

"This?" He pushed the red tail further into the purse and closed the flap. "Nothing. You were saying about money?"

The Earl raised his brows but resumed the conversation. "Once I've paid for this—" he nodded at the bland room in which they sat, "—living expenses, the clothes on our backs – and the rest promised to the King for men and arms – there will be nothing but the leather of my shoes, and that's wearing thin. Felice took the rest with her into sanctuary, and she is guarding it tighter than a maid her virtue. Without money, the garrison at Tickhill will fall, if it hasn't already. And no word from Isobel," he added quietly. "The castle will be taken, and she is close to her time. Pray God she is kept safe."

WARWICK WAITED UNTIL Felice had taken possession of the only chair as if it were a throne. "You should know that the attainder was passed on the Earl. It was uncontested." He thrummed his fingers against the stone sill. "Have you heard from him?"

She folded her hands neatly. "He has declined your offer. He will not submit."

What surprised him was not the Earl's predicted refusal of the clemency offered him, but that he, Warwick, should feel a stab of regret. It irritated him more than he liked to admit. "His title, lands, offices are forfeit to the Crown. He is, henceforward, denied the privileges of rank and the succour of any in this realm. You understand what this means, don't you?" Her passivity galled him. "You lose everything."

"Not my dower lands, my lord. I retain my inheritance for my son."

"Not... necessarily."

Her delicate nostrils flared. "Under what law?"

"Your husband is a *traitor*. Your son is contaminated by his blood, and you, madam, are deemed similarly tainted. You are to be placed under the rule and governance of one trusted by the King until your husband releases you by his death. You might, if His Grace pleases, be allowed to live out your life in a nunnery." He was beginning to enjoy this, while she was white with anger.

"And my son?"

"Placed with a suitable household now that he is orphaned and found meaningful employment when he comes of age – perhaps as a clerk, *if* he proves worthy of trust."

"And who has been given this exalted task of my governance and my son's upbringing?" His expression said it all. She tutted, disdain stamped across her face.

"Wardship of both you and your children has been granted to me, at least initially; but another has requested that singular honour, and I am considering releasing the burden to him." He waited for her to ask him who, but she refused to give him that degree of satisfaction. "It is Thomas Lacey, if you are interested." That succeeded where nothing else had. Her head whipped around. "He has proved himself invaluable, and I am inclined to reward his loyalty. Why, my lady, you're shaking; are you cold?"

"You reward base servitude with *my* governance? With wardship of my son?" She stood, a spasmodic twitching in the delicate blue veins beneath her eye. "Unless you are willing to drag a woman and her infant from sanctuary, there is nothing more to be said. I bid you good day."

He let her get to the door before he spoke. "You are aware that Roche isn't afforded the status of sanctuary?" he said, his voice soft. "It does not have to be this way. I have the power to restore your son's full inheritance, see you returned to your estates, act as your good lord in *all* things."

She stopped. "Such magnanimity comes at a price, I presume?"

For a moment's breath, he wondered whether she thought he wanted something else. Once, perhaps. "It is a small price to pay for the return, I assure you."

"Your assurances have been somewhat hollow of late."

"Then let me make amends, Felice. Pray, be seated." She remained standing. "As you wish. I want you to leave here and return to Tickhill."

Incredulous, she said, "That is all?"

"No, not all. You are to make a public declaration of your loyalty to King Henry and, on her return to the country, Queen Margaret." He noted her guarded calculation.

"You will have me deny my husband, and for that—"

"You and your son are restored to your rightful dignity, yes. His Grace wishes it to be known that he forgives those who have wronged him through the action of their kin and will show munificence towards them. He wants you to be the light of hope and salvation to others – to show them the way." That might have been going too far, but the Countess was more intent on saving herself than demurring.

"Without harm or hindrance – although my husband lives? What expression of faith will you make to me that you will keep your word?"

"Is my word not enough?" She replied with stony silence. He sighed. "Very well, what is it you want?"

"It is not a matter of what I *want,* my lord, but that which I would see… gone."

"Gone. And will you enlighten me, or do I have to guess?" He should have resisted the temptation to resort to sarcasm. The woman's expression hardened, and she fixed her gaze somewhere over his left shoulder. He cleared his throat. "Let us not play games, Felice. Speak plainly, and I will deal honestly with you."

"There is an encumbrance residing at the castle, an embarrassment that dishonours me." Her eyes met his.

"And you wish this impediment… removed?" Her silence confirmed it. "Ah, yes, of course. And then you will return to the castle?"

"And to Court, with my son – the new Earl – and with all his titles and lands intact and without lien."

He pulled at his earlobe then shrugged. "It is little enough to ask, I suppose." With his hat in hand, he made ready to leave. "Tell me, madam, now that we are agreed, what of the Earl?"

"What of him?" She turned her head and contemplated the crucifix on the wall. "Let him lie in his bed as he has made it. It is not of my doing."

Chapter 21

Isobel hadn't been so bored since childhood, when rain had kept her indoors and her mother's declining health prevented her from enjoying the noisy games of chase and seek she much preferred to the stitching she was obliged to undertake. Yet those long hours were preferable to this endless solitude in which she found herself cut off from the world. But at least she had not been abandoned as Cecily was, nor did she wander the verge of madness as Ursula seemed increasingly wont to do. The older woman was quiet enough now, finishing a baby gown and showing Cecily how to make stitches into tiny daisies along the hem. But the least noise outside set her starting and rocking and, in her troubled mind, she anticipated attack with every look, stare, or nod from the men she met on the way to and from the roof where they kept vigil. So now, on this cheerless day, Isobel sheltered behind the edge of the shutter and peered through a crack. Enemy troops patrolled her Earl's land, and at night light from their campfires speckled the darkness like pox. *Her* Earl. Had she really thought that? When had he ever been "her" Earl? When he represented security and continuity in a chaotic world where the order Isobel had known had been turned on its head, and his absence left a hole she had never anticipated, she thought ruefully.

The last of the autumn leaves had been torn from the fingers of the trees and lay lank on the paths of the wilderness. From the window, they had watched the grass grow untended and weeds spill across borders.

Apples withered on the trees as none but the foolhardy risked becoming a target to a bored bowman from across the river. They were besieged in all but name. The watchmen on the roof of the tower remained vigilant, and Isobel smelled their braziers and heard the distant rattle of dice when she stood in the stairwell to catch the morning air. Occasionally, she heard a shouted warning or reprimand to someone straying within bowshot below, and always – *always* – a tension ebbed and flowed that robbed them of any sense of peace.

The baby kicked and squirmed. Breathing steadily, Isobel tried to let the grinding in her womb wash over her, but her inability to escape the baby's persistent attempts to be free wore at her until she could stay still no longer. And she needed to pee. Again.

"I must get out," she told Ursula, returning from the privy and rinsing her hands in the stone basin, wondering how long it would be before the bouncing inside made her want to go again. Few privies were as clean as the Earl's, and Isobel ensured it remained so in his absence. The thought of using another tainted with other people's stench churned her stomach.

"Pee, pee, peeee." Cecily whisked her skirts over her head, making Moth bark and Chouchou look worried.

"And you can come too. You need some fresh air." Isobel held out her hand, and Cecily danced over to take it. "Here, put on your cloak. Where is your hood?"

"It's raining, my lady," Ursula objected, nonetheless helping her with the heavy mantle.

"So it is, but not very hard."

"But you might take a fever, and you are within your confinement. You should be resting, my lady, and you could be *seen*."

Isobel laughed without humour, sweeping the room with her hand. "So, where are my tapestries? Where's my incense? Show me the hordes of priests praying for my safe delivery and the great crucifix from the chapel watching over me. I am no countess, Ursula. Let in the light and the air, and let me see and be seen, because I am nothing, I am no one. I'm *in-vis-i-ble*."

"But the Earl—"

"Is not here. No one is here. Just you and me—"

"And me, me, meeee," Cecily said, dancing, and Isobel tickled her under her chin and she squeaked, "I'm not Mofth."

"No, Mo*th* is far more obedient, my lady," Isobel teased. "Come, let us get out before it decides to rain even harder."

MIZZLE REPLACED THE rain, and the view from the top of the long, steep steps to the bailey was decidedly dreary, but better than being cooped up. Rain-slicked stone stretched downwards, and Isobel tested it with her toe. Not as slippery as it looked.

Ursula scurried up behind them, blinking wildly. "We must wait for Master Taylor, my lady. Lord Langton said you were not to go anywhere without him."

"Yes, but Lord Robert is not here, either," Isobel said rather sharply, irritated to be reminded of his absence. "But at least he is safe," she added in an undertone. "Besides, it will be dark if we wait for Master Taylor to get back, and we will probably meet him in the bailey and he can join us then." She started down the grey-hued stairs with a greater degree of caution than she normally allowed herself, feeling the additional weight of her belly in the joints of her knees and wondering if she looked as ungainly as she felt. There were few people about, and none gave her any more consideration than she did them, huddled as they were against the weather.

The enclosed allées and courts of the fair pleasance were hardly the wide, wilder spaces of the old wilderness garden, but they smelled green and alive under the dead sky, and the freedom Isobel felt was all the sweeter for it. A lone wren pierced the air with song. Clutching her ball in one hand and Nan in the other, Cecily charged ahead and out of sight, chased by the two dogs. Isobel followed slowly, supporting her stomach with her hands. She revelled in the subdued greens and browns of the winter garden and the way raindrops reflected the subtle light, suspended like stars at the tips of branches and caught by the threads of a web. Across the garden, the wren sounded a warning volley. By the time Isobel reached the end of the first allée with her back already aching, Cecily had raced around all four sides. Ursula waylaid her before she tumbled, giggling, into Isobel. "Take care, my lady!" she admonished, and the girl wriggled from her grip and rushed ahead, squealing like a piglet.

"You look like the imp at Lincoln," Isobel called after her. "Watch out, or the angel will catch you and turn you to stone!" The squealing continued, growing fainter as she circled the cloister-like garden, louder again as she drew nearer. Suddenly, it stopped. "I wager she is hiding," Isobel laughed. "Although Heaven knows the dogs are making such a din they will give her away. Let us surprise her." They doubled back, navigating by the occasional *woof*, until they rounded a corner and Isobel stopped in her tracks at the scene before her. Chou hunkered down, growling, her ears flattened against her skull as Cecily stared up at a tall, cloaked man who stood over her, his back to them.

Isobel found her voice. "Get away from her!" He turned as she neared, a pale-eyed man, cave-cheeked and lips reed-thin. She didn't recognise him. "Who are you? What do you want?" she demanded, nearing him. "Cecily, come here." She held out her hand to her.

"He has my ball, Is'bel," Cecily said, pointing. Against the pale skin of his almost fleshless hands, the garish colours of her ball clashed. He held onto it, and Isobel took another step forward, anger beginning to swell.

"Give it back to Lady Cecily!"

"My lady, keep away, keep away!" Ursula tried to pull her back. The man had neither moved nor returned the ball but kept it turning in his hands without taking his eyes from Isobel. She reached for the dagger on her belt beneath her cloak. His eyes shifted to her swollen waist, to her hand now shakily holding the slender blade. Wordlessly, he span around and, dropping the ball, vanished between the gracile trunks of the linden trees.

Ursula let go of Isobel's arm. "Who was that man? We should have waited for Master Taylor. We should have waited!"

Cecily proffered her ball. "Is'bel, that man took my Hector ball."

"Did he touch you?" Isobel asked. Cecily shook her head. "We had better go," Isobel said, feeling the walls crowd and the absence of overlooking windows.

Leaving the seclusion of the garden, they saw no sign of the stranger in the bailey. Chou dogged their heels, but Moth had to be kept on her short lead to prevent her from escaping.

"Where are you going?" Ursula flapped as Isobel headed towards the guardhouse.

"He is not a ghost; someone else must have seen him." Isobel raised her voice as she saw a familiar figure leave the building. "Sergeant!"

If her obvious pregnancy offended him, he hid it well. He shook his large head in slow sweeps as she described the cloaked stranger. "None's been through these gates this side of the day, mistress."

"I did not recognise him. He is not of the Earl's household, I am certain of it. And he should *not* have been in the garden. He took Lady Cecily's ball; he was able to get that close to her."

Cecily wrinkled her nose. "He smelled like wet Moth."

"And this were but a short while back?" he asked.

"Yes, but his mantle was soaked through and his boots wet. He must have been here some time. We did not imagine him," Isobel stated.

"Nor did I say ye did, lass." He eased a stubby finger between his sallet and his skull. "You be getting yersen back to the tower, and I'll tell t'constable what you told me."

"You will find the man?"

"Aye, if he's to be found. An' I reckon I'll tell Philip Taylor to be getting his fat rump up them stairs when I see him, an' all. You shouldn't be about alone, not wi' the Earl gone and the enemy abroad." He hailed two of his men, so Isobel didn't have a chance to tell him that she had promised Taylor she would not stir from the tower until his return and had hoped to be back before he knew she had gone. "These two'll take a turn about and see ye safely to the tower, mistress. You don't want to be slipping now."

Low cloud produced a heavier mist that lay in fine droplets on the weave of their hoods with penetrating damp. Cecily shivered, but between them and the warmth of a fireside lay the long flight of steps to the tower. They were almost to the halfway point – where the stairs hesitated before jinking to the left – when Isobel stopped for the third time, leaning against the stone wall, heaving air. Behind her, she heard one of the men stall and grumble. She looked over her shoulder. "You can leave us now; we are nearly there." They hesitated, and then the older man touched his hand to his brow in salute. "It is not *that* far," Isobel murmured without conviction as the men left them there, and she peered upwards into the intensifying dusk, calculating the number of steps left to climb.

"My lord won't like it. I said my lady shouldn't be out. You shouldn't be out," Ursula moaned, gathering her heavy skirts and waiting for Isobel to resume the ascent. "Take care, Lady Cecily, don't push." Putting out an arm to prevent Cecily from barging past as Isobel puffed up the steps, Ursula knocked the ball from her hand. It rolled down the stairs, gathering speed, with Chou and Moth barking in pursuit. Cecily wailed and set off after them, nimble-footed despite the wet stone. Isobel waited until Cecily retrieved the ball before continuing the climb to the tower. A movement ahead, so slight it might have been a trick of the light; there, at the bend of the stairs with the little platform where the high walls either side deepened the shadows. As she approached the landing, Isobel jumped as a small shape scuttled down past her. A rat. She fervently hoped Ursula hadn't seen it, or she wouldn't hear the last of it. Her breathing loud in her ears, Isobel reached the landing, bending slightly as cramps warned her to slow down, and she put out a hand to steady herself against the wall. The warm wall moved, materialised, became human. Her mouth opened, but a hand clamped her cry, another her arm. Using his thin weight, the stranger heaved her towards the stairs and Isobel felt herself lose balance, topple back. Grabbing the nearest thing to prevent her falling, she heard the man's agonised yell as something came away in her hand. A chunk of fair, thin hair. Steadying herself against the wall, she stared at the hair, at him, his hand against his bleeding skull. He lunged. From behind her, pale streaks shot past as Chou leaped and Moth latched onto his booted calf, giving Isobel a chance to secure her footing. She fumbled for her dagger, cloak tangling, at the same time yelling, "Ursula, protect Cecily!" But by now, her cries were drowned by Ursula's screams and, from the far side of the bailey, the sound of warning shouts and arms drawn. Ursula bounded up the stairs towards Isobel, arms outstretched, eyes glazed, frenzied spittle on her lips, a wild thing, demented. Shaking the dogs off him, the man reached behind his back and Isobel saw his blade. She lashed out blindly with her own knife. Soft flesh tore, and he dropped the dagger, cursing, then, drawing his arm back, aimed a downwards punch at Isobel's belly. In the instant it took for Isobel to bring her arms in front to protect her unborn child, Ursula threw herself between them, taking the full force of his blow on the side of her head. Flung backwards, she teetered on the edge of the top step with hands grappling air, mouth open in a silent scream, and she fell, rolling and sliding in a tumble of limbs.

Soldiers had almost reached the bottom stair. With the dogs snapping at his heels, the man ran down the steps three at a time, over Ursula's still body wedged sideways across the steps, past Cecily staring at her, and pushed through the first guard to reach the stairs.

Isobel vaguely heard shouted commands, the sergeant thundering, "Take 'im alive!" Saw a soldier reach Ursula, cross himself, rearrange her skirts to cover her exposed legs. She was aware of Cecily – floppy and mute – being plucked from beside the body and carried up the steps towards her. Isobel thought she knew the square face approaching from the gloom, felt a strong arm support her, heard concerned remonstrations, but the rest dwindled into a point of consciousness and then faded altogether.

Chapter 22

It was the growing pain in her belly that woke her from the fog in which she drifted. Like the nagging ache of monthly courses, but worse – searing and with intent. In the Earl's bed, Isobel sat up dazed and thirsty, feeling sick. She opened her mouth to call for Ursula, but the woman stared blank-eyed from her memory. Remorse and loss combined, but the discomfort grew until it pushed the grief aside, and it was all she could do not to be overwhelmed by it and the fear that followed close behind. She lay there, panting, until the moment passed, focusing on the single candle burning by the bed and the fire on the hearth by which the dogs lounged. She seemed to be alone. Where was Cecily? Isobel let the nausea subside enough so that she could ease herself from the bed without immediately throwing up. She took one step, two, and a sudden warmth flooded her thighs. She looked down: a dark pool seeped from beneath her kirtle and ran in lines between the tiles. Aghast, she cried out, a cry cut short by a shock of pain. Instantly, heavy footsteps beat the floor, dappled light danced from a lantern, and Philip Taylor emerged from the vestibule, his head swathed in a bandage through which fresh blood oozed. He took one look at the gathering fluid then at her face. "Have ye cramps?" Isobel nodded, not trusting her voice. "Your bairn's on its way."

"She can't be!" Isobel gasped as another spasm struck. "I'm not ready, and… and I have no one in attendance. Ursula… she was… I…"

"Aye, well, it has other ideas." He put the lantern on the table. "Lean on me; I'll get you sorted."

With the wet linen clinging to Isobel's legs, Taylor helped her to the Earl's chair, pulling the cushions from under her before she soaked them. He took a basin and put it on the table, then filled several jugs and a ewer and placed them on trivets by the fire. Now pin-sharp with intermittent pain, Isobel remembered. "Where is Cecily? Where's Ursula? What happened to your head?"

"My lady's safe with the lord steward's wife, and Mistress Ursula... aye, well, she is in the Lord's care now. As for my skull—" he put a rueful hand to his head, "—it were harder than the vagabond expected, but not hard enough. Now then, stay sitting or ye'll fall, and wait; I won't be long. Count between cramps. You can count, can't you?" That remark deserved a pithy reply, and when he didn't get one because Isobel had to clamp her lips tight against the pain, Taylor's expression clouded. "Sit tight and breathe steady now – slow and steady."

Isobel numbered the moments between cramps until she could hear his steady steps no longer and she lost count altogether. She wanted Ursula; she missed her absolute certainty that all would be well, but above all, she missed *her*. She didn't have the opportunity to mourn, because by the time Philip Taylor returned with a woman Isobel had never seen before – broad-shouldered and with arms of uncooked dough – one wave of pain rolled into another, pushing all thoughts into oblivion.

There was no time for introductions. The woman took one look at Isobel's pallid, sweating face and, peering beneath her sodden skirts, jerked a thumb at a bag she had unceremoniously dumped on the table. "Geet me shears and two jugs o' water, an' make them right hot," she instructed the sergeant. Then to Isobel, "This your first birthing?"

Taylor answered when a searing sensation robbed Isobel of speech. "Aye, it is that."

"Let's pray it won't be ye last," she grunted, tossing the shears into the brass jug and setting it close to the fire. Taking a small, linen-wrapped parcel, she bound it to Isobel's thigh, murmured something, then, crossing herself, rolled her loose sleeves above her elbows and thrust her arms into the basin of scalding water he had poured until they turned pink. Kneeling before the chair, she raised Isobel's feet either side of her, pressing the soles against her padded hips. "Keep 'em there, and when I says *push*, push *'ard*. You, master, stand behind 'er and take under 'er arms." She opened Isobel's legs, exposing her to her scrutiny. "Eh, but this 'un's right 'asty to be out, an' no mistake. It'll not be so eager when it gets 'ere, I'll warrant. It'll be bawling to get back in." She cackled to herself. "There's the head. Now ye breathe slow, girl, keep it slow, an' when I says, you push an' pant, got it? Push an' pant."

"My chaplet," Isobel gasped, forgetting she no longer had it, feeling a wave begin to swarm no sooner had the last subsided. "Please… my… beads." She tried not to cry out, to keep the fear from unfolding and stretching and consuming her. Taylor pressed a crude paternoster of wood and bone into her hand, and she clutched it, feeling her body run away with her, out of control as the pain grew, expanded, peaked.

"Push!" the woman said. "C'mon now, ye can do better than tha'. Push *harder*."

Isobel tried to focus in silent desperation, "Have mercy on me. Have mercy on me," repeated over and over.

His roughened chin grazing her temple, Taylor's arms supported her weight. "It's all right to cry out. Cry it out; there's none here but thee and me and the midwife, and she'll not be telling."

But she couldn't; she kept Rob close within her, using the pain to fuel what control she had to keep her from calling his name, so that all she could say between pants was, "Buena. I want Buena," almost sobbing with the excruciating demands of forcing her baby out.

"Yer's almost there. Another push, *now*!" And Isobel strained, almost hearing the tearing as she split like the pomegranate in the Earl's hands.

"That's a fine bairn you have there." Taylor's voice melted into her consciousness, swam, reformed. "Well-favoured. Make its sire proud, all right."

Isobel moistened dry lips. "Rob—"

Taylor grunted. "And its uncle, too, no doubt." A thin cry broke her stupor and ceased as abruptly. She opened her eyes. The midwife busied by the table, her back to them, small rapid movements witnessing to her haste.

"My baby... why does she not cry?" The woman didn't answer. Isobel held out her arms. "Give her to me!" The woman turned around, carrying a swaddled bundle that lay still, and a ball of despair rose in Isobel's throat. The midwife leaned forward, placing the unmoving form in her arms. Unfocused pewter eyes stared from a small red face.

"Eh, I don't know about a lass, but ye've a good strong lad there. See him looking an' looking and nowt but a pig's squeal from 'im an' all."

A boy. His fine, creased skin was already drying in patches, his snub nose blunt, dark hair tufted and unkempt like the discarded feathers of a crow. He was the ugliest thing Isobel had ever laid eyes on; he was the most beautiful being in all creation and entirely beloved. Her child. Her son.

His mouth puckered, his lips moving silently, and his eyes found hers. Her heart crumbled, and nothing else mattered – not Rob, nor the Earl, nor whichever king upon whose head the crown might rest. This was her son, and the world beyond had ceased to exist in the time it took for him to possess her heart and wrap it in threads as fine as silk and stronger than steel. Isobel cradled him and kissed his warm, soft forehead in welcome, breathing in his unfamiliar scent. He mewed, a small sound, kitten-thin.

"Reckon he's goin' to be hungry afore long," the midwife observed. "Let's get ye cleaned up and see what damage's done, and by tha' time the wet nurse'll be ready to take 'im."

Isobel looked down at her child. "Wet nurse?"

"Have ye none?" She made it sound as if Isobel were either a simpleton or negligent. She tutted, muttering under her breath. "Eh, but you ladies are right 'uns."

"That's enough of that," Taylor said. "Know your place, woman."

"I know my place well enough, master, an' I knows that bairns go in the same ways they comes out, whatever their dam and no matter the sire." She sniffed, hitching her skirts and kneeling before the chair again. "You still 'aving pains?" she asked, and when Isobel nodded, she grunted, "Tha'll be the afterbirth comin' and ne'er too soon." And, taking rags, she spread them at the foot of the chair where blood already stained the floor. "I knows a wet nurse in town'll take this bairn and give him suck. She's clean and her own bairn's nigh on weaned now, and she'll be glad of the coin."

Isobel felt an ugly sensation deep in her womb, and her muscles tightened in anticipation of pain. "No," she managed. "I will feed him myself."

"Push it out, mistress, tha's the way." Warmth spread between her legs, trickling, oozing. The midwife scooped up the contents of the dripping cloth and inspected it. She seemed satisfied enough and, putting the folded cloth to one side, began mopping Isobel down briskly. "Oh, so you'll be feedin' 'im yersen, will ye? Suit yerself, but I'll warrant you'll come bawlin' when he starts from hunger and yer milk won't flow – he bein' yer first, like. Before I go, I'll coddle this afterbirth and that'll get yer milk goin' if nothin' else. Mind, now, you ladies are meant fer breedin', not feedin', an' if ye change yer mind, send yer maidservant to me an' I'll get Agnes up 'ere quicker than tha'. You'll be thankin' me, no doubt..." she added with a sideways slide of her eyes.

"You'll be paid," Taylor growled from where he leaned against the wall at a respectable distance. "And you'll leave that caul when you go."

She ignored him. "You send yer servant. You'll be needin' her right enough. There's things need doin' only a woman should see, and he's seen more than he should." She skirted a look at Taylor, who remained expressionless, arms crossed on his chest and immovable. "Well – where is she, yer servant woman?"

"Dead," Taylor said bluntly when Isobel couldn't answer, hugging the now snuffling baby close, her arms aching from holding him carefully but refusing to let it show in case the woman saw her weakness and took him from her.

"Dead, eh? Reckon you'll be needing that caul more'n I will, wi' your luck. Course, if yer gives it to me, I'll make sure I'll get a good price, an' you'll have enough to hire another servant. Can recommend some to ye an' all."

"That won't be necessary. You finished, woman?"

"I 'ave, master, but for a fee I can stay awhile."

Her chatter crowded and confused with twisted vowels and half-eaten words that wheedled, and Isobel wanted her to stop talking and leave her alone with her baby. "Please," she said, "just go. And I thank you for your service to me. To us," she added, softly.

The midwife hefted to her feet, hoisting her sagging breasts within their woollen swaddling. "Aye, well, I'll make that coddle first and be off then – *when* ye've paid me," she added pointedly.

THE ROOM EMPTIED of the midwife's noise, leaving Isobel and her son alone while Taylor – ensuring the caul was left behind – showed the woman the stairs. The baby and Isobel regarded each other, strangers yet bound by ties closer than any, and she hadn't a clue what to do next. His snuffling had become became persistent, and in a moment he would cry. Despite her weariness, she had to find a way to satisfy his growing hunger.

"I should have asked how I must feed him," Isobel said helplessly when the sergeant returned. He looked awkward now that the immediate crisis was over. He waved a stumpy finger in the general direction of her breasts.

"You, er, feed him… there."

She looked down at her sweat-stained smock. "But *how*?"

"I didn't take much notice when my wife nursed our bairns," he confessed. "Her dam showed her how with our firstborn, and then it came to her easy enough."

Isobel wanted to bathe – to bathe and then sleep – but the baby's bow mouth pursed, and his plaintive wail drove rods through her.

Pip Taylor winced. "Perhaps if ye take to thy bed you'll find it easier," he suggested.

He helped her to her feet. She ached: her back from the rigid chair, her legs, her belly. The burning between her thighs had lessened to a persistent throb, but she felt damp and sticky, and could still smell blood and birthing fluid in the air. It was no good. Isobel handed the baby to the startled man and set him clumsily rocking the child while she peeled herself free of the clinging clothes behind the screen.

The dry smock felt fresh against her sore skin when she climbed onto the bed, and when she relieved Taylor of the baby, and the bundle brushed against her, Isobel felt her breasts tingle in response. The baby ceased crying and turned his head blindly towards her chest.

"Reckon he'll know what to do," Taylor said and, excusing himself, left them to find out.

Isobel pulled a breast free of the fabric, the enlarged, sensitised nipple hardening in the cooler air. The baby began mewling again, and she brought his mouth to it. He snuffled jerkily, found it, and immediately began suckling hard. A sensation like warm pins and needles rushed down her shoulders, swelling her breasts, pumping milk to the nipple where his tiny mouth worked. She felt triumphant.

It was only later, once Isobel emerged from fitful sleep to wake and listen for signs of his breathing, that she remembered. "I wish Ursula could have seen you," she whispered to her sleeping son. "You would have made her happy." Emotion pricked her eyes. "Ursula saved me; saved you. She gave her life so that you might live." Listening for his shallow breaths, the signs of life, Isobel hugged him close.

THE NEXT FEW days passed in a blur of waking and sleeping, the stinging between her legs every time she needed to move from the bed vying with the excruciating tenderness of her engorged breasts. The baby slept only a few hours at a time, allowing her to snatch precious sleep before he woke again, crying. By the third day, Isobel could have wept with exhaustion as he fretted at her breast, sucking briefly before turning his head away despite his hunger, his face reddening, his eyes screwed up in disgust. She felt a profound sense of failure. The baby bleated plaintively, and Isobel wanted to wail with him.

"I do not know what to do, Pip, he will not feed."

"Let me send for the wet nurse," Taylor offered.

"I should be able to do this. Other women feed their babies, why can I not feed mine?"

"Perhaps your milk's sour?" he suggested.

"And how would I know?" Isobel said in desperation. "Most other women seem to know what to do."

"Most other women have a dam or servant to show them how, not a bloated pig's bladder like me."

"You have done your best and kept me fed. And you showed me how a baby's napkin should be tied."

He cringed at the memory of the over-tight napkin she had managed to mangle. "Aye, well, he'll be wanting to sire bairns of his own one day. But this won't do, mistress. You need a woman's care. That babe's nigh famished, and you're weak enough with lack of proper sleep. There's no decent servant to be had in town, and none'll serve here in these times."

"I know." Isobel scowled. "No respectable woman would serve the Earl's *mistress.*"

"That's not what I meant. You have nowt to be ashamed of, despite what some'll say."

Isobel coloured. He had done as much as could be expected of a man: made sure she had food to eat and ale to drink. He brought water to heat by the fire for her to wash and saw to it that soiled linen was taken and laundered before it became rank; but he could not attend her as Ursula had done, and there was no one left to do so. And money was running short.

Up until his flight, the Earl had ensured the money from her lands was accounted for and kept secure, an allowance being made to her on a regular basis, not that she needed much; she had little to spend it on. Now, however, when she had approached his steward, Hyde, only a few weeks before, he had frowned at her request.

"No money has been received from Beaumancote, Mistress Fenton. I expected the quarterly fines and dues at the end of November, but they were not forthcoming, nor any explanation why they have failed to be sent." His lumpy forehead formed corrugations of concern as her face fell. "My lord Earl would not wish you to want for anything. Here—" he delved into his own purse, holding out a number of coins, "—take this."

"I cannot take your money!" Isobel said, aghast. "Surely the Earl will lend me some and take what's due when my rents arrive?"

"Forgive me, mistress, I am certain my lord would do so; however, there are certain restraints brought about by the extraordinary circumstance in which we find ourselves."

"There is no money," Isobel had confided to Taylor when Ursula was out of earshot. "Some of the coin has been sent to the Earl in Burgundy, but the rest the Countess took with her. The rents have not been collected or, if they have, they have been intercepted. I did not know things had become so lean."

"Aye, they have. I didn't want to alarm you, but the garrison's not been paid. There's more than one way of weakening our defences, as Warwick knows. He can watch the garrison crumble by starving it of funds, and then it'll take only a few well-aimed cannon to reduce it to its knees. Took six balls to bring Banbrough down. Six. The garrison was ready to fall before the first shot were ever made."

"My lord steward will not surrender," she cut in, "and the constable wouldn't betray the Earl."

"He might not, but a hungry garrison with the promise of full bellies, a heavy purse, and a free pardon to find new employment will persuade even the stoutest heart to make new loyalties."

"But not you. Tell me you will *never* betray Lord Langton."

He scratched his chin slowly, eyeing her. "I reckon I'll stick it out here a while longer. I like me own company, and the food's good. I get a bed to sleep in, and while the ale keeps flowing I've not reason to look elsewhere." She let her shoulders relax. "Mind," he added, "things could get interesting if the rumours I hear are true."

"Rumours?"

"Aye. I've heard that the Earl might be attainted."

"He cannot be! He has not betrayed anyone. He's always been loyal to the Ki—" She stopped abruptly, her mouth still open. She closed it. Taylor nodded slowly, his head bobbing like a heavy apple on its branch caught in a breeze.

"That's right. Which king?"

"And if he's attainted, then... what happens?"

"Then we might be looking for a new place to rest our weary heads." He stood, slapping his thick thighs. "But don't you be worrying about that, now. Many a thing can come to pass before we find ourselves without a roof over our heads, and many a thing surely will. Let's leave it to the Almighty, shall we? He always seems to know what's best, even if we don't know it ourselves." Isobel must have looked surprised, because his stubbly face broadened into a grin. "Never would have taken me for a pious man, would ye? And I'm not. I've done enough in my time to keep me in Purgatory for the rest of eternity, yet I'd say that the best path is on the right side of God, wouldn't ye?"

❦

Isobel circled the confines of the chamber until the baby eventually cried himself to sleep, having driven the dogs from the room, then collapsed across the bed next to him and watched his sleeping face. Even in this last week his features had smoothed, and Isobel searched them for signs of his father. She thought she found him in the shape of his eyes, but she also saw the Earl in the colour of his hair, and she ceased looking for others in his infant face and started seeing him for himself. Although mostly still tightly bound to keep his limbs straight, at times Isobel loosened the cloths and let him wave his fragile arms, seeing him explore the air with fingers splayed. She had learned to tie his napkin and to bathe him in the basin. He liked her stroking his arms and legs and, now that his cord had almost dried and shrivelled, he soothed under her touch when she rubbed his stomach. She and he were all the world, and the world was within these walls. But now, Isobel was too tired to do anything other than monitor his regular breathing.

"He's stronger than you think," Taylor told her earnestly. "You don't need to watch him draw breath – he's doing that by himself. You'd do him better service getting yourself rested."

But she was beyond sleep. Fatigue couldn't blunt her love for her son, but it had dulled her appetite. Isobel struggled to eat what Taylor brought her, and her breasts – although still raw where the infant mouth fought to feed – were less full than they had been. She was losing the battle and would have to relent and let a stranger give him the nourishment she failed to provide. She felt sick at the thought of it. Sick and tired.

Nor could Isobel cope with Cecily's stream of questions and her inquisitive fingers or find the strength to hide from her the tears that sprang too readily when she asked where Ursula had gone. In the end, Isobel had to ask Taylor to take Cecily back to the steward's wife, and suffered the resulting downturned mouth and reproachful eyes that lingered in her mind's eye long after she had left. It wasn't the child's fault. Isobel had come to the end of whatever reserves she had kept in store for the birth of her child. She had never expected to be alone at this point, nor realised how reliant she had been on Ursula and even the solid presence of the Earl, and her son's cries of hunger fed her mounting misery.

Isobel must have drifted into sleep because she dreamed she was at Beaumancote, drenched in sun, chasing dandelion clocks on the summer breeze, and dancing in the long grass between the apple trees trying to catch them to the music of laughter. She heard her mother call her name and looked around, and her dam laughed and clapped and sang in time to her steps, holding out her arms. Isobel ran to her, back to the safety of her past, to a world she thought could never change. But the closer Isobel came the more distant her mother seemed, until all that remained was an impression and the sound of her voice calling, calling. Grief spilled into the garden, the darkness of loss that comes with the knowledge that nothing can remain the same. All must pass.

Desolation engulfed her, deep sobs stealing breath, but the voice kept calling – drawing her back, not letting her go. Isobel clung to it, but it was not her mother's voice now, but one she had never heard before, yet strangely familiar. Isobel tried to open her eyes, as if the grief had stitched them shut and made her blind; but the more she opened them the fainter the voice became until, at last, she surfaced from sleep.

The baby still slept. A candle had been lit and left beside the bed, casting warm light over the surface of his translucent skin. The flame guttered as someone moved behind the bed hangings. Isobel thrust her hand beneath the pillow, already turning to face the threat with her ballock dagger in hand. A figure jerked back, grunting in surprise, and then from the shadows emerged orbs black as charcoal.

Screwing sleep from her eyes, Isobel looked again. *"Buena?"* She swallowed, laughed, felt her face crumple, tried to hide it in her hands but was still clutching the knife. Buena eased it from her grip, placed it on the side table, took Isobel's now shaking hand and placed it against her own face. Warm, sun-tautened skin stretched over high cheeks, pleated around upturned eyes. Real, living, not a phantom of a dream.

"How… how did you get here?" Isobel asked when, eventually, she had scrubbed the last of the wretchedly predictable tears from her face and her voice no longer broke on each word. Buena had done little except watch and frown, but now she nodded towards the door behind her.

"Master Taylor?" Isobel translated her hand movements. "He sent for you? Why?"

Buena looked pointedly at Isobel in her dilapidated state, at the linen lying in pale lumps where it had been dropped, at the half-eaten food abandoned on the table, then at the baby on the verge of waking, hungry again.

"Oh," Isobel said, "I see." Then, "This is my son." She held him out to Buena, who hesitated, looking tight-lipped at the bundle, and Isobel thought she was going to refuse. "*My* son, Ba'na."

Buena took him then, holding him stiffly at first. He began making little sucking movements, wriggling in his bonds. Moving carefully, she loosened the wrap and eased it open enough to let him push an arm free. His hand found her finger and gripped it, trying to pull it towards his mouth. She smiled.

Isobel sighed, settling back against the bolster and preparing to feed him. "He is hungry. He is always hungry." Buena gave him back, and Isobel offered him the less sore nipple, gritting her teeth as he latched on and chewed with his hard gums. Buena watched for a moment. Then she leaned forward, disengaged him and, stuffing a bolster under Isobel's elbow, adjusted the baby's position. He began to wail, but she directed him firmly against her and held him there until more of the nipple was in his mouth and he was fully engaged, then released him. He stayed put, sucking furiously. Milk flowed.

Mystified, Isobel said, "And that is it? That is all I do?"

Buena gave a satisfied nod and, from deep in her throat, laughed.

Chapter 23

Buena had not come empty-handed. On the table by the window, Geoffrey Fenton's scratched and worn seal gleamed in reflected winter sunlight as it rested on top of a letter. The seal felt comfortingly heavy in Isobel's hand. Sliding it onto the silk ribbon, she tied it around her neck where it belonged and, picking up the letter, broke the wax.

It was the first news from Beaumancote for months. Arthur Moynes's agitated hand scoured the page, speaking more eloquently of his anxiety than the words used to convey the news. He had written the letter in some haste, but couched his language as if he expected someone other than she might read it.

> *To my lady Isobel Fenton be this delivered forthwith,*
> *I recommend me to you and send tidings of your estates and your people therein. I give thanks for the use of your honourable sire's seal, safe delivered by he that nobly bore it, and return to you the same.*

Isobel released a slow breath and prayer of thanks. He continued, and the flush of warmth was short-lived:

> *Forasmuch as it shall be said, I send no news that you might take comfort, for without captain nor rule this house and thy lands cannot stand against the tide now turned, for the pike devours the minnow, and all the little fish withal shall seek sustenance*

from others else the luce take them and destroy them, for that which was plentiful is now no more.
I send a good servant known to ye, that she might find a place without offence to her person, and serve thee well.

Isobel became conscious that Buena and Cecily had suspended their lopsided conversation and were waiting, their faces turned to her. Isobel raised her head and straightened her shoulders. "I must go to Beaumancote."

Rocking the baby in one arm, Buena's bony fingers grasped the roll of belly through Isobel's dress, and she shook her head violently. Isobel removed her hand and stood. "I must. I am much stronger now, and my people need me." Buena indicated the baby and patted her own breasts. Isobel stroked his sleepy cheek with the back of her thumb, and he opened his mouth expectantly like a fledgling. "I know, but what else can I do? Without the Earl I do not know how long it will be before Thomas makes trouble again. Arthur says he is already stirring. No wonder the rents have not been paid; people are frightened."

Close to the door, hand as ever resting on the pommel of his short sword and the bandage removed to reveal what should have been a deathblow to his head, Taylor had remained at a respectful distance with an ear towards the stairs to the lower chamber. Now he spoke up. "It's not right to travel so recently delivered, mistress. Besides, you'll not get far with the enemy swarming like ants and the roads not being a place for a young woman."

"Buena made it here safely, and if you are there to protect me—"

"Begging your pardon, but Lord Langton said I were to keep you safe here, and safe is where I'll keep you."

"Lord Langton does not know the circumstances, and *I* am lord of my manors. I have a duty to be there to protect them. If you refuse to help me, I will go by myself if I have to."

"Aye, he said you would say that and all."

Her lips pursed. "Did he indeed?"

"Aye, he did."

Better sleep and a well-fed son had given her energy and purpose, and motherhood a sense of responsibility towards those whose lives and well-being depended on her lordship. Isobel might not be the Earl, nor have her father's wisdom, but she was their lord by right of birth and would exercise those rights in the protection and maintenance of her people. She had watched her father in his governance but had learned the meaning of it from the Earl. She spoke with grave authority. "Nevertheless, Master Taylor, you will do as I bid. Buena, pack as many things as we might need. We can travel in short stages and still make it in time for Yule. We made it to Beaumancote this time last year in half the time, and no one will suspect a woman travelling with her child and servants. They would have no cause to stop us. Anyway," she bent over the baby, kissing his forehead and feeling oddly liberated, "I wish my son to celebrate his first Christmas where he belongs. There is nothing to keep us here; it is time to go home." Buena exchanged looks with Taylor, and he opened his mouth to reply, but a small voice piped up from beside the fire where Cecily sat cross-legged with Chou and Moth.

"Can I come?"

Isobel's heart twisted. In her determination to do what was right for her own people, she had overlooked the little girl. Cecily hopped to her feet and joined them, looking up earnestly. "I won't get in the way, and I can help with the baby."

Kneeling, Isobel took both small hands in her own. "I am not going to leave you behind, and you are not in the way. Where would I be without you?" Isobel enfolded her, and Cecily wrapped her arms around her neck. "We will all go to Beaumancote, and you can meet Alfred, my dog, and help me teach John Appleyard the difference between dandelions and daisies. And I will show you my secret."

"What's your secret?"

"It's a secret."

She giggled, and Isobel hugged her again.

Taylor cleared his throat. "You can't go to Beaumancote, mistress—"

Isobel turned on him, eyes snapping. "Do *not* tell me what I can and cannot do; you have no such authority over me."

He came further into the room. "You cannot go to Beaumancote," he repeated gravely. "It is no longer yours."

Chapter 24

THE MESSAGE QUIVERED a little in her hand, and Isobel put it down again. She had hoped Rob might have written, but why would the Earl's brother have need to write to someone like her? It would only have raised brows and questions, and the fewer of those, the better. The Earl's neat, controlled writing and formal greeting were what she expected, but she detected more in his explanation of the loss of her land than he perhaps meant to reveal: an apology, perhaps? Or was it remorse that she had become victim to his stubborn-nosed politics and personal feud? Isobel might have been mistress of her own manor by now if it hadn't been for him, but then she would be married to Thomas Lacey, and the mere thought of *that* made her skin crawl. How she had changed. Could she resent the Earl for that? Would her father have behaved differently and, for that matter, would she?

Isobel scoured the letter again for news of Rob, which was there almost by default in the "we fare well enough and trust thou dost also," and the Earl asked her to write to him in return. "What shall I tell him?" she asked Buena, more rhetorically than anything else, because she knew what he wanted to hear, what he wanted her to tell him; but she couldn't give him that, so she began with saying that Cecily was safe but that Ursula was not, and that she was delivered of a son but not his name because, as yet, he had none.

It was Cecily who brought the subject of a name to the fore. Buena was changing the baby by the fire. "He likes it when I do this." Cecily blew into the palm of his tiny hand, making him wriggle.

"I am sure he does," Isobel smiled, concentrating on drawing a perfect "d-o-g" for Cecily to copy on her slate.

"You're not looking, Is'bel. Look, he likes it – see? Gowk likes it, don't you?"

Isobel turned on the stool to look at her. "*What* did you call him, Cecily?"

"Gowk." She batted long lashes. "His name is Gowk."

"Gowk." Isobel took a deep breath, counting to ten. "No, it is not. Whatever else it is, it certainly isn't… *Gowk*." She pulled a face.

"But he doesn't have any other name, and you said I couldn't call him Nan!" she protested.

Buena raised her eyebrows. The child had a point.

"Cecily, why, in Sweet Jesu's name, did you come up with *that*?"

"Because he goes like this…" and she imitated a mouth opening and closing, "… when he's hungry. Pip said."

"Do you mean Master Taylor?"

Cecily nodded with enthusiasm. "Pip says he looks like a gowk."

"*Did* he. Hmm. Master Taylor!" Isobel called, and heard what sounded like an ale cup being put down in haste. He ambled in from the vestibule. "*Why* do you call my son 'gowk'?"

He wiped his mouth with the back of his hand, looking apologetic. "Eh? Oh, aye, well the bairn reminded me of one." Isobel must have looked none the wiser, because he elaborated. "A bird, like what you'd call a *cuckoo*, maybe? You know, when he wants feeding… and… such…" He trailed off, thumbing in the direction of the vestibule. "I'd best be getting back."

"Yes, you had better," Isobel said somewhat archly, and to Cecily, "There will be no more *Gowk*, do you understand?"

She pouted. "Then what *do* I call him, Is'bel?"

Isobel had lain awake at night worrying about it, and no matter which way she turned, the fraught question of his name remained unanswerable.

Taylor tarried at the door. "The lad has to have a name; it's only right and his father'll expect it. What about after the King?" he suggested. "That's always popular."

"Which one?" she shot back, and he grinned.

"After his sire then, mistress, or thine?"

Rob's warm eyes swam instantly into view. "No," she said and, catching Buena's perplexed glance, added, "nor my father. All right then," she said finally and with determination. "He was born on the feast of St Andrew. He shall be *Andrew*."

"Aye, Andrew is a good, strong name, and it will please his father."

Buena finished tying the baby's napkin. She began to thread his arms into his fresh, fine linen gown with the embroidered daisies around the hem. Ursula had intended completing the last flower on their return from the garden that miserable day. "And Ursula would have liked the name," Isobel said quietly, going over to the fire and taking him from Buena as she tied the last ribbon. "Andrew." She tried his name, whispering it into the fluff of his sea-coal hair. "And may it please God and Saint Andrew to protect you and your fader." She closed her eyes, seeing Rob in the space behind the lids. He needed to know he had a son. She opened them. "Master Taylor," she said, "I want you to take a message."

"Aye, mistress."

"To the Earl."

His head jerked up. "Ah, now, you know I cannot do that."

"I know what Lord Langton made you promise, but that danger is now past, and the constable has assured me there will be no repeat of the incident."

"Begging your pardon, but I didn't see that bastar… that skinny-limbed ferret until he hit me clean senseless, and I should've done. I failed in my duty to you. And you didn't help thyself, did you?"

Isobel flushed and held up her hand to silence him. "I know, I was a fool, and you did not deserve the blame; you could hardly have known he had slipped into the castle. But now the constable is aware of the danger, and he will ensure our safety – as will Buena." She raised a brow at Buena, who replied with a brief nod and patted the knife on her belt. "And no one – *no one* – dare threaten my baby and my lady—" she gave

Cecily a quick kiss on her curls and was rewarded with a wet peck back, "—or they will have me to reckon with."

He rubbed his chin, considering her, then sniffed and hitched his sword belt over his protruding belly. "I reckon my lord would have me skinned if I turned up out of the blue having left thee here alone. And when Lord Robert's finished, the Earl'll feed my carcass to his dogs, suck my bones dry, and grind 'em for mortar."

She huffed and tried one final tack. "I know it has been a long time since you last fought in battle, Master Taylor, and no one can blame you for being afeared, but…" She stuttered to a halt as his face convulsed, growing first red then purple.

Bending double, he let out a bark of laughter. "Eh, if you'd meant it and weren't a lass, I'd have strung a bow with your guts by now." He wiped his eyes. "Good try, mistress, but I'm sworn to protect thee and so I will."

"But your first loyalty is to Lord Langton, is it not? Then that is where you should be, not minding me but protecting your lord. How else can the Earl receive my letter and the news it contains?"

YULE HAD BEEN and gone by the time the Earl received Isobel's letter in January, stained by the journey and with the poor-quality paper ragged. She didn't say so, but without the fines and rents from her estates, she must be running short of funds by now. He had sent word to his steward to give her what could be spared from the little remaining coin left at the castle, but with his attainder came the cessation of his own revenue, and with that, his ability to protect her. Although she was still at the castle, at some point – if it hadn't happened already – his entire estate would be taken by the Crown, and where would she and his son go then?

"Andrew," he said out loud, testing the name in the empty room, and felt unexpected pride burning his chest. "*Andrew.*" Without Beaumancote, without his protection or that of a husband or father, what would become of his mistress and his son? Where had she left to go?

Portugal.

It came to him in the seabird's call, and he felt the sun warm his face, the breath of sea-cooled air; heard crickets click in the bleached grasses.

She had never been to Portugal and seen groves of olives and oranges and ruby-hued pomegranates hanging heavy from the trees. His son would run beneath them while his parents looked on. Secure, without the burden of choice. It seemed, as he watched himself, that for the first time in his life he would take the unexacting road, an option made easier by circumstances forced upon him. He adjourned his private deliberation as a firm knock at the door brought him back to the present.

Snow falling in damp clods from his boots, Robert entered the room. "The King wants us to join him at Gruuthuse's immediately…" Robert stopped when he saw the broken seal dangling from the linen ribbon that had closed Isobel's letter. "You have heard from Mistress Fenton?"

The Earl seemed to have forgotten he was holding it. "Yes."

"She is alive," Rob stated in an exhalation of relief. "What does it say?"

The Earl held it out. "Read it for yourself."

"Why would I…?" Rob began, then changed his mind and took it to the window where the snow-reflected light could fall across the surface. He read with his knuckles to his mouth, following her words with their wispy letters that would have taken flight from the page were they not anchored by ink. At one point, his brow formed deep ridges and he suppressed a sound, the muscles working in his throat.

He finished reading and handed the letter back without looking at his brother. "A boy. A son. You are to be… congratulated." He sounded anything but pleased.

The Earl repossessed the letter. "I am gladdened by the news more than I expected. I did not think it had weighed so heavily upon me. And I am grateful to you for leaving your man to protect her." He paused. "Robert, look at me." Rob brought hollow eyes to meet his. "I know this must pain you more than you say, but you will have sons of your own one day, when you remarry."

His brother snorted. "Of my *own*?" His mouth compressed, his boot toe tapping on the hard tile floor. "What about Felice? Will she join you here – bring your children?"

"Even if she could be persuaded…" The Earl shrugged, letting Robert fill in the rest.

"And… Isobel?" Rob stumbled over her name, coughed to clear his throat.

The Earl contemplated the toes of his own boots. "I might go to our estates in Portugal, to our mother's lands. It has been too long since I last went there, and I think Isobel will like it. She has nowhere else to go; I have made certain of that." He smiled bitterly, straightened. "If nothing else I owe her that much." The bells from the city square rang the hour. He caught himself genuflecting and lowered his hand awkwardly, relieved his brother was looking the other way.

"I hardly think our mother will make her welcome," Rob said.

"She will have little choice in the matter."

"Will Isobel?" Rob swung out of the chair and kicked a log back onto the hearth, sending sparks flying. "Have you not considered she might want to be someone's wife, not your *mistress*? Do you not owe her *that*?" The bells had ceased tolling. Robert looked around to find the Earl's features blanched. "We'd better go. His Grace is expecting us." He went to pick up his riding mantle where he had left it draped over a stool.

"Has she said as much? Is that what she wants?"

Robert hesitated and appeared to be deliberating, but then he drew the cloak around his shoulders. "She has not said; she never mentioned you."

HIS FACE ALMOST vibrating with excitement, the King spun to face the Earl as he entered. "This is what we have been waiting for. Duke Charles will have no choice but to give us the support we need. Louis has repudiated the Treaty of Pérrone, and the Duke's French lands are declared forfeit to France. Charles has been playing both sides and has discovered you cannot play the Devil at chess and expect to win."

"Duke Charles has finally declared for Your Grace?" the Earl asked.

"Not openly, but he will. He has agreed to meet with us at his court at Aire. If he wants an ally against the French throne, he'll first have to help me regain mine." He clapped his hands and rubbed them briskly together. "My lords, gentlemen, prepare in earnest and make keen your swords. Let us put an end to this exile and find a way back home."

Chapter 25

FELICE'S PRACTISED SMILE gave nothing of her inner thoughts away. "You failed to deal with the problem."

"Yet, madam, you grace us with your presence at Court." Warwick acknowledged Scrope's passing greeting with a nod. "You have taken your leisure in coming forth; is Roche a little cold at this time of year?"

"Since it proved to be beyond your reach, my lord, I will eradicate the problem myself. And now she has borne a whelp you double my task."

Warwick pursed his lips and inhaled. "I pity the girl. I wonder she has lasted this long. Still, she must have something to offer for the Earl to have kept her in his bed so long."

"*Former* Earl," Felice said, not rising to his jibe.

The old king's thin hair looked limp beneath his crown, and the flat grey of its hue aged him further. He made to rise but then sat down again. His left hand shook a little, Felice noticed, and he gripped the ermine edge of his robe, his eyes darting about the room until he found Warwick. He raised a querulous hand.

"The King is looking tired," she remarked. "No doubt Queen Margaret's arrival will be a great comfort to His Grace. And how long is it since he has seen his heir? The country awaits its Prince with eager anticipation, as must you, my lord. Young blood will give the people heart." Her wrist itched, but she resisted the temptation to scratch.

"How is the Duchess of Clarence? Isabel must be delighted her sister Anne has married a prince. I envy your gift for selecting husbands for your girls. Few can claim they have fathered one potential queen, let alone two. You must tell me your secret, my lord."

"They will be here as soon as the time is right," Warwick said smoothly, "and I see no lack of love for the King among the commons."

"Although the room is a little spare of lords, despite His Grace's generosity with pardons."

"It is a pity your husband did not accept one when he had the chance. How does he feel knowing that his wife has made her peace with King Henry and reaped the benefit of his estates?"

"My *son's* estates," she corrected, looking straight ahead.

Warwick studied her profile; had she been a man he would have found her intimidating. "You have not told him, have you, Felice?"

"The King beckons, my lord."

His eyes lit. "Hah! The Earl doesn't know. Well, well, and how hard did you try to persuade him to accept the pardon?"

"You should know, you have your informers." He didn't deny it. "Then there is no truth in the rumour that Edward of York makes ready to sail?"

"If he does, I have ensured he will meet with a warm welcome. All ports are covered, as are landing areas up and down the east coast, and Wenlock has Calais alerted for any signs of movement. York will find our hospitality generous should he decide to chance these shores again, but he has little support among the people. If he tries, he will fail."

Felice viewed him with curiosity. "You sound as if you would welcome the attempt."

"Let's say it would clear the air." He cast a sideways look at her. "And you, madam, would you embrace the chance of seeing your husband again and taking your place at his side, providing, that is, the *encumbrance* is no longer an issue?"

She moistened her lips, removing a fine film of whitening paste from around their fullness, making her mouth look faintly bruised. "As I have said, my lord, on my return I will ensure the castle is no longer troubled with vermin." She neglected to comment on her willingness, or otherwise, to resume her role as wife. If so, it would have to be in a world far removed from the one Warwick envisaged, and she was unwilling to voice in so public a place the possibility that Edward of York might one day again be sitting where this decrepit old man now sat, vacantly inhabiting his throne. "Come, my lord, the King awaits. I have done my obeisance; now it is time to do yours. Or is it the other way around?"

"Mm, how the Earl must miss your wit." He snapped his fingers in mock surprise. "I forget, he no longer bears the title, does he? I am surprised he has not requested you join him in exile. I believe Edward holds a merry enough court and, although funds are a little low, the faces are fresh and willing." He bowed and joined the King as her skin flared beneath the veil of paste she had so carefully applied to disguise the encroaching storm of lines around her eyes and mouth like cracks in drying mud. The King saw her looking and, revealing discoloured teeth, smiled in recognition and waved her towards him. She approached and sank low.

"Lady Felice, we greet thee well. How fares your husband, the Earl?"

She tried not to let her surprise show. "He is abroad, Your Grace."

"Pity, pity, we have missed him at Court. Tell him we shall look forward to his return."

Warwick leaned towards the King. "Your Grace, the former Earl is in exile with Edward of York. He is no friend; he fought against you."

"Then offer him pardon. We miss him and would have him with us."

Warwick rolled his eyes. "Highness, Langton is a traitor; he is attainted by Parliament. Your Grace commanded it."

"Did we?" Transparent fingers fumbled for the gold paternoster at his waist. "He must do penance for his sins, or we will have his head upon Micklegate as we did his father." He mumbled something that sounded like a prayer and then broke into a smile. "Ah, Lady Felice, we welcome you. Have you seen our queen?"

"Her Grace is in France, Highness."

"Is she? What is she doing there?" Frowning, his head swayed, and he began to ramble. Warwick signalled to two burly attendants. They almost lifted the King to his feet.

"His Grace will retire," Warwick announced, as the old man was bundled from the room, leaving Felice still kneeling before his empty throne.

SAWCLIFFE WAITED FOR her in the crowded vestibule with the air of one eminently amused by everything and everyone around him. Dressed in black, he reminded Felice of a skinny spider with webs strung among the various conversations in the room, listening to the vibrations, waiting for a morsel of information he could consume. He inclined his head on her approach. "I trust my lady found the morning enlightening?"

She looked on his bowed head with indifference; she could never decide if she liked him or not. She certainly didn't trust him. She received fine cream gloves lined in red silk from her servant. "We return to the castle to take residence immediately."

"His Grace has granted a pardon to the Earl?"

"His Grace has seen fit to entail the earldom to my son with immediate effect, and for him to be under my governance until he comes of age." She allowed herself the slightest smile of satisfaction at the surprise in the man's face. He might be ears and eyes to her husband, but she had remained one step ahead of him in this game.

ROBERT SAW THE sword as it arced towards his head and ducked sideways, hearing the air severed by the blade. A sigh echoed from the watching group, followed by a slow clap.

"Well played, my lord," the King called from the stalls.

"Nearly had your ear, brother." From a comfortable distance, the Earl wiped sweat from the back of his neck with a cloth. "Wouldn't want it to be your head." Robert measured the distance between himself and his older brother without answering. He advanced, sword raised in challenge, and the Earl dropped the cloth and took up a defensive position. Several women of Duke Charles's court exchanged whispered comments behind their hands and tittered.

"The ladies are raising a wager, my lords," Edward remarked, "on who will win this round – but don't let that distract you."

Maintaining eye contact, the two men moved forward. Robert made a sudden lunge, and the Earl neatly parried the blow, using the weight of his sword to knock Rob's blade aside. In a blink, the Earl thrust his sword towards Robert's stomach, stopping a finger's breadth from the padded jack that was all that stood between steel and flesh. The women clapped in delight, chirping something in French too indistinct to be heard from the stalls.

"Les Mesdames salute your move, my lord Earl, and wish to know whether the winner will entertain them tonight?"

The Earl countered Rob's attack before he could reply, and this time Robert's sword came within a breath of his arm, the men grappling before pushing the other off. Without breaking step, Robert moved back, recovered his stance, and attacked, again narrowly missing the Earl's groin as the blade sliced at an angle across him. Pushing the sword away with his arm, the Earl frowned as Rob circled, all humour gone. From the stalls, the King exchanged a remark with William Hastings. Something glinted in the King's hand. "You might have need of a second blade." He tossed a dagger to the Earl, who caught it in his left hand. "I'll wager experience over youth," he said, chucking one of the girls under the chin and grinning sideways at his younger brother. Gloucester pitched his own dagger to Rob. He caught it unsmiling, rotating his wrist to limber the muscles without taking his stony gaze from his brother's face. The two men measured the other's intent. The Earl feinted to the left, parrying Rob's sword and bringing the heavy pommel around and grazing his cheek. The women applauded, but before the Earl could follow up, Robert used his shoulder to knock him sideways, and it was only the Earl's agility that saved him from falling victim to Rob's blade. He pivoted on one heel, regaining his balance, surprise on his face. One of the women squealed, and brittle laughter broke from the watchers. Edward took his arm from around the girl and leaned forward on the stall. "My lord Langton, have mercy and spare your noble brother, I have need of him." His grin fell away as, without hesitation, Robert rounded again with deadly intent. "My lords, enough!" Steel slid against steel, Robert catching his brother's blade and twisting the sword from his hand, sending it cartwheeling to the ground. "Well played!" the King bellowed. "But enough."

Gloucester leaped over the stall rail, scattering sawdust. Holding out his hand, he spoke quietly. "My dagger if you will, my lord."

Robert hesitated, gave a short nod, wiped the blade, and gave it back.

Stooping to retrieve the fallen sword, the King joined them. "What games we play, my lords – but save it for battle. That was a neat move you made, Langton, but you've been too long without the company of women – your blood's running high. One slip and you would have gutted the Earl. You've won the bet—" he leaned down until his mouth was level with Robert's ear, "—but don't make the same mistake again." Straightening, he handed the sword to the Earl and, raising his voice, said, "Come, my lords, these ladies are eager to test your mastery in more pleasurable ways, and I can vouch for their prowess." He cocked a finger to the women, and they giggled their way from the stalls, straw catching in the furred edge of their gowns as they glittered like starlings towards them. But Rob had already turned away, seizing his scabbard from where it leaned against a stall and sheathing his sword without stopping to buckle it to his belt.

Edward watched him leave the practice yard with an expression of puzzled amusement. "Langton seems not to be himself of late and is as ill-humoured as an ox, so I must forgive him his lack of courtesy."

Something caught the Earl's eye, and he bent down and lifted it free of the sawdust. He held it in the palm of his hand, brow furrowed, then looked to where his brother had been just moments before.

"I can think of only two things that can occupy a man's mind to the indifference of his king and of passing beauty, hey my lord?" The King squeezed the dark-haired girl's neat bottom through her gown, and she simpered. "He's either lost his soul to God or his heart to a woman."

"Do I KNOW her?" the Earl asked when they were alone.

"It would make no difference if you did," Robert replied, and dismissed the subject.

THAT NIGHT, WHILE his brother slept, the Earl held the coral and jet chaplet with the little lindenwood acorn to his lips before slipping it into the purse from which it had fallen. He stood for a moment observing Rob's troubled rest, the bruise on his cheekbone a smudge against his pale skin, and then went to seek his own oblivion in sleep.

The Countess slipped on an icy cobble as she stepped from the covered wagon and was saved from falling by one of Warwick's liveried men who had accompanied her from Roche in some splendour that morning. She said something that had him remove his hand from her arm and step back swiftly, and she looked up at the tower. Despite the distance, Isobel could clearly make out the downturned set of her mouth and the way she scoured the windows for signs of movement.

"Now what happens?" Isobel said as the Countess moved across the courtyard to her own apartments, followed by the steward. Her servants piled from the wagons and packhorses and began to unload carts. "I expect she will want Cecily to join her." Isobel turned to Buena standing behind her. The little girl played quietly near Andrew as he slept in the cradle of furs and cushions she had helped make for him. At two months, he was already lifting his head and could sit on Isobel's lap for a few moments without toppling over. Cecily had chatted away to him and pulled faces until he gurgled and cooed himself to sleep, and now she entertained herself by walking Nan up and down Chou's back. Isobel marvelled at the tolerance of the dog, whereas Moth needed restraining in case she ate the poppet. She doubted the Countess would show such indulgence to her own daughter, if she paid any attention to her at all. "We must bar the door."

The information gleaned from the sergeant at the gatehouse did little to lighten her mood. "It's like this," he said, but hesitantly, as if he didn't want to spill the news. "My lord's not been pardoned – nor Lord Langton, neither – but the attainder's been lifted."

"That does not make sense."

He drew her to one side of the now sparsely populated guardhouse, where they might speak without being overheard. "Well, it seems that it does, mistress. The bairn's been granted his father's titles and lands: he's the new Earl, and the Countess will mind him until he comes into his own, like."

"And where does that leave me?"

"I can't say."

"We cannot stay here. Even if the Countess lets us I have nothing left to pay my way – only this." She lifted her father's seal on its ribbon. "Or my son's caul." She thought quickly. "If I give you my fader's seal, could you sell it for me?"

"If I turn up with a gold seal like that, they'll take me for a thief. And I reckon thy lad'll best be keeping his own caul than letting some other have the blessing of it."

Isobel couldn't imagine Andrew ever being old enough to go to sea. "He will have no need of it; I will keep him away from water."

"I expect that's what my lord Earl thought and all."

She shuddered, remembering the agony in the Earl's eyes at the loss of his son. "So…?"

"So, you stay here, mistress, in the tower, and until Pip Taylor gets his backside on a horse and back here to protect thee, I'll do what I can to keep thee and thine safe until my lord's return."

"You think he can return? How?"

"You don't believe they'll leave it there, do you? Folks'll blow with the wind come what may. It makes little difference to them who's on the throne, as long as they've bread on the table and crops to sow. But to my lords, now, and all their kin, they've nowt to look forward to unless it be in the rule of their own lands and their people, and to do that they'll have to win them back."

"And do you think King Edward will try?"

"I think there's too much to lose if he don't. And in the meantime, I have to keep ye safe or the Earl'll flay the skin off me back when he returns. I'll bring thee news when I can. Is there no kin you can go to?"

"None."

"Then there's only one thing to be done, and that's bide here and pray that the kingdom's worth more to King Edward than the risk to his neck."

Chapter 26

"THEY'VE LANDED!" The sergeant came into the room carrying with him the smoke of guardroom gossip, his usually placid features alive with tension.

Isobel stood, dislodging the dried beans she had been shelling and scattering them across the floor. "Where? When?"

"Ravenspur – on the tip of Holdeness at the mouth of the Humber—"

"Yes, yes, I know where Ravenspur lies. Is Lord Langton with him? And the Earl?"

"Aye, as far as I know, but the report's scant for want of testament. I do know they made to come up the Humber through Lincolnshire, but the place is swarming against them, and they met with a force led by Martin de la See, and he stopped their progress."

Isobel felt her face pale. "They have fought?"

He swung his boulder of a head. "Not that I've heard. The King told them he has only come to claim his rightful inheritance as Duke of York, and showed him some friendly letters from the Earl of Northumberland, and the gentleman let him pass!"

It took her a moment to translate what he had said into something that made sense. She shook her head to clear it. "This… de la See, just let King Edward through? Without further challenge?"

"Aye."

"And where is the King now?"

"Last I heard, he were in York. Refused entry at first, but he made the burghers see sense and they let the whole army in next day. I don't know what he promised them, but they believed him all right. Luck of the Devil, that one has."

Isobel recalled the King's self-assured charm and quite believed he could conjure victory from defeat with it, but her father would have added that townsmen require something more tangible than the promise of a king's smile, no matter how golden.

"Might His Grace come here?"

"Eh, I don't know, mistress, but I do know he'll have to raise a gert deal more men if he's to stand a chance against Warwick and Clarence, and there's nowt certain on the field, as His Grace and my Earl knows right well to their loss."

"Perhaps… perhaps it will not come to that?" And leave the ultimate question unanswered? Whom was she trying to fool? His expression said as much.

"There's a kingdom at stake and more than that – lives too. There can be no peace 'til it's settled, and it best be settled afore Warwick and Anjou can join forces. Enough lords are holding their peace 'til they see which way winds blow. Warwick's got some he can call on, but not all – aye, not all."

"What about the King – Edward, that is; will any come to his standard? And the Earl's affinity – surely they will not abandon him. He has always been a good lord, and is he not well-loved?"

"Aye, by me and my likes, but that's a good question," he said, eyes narrowing. "He's not the Earl, is he, but his wee boy, and his dam has charge over him, so she stands to lose if her husband returns to claim his titles and rights, eh? And what did she have to do to get it, if you see what I mean?"

"King *Henry*?" Isobel said, shocked at the thought.

"Not *him*." His eyes rolled. "I'm not one for talk, as you know—" he chose not to see her raised brow, "—but at one time my lord and the Earl of Warwick were as close as kin, and Warwick were a frequent visitor here."

"My father said that such smatter is for idle tongues and simple minds," Isobel said with gravity. "It never leads to good but often harm." She sucked her cheeks, trying to resist – and gave up. "So? And?"

He winked. "And the Earl was not always at home when Warwick came visiting, if you get me. There might be nowt to it but jangle and such; you know what people are like." She did indeed, and she didn't like it. "Anyhow, our Earl won't have Warwick inside these walls. He'll kill him if he steps a foot past those gates, make no mistake. Once he's taken a dislike there's nowt in this land that'll stop his wrath, mark my words."

Echoes of her father's warning so long ago reverberated around her skull like bells. Isobel studied the figures on the painted screen depicting the Earl's long lineage until she met the cool eyes of the Countess and looked away. Perhaps the Countess had given the Earl cause to shun her after all? Isobel couldn't imagine any man being able to warm her. And then she considered her own position, and the cold contempt in which she held the Earl, and thought that what she had done was not so far removed from treachery after all. But had she loved him there would be no question of betrayal; as it was, he denied his brother's right to happiness and for that, Isobel could not forgive him. "What will the Countess do if he is restored?" she said almost to herself. "Surely she will not expect him to forgive her?"

"I don't know about *forgive* as such, but blood is thicker than water, and thicker still the bonds of marriage – they can't be broken that were given in law." The sergeant squared his shoulders inside his wool cote. "It's not what he'll do if he gets what's rightly his, but what *she'll* do in the meantime – that's the question."

Isobel met his eyes directly. "She will wait," she said with certainty. "She will want to see where the tide runs, and she'll wait. She will not come after me again while her future is uncertain."

He eyed her with appreciation. "I reckon you're right, there, mistress. I hope you're right."

Chapter 27

14th April 1471

"It was always going to come to this." The Earl adjusted his position, taking care not to let the metal poleyns protecting his knees chink against the cuisses on his thighs. "Warwick would not accept Clarence as intermediary – and who can blame him after that brazen affront? Edward might be able to persuade himself that Clarence was *misled*, but Warwick? There was never any chance he would accept an offer of a pardon – he has gone too far for that – and the King chose the one person to deliver the message with whom he knew Warwick could not negotiate. Once Clarence came back to the family fold bringing with him his four thousand men, there was no point in Warwick delaying open battle any longer."

Robert hugged his mantle closer over his armour. "Which brings us to this sleepless dawn encamped by the road without the comfort of a fire, nor the benefit of light. I hope Warwick is suffering equally for putting us here."

"We will make him suffer," the Earl offered grimly. "And he knows it, which is why he cannot afford to lose, and we must not risk him knowing how close we are to his own camp. Lack of warmth and hot food is the price we pay for the advantage of surprise. Quiet there!" He barked in an undertone as a pole-arm was dropped, rattling, against a mailed leg. "This mist affords cover only as long as fools do not give us away."

A hooded figure searched among the men and, finding the Earl when he almost stumbled upon him, whispered behind a closed hand. The Earl nodded, and the man was absorbed into the mist from whence he had come. Standing and stretching his back, he murmured, "His Grace is hearing mass and bids us join him. I am undecided whether making battle on Easter Day will gain God's approval, but I suppose only the outcome will justify the means."

MEN RECENTLY ROUSED from sleep coughed into their sleeves and spat into crushed grass. "They seem unaware of what could lie ahead," Gloucester said.

"I think they know, Your Grace, but sleep is a way of disarming fear. Nor do they have the responsibility of lordship; there is security in being governed by another. And they are well paid for it."

"There is greater loyalty in such sacrifice than a day's wage can account for, and yet they walk towards death at our behest."

"And we ride towards it and get there quicker and share the same fate. Death is no respecter of birth."

"As I know all too well," Gloucester said quietly. The first hint of dawn lightened the thick fog. Gloucester scoured the remains of the night. "The King sees this mist as a blessing from St Anne, a sign of God's favour."

Robert steadied his horse. "It might be if we can use it to our advantage, Your Grace."

"On Palm Sunday – before we entered London – a statue of St Anne revealed herself to Edward at Daventry, and thereafter all opposition fell away before us, and he was welcomed into London where he took possession of the old king." He paused.

"Yes, Your Grace?" Robert prompted.

"How many times might an omen be effective, my lord, before the blessing is deemed spent?"

Robert detected the nervous glint in the young man's eyes. Mist clung to his dark lashes, framed his face, deathly pale in the eternal phantom of the fog. "A swift death honourably won in battle is the best we can hope for. Anything more is a miracle." He closed his eyes and brought Isobel before him, reaching out to touch her cheek, feeling her lips in the palm of his hand, her breath on his skin as he caressed her. She evaporated like a spectre, and with a jolt Robert realised the Duke had asked him a question. "Your Grace?"

"Do you believe God is with us?"

Rob felt for the chaplet at his wrist; it was still there, safe. "I have to believe that our cause is right, and God favours the just. Yes, I believe."

"I wonder whether my brother Edmund thought the same before he rode out with our father from Sandal." His horse, sensing his agitation, began to pull against the bit, and the Duke wrestled to quieten him. Langton made out the dread in the youth's movements, in the tenor of his voice. Why was he not also afraid? He should be afraid. He should be sensing his bowels loosen as his gut constricted with fear and the muscles of his throat tauten until swallowing became nigh on impossible, with the only thing preventing him from throwing up inside his helmet the greater fear of drowning in it. Fear was not to be shunned at a time like this. Fear made a man sharper in battle. But he was not afraid.

The signal went out like a fever among the ranks. "Your Grace, it is time."

Taking as deep a breath as his lungs would allow, the Duke nodded and, with the donning of his helmet, raised his arm and signalled the advance.

BURGUNDIAN GUNNERS AND bowmen had cued the assault and through windows in the mist the Earl made out the King's broad back chopping his way towards the thick of the fray on horseback. The Earl had forgone his mount a while back, and now he fought his way towards him on foot, catching against discarded lances, almost falling over the amputated body of a man lying disguised by blood and mud. He found his footing, ducking before a broadsword removed his head and returning the blow as the knight regained his balance, bludgeoning him until he fell to his knees, then he delivered the death blow in a single swift thrust of his dagger. He lost sight of the King again in the parody of dance and the music of death as a wave of men surged sideways, and he tried to move against it but found his way blocked. "Langton!" somebody shouted at him, and he saw Henry Lynes cutting a swathe towards him. "My lord, Oxford's crushed Hastings' left flank. He's on the run!"

The Earl swore, looking over the broken ranks of struggling men to where he had last seen the King hacking his way through Montagu's griffins. He could make out nothing beyond. "Is Gloucester holding?"

"I have no knowledge of it." A blow to his shoulder from behind almost knocked Lynes to the ground. The Earl managed to parry the next attempt before Lynes could turn and defend himself, the wrong-footed assailant falling and bringing Lynes down with him. The Earl brought his foot hard against the man's skull, stunning him long enough for Lynes to wrench the visor from his face and drive his dagger through his mouth. Blood frothed around the blade as it was drawn free.

He hauled Lynes to his feet. "Find the King. Tell him about Hastings." Not waiting for an answer, he located his own men in a knot at the edge of a heaving flank of Montagu retainers. Smoke from the Burgundian guns lingered, mingling with the impenetrable mist in a choking miasma. He lost sight of his retinue and found himself surrounded by men displaying Warwick's bear and ragged staff. He took the foot off one man with a backward sweep of his sword; slashed blindly at another attacking from behind, feeling his blade oscillate against metal and bone; disarmed a third with a twist of his dagger. Through the breaking mist, a figure swam into focus among the straggling men, was lost, but then reformed into a yellow pike on a blue ground. *"Lacey!"* he bellowed. With immense effort, he reduced the distance between them. "Lacey! You son of a *whore*!"

At the sound of his name, Lacey looked around, anchored for the moments it took for the Earl to reach him, covering his head with his arms to take the falling blade, eyes bulging with fear behind his visor. But a blow to his shoulder had the Earl spin to defend his rear, reacting before he recognised one of the King's men. The man staggered back, dropping his axe and raising his arm in defence. "My lord, I thought you were Montagu!"

He span back ready to strike, but Lacey was barging through the heavy throng of Warwick's men, fast retreating beyond his reach.

"Coward!" the Earl threw after him and without caution pressed on in pursuit.

❧

BLACK-FACED, THE Burgundian gunners retreated as the last shot echoed across the heads of the men and the volleys of arrows, shot in quick succession, had either found their mark or else punctured the ground like spines through which the silvered bodies of the Duke of Exeter's retinue now laboured towards them. Eyes snapping, his body quivering with tension, Gloucester leaned forward over the high pommel, readying himself.

"Keep together," Robert warned. "I'll watch your back." No matter how many hours had been spent in the practice yards, nothing could prepare for that first clash. Voices of steel rose in a wall of sound, and the impact of armour and weapons sent shock waves through the ranks and the Duke's horse jittering back. "Steady." Langton caught the animal's rein. He noted the position of their men – good men, all of them – fighting their portion of the field to protect their Duke's flanks while the young man found his bearings and his courage. His youth and title were no protection against a blade, and his inexperience and slight build made him the more vulnerable.

A weathered man-at-arms picked the Duke out as an easy target, swinging a mace in an arc at his leg. Robert lunged his horse forward, intercepting the blow and using the animal's armoured weight to knock the man back. With a low swipe from his saddle, Robert's sword found an exposed joint, severing a tendon. He silenced the man's pig squeal with a thrust of the point into his throat, ramming it home with the flat of his hand. Wheeling his horse, Langton pinpointed Gloucester moving ahead of his body of men, engaging blows with a burly knight twice his size. Smashing the hilt of his own sword into a pikeman's face, spilling teeth and spittle, Robert wove towards the Duke as the knight began to gain the upper hand, reaching him as Gloucester dodged the falling blade and in a swift, elegant move sliced through the knight's knee. He had the blade inside the visor and the man dead before he knew what he was doing. He looked around as Robert joined him, and in that one, hollow moment, Rob recognised in his eyes the shock of first blood. There was no time; Exeter's men were upon them out of the mist, and the Duke was hunting his next kill, fire igniting his blood, taking on any who came within his reach. "They're retreating!" he yelled, voice magnified within his closed helmet.

"We're pushing them back," Robert amplified. He didn't see the billhook until it rammed into his side, knocking breath from his lungs, but he managed to grab the haft before the lethal hook could pull him off his horse, yanking hand over hand and breaching the man's startled face with the heavy hilt of his sword. Dizzy, he dragged himself upright. The mist broke, and before it reformed he saw their quarry. "Exeter!" Robert indicated with his sword. Gloucester followed the direction, craning through the melee, identifying his despised brother-in-law's banner among his close bodyguard.

"Your Grace, stay close!" Robert bellowed, but Gloucester was moving in the direction of the duke, gathering as many of his retinue as heard his call to arms, fighting their way up the shallow slope blow by blow. Robert tried to follow, but the billhook had stolen his breath, and each movement jarred. His vision blurred. He couldn't tell which way he faced. "My lord!" He peered through the shifting mist and saw Lynes, hardly recognisable except for the remnants of his surcoat, moving towards him on foot. "Langton, you're hurt?" Robert shook his head, finding he could think again. "Montagu's dead, my lord. Warwick's men mistook Oxford's star for the King's Sun, and by the time they realised their mistake Oxford had retaliated, thinking he was betrayed. Montagu's dead," he repeated, "Oxford's in flight, and Warwick has ordered men to hold Exeter's line. The King's sent out instructions to capture Warwick alive."

"Have you seen my brother?"

"The last I saw he headed after Thomas Lacey."

"Where was that?"

He pointed behind him where the mist was at last beginning to disperse, allowing the sun to bleed through the gaps between. "Into Warwick's lines. I haven't seen him since. I have orders from the King. God speed."

A yell went up from the direction in which Gloucester had forged ahead of his own knights, and renewed sounds of steel and cries of men rolled down the slope towards them. Rob spied the Duke in the thickest part of the fighting, avoiding the heaviest blows he couldn't hope to survive and making every stroke count. Almost unseated by a bigger man on a heavily armoured horse, the Duke regained his defensive position in anticipation of his opponent's next move, only to find his own mount slipping in guts and throwing him off balance. The man drove his animal against Gloucester's, swinging a morning star towards the Duke's head. Gloucester rolled sideways, using his saddle to pivot, then used the forward momentum and the man's own weight to drive his blade through the man's groin. Wresting the blade free, he turned and sliced down at an angle, taking the nose off a foot soldier reaching up to pull him from his saddle. But Warwick's reinforcements were taking their toll and threatening to overwhelm them.

Rob rammed his horse through the jostling men. "Your Grace! We must leave!" He kicked a sergeant bearing Warwick's badge in the face and finished him off before he could recover. "Your Grace!"

Hauling Gloucester's horse by its harness, he managed to extricate him, only to be met by burning orbs and "I'm finishing it" squeezed through a grid of teeth. In the shadows of the helmet, Gloucester's eyes focused behind him. Rob automatically raised his sword, but the maul wielded by a man-at-arms glanced off his forearm and broke his grip, rendering the sword impotent. Robert lurched off-balance, unable to defend himself from the following blow. "No!" Gloucester roared, and from the corner of his visor Rob saw the maul smash the Duke's arm as the young man intercepted the attack.

The Earl heard the cries of *treason!* before he witnessed the rout in disarray of Oxford's men, scattering into the mist pursued by Yorkist troops. Towards the centre of the fighting, where thickets of men fought shoulder to shoulder with barely space between them to wield a sword, both the King and Warwick appeared oblivious to the broken lines, maintaining order amongst the ranks and directing them with absolute authority. Among Warwick's retinue, the Earl distinguished Lacey's men, and he singled them out and cut them down with the sole purpose of locating Lacey himself. In the confusion, the Earl had lost contact with his household knights and found himself in soft ground, mired mud sucking at his feet, alone and on the edge of battle. Thirst desiccated his throat, the smell of piss and sweat and guts hung in the thinning mist surrounding him. He wrenched off his helmet, gulping air, and looked down at his feet. With the clearing air came a shaft of sun, and what he had thought water was blood – pools of it – congealing, glistening, over the bodies of the dead and dying. Mist clung in patches masking men, and unidentifiable mouths gaped, the rising sun reflecting in blind eyes. And not far from where he stood, another, with his leg severed below the knee, dragged himself with soft moans meaninglessly towards oblivion. As the sun strengthened, it illuminated the slumped figure of an old soldier with his bare head crowned with light. His great sword lay across his legs with his hand resting on the hilt ready to take it up again. A cry escaped the Earl's parched throat, and the figure moved, holding out his hand in supplication, his mouth moving soundlessly, calling his name. The Earl tried to lift his feet free of the morass, but iron bound his legs and he fell forward onto his hands, casting other men's blood in molten drops into the air, tasting death on his tongue. This was Hell, and he had fought his way into it. He heard his name again, but fainter now, dissolving with the mist. "I'm coming," he called, struggling to free himself. He half-crawled and groped his way towards the man, only to find him motionless when at last he looked into his face, rigid in death, long drained of life. Not his father at all. He became conscious of the battle still blazing, the new sun revealing the relative positions marked by banners, saw the King's sun in splendour, Warwick's bear and ragged staff, the white boar of Gloucester, and, nearby, Clarence's black bull. But, creeping from thicket to stump in an attempt to remain unseen, Thomas Lacey skirted the edge of the fighting. He had torn his surcoat from his armour and was trying to strip himself of the vestiges of nobility to avoid detection. Fuelled by rage, the Earl escaped the bog and hurled himself in the direction of his revenge.

Crouching part-dressed and linen soiled by fear, Lacey's head jerked up as he heard the Earl thunder his name, and he lurched for his sword. The Earl raised his own blade. "For my father, for Isobel—" He didn't see the assailant but felt the resounding blow against his back that sent him flying onto his face. Stunned, he lay there deafened by blood pounding his ears. His sword had fallen an arm's length away. Pain searing his side, he reached for it, but a foot pinned the blade to the earth.

"Kill him!" he heard Lacey screech. The Earl managed to roll onto one knee and looked up at the thick-set man with a broken nose.

"You don't remember me, do you, my *lord*?" he mocked. The Earl's eyes widened with recognition, and the man grinned. "Ay, Beaumancote."

Lacey found his voice. "Kill the bastard, George!" Feeling the weight of the war hammer, the sergeant adjusted his grip. Without taking his eyes from the man, the Earl felt behind him, remembered he had dropped his dagger in the mire. The pounding in his head grew worse, he wanted to shake himself free of it, but it became louder, became metal feet, the sound of someone running. He refocused beyond the sergeant's back on the armoured figure rapidly approaching. George swivelled as Robert came to a halt spitting distance away. For a moment, for the merest beat of his heart, the Earl thought he read hesitation in his brother's eyes, but as the sergeant began to swing his weapon to defend himself, Robert took a step forward, and with a blow brought the sergeant to his knees, then with a second removed his head. The hammer had fallen by the Earl's foot. He picked it up, but where Lacey had been standing only minutes before, there was nothing but a discarded pile of armour and his stink.

Chapter 28

Stripped of his gilded armour, Warwick's body looked like any other, and it had taken some time to identify him. Now he lay next to his brother in the privacy of a mortuary tent under the eyes of his cousins.

Edward's head grazed the canopy. "There could be no other outcome: it was them or us."

"They should have been left untouched."

"They were spared mutilation, which is more than can be said for some poor bastards." He took in Gloucester's exhaustion; he could barely stand. "This is hard, I know, we were close once – kin. Warwick was there from the beginning, and I trusted Montagu with my life, even when his brother turned against us." Richard's gaze remained fixed on Warwick's face, his own pale as alabaster; but he showed no desire to leave. "He will be treated with dignity, and after their bodies are displayed in St Paul's—" His brother flashed an angry glance. "They must be seen to be dead, Richard, or none of this will end."

Gloucester swallowed carefully, his throat raw with battle cries and gun smoke. "I know."

"I will have their bodies released to their families, and they can be buried with all due honour at Bisham. It's where they wanted to be." Edward frowned as Richard cradled his left arm. "Have you had that seen to?"

Richard immediately released his arm and attempted to straighten it, but the action had his face crease with pain. "It is nothing; it is merely jounced." He cast another look at the bodies laid out before them.

Edward felt a wave of gratitude. "I thank God your life has been spared. You fought bravely and acquitted yourself in a manner that would have made our father proud. Sweet Jesu, *I* am proud." He resisted the temptation to ruffle his brother's hair and embraced him instead. "My little brother is not so little after all. It will give me great pleasure to see your loyalty rewarded."

"There are others I would have recognised for their services – Ashby, Robert Langton, Francis—"

"And they will be. For the love of the Saints, get yourself some rest; you've earned it."

"As have we all," said a voice behind them. "I couldn't find you in your pavilion. Have you come to see the fruits of your victory and mock the vanquished?" George Clarence cast an indifferent eye over the corpse of his father-in-law.

"Have you?" Gloucester said brusquely. "Some mark their passing with greater respect."

Clarence could sneer for England; he did so now. "You look half dead, brother. *Merde*, you are getting blood all over the place. Oh, no, it's not yours, is it. I did not see you fight; were you there?"

Edward placed a restraining hand on Richard's shoulder. "Where have you been, George? I sent for you before noon."

Clarence had walked around the side of the temporary funerary trestle draped in Neville banners and was now canting his head to get a better look at his cousins. "Writing to my wife before somebody else tells her the news of her father's death." Gore matted Warwick's hair. George skewed his mouth in displeasure. "She will be heartbroken," he added without emotion.

"I'll expect you to be present when we enter London and give thanks at St Paul's, is that understood?"

Clarence raised his brow, as if the thought of being anywhere else had never crossed his mind. "Of course."

"And you will be seen to love us."

George placed his palm against his chest. "Do you want me to go on my knees in front of the citizens of London and beg forgiveness and pledge undying fealty to Your Highness?" he asked with mock solemnity.

"Well, do you?" Edward asked, without a glimmer of humour.

The smile dropped from George's mouth. "Am I to be rewarded for *my* loyalty and my four thousand men? Without me, your fortunes would be reversed." He kicked the nearest trestle, and Montagu's arm fell stiffly and hung suspended over the edge. Edward looked at his brother then at the dead men.

"Believe me when I say that you will be rewarded according to your true service. Without the intercession of our lady mother, our sisters, and our younger brother, we would not be standing here having this conversation. And this is not over yet. We might have the old king secure in the Tower, and God knows there is nothing left in him to provoke any feeling of accord among his former allies, but the She-Shrew he calls wife has a son she wants crowned, and they make their way to these shores as we speak. Those traitors, Edmund Somerset, Devon, and that slippery bastard De Vere, have everything to play for and more to lose – as do we. So, brother, I ask again: do I have your loyalty?"

George's eyes slid to the corpses and then back to his brothers. "Of course, Your Grace. My loyalty is assured, as I have much to gain from your generosity."

"Do not try my patience, George. You've not grown so great that I cannot quash you."

"With our dear cousins dead, who now inherits the Neville affinity, Edward? Can you trust Harry Percy to come to heel when you call, now that there is no one left to keep him in check? Northumberland is a powerful friend when he chooses, but he is a man consumed by contradictions and swayed by ties that extend far beyond the Crown."

"Do you threaten me, George?"

"I intend merely to advise, Your Grace. You have in me a natural ally bound by kinship. My wife is Warwick's heiress, and I am—"

"*Co*-heir," Richard cut in. "Anne inherits half his estates and is as much a Neville as Isabel."

Clarence's smile soured. "Yes, but she's married to Edward of Lancaster, or had you forgotten?"

Richard opened his mouth to reply, but Edward interrupted. "*You* forget, Warwick's estates should be forfeit by attainder to the Crown."

"You cannot deny my wife her inheritance!"

Edward's eyes became hooded. "I can and I will, unless I can be persuaded otherwise." Turning his back on Clarence, he left the threat and the promise hanging. Richard had grown visibly greyer over the preceding minutes. Edward frowned. "I cannot afford to lose you; that arm needs attention. Come, we've been in the presence of death long enough."

As Edward bent to leave the tent, George called out, "The manner of our conversation made me forget the reason I sought out Your Grace."

The King stalled, looking back. "Which was?"

"French ships flying the English standard were spotted short of Weymouth last night. Anjou is expected to make landfall today with the prince." For a moment, it looked as if he had pushed Edward too far, but he ducked out of the tent without another word, leaving Clarence to smile and say softly, "I thought you would want to know."

Louys poked his head inside the Earl's pavilion and, seeing him there, stepped inside. "My lord, Thomas Lacey's been caught on the road south. He's been taken before the King."

The Earl halted the ministrations of the doctor and waved him away, pulling the linen shirt over his head and wincing as he stood up. "Where is His Grace?"

"By my lord Warwick's mortuary tent." Louys crossed himself. Even in death Warwick commanded a degree of respect many others lacked in life.

The Earl's shirt stuck to the salve spread over the deep bruise under his right shoulder blade. He caught his breath as he reached for his sword and moved with greater caution. "Send to Lord Robert."

"It was Lord Langton who sent me, my lord. He was with the Duke of Gloucester when Lacey was brought in."

Lacey was in the position most suitable for a traitor caught on the run – face down and prostrate before the King. He had only to kneel, and his head would be the perfect height for removal. The Earl fingered the hilt of his sword and moved closer, but with the slightest movement of his hand, Robert issued his brother a silent warning. He stood behind Gloucester, who listened intently to the King.

"… this pardon is granted in honour of Christ our Lord this day, subject to the conditions laid before you: that you do freely submit to our authority and offer fealty in the manner described on pain of forfeiture of your life, title, and property—" the Earl grunted his disbelief, "—that property being the most part the title and manors of Beaumancote, Great Stanton, Corti—"

The Earl didn't stop to hear the rest. Blinded by fury, he stormed across the shredded ground back towards his tent. Behind him, he heard Louys following. "Get the horses," he slung without looking around. A hand reached for his arm. Enraged, he rounded with fist raised. Rob fielded the blow.

"Where are you going?"

"Home. Portugal. Anywhere that whoreson isn't breathing in my face. Get out of my way." He pushed past his brother.

"The King expects your attendance—"

"The King? The *King*?"

"For the love of God, keep your voice down!" Rob hissed, pulling his brother further from inquisitive ears. "His Grace is displeased you left in such a manner. He commands you attend him. Now."

In the relative privacy of the royal pavilion, the King broke step only to sign a document. He let the quill fall, ink drops staining the cloth, and waved the document away. His secretary left, leaving Gloucester as witness to his brother's rising temper. "What makes you so bold as to question my judgment, my lord Earl?"

The Earl was in no mood to be thwarted, even by his king. "Your Grace will be thought weak if men like Lacey are not punished for their treachery."

"You think me *weak*?"

The Earl governed his own temper. "Lacey betrayed you once before; Your Highness said he would not be permitted to do so again."

"Ah, so now I am both weak *and* inconstant?"

"I do not say so, Your Grace. The moment Warwick crooked his finger, Lacey came running, and this time his treachery is rewarded not with the punishment he deserves, but with a pardon and the lands which he came by unlawfully."

"Christ in Heaven! You now seek to teach me *law*?"

"It is *your* law, Your Grace. What other protection do we have against those who would harm us and seek arbitrary pardon for the offence? Why him? Why allow Lacey to live when not two months past you would have gladly seen him dead?"

Quiet, watchful, Gloucester said nothing.

"Two months ago, we were not in a position to take back this crown. Now we need any who would pledge their support. Lacey fought for Warwick. Warwick is dead. The West Country is being raised for Anjou; I cannot afford to lose one lord who can bring men to our cause. This battle is ours, but we are not secure until we have removed this last threat."

"But to disinherit Fenton's daughter and allow Lacey to keep her lands… Beaumancote… which could still be used against Your Highness? What madness is that?"

Picking stubborn blood from around his nail, the King allowed the last part of that comment to pass, but he noted it. "Was it not you, my lord, who perceived the weakness in having an unwed heiress in so vulnerable a position?"

"I secured the Fenton lands—"

"By securing the girl? Was she not already promised in marriage to Lacey? Some would say your motives were questionable. Would the threat to the area have remained had you not interfered and prevented the marriage?"

"Your Grace, Thomas Lacey was, and still remains, a threat. His wife is sister to Warwick's man. He bears no love for the House of York, and you have allowed him to retain the basis with which he can build his affinity against you—"

"Enough!" The King boomed. "I have given him reason to serve me, reason you denied him when you refused his offer of service." He

stabbed a ringed finger in the Earl's direction. "It is *your* feud, my lord, this enmity between you has sown the seeds of discord you now reap." He let his sudden anger settle and took on a more conciliatory tone. "Come, my lord Earl, let us not quarrel. You have served me well, and I will reward you for it. Be content and let the Lacey matter go."

GLOUCESTER WAITED UNTIL they were alone before turning to his brother. "What of Isobel Fenton?"

Tetchy, Edward said, "What of her?"

"She has also done you great service and yet is robbed of her inheritance. Can you afford to let this injustice pass? What will be said of the King's law if a loyal heir can be so arbitrarily disinherited? Who is the guarantor of his subjects' peace if not the King?"

"I do not need reminding of my duty, Richard! I was doing my *duty* out on the field of battle this day."

Richard met his brother's anger with his steady gaze. "I would not seek to remind you but know you would wish to be counselled of it when pressing matters of state drive it from your mind."

Edward pushed his upper lip forward as he regarded his brother thoughtfully, then asked, "And what would my wise counsellor suggest his king do?"

"Reinstate the lands to Isobel Fenton."

"Did you not just hear my judgment on the matter!"

"I did," Gloucester replied evenly, "but the problem is not the Earl, for he has only ever sought to serve you. The problem lies in an unmarried heiress and an entailed inheritance to a man whose sole interest is the reversion of the property to his family."

"So, let him have it and be done with it!"

"But his interests are not ours, Edward. He will use the Fenton lands against us, be sure of it."

"So?"

"So, secure the inheritance by finding Isobel Fenton a suitable husband whose loyalty is beyond question."

"And Lacey?"

Gloucester's eyes hardened. "He keeps his head. That is more than he deserves."

THE EARL DREW his hand slowly over his face, his voice thick with fatigue. "So, Lacey keeps his head but loses the Fenton lands after all. What changed the King's mind?"

"Gloucester." Robert joined him at the small campaign table in the Earl's tent and washed his hands. He tore the flattened round loaf and offered his brother the larger half. The Earl laid it on the table before him but didn't touch it.

"Why?"

Rob coughed carefully, feeling it in his bones. "I know not, he didn't say. Perhaps he thought an injustice had been done to Isobel."

"By whom?"

Robert didn't rise to the challenge in his brother's tone. The Earl was clearly still angry after his confrontation with the King, but something else rankled. Now was not the time to tell him the condition that sealed the return of her lands, something he had yet to come to terms with himself. The Earl hacked a piece off the bread. "Gloucester must be grateful for the service you've done him today."

Robert chased bread with wine. "Why do you say that?"

"It was his first battle. I have seen bigger men than him piss themselves." He discarded the bread. "This tastes like rubble; you could use it to build walls."

"He took his injury saving me from a butcher with a glaive," Rob said quietly. "He did not hesitate."

The Earl noted his brother's cautious movements, remembered the fleeting hesitation before he raised his sword and struck the sergeant down. "I did not realise your injury. I owe the Duke a debt of gratitude in more ways than one."

Rob nodded without meeting his eyes. "The King wants to leave for London without delay. We've taken casualties, and he will call for as many fresh troops as he can muster before Anjou makes land. Do you intend to leave, or will you join us, brother?"

We? Us? When had Rob ever identified with anyone other than his own family? When had he lost his brother to another lord? With shock, the Earl recognised a fundamental shift in something he had always taken for granted. The bread on the table, the wine in his cup became torn flesh, shattered bone, blood, and his stomach heaved.

"You fare ill?" Robert asked as the Earl sat heavily, swallowing wine to clear his mouth, shaking the memory of the old man from his head.

"It is nothing sleep cannot cure," he said gruffly; then, more like his usual self, "I had better send a message to Felice before she celebrates mass for my untimely death. And we need more men, Rob, and we need them now. Let us see who remembers their old loyalties and comes to our banners. These next weeks will sort the wheat from the chaff."

Chapter 29

FELICE CRUSHED THE paper until it resembled a discarded rag stained with her husband's words. She dropped it into the fire and watched it burn. The message had eventually reached her from Roche after some confusion. It was clear that the Earl still believed her to be in sanctuary and was unaware of the arrangements she had made with Warwick regarding the estates. As far as she could see her options were now severely limited by his imminent return, and she had to move swiftly if she wanted to have any say over her future. Richard Neville had failed her twice: by not fulfilling his portion of their agreement, and by getting himself killed. The thought of him no longer being part of their lives left her feeling awkwardly empty, an absence she had not anticipated. He had been a heartbeat in her life, in the country, and now, even despite his death, much hung in the balance. In some ways he had been an anomaly – almost a distraction – upon whom neither king could entirely rely as ally or foe. His passing left a void that had to be filled and, even as she pondered this, Margaret of Anjou and the young Prince Edward, with the Duke of Somerset and the Earl of Oxford – carried on a bow wave of support from the West Country – swept towards the York king. Buoyed by his recent victory, Edward of York amassed more troops daily. Whatever the outcome, Felice had to safeguard her future and that of her son. She had to move fast.

"WHAT IS TAKING so long? I am starving. Drew's content enough; all he has to do is open his mouth and I feed him." Isobel smiled at the baby sleeping in the middle of the Earl's bed and the dogs – tethered to prevent them from jumping up beside him – on guard close by. His face was filling out and taking on distinctive Langton features, but his straight nose came directly from her father, for which she was thankful. Buena made eating motions and pointed to the child, then expanded the space between her hands in stages. "Yes, he is growing fast; it is difficult to eat enough to give him the milk he needs. Then again, if not for my lord steward we wouldn't have even that, so I suppose we must be grateful." She wrinkled her nose. "At least Cecily will be getting enough food in the nursery. I do miss her; I hope she fares well." She went to see if her kirtle was at last dry enough to wear. It wasn't. Beside the bed, Chou raised her head and hummed. "That must be the kitchen boy, Buena. Take the food but do not let him in, I am not modest."

Buena unbolted the door and peered out then bent and picked up something lying across the threshold. Rough wool wrapped a long, thin shape.

"What is it?" Isobel asked, holding out her hand. Buena gave Isobel the object. She unwound the cloth and extracted a wooden rod, half a yard in length, painted white. Puzzled, Isobel held it up for her to see. "Who left it? What is it meant for?"

Buena's eyes opened wide, and she coloured the same shade as the stick. She tried to snatch it from Isobel's hand.

"What do you think you are doing? It's mine, let go!" Isobel laughed in consternation.

Making odd sounds in her throat, Buena tried to tug it from her hand. Then without warning, Buena let go, her attention fixed on the door behind Isobel. She reached to slam the door shut as Isobel spun round, but it was too late.

"Who are you?" Isobel said in alarm as a man with a notched ear pushed into the room, followed by another with blotched skin. She dropped the stick and tried to cover herself with her hands. "Leave!"

"Take her," the first man said, then to Buena, who attempted to block him, "Out of my way, woman." He shoved her aside and she fell sideways awkwardly against the Earl's aumbry with an unwholesome *crack*. She lay still.

"Buena!" Isobel cried, then to the men, "What are you doing? How dare you... take your hands off me!"

Notch-ear secured her wrists and started pulling her towards the door as the other went towards the bed. He reached for the baby. "No!" Isobel screamed. "Don't touch him!" She sank her teeth into Notch-ear's hand and rammed her knee into his groin. His legs buckled and he swore violently, but he maintained his grip. "Keep still!" Then, to his rough-skinned companion, "Leave the tyke."

"We were to bring him..." Blotch-face hesitated as the dogs snarled and snapped, their tethers straining as they repeatedly lunged for him.

"There's time enough to deal with the ket."

Blotch-face shrugged, picked up the white stick and, stepping over Buena's prone body, followed them.

"Buena!" Isobel struggled to free herself from his grasp. "Why are you doing this?"

The man shook her roughly. "Quiet." And he pushed her towards the stairs, leaving the dogs barking furiously and the baby beginning to stir.

She heard them before she saw the crowd gathered in the bailey, and the mob noise became jeering as she was propelled into view at the top of the uncovered steps. Blinking in the glare of daylight, bewildered, she caught glimpses of writhing faces, snatches of phrases that coalesced into bile.

"You forgot this." The rod was thrust into her hand. He gave her a shove in the back, and she stumbled forward. "Move," he said as she looked down the steps at the raised faces of people crowded before her. She reached the bottom and looked back at him, but he gave no explanation, no hint that he would relent and let her retreat. "Walk," he ordered, and the gathering crowd slowly parted before her, making a crude path to the far gate towards which she slipped on greasy cobbles. She clasped her arms over the thin smock barely covering her breasts as freezing drizzle soaked the material, making it cling.

"Sssssssssss," quietly at first, building in momentum until, "Slut!" a woman bayed, then, *"Whore!"* Her voice was echoed by a rising chorus of barks and whistles, and someone close by set a rhythmic metallic beating – ugly, discordant – taken up in a slow clap and hiss and spreading like fire as she faltered down the path of people that drew in behind her. Blinded by shame, mute with fear, Isobel recognised barely a handful of the faces around her until she saw one that was familiar.

"Joan!" she called. The woman detached from the line and, for a second, Isobel thought the hand she held out was to steady her, but instead she reached over and poked something scratchy down her cleavage.

"Bitch," Joan hissed, stepping back and adopting the same slow chant as the others. Cold sweat replaced the chill, her skin burning, and through the eyes of the onlookers Isobel saw Ursula's scalded, shrivelled hands, pictured the bloated body of the girl floating in the millpond, and knew instinctively where this was leading.

Whatever it took, she couldn't leave Drew unprotected. Isobel turned, not caring now what anyone said, and began to sprint bare-legged back towards the stairs and her son, accompanied by whoops of ridicule. Dodging snatching hands, she made it to within spitting distance of the steps when she was brought down with a punch to her head. She skidded onto her knees, feeling the skin tear from the heels of her hands against the stone. Still dazed, she was hauled to her feet and pitched in the direction of the gate's gaping Hell-mouth waiting to consume her and disgorge her into the void. Guards leaned over the parapet to watch, and figures by the gate observed her progress towards them – the porter, and another, dark-robed and smiling.

"Master Sawcliffe! Please, help me!" But she was grabbed from behind.

"Yer won't need this where you're goin'." A rough hand pulled her hair into a tangled rope, another wielded shears and began to hack off crude hanks. The sawn hair was held aloft like a trophy accompanied by heckling applause. She looked wildly about the range of buildings. From across the court a figure moved in the extravagant solar window of the family chambers, and Isobel made out the gleam of the Countess's white face. A hood – a red hood, a whore's hood – was crammed over Isobel's naked head, and she was prodded towards the entrance.

"Master Sawcliffe, *please*! Protect my baby!" If he heard her, he made no indication of it and instead seemed distracted, turning away to look through the gate towards the drawbridge. The swell of people behind compelled her forward, sizzling with anticipation, greedy for the show.

Shouts from the guards on duty on the tower roof joined the raucous voices below, drowning out her own cries for help. A low rumble, indistinct at first, then recognisably metal shrouded by stone blotted out all other sound, reverberating within the confines of the gatehouse as the windlass took the weight of the drawbridge's great chains. From the guardhouse, men tumbled dragging sword belts around their waists, grabbing polearms, and throwing spears from wall racks, passing her as if she had become suddenly invisible.

Crows of alarm replaced jeers, people scattering like a shoal threatened by a pike, making for the shelter of the buildings. Isobel shrank against the damp stone, snatching the hood from her hair and using it to cover her breasts as she backed away from the gateway unnoticed. "Get behind me and stay hidden," a gruff voice said, and the sergeant-at-arms moved between her and the gate.

"Sergeant, help me!"

"Quiet," he warned.

Isobel took Cecily's scratchy poppet from where it had been wedged in her smock and grasped it to her. "I must go to my baby—"

He spoke from the side of his mouth. "Hold still, lass; no one'll be interested in you now." She looked over her shoulder towards the stairs to the tower. There was no sign of either of the two men. Had they returned to the tower for Drew? Fear unlocked her legs, and she began to move towards the stairs, but the sergeant uttered an oath and his hand went to his sword as the portcullis grated and the gate began to swing open. She froze. Horseshoes rang against stone, and the breath of animals stained the air. The sound of running and agitated voices that had filled the bailey came to a sudden standstill and was replaced by hush. She strained to see what was happening, but the sergeant's bulk obstructed her view. The horses grew closer.

Without warning, the sergeant dropped back on one knee, head bent, leaving Isobel standing like a leafless tree in the fen, alone and conspicuous, staring at a gilded spur.

Chapter 30

SLOWLY, SHE LOOKED up to be met with the Earl's dispassionate gaze. He scanned her shivering, drizzle-drenched body, the hood and rod clutched in vain protection. He took in her shorn, rain-lank hair, the doll crushed to her chest. His eyes scrutinised the courtyard, dropped to the length of hair lying bedraggled and forgotten, honey against stone, and his mouth tightened. Without a word, he heeled his horse forward towards the great hall.

The courtyard exploded into activity. "Better get thee covered and then back to the tower," the sergeant advised, taking her by the elbow and hurrying her towards the guardroom with a weather eye on the Earl's back. "My lord wasn't expected, and there's going to be trouble." It had begun to rain again. He went to the rear of the room, found a cloak, and she huddled into the mantle reeking of wet wool and wood smoke as he led her back outside and towards the tower stairs.

She ran up the steps, never more glad to be within the confines of the tower than now, pausing only to pull air into her straining lungs before continuing to the council chamber, crossing the floor, and making the final flight of stairs towards the privy chamber. She entered the vestibule, greeted by neither the crying of the baby nor the whining of the dogs. The door was still ajar. Heart crashing, she pushed it wide.

Buena sat propped against the cupboard, knees drawn to her chest, holding her hand to the side of her head, her eyes vacant with shock. On the other side of the room, both dogs were mute. Isobel stared at the confusion of pillows thrown to one side, bedclothes pulled awry. She couldn't see the baby. She let out a strangled cry and ran to the bed, dropping the doll and hood and rod. Drew lay there in a tangle of cloth, arms and legs blue-tinged and bare, his eyes wide open.

"Andrew!" she cried, using the last of her breath. At the sound of his name, he beat the air with his limbs, and Isobel scooped him from the bed, holding him to her, feeling him all over and weak with gratitude to find him cold but unharmed. Wrapping him snugly, she kissed his fluff of dark hair, breathed in his scent, felt his baby-soft skin against her own cool, wet flesh. "Thank Jesu, thank Jesu," she said over and over again, her eyes closed, holding him tightly until he began to squirm and search for food.

Behind her, the sound of a stool falling had her swing around. Buena struggled to her feet, swaying. "Stay still!" Isobel said, righting the stool and helping her sit. "Let me look at that." She laid Drew on the bed and, removing Buena's headdress, inspected the side of her head where a distinct line beneath the dark hair reflected the unyielding edge of the cupboard. Buena focused unsteadily as she took in Isobel's dilapidated state. She touched the massacred hair, her face creasing in distress, saw Isobel's torn hands, the bruising on her wrists. "It matters not; my hair will grow and my skin will heal. Sit there, and I will make you a poultice for your head."

Buena took Isobel's hands and, kissing them, climbed to her feet, gesticulating.

"I am fine, just a little cold. We are both cold." But, at her insistence, Isobel took Drew to the welcome warmth of the fire, while Buena filled the copper basin and washed first one hand and then the other, taking care to ease the grit from the ragged skin. "The last time you did this I had skinned my elbow on the garden path, do you remember? I must have been about seven." She gave a little smile. "That seems a very long time ago. A lifetime away. What would my lady mother say if she could see us now?"

Buena finished drying Isobel's hand and picked up the basin without comment, and Isobel was left to interpret her silence. Cradling the baby, she inspected a tag of loose skin that stung her palm, but a harsh crash of metal hitting stone had her spinning to her feet, expecting to find Buena collapsed.

"Buena! *NO!*" Water from the basin swam at the room's entrance as Buena blocked the doorway, arms outstretched, dagger positioned so that two steps further would have driven it into the Earl's heart. "Buena, get back. Now!" Isobel grabbed the arm with the knife. "It was not him. He did not do this to me."

The Earl's initial surprise turned to anger. He raised his hand, eyes blazing.

"Buena!" Isobel snapped before he could strike her. With deliberate slowness, the woman stood back, eyes locked on the Earl's face, her lips drawn from her teeth, an animal guarding her young.

"My lord, she is just trying to protect us," Isobel interceded. "She was hurt trying to stop those men. Look at her head – she is still confused."

The Earl cast a look at Buena's reddened scalp, then at Isobel and what she carried, and his expression changed. Stiffly, as if he had been long in the saddle, he moved towards her. "My child?"

His child? Silently she begged forgiveness for the lie, and nodded. He reached out and, carefully folding the cover back from the infant's face, touched his finger to Drew's cheek. Instantly, the baby's mouth came around seeking to suckle, and he stroked his skin gently.

"Andrew." The Earl's expression melted into one of wonder. "My son."

A BRIGHT WIND had sprung up during the night, clearing the low cloud and drying the stone flags of the bailey. It was packed and, in contrast to the previous day, the noise of the crowd gathered around the temporary scaffold was subdued despite the sun. The second of the two men, his face noticeably marked, hands bound behind his back and rope around his neck, balanced on the ladder next to the suspended body of the ear-notched man. He glanced at the solar window as the constable gave the signal and the ladder was removed. He swung, twisting and jerking, for as long as it took for his life to be choked from him, and a sigh rose from the onlookers, swept by the wind through the open casement of the Countess's window from where the Earl watched the proceedings. He waited until the sergeant-at-arms checked for signs of life, the bodies were lowered to the ground, and the company, assembled to watch the executions, began to disperse. The Earl closed the casement and faced his wife. She continued looking straight ahead into the fire.

"Did you really think I would not act?" She declined to respond, and the rage he had contained since returning home began to smoulder anew. He slung the red hood and rod at her feet. "The fruit of your labours, madam. Two men have died, and another awaits interrogation. Did you think I would not find out who lay behind these attacks? Or did you hope I would fail to return at *all*?" Her eyes slid to the items on the floor by her feet and then to his face, tight with discomfort from cracked ribs causing him to break for breath.

"How could I allow her to remain under the same roof when her presence brings shame on your wife and your heir? I could hardly hold my head up at Court. You were not here to defend us, so I had to make of the situation what best I could."

"Is that what you call crawling to the enemy? *Making the best* of it? What other arrangements did you make with Warwick in my absence?"

She gave him a quick, sharp look, gauging his mood. "I saved *your* title and *your* lands for your *heir*. If it were not for me, they would have been forfeit to the Crown—"

"But as it turned out you gained complete control over them. How my return must have inconvenienced you. You will have to wait a while longer before you have such an opportunity again. Let me make it very clear: should I, by some misfortune, die before the child comes of age, my brother will be custodian of his inheritance, not you. I will not risk Langton titles falling into enemy hands."

"You talk about your son yet never mention him by name. You have barely seen him and regard him even less. What place do your whore and your bastard have here? Do you know she suckles the brat like the base-born harlot she is? Is that what you want – to debase your blood with *that*?"

His hands tingled; he felt the urge to reach out and take her by her fine white throat, to feel his fingers curve around her soft, cool skin, to squeeze the breath from her until her eyes bulged. He curled his fists and consciously released the tension in them.

"I warned you not to harm her, Felice. I told you I would not let it lie." He left the threat hanging and went to fulfil the promise he had made earlier that morning.

HIS SUBDUED DAUGHTER stood in front of him, waiting for a rebuke. With difficulty, the Earl kneeled, bringing himself to her height. "I believe this is yours." Cecily took the still-damp object from his hand. She smoothed the tatty dress. "Mistress Fenton said she will make a new gown for your poppet, and she has braided its hair." He expected a response. She said nothing, just looked, and he frowned. "Are you not pleased to have it back?" She nodded, then surprised him by throwing her arms around his neck, almost knocking him off balance. "Careful!" he said sharply, regretting it as her body stiffened and she began to retreat. Awkwardly, he stroked her hair. "Your father did not mean to shout. He is… I am pleased to see you." Still no response. "Cecily?"

She pushed his arm away. "When can I see Is'bel and Gowk and Moth and Ba'na?"

He held her hands. "There is no room for you in the tower. You will stay here with your lady mother and your servants." Cecily's lower lip trembled. "Now," he said briskly, intercepting tears, "you must take better care of your poppet and not lose it again. Mistress Fenton might not find it next time."

The child cast a fearful glance over her shoulder at the ample attendant, who seemed to be busy at her work nearby, and dropped her gaze. "That is better. The daughter of an earl does not cry, does she? She is always dutiful and brave." He kissed her on both cheeks, avoiding the dark eyes that pleaded with him. "You may embrace me, and I will carry to Mistress Fenton your thanks for her kindness." She placed a tiny, wet kiss on his cheek, and he resisted the temptation to wipe it, instead climbing carefully to his feet. "Be an obedient girl, and I expect Mistress Fenton will want you to attend her soon."

Cecily's chin jutted. "Joan won't let me."

"Joan will do whatever she is told, as will you."

"But I want to learn my letters. Is'bel teached me."

"She is too busy with Andrew to instruct you now. You will learn here."

"But I want Is'bel to learn me," she screamed. "I want Is'bel!" And she threw her poppet to the floor and ran from the room, leaving her father dumbfounded and Joan smirking.

"Who is Gowk?" he queried when he returned to his chamber in not the best of moods. He sat with caution, and Isobel left the window where she had watched proceedings in the bailey with a mixture of horror and fascination and fed cushions behind his back to support his aching ribs.

"You have seen Cecily, my lord?" she said, surprised.

"You asked me to," he responded gruffly. "She was in a contrary humour. I do not understand her."

"Did you give Nan back to her?"

"*Nan?* Is that what it is called? Yes, but she did not seem thankful."

Isobel tucked a cushion under his arm, and he rested it gratefully. "My lord, you do not know her. She is a loving girl and very quick."

"She has a quick temper."

"As does her fader," she reminded him. "She misses her sister and is lonely." She slipped onto her knees in front of him, ignoring the bruising from the previous day. "My lord, Cecily is unhappy in the nursery. Might she not be found a room here in the tower? Then I can oversee her lessons, and Buena will care for her far better than anyone else."

"She remains where she is. You are not her dam, and you have other duties looking after my son. Which reminds me, a woman in your position should not be feeding her own child; it is not meet. You should have found a wet nurse for him."

A woman in her *position*? Isobel slowly exhaled her exasperation. "I had no money, and no respectable woman would serve me here. And I would not have Drew nursed by a stranger in town even if there had been someone I would entrust him with. He is *my* son."

"And I am his father and your lord, and I will say how he is to be cared for. Do not look at me in that manner, Isobel, I want what is best for both of you. Moreover, I have been informed that Master Taylor attended the birth. That is not something that should have happened."

"But Ursula was dead, and I had no one else. And if it was not for Pip, I wouldn't even have had the midwife—"

"If Taylor had done his duty, you would not have been put in that position in the first place, and Ursula would still be alive. He failed to protect you and should be punished."

She thought of those men swinging in the bailey, and the possibility that Pip might join them was too horrific to contemplate. "It was not his fault. I did not wait for him as I said I would but went for a walk."

"Nonetheless."

"But it wasn't his *fault*!" She all but stamped her foot. "It was mine, and the Countess..." She came to a halt as the Earl's mouth became iron at the mention of his wife.

"As he is my brother's man I will take no further action against him, but I will recommend he is replaced. I had not realised things had become so lax, nor you so poorly served, Isobel, and I am to blame for leaving you overlong in unsuitable company. But I will make amends and secure a servant for you. I did not expect to see that... female... here." He gestured towards Buena on the other side of the chamber, gathering Isobel's things while watching over Drew as he slept. Isobel rocked to her feet, making the Earl start, her eyes glistening ominously bright. "Where are you going? I have not given you permission to leave." Her fists scrunched until her knuckles blanched, and he wasn't certain whether she was on the brink of tears or about to scratch out his eyes as she struggled to compose herself.

"Why do you dislike her so? My lord, I have done everything you have bidden since coming here: I lost my chance to marry, have submitted to your will, and I keep your bed, but I will *not* give up Buena again. She is *my* servant and my mother's before me, and if you send her away, I will go too and take Andrew with me. And feed him myself," she appended in case he had other ideas.

Rising to his feet, he stared down at her. "Will you now?" he said with an undercurrent of threat. "And where will you go with *your* servant and *my* son?"

She wanted to say, *he's not your son,* and *I'm taking him to his father where we belong;* but that would have been madness, so she bit her tongue and instead said simply, "Not here," and waited for the flash of his temper to whip her into order.

"Why not here, Isobel?" he asked, his voice dropping. She hadn't expected that. "Why do you not want to be here?"

"I... I do not belong," she faltered.

"And would it help you to *belong* if I allowed your servant to stay?" She viewed him warily, suspecting a trap, and nodded quickly. He paused before answering. "Then she can stay."

"And you will let me nurse Drew myself?" she ventured.

"As long as I can watch." He sat again, picked a wafer from the nearby dish, and demolished it as her anger evaporated. Detecting a source of food, Moth bounced up to his elbow. "I did not say that the tyke could remain, however. It offends me." She was about to defend the dog when he raised a sardonic brow, and she realised he teased. "I can hardly separate the two of you. It had better stay; it has the makings of a good guard dog." Canting his head, he asked, "Have you nothing to say to me?"

Twisting her hands, she murmured, "Thank you, my lord."

"And… is that all?"

All? What else did he want her to say?

"Come here." He took her hand and pulled her closer. "Did you not miss me these many months?"

"I prayed for you every day, my lord."

"You prayed for me. Does that mean you regretted my absence?" She avoided his eyes. "You said your Paternoster and Aves for me, did you?"

"Yes. And for the King and the Duke of Gloucester."

"Yes, of course you did. You are dutiful, as your father once told me." He surveyed her thoughtfully. "And my brother? Did you pray for him too?"

Heat rose to her hairline, but thankfully Drew began to wake and wriggle, giving her an excuse to escape scrutiny, except the Earl held onto her hands. "Well?" he asked.

She nodded, looking down. "Yes, and for Lord Robert."

"As indeed you should." He watched her avoid him for a moment longer then kissed her knuckles. "We need your prayers, and I pray that war will not separate us again."

"War? But is not the country settled?"

"Far from it. Warwick might be dead – Montagu as well – but Anjou and her son are still gathering men to their standards, and they will need to be defeated before a decisive victory can be declared. Why?"

"I thought it was over."

"Isobel, you are shaking. Come..." He balanced her on his knees like a father with a young child. "There is no need to be frightened. I cannot leave until my ribs are healed, and that will be at least a month yet, and by then the victor will be decided."

"But what if King Henry is victorious? What if King Edward is killed, or his brother, or... or..."

"Mine?"

"Yes," she whispered.

He touched her temple where a short stray hair caught in her eyebrow and stroked it clear. "If the tide turns against the House of York, I have plans to preserve us." He kissed her hand again. "Until then, our best course of action is to trust in God and prayer. You will continue to pray for the King, will you not?"

"Yes, of course."

"Then you will need your beads." His voice dropped lower. "Where is your chaplet, Isobel?"

Without thinking, her hand went to her waist before she remembered, and her thoughts scattered like finches. "My chaplet?" She located that part of her mind still in control. "I... gave it to Lord Robert when he went into exile; he had none." And without a moment's hesitation, she followed with, "Please forgive me, I know it was a gift, but I also sent the Duke of Gloucester my games box. It was the day of his nativity, and I thought you would deem it fit for me to do so." When had deceit become part of her vocabulary? When had lies slipped so easily off her tongue? Or, if not lies exactly, her intent to hide from the Earl that element of her bound so tightly to his brother that she could no longer perceive the truth in her mind.

"I am sure it was received in the spirit in which it was given," he said measuredly, and Isobel threw him a quick look. Whom did he mean – the Duke or his brother? Did she read into his words something that wasn't there because of her own guilt? Isn't that what her father used to say, that men judged others by their own standards?

"I wanted His Grace to remember us kindly."

"As I am certain he does."

Drew started up his *I'm-starving-and-neglected* routine, and any response she might have made was negated by his steadily rising wail.

Buena put Isobel's bundle of clothes down and picked him up. The Earl loured in her direction. "What is the woman doing with your clothes?"

Isobel stood up. "Taking them back to my… to the armoury, my lord."

"That is not necessary. You will stay here." He rested his head against the back of the chair and closed his eyes against the pain. Pallor leached his sun-washed skin, the creases between his eyes incised more deeply. Exhaustion paved the way for sleep. She looked around the room that had been hers for nigh on six months and felt its walls shrink.

"But I… I am still nursing."

He opened one eye, looked at her, closed it again. "Yes."

She collapsed onto the stool, raising her palms in a gesture of abandoned hope, and Buena – placing Drew in her arms and keeping an eye on the Earl – raised two fingers and made them dance. In a final flourish, the little finger wound around the bigger forefinger, bringing it to a standstill in a stranglehold. Isobel studied the fingers and then the sleeping Earl, and Buena cocked a brow.

Chapter 31

ALREADY HOT, THE mid-June sun skirted benign cloud, raising the vapour of overnight rain from the broad wood beams of the drawbridge over which Robert Langton had crossed so often in the past that he had lost count. This time felt different.

Bringing his horse to a standstill, the Duke waited for Robert to catch up. "Much has changed since we last left these walls, has it not, my lord?"

Rob gave a mere nod in acknowledgment of Gloucester's dry observation and nudged his horse forward, hearing the changing melody of hooves upon hollow wood as together they crossed the bridge and under the grim-arched gatehouse, where banners flew in acclamation and challenge.

The constable greeted the small group of mounted men, and the bailey came alive. "We did not expect Your Grace. My lord—"

Rob flicked a look at the tower gleaming white in the early morning sun. "Is my brother in residence?"

"He is, my lord. I'll send word to the Earl of His Grace's arrival, but—"

"No matter, I will do so myself." Dismounting without ceremony, Robert and Gloucester crossed the bailey and mounted the steps to the tower two at a time.

A fire had been laid but remained unlit in the council chamber, and the casement had been opened to the sun. From the battlements, doves' mellow voices softened the chatter of sparrows. Footsteps on the stairs preceded the steward, and he appeared, puffing and apologetic. His servant ran ahead, disappearing through the door and up the steps in the thickness of the wall to the Earl's privy chamber, as the steward, sweat at his hairline, ordered refreshment.

Above them a door thudded open and, yelping with excitement, Chou and Moth rattled down the stairs and into the chamber towards them, eyes bright and tails thrashing. Gloucester bent to ruffle their ears. Moments later the Earl appeared, long gown pulled around him, his hair unkempt, his chin still roughened with the night. He bowed – a little stiffly, Rob thought.

"Your Grace has caught us unprepared. Forgive my state of undress. You are most welcome to whatever hospitality I might offer."

"It is I who have breached courtesy, my lord, by not giving you greater warning, but I am on my way north and persuaded Langton to allow me to repay my debt, and so we find ourselves here unannounced." Gloucester handed his dust-edged cloak to a servant.

"Debt, Your Grace?"

"Indeed, for your hospitality and to Mistress Fenton for our comfort. The latter might need greater explanation," he added, grinning at the Earl's perplexed look.

"In which case I urge Your Grace to stay and elaborate over breakfast. I need no thanks, and Isobel will rejoice at your safe return." He bowed his head then addressed his brother. "Rob, I thank Almighty God for your safe delivery." He embraced him warmly, if carefully, then, standing back, examined him. "You took no hurt at Tewkesbury? You look in need of rest and meat."

Tired? Yes, he was tired. His bones ached and his muscles screamed for mercy, but the fatigue he felt went far beyond his body. It ate at him, at his soul. On the contrary, his brother looked better than he had seen him in a long while. Rob raised a smile. "None other than bruises and a sight less than the enemy."

"I wish by all the Saints I had been there. After everything they have put us through, I would have liked to have seen the Lancaster whelp culled – Somerset and Devon too." Food had begun arriving from the kitchens and was being laid discreetly on white linen cloths using the table dormant as a trestle. Rob noted a tray laid with dishes and ewer being taken upstairs to the privy chamber. Distracted, he traced the footsteps to the room above, imagined Isobel there in his brother's bed, perhaps waking, her long hair tumbled from the night. Chou thrust her muzzle into his hand, breaking his thoughts. The Earl was asking Gloucester about the victory at Tewkesbury as the Duke washed his hands assiduously in the stream of water pouring from the jug held for him over the silver basin.

"It has taken the fuel from Anjou's fire. With the old king now dead in the Tower and her son killed in the field, there is little left to fight for and no one left to do it. But they led us a dance before it came to battle, and our victory was never assured until it was won." There was little sense of triumph in the way he said it, as if after only eighteen years of life he was already weary of it. Gloucester flexed his fingers in the warm water, softening the sword-worn callouses. "By God's will it might as easily have been our lives taken that day, not theirs. You are healed of your injury, my lord?"

The Earl felt his ribs, still tender through the figured red velvet of the gown. "I am in most part, Your Grace; and you also?"

"Well enough to fight." The Duke smiled a little ruefully, taking the cloth presented to him. "We could have done with your sword."

"The outcome would have been little changed."

"The outcome, perhaps, but your presence would have stiffened our troops' resolve and cast doubt into the hearts of our enemies."

"I think Your Grace flatters me."

Dropping the cloth on the table, Gloucester looked at him sharply. "I do not squander words, my lord. Our victory was won at great cost to ourselves as well as to our enemy. Do not underestimate the value I place on loyalty. We have seen little enough of it these last years. As it is, I have much for which to thank Langton fealty," he said, looking at Rob as he sat down at the table.

Robert shook his head. "We watched each other's back, Your Grace, and I am well-rewarded for it." He waited for his brother to wash his hands before doing the same, although he had no appetite for food.

While Gloucester and the Earl ate and discussed the uneasy peace now settling upon the country, Robert picked at the salted fish with limited enthusiasm. Moth had been investigating his boots with an exploratory lick or two, but now her ears pricked and, without warning, she skipped long-legged from under the table, through the far door, and up the stairs. Rob thought he heard the faintest cry through the heavily timbered floor, but it was silenced before he could trace its origin. A bee entered the room before unhurriedly exiting the way it had come.

"Well, my lord?" Gloucester asked.

"Your Grace?"

Gloucester dipped bread into wine. "Your brother asked what your plans are now we have secured peace."

"Plans?" There, that sound again – tiny, almost a squeak. He strained to hear it again.

The Earl almost laughed. "Yes, *plans*, unless you wish to remain unwed. You will make a better match with these new offices you've earned."

Robert wasn't listening. A noise – distinct this time – a baby's cry. He half rose to his feet, but his brother beat him to it. Wiping his hands and excusing himself, the Earl left the room with Chou at his heels. Gloucester made some comment, but Rob didn't hear him, the pounding in his ears expanding until it deafened him. Remains of food lay like scattered bones on dishes, blood wine in pools in the base of glasses – all rank with death. Through the lions in his head, he made out his brother's returning steps, Gloucester rising from the chair, and then a cheerful demand he look at what the Earl carried. Slowly, Robert raised his head. From his brother's arms a tight-fisted infant gazed back at him, round-cheeked with wisps of charcoal hair and searching steel eyes. They stared at each other. The baby frowned uncertainly, wobbled, then broke into a wide beam revealing bumpy pink gums. He reached a chubby hand towards Rob's shiny boar badge attached to his doublet.

The Earl laughed. "He is your bond man already, Your Grace."

Not entirely certain how to respond, Gloucester smiled diligently, holding out his finger, which the baby eagerly grabbed. "He is a fine boy, and the King will no doubt be pleased to stand godfather to him and grant him a position at Court when he reaches an age."

The baby let go of the Duke's finger and rocked to one side, trying to reach the silver badge again, kicking against the Earl's ribs as he did so. The Earl winced and shifted the baby to his other arm. "Not my son by the Countess, Your Grace. This—" he said, "—is my son, Andrew." His voice vibrated with pride, and Rob's heart recoiled from its warmth, shrinking into a hard ball of iron that burned away in his chest.

The child's gentle burp disguised Gloucester's momentary surprise, and the baby wrinkled his nose and laughed, cramming his fist into his mouth. The Duke recovered. "He… has your likeness, my lord, but is more inclined to good humour than his sire, would you not agree, Langton?" But Robert had frozen, and the Duke, following his line of sight, spotted a figure in the shadow of the door. He beamed in recognition. "Mistress Fenton, well met! We are admiring your son."

Avoiding Robert's eyes, she entered the room, dropping into a curtsy before the Duke amidst swathes of richly embroidered cherry silk, light reflecting from the snug, elaborate headdress worked with metal wire and pearls as she bent her head. Gloucester helped her rise. "I have come to thank you for your service to us. It pleases God we meet in better circumstances than of late." He swiftly kissed her on both cheeks. He tilted his head, appraising her. "You are yet more fair than when last we met."

She was. Rob saw that her clear skin had warmed from the Duke's attention, her blue-green eyes brightening as she lifted her wriggling son from the Earl's arms. She had regained much of her vitality and moved with the fulsome confidence of motherhood. If she wasn't the same girl he had met in her garden – her hair drawn neatly from her brow, and the fingers that swept the baby's dribble from his chin now smooth and free of sap – she nonetheless exuded the same light, bringing the memory of that first meeting surging back, and it hurt. It must have shown because she chanced a look at him as she turned, and he saw his pain reflected in her face. Just in that moment, that fleeting heartbeat of time, before she disguised it with a smile.

The Earl was tickling the baby's cheek, smiling as Drew tried to mouth his finger. "Isobel, His Grace sees Andrew's resemblance to his sire."

"It is the drivel that does it," Gloucester shot back, fingering his chin and indicating the child's drool. Isobel laughed and nuzzled her son's ear until he chortled, and their combined joy cut Rob like scythes.

He'd had enough. At the first opportunity he left them, with his brother trying to feed the baby pieces of flaked fish and Isobel laughing and protesting, and went in search of distraction – anything, rather than face the possibility that his brother made her *happy*.

Rob's abrupt departure left Isobel floundering in confusion. She took herself to the window seat overlooking the bailey, welcoming the stream of warm air and the sounds of life outside. The scaffold had long since been dismantled, and where bodies had swung several esquires now practised arms. She recognised Martin sparring with the Duke's esquire, and curly-haired Louys looking on, and by the guardhouse Pip exchanged gossip with the sergeant-at-arms. Evidently, Rob had disregarded his brother's advice to dismiss Pip. At the thought of the haunted look on his face when he saw his son, the misery that had dogged her bubbled closer to the surface. She had registered the Earl's brief words to her with a varnished smile as he, too, departed the room, and she was now left with her doubts and fears ready to split the calm exterior she struggled to maintain. Squeezing her hands together, she adopted a benign expression she had often observed in her mother before she was old enough to understand what might lie behind the mask of passivity.

The Duke joined her, and she saw he noted the fierce tension in her hands and made an effort to relax them.

"I came to offer my thanks for the service you did me, and to return this." He placed into her hands a leather box of about two hands' span wide and the same deep, the hardened surface embossed with foliate designs picked out in greens and reds, and gilded with idle lilies and white roses. A gilt metal lock secured the two halves of the box. He handed her a key in answer to her puzzled look. "Open it."

The key turned smoothly, and she pulled the two halves apart. "My games chest!" she said, surprised.

"The sea crossing was a little rough and the bag damaged beyond repair. I had this made in Bruges in the hope I might return your gift in person one day. Here, can you see what hides among the vines?"

She squinted, making out the ridged back and tusks of a wild boar. She smiled, despite herself. "It is more than I deserve; thank you, Your Grace."

"I would have included your own device, but do not know it."

"I do not have one."

"Oh." He frowned, then smiled. "Anyway, I had lilies placed among the roses instead." Lilies of virtue: the symbol of the Virgin. Given her state of pregnancy when he had last seen her, the irony was not lost on her. Nor, it would seem, on him. "Lilies for the pure of heart, Mistress Fenton," he said, regarding her earnestly and without his customary humour. In the bailey, Robert had joined Martin and the other youths. "And for those with good intent." He gave her one of his broad, unguarded smiles, and she offered a quick nod in response.

"Did you recover your chess pieces, Your Grace?"

"No. The King has made me a princely gift of a set, but I still carry this." He pulled the king with its chipped crown from the pouch at his waist, looked at it as if reminding himself, then replaced it in the bag and took a folded document from it instead. "There is something else I must return to you." He proffered the sealed parchment.

Isobel opened it, read the first few lines, and looked up, her brow forming corrugations. "I do not understand..."

"It is a letter of intent. The King has determined your lands be returned to you. They were granted to Thomas Lacey unlawfully, and they are yours for you and your heirs to do with as you wish."

Her heir. Isobel exhaled. Now she had something more than his bastardy to leave her son. "Does the Earl know?"

"He does." The Duke paused, weighing up whether to continue. "He risked the King's displeasure in the pursuit of justice for you." Isobel reread the letter and the signature at the end, unscrambling her thoughts. On the floor between them, Moth rolled onto her back, taking up all the space and lying on the Duke's feet with her tongue lolling. "As a woman of estate and good birth you might give heed to a symbol of your own – a lily, perhaps?"

Checking to see whether he teased, Isobel saw he was serious. "Not a lily, Your Grace, I am not worthy of it."

The Duke stretched his legs out sideways past the dog, who stirred but didn't move. "What, then? A lank-limbed hound?"

She studied her hands. "A dove, Your Grace." She smiled up at him. "I would have a dove."

He considered it for a moment in the particular way he had - turning his thoughts inward - before looking at her directly again. "For constancy and the pure of heart. The choice of a device is not to be taken lightly; you have chosen well." He smiled and might have said more, but metal clashed in the bailey, catching their attention. Rob had disarmed one of the youths who was rubbing his arm, and now demonstrated feint and parry to the esquires, tossing the sword to Martin and standing back to let them work the moves.

The Duke watched with intelligent interest. "Lord Robert is not someone to cross on the field of battle – he lends a certainty to any outcome. I was glad to have him by my side."

Hearing the respect in the Duke's voice, Isobel marked the intricate manoeuvres being mapped out below. She had never seen Rob in the practice yard before and had avoided imagining him in battle. She had witnessed the results of war in her father's mutilated body and the lifeless eyes of Ralph Lacey and never wanted to see it again. But not once had she considered that Rob might be the one delivering death. "Is that what battle does to you, Your Grace, make things more certain?"

"Is that how it seems? No, you value life all the more because it can be taken away from you by another man's sword."

Louys misjudged a lunge and ended up on his back with a dagger to his throat. Isobel thought she could see the white of his eyes. "So much anger, so much… *hate*," she said almost to herself.

"Do you think so?" Gloucester asked. "I remember fear, excitement, relief – and confusion, so much confusion. But not hate, nor anger, even, or nothing that lasted more than a few moments. I did not know the men I killed."

"Would it have made a difference if you did?"

"Yes, probably. But you do not think, you just react, and all the years of training take over. It is not the man in a gambeson or behind the visor you see, only the sword or billhook they hold in their hand. You kill the sword, not the man."

Caught in a line of web across the corner of the casement, a small brown butterfly beat in a vain attempt to free its wings, reminding Isobel of the lurching bodies of the two men on the scaffold. The Duke leaned forward and broke the web. The butterfly sat on his finger to recover while Gloucester picked a stray thread from the creature and watched it lift into the free air beyond the window. "In battle, you do not have time to consider the men you fight until it is over, and then it is all you can think about. You see their face in the moment before death, imprinted on your memory. Langton warned me not to look at Warwick's corpse, but I did. Now it is all I can see, and I cannot remember what he looked like in life." In raising his eyes to the unsullied sky perhaps he hoped to obliterate the image of the mortuary tent. He looked young and oddly vulnerable, and Isobel couldn't imagine him facing death on the field. Without thinking, she touched his arm, feeling the iron-bound muscles move beneath the light fabric.

"Your Grace, he flew too close to the sun."

He blinked. "Yes." He levelled his eyes to meet hers, and she was relieved to see his usual resolve restored in their clear depths. "Sometimes we have to break something to mend it."

"But in breaking it, it can never be the same," she ventured.

"No, it cannot. War changes men and drives them to do things they abhor in others – love also." He paused at that thought before continuing. "War brings change, and we must change with it if order is to be restored." He smiled at her sombre expression, dissolving the chill that had gathered about them. "But not all change is for ill, is it? Look at your son; that is one altered circumstance that has made his sire glad." He nodded in the direction of the bailey, and Isobel saw that the Earl had joined Rob. As she watched, he dismissed the esquires and the brothers entered into close discussion. At one point, Rob broke away, striding a few yards, then returned in short, angry steps. He gesticulated towards the tower, and the Earl placed a hand on his shoulder in what looked like appeasement. Without warning, Rob took a backward step and threw a punch.

The Earl found Rob in the bailey taking several of the esquires through their paces within the roped-off practice yard. By the time he joined them, Louys had come off worse in a contest and was nursing his arm while watching from the relative security of the temporary wooden post from which the rope ran. The Earl could tell from the set of his shoulders that his brother was in no mood to give quarter.

"My lord," he called as he neared. "I would speak with you." He waved the esquires away as Rob wiped sweat from his top lip, clearly resenting the interruption.

"What is it?"

The Earl closed the gap between them, ensuring they couldn't be overheard. "Come inside. There are matters I wish to discuss."

"Matters?" Robert shrugged. "There is nothing that cannot be said out here." He loosened dry soil from between the flagstones with the point of his sword and crushed it into dust beneath his heel.

"This concerns Isobel—"

"And why would I want to discuss *her*?"

"That is precisely why we have to talk. This involves you also."

Abruptly, Rob stopped his excavations. "How?"

"Come inside," the Earl insisted, but Robert remained stubbornly rooted as he might have done at fourteen. The Earl sighed at his brother's obstinacy. "Very well. The way you behaved towards Isobel earlier—"

"Did she send you?" he butted in.

"No, of course not. I wanted to say that I understand how difficult it must be for you seeing my son—"

"*Your* son!" Rob paced a few yards, hand gripping the pommel of his sword, shoulders hunched.

"… but that I do not want you holding it against Isobel. Whatever happens, she is not to blame."

Wheeling around, Rob returned to face his brother. "Blame Isobel? For what?"

"We keep this between ourselves. No one must know about it, not yet—"

"By all the Saints, know *what*?"

"I should have done this a long time ago – I owe it to Isobel, to our son – and of course I will ensure provision is made for Felice and the children. She ceased to be my wife in all but name years before all… this. Cecily will have a good dowry, and Bess bears her husband's name. As for the boy, I will make suitable arrangements."

Colour leached from Robert's face. "You intend to put Felice aside."

"Yes." The Earl put his hand on his brother's shoulder. "I know this comes as a surprise—"

Robert threw him off. "You've lost your wits!"

"Keep your voice down."

"Does Felice know? Does Isobel?"

"I have said nothing yet and nor will you. I cannot forgive Felice for what she has done. Warwick—"

Rob snorted. "You do not really believe Meg was his child?"

"I am not talking about that, nor that Felice so willingly betrayed this family for her own ends, though God knows it is enough. I am talking about what she tried to do to Isobel."

Rob ceased pacing. "To Isobel? What did she do?"

"She determined to have her killed. When she was great with child. One of Warwick's men – part of their *arrangement*." His lip curled. "Instead, it was Ursula's neck that was broken trying to protect her."

Rob linked his hands behind his neck and, blank-faced, stared at the sky. "I left Taylor here to preserve her. She should have been safe."

"Yes."

He brought his arms down and ran both hands over his face. "Is that what he meant when he said he had failed me?" he muttered. "And the matter of the whore's hood and harlot's rod – that was her, too?"

"It was."

"Why did you not tell me?"

"What is it to you? You have seemed too preoccupied with your own affairs of late to need be concerned about mine. I have to make it right."

"By eschewing your wife and keeping your mistress in… in bondage and her son a bastard to her shame and yours? After everything you have ever said about duty, about family honour?"

"Honour?" the Earl whipped, lips drawing back over his teeth. "I have renounced *everything* for the sake of family honour. I have forsaken my own peace to fulfil the expectations placed on me, sacrificed the happiness of another. I have changed; our time in exile taught me I cannot run from the past. I do this to fulfil my obligations to Isobel. For me. I do this to honour *her*." He didn't see his brother's fist until it was too late, and the blow to the side of his head sent him reeling backwards. He put out a hand to stop himself falling and felt his new-healed ribs crack. His arm protecting his chest, he regained his footing, saw the fist as it arced towards his head again, and ducked sideways. "In Christ's name, what are you doing!" He stumbled, righted himself, his chest screaming in pain as he grabbed the nearest practice sword from the stand. "Rob, stop, what madness is this?" He was vaguely aware of the shouts across the bailey, of the esquires and men-at-arms converging, but he couldn't take his gaze from the rage in his brother's face, the fury in his eyes as he prepared to attack.

"Rob, *no*!"

At the sound of her voice from the tower steps, Robert froze, arm raised, blood staining his lip where he had bitten it. Gradually he lowered his arm and then, without looking back, he turned and walked away.

Chapter 32

"Rob, wait!" Isobel caught up with him by the stables, panting, clutching Andrew to her as she ran and trying not to trip over her skirts. "You are hurt – let me look."

"It is nothing."

"You're bleeding." She reached up and wiped the blood from his lip, revealing torn skin.

He jerked his head away. "Leave it, Isobel," he snapped, cursing himself as she flinched. "I have to go. You must not be seen with me."

"You cannot go without seeing your son. You have not even held him. Look, he wants you to hold him." She lifted Drew towards his father. She thought he was going to take him from her, but instead he lightly touched the baby's hair and, changing his mind, withdrew his hand.

"He looks like him," he observed, and Isobel withered from his rejection.

"Of course he does, you are brothers. He also looks like you. Is that why you attacked the Earl, because Drew looks like him?"

"No." His lips moved, and she detected he wanted to add something to his bald statement, but he clamped them shut.

Unable to reach him through the stone wall of his silence and her frustration mounting, she blurted, "You knew he had been recently injured and was unable to defend himself. Why did you have to humiliate him in front of everyone?"

"Is that what you thought I was doing? Humiliating him? After what you have been through, you ask me *that*?" He held his fist to his mouth, fighting for control, then spoke slowly, deliberately. "There was a time at Barnet, Isobel, when I hoped he would be killed. I wanted him dead. Do you understand? *Dead.* How can I live with that, knowing he will not let you go and with my son growing up thinking he is his father? If I stay, I will end up telling him the truth, and if that does not kill him, I *will.*"

Andrew began to whimper. Shocked, Isobel stared at Rob. "You cannot mean that. If you leave, I will have nothing—"

"You have him. And our son. He can give you more than I can."

"I do not want your brother. I never wanted *him.*" Shaking with rage and despair, points of carmine rose on her cheeks. "I am not *his.*"

"That is not what he thinks. Here, take this." He thrust something into her hand.

"Rob, I gave you my chaplet to protect you."

"From what? From this?" He indicated the castle with a sweep of his eyes then held out his hand. "Come with me, Isobel. Now, while you can. We can be away from here and married before he knows we have gone." His words burned like fire through a field of stubble – promising new life from old, riches of love beyond wealth. But his fire would consume more than it made. She shrank against the wall.

"I… I cannot do that to him; it would break him."

"It would break *him*? We swore to love each other – we exchanged promises. What has he ever done to deserve your loyalty? I am offering you the chance of freedom from all this; I am offering you – our son – my *name.*"

"I cannot," she said again and, spinning around, fled the way she had come.

"THEY HAVE GONE." The Earl walked carefully to the long bench between the windows and sat down on the red velvet cushion. The new strapping made it difficult to breathe but gave him considerably more freedom to move without his ribs grating. His temple ached where Robert's fist had driven into it, the reddening already darkening to purple around the small silver scar, but the pain of the bruise was nothing compared with the reason for its presence. That would take longer to heal. He felt weary, bone-tired, old.

At the sound of the Earl's voice, Andrew kicked and cooed in his elaborate cradle, making the blue and yellow silk hangings shimmer in the afternoon light. He rattled his coral teether. Isobel remained kneeling before the crucifix, her head bent and eyes closed. A line of moisture along her lashes reflected as the lids squeezed tightly shut, and her lips moved silently against the chaplet wound around her hand. He studied her for a moment. "Did he say anything?"

The movement in her lips ceased, but she didn't open her eyes. "Who?"

"My brother – when he returned your chaplet. Did he say anything to you?"

She crossed herself and pushed to her feet in a slide of silk, avoiding his eyes. "No."

He was too hot in the strapping. It pinched under his shirt and already sweat pooled under his arms. "Will you help me take off this doublet?" Wordlessly, she undid the chased gold clasps securing the quilted blue doublet, too heavy for a fiery June day. "He did not mean to offend you, Isobel. His anger was not directed at you, but at his grief." Her lips remained tight, and he could not read her mood. "Isobel?" The last clasp was proving stiff. She struggled to unhook it. "Do you hear me? Seeing Andrew reminded him of his loss, and I also suspect he has formed an attachment that is not returned." She jerked, her fingers slipped. She yelped, sucking the side of her forefinger. "Let me look." He inspected the scrape then brought it to his lips, tenderly, and cradled her hand against his chest. "Forgive him, Isobel. Love and grief can drive a man from his mind and make him do things outside his nature." With the tip of his finger, he swept her lashes free of the remaining tears. "Forgive him, and in time he will accept the decisions I have made and perhaps also find contentment in a new match, as have I."

"Decisions, my lord?" she asked, dully.

But he stroked the side of her face with his thumb. "You are too pale, my Bel. When I am able, we will ride out. I have a pretty little falcon you can fly. It will be good to be free of our cares for a while."

Chapter 33

HAVING EXPLORED THE bumps in the blanket rolled out over the grass under the cheerful dagged canopy, Drew made a bid to escape. He crawled off the edge of the soft velvet and onto the prickly turf, looked surprised, stopped, and swivelled onto his padded bottom. Isobel stretched and ruffled the yellowing tufts. "Grass." He bounced, waving his arms and blowing bubbles, and attempted to copy her movements. She laughed. "That's right – grass." Chortling, he grabbed a handful and tried to eat it. Isobel intercepted before he could cram it into his mouth and brushed a trapped ant from his skin as it ran down his wrist. It was too hot for clothes, and he wore a short smock over his bulky napkin, his knees pink from crawling over the rock-hard ground. Moth sniffed and nudged his neck and took a surreptitious lick.

"Leave. Lie down." The Earl pointed to the ground, and Moth sank gracefully beside the child, leaning her long muzzle on her paws. Isobel marvelled at the control the Earl exerted over the animal. He had spent a few short weeks training the dog and achieved what she had failed to do in as many months. "If the hound has to stay, it must learn manners," he had growled when Moth had, yet again, helped herself to his favourite wafers under Isobel's indulgent eye. "If you spoil her, she will control you and be of no use to anyone."

"She is pretty, though, is she not?" Isobel had replied, admiring Moth's fine limbs and long silky fur and brown eyes that followed Drew everywhere.

"For a gam-legged creature she looks well enough," he admitted, "but a *mignon* might be pleasing to the eye and of no benefit to its master." After that he had taken her training upon himself, and now his wafers remained unviolated.

Under the awning, the strong August light made shadows of the branches of the apple tree under which they rested. Just over a year ago, Isobel had leaned against the same rough bark and taught Cecily her letters before Rob had found them there. She sighed. Only a year ago.

Linking his hands behind his bronzed head, the Earl contemplated the dancing leaves silhouetted by the sun, the soft breeze lifting and shunting the canopy above them. "What is it?"

"Nothing."

"If this weather holds fair, we can go hunting again. It will be cooler in the woods. Summer cannot last forever. We must make of it what we may."

"Mmm." She kept close watch as Andrew eyed a premature apple, ejected from the tree before ripeness could make it fall. He dribbled.

The Earl waved a fly away. "If the arrases arrive in time we could use them at the Lammas feast." In her head, Isobel counted the days until mid-August using the date of her last courses. Two weeks. "You will need a new gown," the Earl continued.

"I have no desire for more gowns, my lord, nor headdresses, nor shoes, nor enamelled girdles and gold-worked purses. I have everything I need."

"I like to see you in the finery you deserve. Anyway, the King might join us if he passes on his way north. I will ensure we are prepared, and you will wish to be suitably attired if he does."

Isobel writhed at the thought. She always felt exposed on the dais next to the Earl when he held court in the great hall, but he had brushed aside her objections and the snide comments she suspected his guests and household made when they thought he couldn't hear them. "I am only your mistress, my lord," she had whispered to him, squirming. "They expect to see the Countess by your side, not some…" She ran out of words.

"You are where you belong, Isobel." And, as if to make his point, his hand had closed over hers, pinning it to the arm of his lord's chair.

That was then. Now, and despite her inattention, the Earl was still talking. "I doubt Clarence will attend, but Gloucester might accompany the King, and with him, my brother."

Hearing the note of hope, Isobel brought herself back to the present. The Earl rarely mentioned him since they had fought, but he missed Rob, and he used his sources to garner any information he could. His mouth twitched, and he flicked at the fly that sought to settle. "He is expecting to make a match. Have I told you?"

It was the news she dreaded. She made a point of focusing on Drew's chubby back. "With whom?" she asked, tight-voiced.

"A girl of good blood from Norwich, known for her pious chastity and huge fortune." He drank from his gilt cup, staining his lips. He wiped them. "Does it matter?"

"It used to matter to you, my lord, when he was your heir."

"Had I not interfered, perhaps he would have made a better match when he wed before and still be married today. He did not listen to me then; he certainly will not now." The fly landed on a brocade cushion nearby, and he watched its small, jerky movements, thinking. The wind flapped the awning, and the fly took fright. The Earl rolled onto his elbow, his hand reaching for hers. "Isobel—" he began.

"Andrew, *no*!" She grabbed the baby's arm, but he had already popped the tiny green apple into his mouth. His cheek bulged, his eyes round. She inserted her finger, fished the apple out covered in drool, and threw it as far as she could. Moth sprang to her feet in pursuit. Drew's mouth opened in a wail of protest, exposing the cusp of a new tooth. "Look, here is your rattle, chew that." She pulled him onto her lap, and he sucked the coral branch, turned the rattle over, and ran the embellished gold handle over his gums instead. "His tooth is nearly through," she commented to no one in particular. "Perhaps this was not the best place to sit." She motioned to one of the servants and instructed him to check the ground for further hazards.

The Earl withdrew his hand and fed the cushion's gold tassel through his fingers instead. "I know not why you wanted to sit near the tree in the first place."

"Because the fair court is being replanted. Anyway, the Lady Snake tree is Cecily's favourite place."

"Isobel, Cecily isn't here." He yanked the tassel, and it came away in his hand.

"I know," she said a little crossly. She had last seen Cecily at the window of the nursery overlooking the bailey – just a pale smudge – and then she was gone. Dropping the rattle, Drew grabbed the ribbon around her neck and mouthed her father's seal.

"And why *Lady Snake* tree?" he asked, scowling at the coiling figure coolly observing them only feet away. "What a ridiculous name."

"No, it is not," she objected. "It is what Cecily calls it: *Lady Snake*."

He grunted. "You indulge her, Isobel."

"And you do not, my lord," she threw back.

Where before he might have chastised her for contradicting him, this time he chose to overlook her remark. He chucked the tassel to one side and picked up his beaker, drank. His face twisted in disgust. "This wine is tainted; do not drink it." With a flick of his wrist, he threw the contents on the grass. "It is not *Lady Snake* or whatever she calls it; it is Eve."

She forgot to be cross. "Why?"

When he didn't answer immediately, she looked back at him. He had found a longer blade of grass and was now peeling it down its length.

"My lord?"

"Eve betrayed Adam." He discarded the grass and met her eyes. "She was the downfall of Man."

Drew patted her mouth with an open hand, and she kissed his sticky palm. "Is that how you see women – as Eve?"

Swifts screamed overhead, making the baby start. The Earl followed their progress. "When swifts fly, the house will fall," he murmured.

"My lord?"

"Mmm?" He looked at her then, as if having come from deeper thoughts. "Swifts make good mothers," he remarked, and then sat upright and leaned over, taking Drew from her lap. They regarded each other, the baby wobbling on his stout legs, his pink feet curling as he balanced on the Earl's hard thighs. "Women cannot escape their inheritance of Eve's imperfection any more than men can avoid the sin women incite. One does not exist without the other, Felice." The birds were wheeling above them, catching insects and calling to one another, so she might have misheard.

"What did you call me?"

"Call you? What do you mean?" He smiled at Drew, pulling a face and making him laugh.

"I thought you..." She shook her head. "It matters not. So, all women are a necessary evil, which men cannot avoid?" she challenged.

The Earl brought Andrew to his chest, holding him comfortably as he spoke over the top of the child's head. "And where would we be without Eve, without the pain of love? What life is that?" He looked down at the baby, who had managed to create a patch of dribble on the pale blue silk of his open doublet and was now trying to suck the fabric. The Earl caressed the wisps of hair. "This life we have is so fragile, this love... if I could live again, I would live differently. I thought I could change the past, undo what I have done by... by loving you." Drew gave up on the silk and began to fidget, and the Earl put him down to let him find his own amusement, batting at flies as they escaped the sun and babbling happily to himself.

By loving her. Could she, in all honesty, say the same? Would she – given the chance – turn back time and undo what she and Rob had done, the evidence of their treachery yawning and grizzling intermittently as he tired of play and inched towards sleep? Is that why she had refused to leave with Rob? She couldn't undo their betrayal, could not escape the past; had she, in reparation, denied the love between them as self-imposed penance? Except she had done so out of guilt and punished Rob with it: withholding his son, abandoning her heart. Was his marriage his revenge on her tyranny, and could she ever, *ever* forgive herself? The breeze billowed the awning, letting in shafts of sun like spears. The Earl winced and shielded his eyes. He seemed different today, reflective. He saw her looking and invited her to sit by him so together they could watch the baby sleep. She curled her legs on a cushion and arranged her skirts modestly.

"If I am wicked Eve, what does that make you?" she asked him.

"Foolish Adam." He smiled at her surprise. "Or if not Adam, how about Adonis, for he was loved by two women?"

"But Adonis was betrayed by envy. Am I Venus or Persephone?"

He didn't answer immediately, removing the long pins securing her headdress and releasing her hair. It fell to her shoulders in a straight line, and she put a defensive hand to the shorn ends. She darted a look around them, but his servants had taken themselves from sight and they were alone. He lifted a handful of hair to the rays of sun now steadily breaching the edge of the canopy, and inhaled rosemary. "Like honeyed wine and as sweet. It has grown." He smoothed it, his sharp grey eyes softening. "Isobel, I want you to take this." With some difficulty, he inched his sard intaglio ring from his finger. It left a deep indentation.

"I cannot take your ring!"

"It is mine to give to my heir, as my father did before me, and he by his sire. I want you to take this for my son." He pressed the ring into her hand, and for a fragment of time Isobel thought he had confused her with his wife again. Seeing her misgiving, he took the ring from her palm and slid it onto her forefinger. It was too loose. He tried her thumb. "Wear this for Andrew. I have no need of secrets anymore."

The heavy ring swamped her hand, but his own looked naked, as if he had abandoned a part of himself. "My lord, you speak in riddles."

He silenced her objection with his finger to her lips. "In my grandfather's time, these figures carved upon this stone were held to be Adam and Eve in remembrance of their disobedience to Almighty God, and not Adonis and Venus as they were meant to be by the Roman who carved them. But I have always fancied them to be Tristan and Iseult, and so I give it to you, my love. With this ring, I pledge myself to you and none other. Say you will do the same."

Isobel's mouth fell open. "I… I cannot… the Countess—"

"… is of no importance. It is you I love – have always loved."

"My lord, you cannot speak in one moment of arras and the King and the honour of your family, and the next make a pledge to your *mistress* when you are legally bound to your *wife*. It will bring shame on your name and that of your children. Think of Cecily and Lady Elizabeth, of your son and heir. Remember your duty to *them*." She started to remove the ring, but he stopped her.

"Isobel, duty to my family brought me to this point. We will leave, go abroad where we are unknown, to the gardens of my mother's house where the pomegranates grow. We will plant sons – and maids, too – and they will know only freedom in Éden… Éden… No more secrets, Isobel." He broke off, pressing the heel of his hand against his temple, his eyes screwed shut.

"Your head hurts again, my lord?"

"It is nothing." He beat his head several times then opened his eyes and tried to smile. A drop of fluid gathered on his top lip from his nose. He wiped it with his hand, looked at it, surprised. Another replaced it, and then several in a rush. He fumbled for his handkerchief. "Too much wine and too much sun," he said, his face greying. "My stomach sickens. Let us go inside and you can make me your dwale."

"And you can tell me about your mother's garden," she suggested, wanting to please him now and helping him stand. She beckoned to a servant.

"No, I can manage." He pushed the man away. He found his feet, straightened his shoulders, and took a step. "Isobel…!" he gasped and, legs buckling, slumped to his knees.

"My lord?"

Slowly his physician's bony face came into focus, skull-white and concerned. The Earl tried again, but his mouth wouldn't form the words and his tongue laboured. He coughed. Immediately a cup was placed to his lips. The pale liquid spilled from one side of his mouth and tasted foul, but it enabled him to speak. "Head… hurts."

"I suspect *syncope*, my lord, brought on by too much sun on the brain. If you will allow me to bleed you a little, it will relieve the pressure."

His head? Is that what it was? His head burned like a brazier, and the air was difficult to breathe with a thick stench making him want to vomit. "Windows," he murmured.

"They are shut, my lord."

It was too much effort to correct the man, who had already selected an area of his exposed arm for bleeding. He felt the nick, but somehow couldn't make it connect with his body as he floated in a dream-like state where the blurred faces around his bed moved with exaggerated slowness. She wasn't there.

"Wheresshe…?" Damn his words. A figure moved closer, materialising into the broken face of his steward.

"Lady Felice has been informed, my lord."

"Is'bel…" His voice sounded strange to his ears.

"The lady is outside. Do you wish me to summon her?" The Earl moved his head enough to indicate *yes* without making him want to throw up. Patches of clarity had begun to form in the room, as if someone had polished windows into the surface of a frozen pond. He could see the perch he thought trapped in the ice, but as he hammered away with the stone, with a flick of its tail it was gone into the depths, leaving him with fractured ice and a bruised hand. He could hear Duarte laughing from the banks where the frost-limed rushes broke the surface like spears. Duarte. *Dudu.* He had not thought of his older brother as living in all these years. He had always been dead to him.

"Duarte, my lord?" The steward's voice had softened and taken on a musical note. He opened his eyes to find Isobel beside him, her brow deeply folded. He must have spoken his name out loud. She would be confused, and she looked frightened. He didn't want her to be afraid.

"I-so-bel," he said carefully, and tried to sit up but found he was weaker than he thought as his head pounded with deafening waves against its bony shore. His grooms helped him, and he had to wait until the room ceased gyrating before attempting to speak. "They have sent for my chaplain. They think I am dying, and they might be right." He moistened his lips. "There... are voices... in my head... all talking at once. Angels..." He breathed with difficulty as pain swarmed, and she took his hand, holding it tight, willing the pain to pass. "Windows..."

"Open the windows," she told a groom. "Do it," she insisted when it looked as if the physician might counter her order. She turned back to the Earl. "There, you can breathe now."

"I have so much to say to you, so much... regret... things I never intended..." Becoming agitated, he tried to raise his hand to pull her to him.

She brushed the dark hair from his eyes. "Shhh, do not speak; it does not matter. None of it matters."

"I've tried to make it... right." His hand sought hers, feeling for the ring she had turned inwards to her palm. "My pledge to you – r'member."

"I remember." She had never seen him so weak before, vulnerable, and she fought unlooked-for tears. "Rest now."

His mouth rose in an attempt at a smile. "I'll have enough rest if God grants it." He indicated his belt and pouch with a look. "Take my key, go to my aumbry. There is a... sealed paper. Fetch it."

She did as bidden. Inside, on the shelf next to the toy horse with its ever-vigilant knight, lay a slender thrice-folded document sealed with the very ring she now wore. In reaching inside, she dislodged something else behind it. Isobel canted her head and peered into the dim depths. She took hold of something cold that rattled and withdrew the object. As she looked at it, curled like a glossy snake in her palm, her pulse stumbled and blood drained from her heart, leaving her cold.

"Have you… found… it?" the Earl asked from the centre of the room. When she continued to stand by the open cupboard with her back towards him, he found the strength to raise his voice. "Isobel, bring it here." She did so without thinking, because all thought had been driven from her mind by tiny hammers of alarm and confusion. Standing by the bed, her eyes darted to his and back to what she held obscured by her skirts. A touch of his old impatience, but just a touch and no more. "You have the document? Where is it?" She opened her hand enough to let him see what she kept hidden: a coral and jet paternoster with a glass pilgrim's token – identical in every way to her own except for its length.

His eyes met hers, revealing naked honesty. "Isobel, I want to tell you, I wanted—" The door swung open, cutting him short.

"What is *she* doing here?" the Countess demanded as she crossed the room towards them, the wet nurse with the infant in her arms puffing to keep up. "Get her from my sight."

"You best leave, mistress," the steward said quietly, taking Isobel by the elbow.

"She stays," the Earl said, his eyes still locked on hers.

Felice attempted to bustle between them, but Isobel stood, rooted and stone. Thwarted, the Countess went to the other side of the bed where the physician hovered. She pushed him out of the way. "It is not right. Whatever way you would have it, *I* am your wife."

"She… *stays*." He lifted his head. "Thir-sty." Isobel held the cup to the Earl's lips, and a little of the bitter liquid escaped, gathering at the side of his mouth. She wiped it gently with the tip of her kerchief. "My son. I want to see my son."

Crooking her finger at the wet nurse and adopting a beatific smile, Felice swept close, swamping him with jasmine. "He is here, my lord."

Isobel began to stand back, but his fingers clenched her wrist with surprising strength. "*My* son, Is'bel. Bring Andrew."

Felice's expression congealed, capturing the moment between ecstasy and bile. "*Your* son awaits his father's blessing." Eyes blazing, she seized the child from his wet nurse and thrust him towards the Earl, the baby's legs dangling over his chest. "Your son, my lord, your *heir*." Shaken from sleep, the startled boy began to cry, the thin sound building within the confines of the room.

The Earl tried to push her away but only succeeded in raising his arm from the bed. "I said I wish for my son." Chou began whining, standing on her hind legs and trying to lick her master's hand.

Felice recoiled, her lips writhing. "His wits are addled. There is no sense in him. Bear witness, my lord steward, my husband is not in his right mind." She shoved the dog out of her way. Chou turned and snapped, narrowly missing the Countess's hand. "And get that animal from here."

Hyde bowed solemnly. "Madam, I see and hear all. Perhaps it is best if you step away – for your own comfort." He spoke quietly to Isobel. "My lord is becoming distressed; it is best you send for your child. Shall I give word?"

She nodded, adding, "And Lady Cecily. Is the priest near?"

"Master Sawcliffe is sent to accompany the priest. He will not be long. I will have Lady Cecily fetched and will return forthwith." He left the chamber. The two women faced each other over the bed, then the Countess tutted her disapproval, turned her back, and stalked to the fire.

"Is'bel..."

She leaned close. "I am here, my lord."

"My beads... *her* beads," he murmured, "give them to me."

She placed the string of beads in his hand, and he held them against his chest as if absorbing them through his skin. "Isobel, your mother—"

"What are you doing?" Felice demanded from the fireplace. "Get away from him; can you not see he needs the comfort of a priest, not a whore?"

His fingers found her cheek, her hair. "You are her image. God forgive me, I loved her before I knew any other. We made pledges to each other, do you understand? She was mine."

A coldness bled into Isobel's veins. "You were contracted with my... mother?"

"I had to put her aside, to do my duty. When my brother Duarte died… when I became heir… I had to marry Felice."

"What are you talking about?" Felice hissed, catching her name and straining forward to hear. Chou emitted a low growl, and the Countess backed off.

"My father – the old Earl – persuaded Geoffrey Fenton to wed her… my wife, my Bella… You are so like her. Isobel…" The words caught in his throat, his eyes moist.

Her numb lips moved of their own accord. "Y… you thought I was my *mother*?"

"No… yes… perhaps I thought I could capture her in you… and then all I wanted was you. I knew I was forgiven when we were blessed with a son. My son, our son." She tried to pull away, shock registering at last, but desperation haunted his eyes. "All these years. I've done my duty… God has forgiven me, Isobel. He sent you to me and gave us a child." He held up her hand, the light making the tawny seal ring glow. "I have made it… right." He brought it to his lips. "You are my true love."

She took a desperate look at Felice. "But the Countess, your children—"

"Yes," he said simply. "I must make it right." He beckoned Felice to the bedside, and she walked stiffly over without looking at Isobel. "I have wronged you, Felice." His voice weakened to a broken whisper. "Forgive… me." His eyes closed, and his mouth worked wordlessly.

She looked at him with contempt. "You brought this *whore* into our marriage, and you ask for forgiveness, yet she stands here still?"

The Earl opened his eyes, and a deep *V* formed on his brow. He attempted to move his head from side to side on the pillow. "No… there was another… before we wed… another…"

Bleaching with shock, her lips thin and bloodless, she said, "Your father arranged the match, we were married, the contract made—"

"My father made me vow never to reveal it. He had me put aside my wife… deny her… abandon her. I had… no… choice. No choice." His eyes pleaded with her to understand, but she drew to her full height, then her mouth curled into a sneer as she leaned close to his ear.

"Wronged me? For all these years, you have made me no better than this strumpet and your children bastards. I was loyal to you and bore your slights and your indifference. What have you left me? Not even the honour of being your *widow*. Forgive you?" And she drew her head away, gathered saliva, and spat at him. Spittle slowly ran down his jaw. He blenched, and moisture gathered at the edge of his eye, marking its way down his colourless cheek.

"Have pity!" Isobel snarled, wiping the spit from his face and spreading out her hand as if to protect him from her spite. Felice stared at the ring on Isobel's thumb. Slowly, the Countess stood upright, aware of the rising interest of the grooms and the physician outside the room.

"Close the door," she barked at them. "I will send for you if my lord has need of your service."

Isobel met the woman's stare, saw the calculation in her eyes. As the door began to close, Sawcliffe and the priest entered. Felice accepted the secretary's obeisance and, with a jolt, Isobel realised that the Countess intended to continue as if nothing had changed.

Sawcliffe bowed again. "Madam, we must allow my lord the privacy of receiving holy office." He indicated the door, but she turned her shoulder towards him.

"I will not leave my husband in his hour of need but will make my devotions at the foot of the cross." She took herself to his prie-dieu next to the aumbry, and sank gracefully to her knees, her ornate paternoster of black onyx and pearls already in her hands before he could insist she leave.

Sawcliffe arched an eyebrow at her back, then said, "Mistress Fenton, if you will?" Isobel cast a doubtful look at the woman's inclined head, and to the Earl, whose troubled features betrayed his distress, and she hesitated. "You may return if my lord wills it, mistress." She waited in the vestibule with the groom of the chamber, both silent, both deep in their own thoughts. Vapour of incense slipped through the cracks, carrying with it the mumbled conversation of penitent and confessor, the ting of the bell. What was he confessing after his lifetime of sin: adultery? Bigamy? Murder? *Rape?* Could he confess those away and be left absolved, and how long would he serve in purgatory before he was allowed to enter eternal life? Suddenly, the weight of his sins became overwhelming, the thought of the torment he would have to endure greater even than anything she had suffered at his hands. All the darkness that followed him had stemmed from the love he bore her mother and was not darkness at all, but sorrow. The enormity of his confession hit her, a ball of stone in the pit of her stomach. Clutching her chaplet, she tried to pray. Behind closed eyes she saw her mother holding the same chaplet as she lay dying, and then the Earl with his, and it all became too much and she gulped back a sob, and then another. The groom gave her a pitying look and averted his head.

From below she heard noises, and within moments Cecily and Moth bounced up the stairs towards them, followed by Buena holding Drew, and behind them, pinch-faced, Alice. Isobel took her son into one arm and held Cecily tightly to her with the other.

"What's happening?" Cecily asked, squirming free. "Why are you out here?"

Isobel bent low. "Your fader is very ill," she said gently.

Cecily's mouth turned down. "Like Meg?"

She wanted to say more, tell her that everything would be all right, but all she could say was, "Yes," and she felt her throat constrict at the thought of what was to come. The door opened behind her, saving her from having to say anything else.

How is it that incense smells of death? It lay forming an invisible fume mingling with the scent of candles and jasmine. Felice waited by the aumbry, and the Earl lay very still. For a moment, Isobel thought he had died, but on hearing Drew's baby babble, he opened his eyes and moved his lips. Isobel urged Cecily forward and followed. At the sound of their movement, Felice rose, eyes hardening as she saw the baby in Isobel's arms and her own daughter approach the bed, and she took herself to the other side of the room to stare through the window with her back to them.

Cecily climbed up beside her father, still holding her poppet. Without speaking, he caressed her curls with small jerky movements, then touched Nan and gave a lopsided smile. Cecily beamed and threw her arms about him. Over the top of her head, he met Isobel's grateful gaze and beckoned to her. Cecily climbed down and went to join Buena, and Isobel placed the baby carefully by his side. He didn't speak for minutes while Andrew played with the edge of the Earl's shirt, and then he said, "For my son," and he found Drew's small hand and gave him the chaplet. "I regret… nothing." He stopped suddenly, and a look of wonder crossed his face, bringing with it a peace she had never seen in him before. "Is'bel, the angels are calling—" He coughed, choked, his breathing becoming ragged.

"William!" She took his hand and held it fast.

He blinked, looking surprised. "You called me… by my name…" He smiled, but his eyes lost focus and, voice fading, he whispered, "Make me hypocras, my Bel." And his hand went slack.

She clamped her palm over her mouth as Drew chewed the coral and patted the Earl's chin, cooing. Sawcliffe genuflected and bowed his head, voicing a silent prayer.

"He is gone?" Felice said without emotion. She adjusted her wide sleeves, pulling them down over her wrists. "Master secretary, send for the steward and then return. I wish a message to be conveyed to the King informing him of my lord husband's death and the succession of his son and heir." She challenged Isobel to contradict her, waiting until Sawcliffe had left before swiftly crossing the room to stand in front of her. Lips taut over her tiny teeth, she hissed, "This alters nothing. There is no record, and there are no witnesses. As far as anyone is concerned, I am his widow and you his mistress, and anything else is the mania brought on by his malady. No one will believe you if you say otherwise, and it will only add to your shame and that of your bastard child."

Isobel picked Drew up, handed him to Buena, and ushered them towards the door before rounding on Felice. "Will you not mourn him?" she asked incredulously.

Felice cast a look of contempt over the body of her husband. "Mourn? I grieved from the first day of our marriage. He was never mine, and he has made whores out of both of us and bastards of our children." She made a dagger of her finger and repeatedly stabbed Isobel in the chest. "Had I known, I would have carved out his *wife's* heart and made him eat it. Mourn?" she said again, with a final hard prod. "You should be *celebrating*."

Isobel lashed out, the heavy ring tearing skin from the woman's face. Felice reeled back against the bedpost, one hand pressed against her cheek from which blood escaped through her fingers. A groom ran into the chamber to be joined almost immediately by the steward and Louys. "She assaulted me!" she shrieked as soon as she saw them. "She stole my lord's seal ring, and when I tried to stop her, she attacked me like a maddened dog. Look, she wears it now!"

The steward assessed Felice's state, his Earl lying dead and devoid of authority, Isobel's fury in the stripes of colour on her ashen cheeks. "See to my lady's wound," he instructed the physician hovering uncertainly, and to the priest, "Instruct the Offices of the Dead for the comfort of our lord's soul." He took Isobel's arm. She attempted to pull away, but he was surprisingly strong.

"I did not take the ring."

Cecily tugged at his arm. "She didn't, she didn't!"

Felice rounded on her, grasping her arm and shaking her. "Cecily, be silent!"

Hyde marched Isobel from the room to the vestibule where Buena waited. "Remain here," he ordered and returned to the hubbub of the privy chamber. From behind the closed door, Isobel could hear the Countess's shrill demands for her immediate arrest and Cecily crying. It took Isobel less than two beats of her heart to come to a decision. Grabbing Buena, she propelled her down the steps in front of her, across the council chamber where members of the Earl's household waited for news, down the last flight of stairs, and out into the stone-baked air at the top of the tower steps. "We leave, now – without delay," she panted, catching her breath. "We are in danger every moment we linger. We take Drew, and we head for Beaumancote." Her lips pressed into a determined line. "We are going home."

Chapter 34

News of the Earl's death had not yet reached the constable, nor word issued to stop Isobel from leaving the castle. She had her own palfrey saddled and another for Buena in the time it took to fabricate a jumbled story that would fool no one but the overawed stable lad.

They rode from the castle as the first of the bells began to toll the Earl's death, pursuing them past the millpond and through streets surly with heat. Even when they made the road, metalled by summer drought, the doleful tones could be heard, and long after they moved beyond earshot, it was all Isobel could hear in the numb cask of her mind. Only when darkness swallowed day and they were forced to shelter among the thickets bordering the road did the ringing stop, and only then because silent grief consumed her.

They huddled together without drink or sustenance, keeping inquisitive night insects from testing Drew's tender skin, ever vigilant for the ring of hooves against the ground.

At some point – long after dew began to form and the baby had suckled himself to sleep – Isobel woke to a moonless sky studded with faint stars. A moth escaped the tangle of her hair as she listened to the night noises, ears stretched into the shadows of the trees around them. There – again – padded steps and a tiny sound, like brittle stems of grass breaking. She was about to wake Buena when a form broke cover, rushing towards them out of the dark. A long tongue and a wet nose covered her face and hands, and she felt a broad collar as she attempted to push it from her. "Moth!" she sobbed, hugging the dog until the animal broke away and lay down next to them, ever vigilant, on guard.

THEY WOKE AS the first birds breached dawn. Dew-damp, they rose, stretching stiff limbs. Isobel's stomach ached with hunger, and Andrew fought at her breast for milk. When she finished nursing him, he left her skirt damp and smelling of urine. She had nothing to change him into. "We cannot be far from Owston Ferry; we can cross with the horses there. I doubt anyone will be looking for us; they have greater concerns now." An unwelcome image of the Earl lying dead flashed before her, and she scrubbed her eyes to clear it. "We must go."

Dragonflies swam and dipped over the dying pools of standing water on either side of the baked peat paths, and clustering gnats gathered around the horses' heads and whined around Isobel's ears, competing with the larks. She flapped them away from the baby's face. "I can hear a church bell. What day is it? And I can smell the river; we must be near." Sensing free-flowing water, the horses quickened their pace towards stands of trees marking the river's edge and the village of Owston Ferry. The flat call of a single bell rang for the feast of St Lawrence from the chapel across the river at East Kinnard. Isobel crossed herself and prayed the ferryman would take them across the Trent on a feast day.

THEY HAD SOUGHT alms of bread and small ale at the chapel on the opposite bank, and the larks were still singing when at last the walls of Beaumancote crested the gently undulating land, but any sense of relief soon diminished as they crossed demesne fields empty of people and fallow of crops. Only a scattering of strips looked as if they had seen a plough. Last year's furrows blossomed with poppy and vetch, and long strands of yellowing grass blurred the edges of narrow fields alive with crickets. Their misgivings deepened as they neared the gatehouse: no shout went up from the walls, and no one ran to open the gates to greet them. There came no welcoming bark.

"Lady Lacey wouldn't have Alfred in the house, my lady. She said the old dog reminded her of Fenton stink." Arthur's normally benign features morphed in undisguised loathing. "John Appleyard took him in." He looked around the great hall – what was left of it. "When the order came for Lord Lacey to leave, they took everything, even your father's silver cup."

"They left you," Isobel said.

"Aye, well, they couldn't very well take me; I'm a Fenton man. I only stayed because I wanted to see your manor protected in case... well, in case you returned."

Isobel smiled tiredly. "And I have."

Moynes crossed himself. "I am saddened to hear of the lord Earl's death. His good lordship is a grievous loss. And... I'm sorry for your own grief, my lady, and for your son."

Isobel studied the naked floor where light fell through the coloured roundel set in the window staining the stone red and blue and gold, rather than see the sympathy in his eyes. "Yes, thank you."

"We felt my lord's absence last winter when he and the King were in Flanders. The manor suffered for it."

She was grateful to return to the subject of her lands. "The fields have not been sown and are riddled with weeds. And where are my servants? Why was nobody on guard? Where is George?"

Moynes grunted. "Him? Were you not told, my lady? He took Lacey's part and nearly killed the Earl at Barnet." His dull eyes gleamed. "Lord Langton saw to it he didn't succeed. Did you not know?" he asked again.

"No." This secret world men kept to themselves. Even those closest to her. "Nobody told me."

Where the lord's table used to sit in front of its painted screen, a trestle of sorts had been conjured from a few planks of rough-sawn wood. It wobbled on its uneven legs as Moynes's knees knocked it, shaking the remains of the coarse trencher of bread, from which she had eaten a modest supper, to the floor. Moth darted between them to wolf the crumbs.

"It is not women's business to know such things," he said earnestly. "My lord would not have wished to distress you. We heard it from the Duke of Gloucester's man as the Earl himself told the King. Lord Robert fought like a wolf, he said, like a man possessed." Isobel detected the note of awe in her steward's voice, but all she could remember was the expression on Rob's face as he attacked his brother, and his last, hollow look as she turned and fled back to the Earl. She swallowed. Where was he now, and how would he come to terms with his brother's death with so much unresolved between them?

"My lady?" Moynes leaned towards her with concern.

"The Duke of Gloucester's man?" Isobel queried, refocusing. "Why, was he here?"

"His Grace sent a messenger with notification that your lands were to be restored and an escort of armed men to ensure the delivered message was… ah… received and acted upon. Lady Lacey threw a small ewer at him. It missed, but the window suffered for it." Mismatched pieces of glass in the nearby casement bore witness to her temper. It was the same window where Isobel had first seen Rob, his hair coloured warm oak by the sun. She looked away.

"But His Grace said it was the Earl who made sure my lands were returned to me."

"My lady, the Earl might have made the case to the King, but it was the Duke of Gloucester who ensured the decision was enacted." Arthur's face rumpled. "Lacey took some of the household servants with him – the cook for one – and those who would not leave, he threatened. Others drifted away thinking… well…"

"That I would not come back?" She pursed her lips. "The Earl was always so particular about my estates, so careful."

Lugubrious, he nodded. "The Earl was a careful man, may he find eternal peace." He genuflected again. "He must have been consumed with the security of his own estates, or perhaps…" He faltered.

"Perhaps…?" Isobel prompted.

"Forgive me, my lady, but perhaps the Earl thought that you would not wish to return." His glance dropped to the ring she still wore. She twisted it until it sat straight on her thumb, the significance of the carved lovers so painfully sharp it hurt. Until yesterday, she might have replied with some vehemence that Beaumancote was the only place in the world she wished to be. Now, however, as she looked around her, she could no longer recall the yearning she once felt for the place. It had lost its allure, or maybe it was she who had changed and no longer belonged. But poor though it might now appear, it was all she had. She startled her steward by rising abruptly.

"Well, I am here now, and we have work to do. I need an inventory showing all remaining goods and chattels, stores of provisions, livestock. And bring me a list of people, indentured or otherwise, who still serve me. I want to know exactly what resources remain on which we can draw. Oh, and Arthur, ensure the bailiffs of my manors know of my return. I expect their absolute loyalty and will reward it well." Although with what was another matter. Moynes's expression reflected the same doubt. She needed time to think. "If you need me, you will find me in my garden."

Evening tempered the day's heat and softened the light, stretching shadows as they traced the path to the garden where honeysuckle mounting the walls fragranced the air. Isobel pointed to the entrance. "This is my garden, Drew, *your* garden." She ducked under snaking stems hanging across the door and tested the latch. It took more force than she expected to dislodge the rust, and the door grated on its hinges as it opened. Forgetting to check the secret nook, instead she stood stock-still at the sight that greeted her. Behind them, Buena let out a moan of dismay. Fat orb spiders had spun webs criss-crossing the paths between greyed heads of unclipped lavender, untamed roses flung haphazard stems in flagrant disregard of their former order. Raised borders heaved with tangled weeds. Moth barged past their legs and disappeared into the forest of growth. Sensing his mother's distress, Drew's mouth bowed into a whimper and she hugged him tightly, unable to speak.

She sank onto a stone bench, crushing sprawling hyssop. "It is all gone," she whispered. Everything she had kept hidden for so long vented in a lesion of grief. She wept until the agony in her chest eased and her tears no longer burned but spilled out in sobs that shook her from chin to toe. Buena held her to her breast as she had done in the days after her father's death, stroking her hair and rocking back and forth while humming a foreign lullaby. When Isobel stopped shaking, leaving her drained and empty, they merely sat in silence.

Drew's head turned as Moth crashed out of the border in long jumps accompanied by the harsh reprimand of a blackbird. Feeling hollow, Isobel straightened and hunted for her kerchief. She found instead the Earl's and fingered the griffin embroidered there. She dried her eyes and rose slowly, breathing out an unsteady sigh and taking a longer look at her garden.

"I never thought it could change even when I knew it was no longer mine; somehow it would remain..." she sought the word, "... uncorrupted. But it was never as I thought, was it? It was all based on lies, even this."

Buena made a throaty sound and made her hands speak for her.

Isobel shook her head in answer. "*I* am a lie. All those truths Fader taught me, *'Always tell the truth, Isobel, lies darken the soul.'* Remember? He understood that better than anyone because he lived a lie, and every time he thought of my mother – or me – he saw it. He must have died a little each time he met the Earl. And now I cannot think about my mother without seeing *him* with her. Did she love him, Buena? Did my mother love the Earl?"

Buena's hand went to her mouth, and she gave one simple nod. Isobel released the breath she had been holding. "When I think of him, I remember the injustice he did me; but I cannot hate him for it, not now, not after this. He loved me. In the end it was *me* he loved, and I betrayed him..." She stopped long enough to let the burgeoning emotion subside, ignoring the questioning look that crept over Buena's face. She bent to pluck prickly burrs from Moth's coat. "Buena, you knew about them, didn't you," she stated without condemnation. "You have known all along. That is why you hid from him that day when he injured himself hunting, and why you did not want me near him. He didn't like you because of what you knew. Did he make you swear to keep the secret?" Buena held Isobel's stare, then looked away. "My fader? Mother? Buena, what are you not telling me? Were you silenced?" A sudden thought occurred to her. "Did the *Earl* have your tongue cut out?"

Buena shook her head with vehemence, her hands dancing, then she opened her mouth and made a sawing motion with her fingers. "*You* cut out your own tongue?" Isobel felt sick. "Why? Why would you do that?"

Buena drew pictures with her hands and then lightly touched Isobel's face, her heart, and made a cradling gesture with her arms crossed on her bony chest. Her eyes creased, and for a moment it looked as if she might cry. "Because it was the only way you would be permitted to stay with my mother? So, you lived this lie as well. Who else knows? Does Arthur?" Buena shook her head. "No one else here, then. That leaves you and me – and the Countess. You know what that means, don't you? It is in her interests to silence me, or she must forever live in fear that I might reveal the truth." A wry smile briefly lifted her mouth. "For once I have something with which to barter. It makes a change." Isobel snapped a silvery paper disc of Peter's Pence – the irony of its alternative name, *honesty*, not lost on her – and gave it to Drew. She looked around at the wasteland of her garden. "Perhaps there is something to be salvaged from this after all."

"THAT IS IT? That is the sum of fines and rents from all my manors for the last quarter?"

Arthur coloured under his thinning fair hair. "Since Epiphany, my lady. Lord Lacey—"

"Yes, I know, since Thomas took my estates and emptied my coffers to further his ambition. And I take it that the rents since midsummer are not recovered enough to pay the wages of the husbandmen needed to plough and plant the land?" He shook his head in familiar slow swings in a manner she was finding increasingly irritating. She ground her teeth and continued to read his thorough report, pulling the coarse wool cloak further over her shoulders against the chill September air. It was worse than she thought possible. "And this is all the labour I can expect? What about John Yeland or George Fuller and his son?"

"Gone, my lady, or dead." It had been the same story from each manor. She rattled her nails on the trestle.

"Do people not know I have claimed my inheritance and returned to my manors?"

"Yes, my lady, but… but…" He squirmed in front of her.

"Arthur, what?"

"Forgive me, but you are not a man. My lady, please!" He held up his hands, palm out, in a gesture meant to restore calm as her eyes flashed wide. "Let me explain. Without your father or the Earl there is no one to guide you—"

"I need no guidance," she fumed, "I need them to obey and serve me."

Arthur bent his head and exhaled. "Forgive me for being blunt, my lady, but without a lord to protect your interests, these lands will fall prey to the abuses of any who seek to usurp your position."

"The King was supposed to restore justice."

"He cannot be everywhere. The Earl provided that protection—"

"And now he is dead – is that what you are saying? There is no one to administer justice as he once did."

"Until his son is of an age, the Countess will act in his stead."

"*She* is a woman," Isobel said, acidly.

"My lady, the Countess has her husband's affinity and the wherewithal to support it. You have neither and little chance of building it without a husband whom they can call *lord* and who can wield power on your behalf. And there is one other thing."

Wearily, she looked at him. "Which is?"

"At Epiphany, when it seemed likely King Edward would attempt to reclaim the throne, Lord Lacey wanted to ensure he had enough men and arms, and he… he sold Long Acre Field and the land east of Winterton to fund them."

Her jaw slackened. "That is why the return on the rents has been so low."

"That, and the matter of your tenants being warned against serving you."

"Why? Because I am a woman?"

"No, because it is thought you won't hold your property long enough to make it worth their while."

She felt her face pale in stages and then flush with outrage. "And who is going to take it from me?"

He shrugged. "That, my lady, I cannot say."

"But I can guess," she muttered, regaining control. "Arthur, this is all I have left, all I have to leave to my son, and I must make of it what I can – work the fields with any husbandmen we can find until it pays enough to buy back my land. I can see no other way forward to secure funds, for I have nothing to sell except my father's seal."

"My lady, you need that as a sign of your authority."

"Because I have so little of my own?" She rubbed crossly at her hairline where new growth pushed through; there was no point plucking it now.

He didn't deny it. He indicated the Earl's ring. "Could you not sell that? It would fetch a fair price."

Isobel pressed her thumb into the textured surface. "No, it is not mine to sell." What about Drew's caul, wrapped and tucked in the purse at her waist? She mentally shook her head: it was his, and he might need it one day. She was at a loss.

"There is another way, my lady," Arthur said gravely. "You could marry."

Chapter 35

ISOBEL PARTED THE long grass beneath the apple tree and located the rough mound crowned with Herb Robert and a crude cross.

John Appleyard shuffled beside her. "It were his favoured place, my lady. I thought you'd want him here. I buried a bone wi' him," he added. "He liked his bones, he did."

"And windfalls," she said, placing one on the grave. "You chose well, John. Alfred would like it here." She gave the ground a pat, releasing a spicy scent from the red-bruised stems of the plant, and stood up, brushing fragments of soil from her hands. "We have much work to do."

She meant nothing more than she said, but John's ruddy complexion deepened further. "I were only thinkin' of me family. I couldn't stomach staying on wi' he and his wife, wi' her takin' such dislike t'old dog an' all, and me sayin' as such."

"I understand."

"An' the Abbot at Thornton, like, was lookin' for labour on account of shortage due t'war. It were a steady wage, an' not knowing if ye would return… an' thinkin' of my family – yer see?"

"I do." She offered him a faint smile. "It's all right, John, you have your wife and children to provide for, and the abbey will give you guaranteed work and a better wage than I can."

His expression clouded. "Tha's not what I'm saying. When Lord Lacey left, we 'oped you might come back, but Harry Johnson said there's nowt to come back to, not with ye bein' so fair wi' the Earl and having his bairn, like. 'What's there to come back to?' he said, 'when tha's livin' in't castle and supping with princes like a countess? Why would she want to come back 'ere and live among us poor folk after livin' like that?'"

"Is that what Harry Johnson said?" Isobel said quietly. "And what do you say, John?"

He hawked and remembered not to spit. "I say my lady will want to come back to look after her people, and they that remember thy fader's rule, want nowt but the peace he brought."

"I am not my father, John."

"Nay, but tha's thy fader's lass, and that's good enough for most an' is good enough for me. I'll serve thee if you'll 'ave me."

Her heart expanded with gratitude. "Gladly. I would have no other. I will endeavour to be a good lord to you, but without the Earl..." She felt a swirl of pity mingled with regret at the thought of him and tugged at some grass around Alfred's grave to cover the moment.

"Aye, well, I've had nowt to do wi' great lords – except Lord Langton, and then only in passin'. Lord Langton, now, is right fair-minded; he said he needed loan of me sacking cloak I keep here in't outhouse." He thumbed over his shoulder to the lean-to shed, largely hidden by woodbine. "And I were glad to gi' it and welcome; but before midsummer, he sent me five ells of green kersey, too fine for t'garden. Me wife's made gowns for hersen' and the bairns from it. He sent a message wi' it an' all."

"What did it say?"

"I don't rightly know. I were going to show it to Lord Abbot, but..." He shrugged, looking abashed.

"Bring it to me, and I will read it for you."

His face brightened, and he fumbled in the large pouch at his waist where he usually kept his hone and paring knife and loops of twine, producing a small square of paper from a protective wrap of waxed cloth, carefully folded and with the seal still intact. She broke the seal and read the short message, hearing Rob's steady voice.

"My lord thanks you for the service you have lately done him, and bids you remember him in your devotions." She looked up. "He signs it in his own hand."

John scratched the back of his neck, looking embarrassed. "There were nowt to it – only t'old cloak an' keepin' watch like."

"He obviously thought otherwise." She smiled. "He must have liked your gardening."

"Lord Langton wanted to see it specific like."

"Did he? Did Lord Robert say why?"

"Not to me, m'lady, but he wanted to be alone an' I let him." Isobel pictured Rob as she had first seen him, when she was very young and he fresh from his first battle. Then the last time they had been here together, when the frost snapped and they had studied the stars and, in those moments, found peace. Where was he now? Did he still mourn his brother, or had he found happiness with his new wife and already forgotten the past, forgotten her? An apple dropped close by, landing with a dull thud and rolling into the gold-stemmed grasses. John was looking at her with curiosity, and she realised she must have said Rob's name out loud.

"Make a start on the weeds and scythe the grass, John. We cannot put sheep in here with so many windfalls. I will see what can be redeemed among the herbs, and then we will harvest the hard fruit and the nuts. We will need it over winter. At least Lady Lacey left us that much; she has taken everything else."

"Only 'cos it weren't ripe," John muttered.

She left him to organise the few men and boys available and willing to work the garden and, collecting the basket of sage she had gathered earlier for drying, made her way along the overgrown paths, ruminating that the garden no longer resembled the one she had left two years before. At the gate, a thought sprang from nowhere and, standing on the tips of her toes and wiggling the loose stone from its nook, she felt with her fingers the dry-dished place of secrets. Something rustled, and she removed what felt like stalks. A sprig of rosemary. Withered and warped, the brown-edged spikes still resonated with pungent scent, as it must have done when Rob picked it and placed it there for her to find on a day such as this.

By THE FIRST frost around Michaelmas, it was clear much of the garden needed replanting. Buena helped her take cuttings of rosemary, sage, gillyflowers, and lavender, pruned roses out of season, and gathered what seeds remained in papery heads, all watched by Drew in the enclosure of willow hurdles John had made for him, guarded by Moth. When it rained, she pored over inventories and lists with Arthur and wrote letters drawing on the years of goodwill her father had developed with merchants in Hull and the Guilds in Lincoln. But the offices he once held had passed to others, and she had little to offer in return. She was thankful to be kept busy. Busy kept her too tired to hear mass in her church where she would have to face her parents' tomb and the lies that lay there. Busy meant she didn't have to think about Cecily at Tickhill, nor Rob with his new wife.

DRIVING WIND THREW occasional pebbles of hail against the oriel window. The day was dark, although it neared noon. Woken from his morning sleep, Drew's babbling contentment made their lonely existence more poignant. On days like this they kept to her parents' solar – now her own – where the frequently fed fire combatted the cold squeezing under the door. Her father's books had gone, and the hangings around the bed also. His tables and chair were undoubtedly gracing Lacey's hall, and she now perched on a stool topped with the crudely embroidered cushion she had made when a child – all that was left to remind her of contented hours spent with him on days such as this.

Andrew scuttled on all fours towards Moth resting by the fire. Isobel scooped him up and blew reverberating kisses under his ear, making him laugh. "Let Moth sleep. Look, we can make a tower." She kneeled on the floor and stacked the small blocks of applewood John had made for him, one on top of the other. Drew leaned forward and promptly demolished them with a delighted squeal. "Hmm, I build and you knock down." She tried again. "Take one block and put it on the next – like this." He watched her carefully, picked up another block, and threw it, narrowly missing Moth's head. Buena gurgled a laugh and Drew chortled, rumpling his chin and exposing his baby teeth. He bent over, selected a block, and this time crammed as much as he could in his mouth and gummed it.

"That tooth is taking its time to come through," Isobel reflected to no one in particular.

"My lady?"

She hadn't heard Arthur's plump and pleasant wife come in. She seemed nervous. "What is it, Agnes?"

"You have a visitor, my lady." For one wild moment, Isobel's heart vaulted at the hope it might be Rob, but the woman continued, "It's... Lord Lacey."

Thoughts scudded one after another, finishing with an abrupt, "I do not wish to see him."

"I said you were not minded to see anyone, my lady, but he won't leave until he's spoken with you. He is resolved to it. Master Moynes sent me to enquire if you will come."

Isobel arranged her skirts, straightened her simple headdress, and counted to five before entering the great hall, resenting the waste of precious wood as Thomas warmed himself by the new-lit fire.

"Isobel!" He strode towards her, kissing her on both cheeks before she could draw away. She scrubbed the feeling from her skin with the back of her hand, making no attempt to hide it, but he disregarded the gesture, appraising her. "You look well despite this weather. Brrr, it is *cold*." He rubbed his gloved hands together, making the fine embellished leather squeak.

"What do you want, Thomas?"

"To see you, of course, and to welcome you to Beaumancote. It has been a long time since we last met." Biting her tongue, she increased her count to ten as he began removing his gloves finger by finger, looking as if he might stay. "I could do with a cup of clarry to warm me."

"I have neither wine nor cup," she replied tartly, "and I am busy. Say what you must, Thomas, and then leave."

His mouth flinched into a smile. "Ah, I see I am not welcome. You have perhaps forgotten our previous bonds, but I have not. Well then, as old *friends*, I wanted to ensure that you have what is needed for your comfort."

She gave a harsh laugh. "My comfort. All that you see is all you left me. How do you reconcile *your* acquisition of *my* goods with assuring my *comfort*?"

"I understand how it must seem to you—"

"Oh, do you," she said with a caustic grimace.

"—but you have to understand I could not risk leaving the contents of the manor when it was so poorly defended," he finished seamlessly.

"Poorly defended because my sergeant-at-arms betrayed my father's name and fought for you against his lord, not to mention the loss of other men whom you enticed from my service, or those too frightened to stay."

"I had no notion of when – or if – you might return."

"You do not for one moment expect me to believe that, do you? Thomas, you betrayed the King. You would still be here at Beaumancote had Warwick not been defeated and you left with no other choice but to beg for mercy."

"What makes you think *I* asked for mercy?"

Isobel thought it prudent not to reveal the full extent of her knowledge. "You mean the King granted you pardon because he *likes* and *trusts* you?"

Thomas inspected his fingernails, avoiding her glare. "The King values my service. I no longer required your manors and asked His Grace to restore them to you. He felt able to grant my wish," he finished airily. He cast around the bare room, where the marks of previous furnishings ghosted the walls. "It is a dismal place in winter. My wife frequently remarked on it."

"Then you will not wish to stay longer than necessary," Isobel fumed.

"It suited our purpose well enough, but I prefer my current dwelling – it is more fitting to my station and where I might conduct my business in more… amiable surroundings. Perhaps you will honour me by visiting one day?" He smiled down at her, but it seemed to Isobel his pleasure was at her cost. She scowled back at him and wondered what it would take to make any impression on his sense of superiority – bred, not earned, she noted. A few of Moth's silky hairs had managed to attach themselves to his sleeve. He picked the fabric free. "I will arrange for the return of your goods. I regret several pieces had to be burned. My wife would not have them in the house. I'm surprised you had failed to notice how wormed they had become. Still…" He smiled again, as if that somehow would make it all right.

"And Long Acre Field and my land east of Winterton? Will you make reparation for my loss?" she pushed.

"Isobel, you must understand that in times of war it is sometimes necessary to make difficult decisions." It was meant to end the debate, but it only served to make her blood seethe and want to goad him further.

"You used my land to fund your treachery."

His pale eyes turned on her. "Treachery? *Your* land? You forget this manor was granted to *my* family by *King* Henry II, Isobel. *My* family held it until the old Earl stole it and gave it to your father during the King's absence. I watched my family be driven from our lands into obscurity, and I watched while my uncle was murdered at Beaumancote's gate by the Earl with your father's blessing. I remember, Isobel; I was there. Tell me, who betrayed whom? I took back what was rightfully *mine*." His closed fist knuckled his own chest, a strand of clay-yellow hair stuck to spittle at the corner of his mouth. He straightened slowly, regaining control, and wiped the foam carefully with the pad of his thumb. "You have made me lose my temper; I did not come to quarrel. What is done is past. I have found favour with King Edward, and you have returned to Beaumancote. We are neighbours; let us also be friends." He made to kiss her, but she twisted her head away.

"Your wife will be awaiting your return," she said, icily.

Pulling on his gloves, his mouth pinched. "My wife is dead these last three months. I am surprised you did not know. The child died with her."

"Your pardon," she faltered. "I was not aware."

"Obviously." He formed a tight smile. "It seems that we have both been subject to recent grief. Perhaps you will favour me with your time before too long, else we are called to Almighty God without making amends for our past offences." He hitched his shoulders in the way she remembered from years ago when he was being defensive. "I will send wagons on the morrow."

He left her without making further comment, and she wondered what offences he believed she had committed for which she must make amends.

"Summer cannot last forever." The Earl's words woke her from troubled sleep. *"The house will fall."* She lay thinking about those last few hours

spent under the canopy by the Lady Snake tree, how eternal they appeared then and how transient now. If she traced back, she could pinpoint the times when he seemed not himself. How far were the words of love he lavished on her in those last months the malady of his brain that killed him? Or had he finally come to terms with the loss of her mother and found some reconciliation in her daughter? She might never know. One thing she did conclude, however, was that his mistrust of Thomas Lacey lay untarnished to the end. But had it been entirely justified?

Thomas had returned her goods – or some of the lesser ones – as promised. He also visited on a number of occasions, avoiding subjects of dissension and being careful to note the improvements she slowly wrought on the manor with the limited means at her disposal. She was mindful that, no matter past grievances, she had little to gain from continuing them. And when he brought little gifts for her and endeavoured to engage Drew in play, she wondered whether Thomas Lacey was not also changing and growing into the man her father had wanted her to marry.

Her parents occupied much of her thoughts, prompted as she constantly was by the skeleton of the garden being fleshed out by new growth, and the remains of her father's library, now sadly depleted, kept carefully protected from damp and worm. Reminders were everywhere, memories tainted with the truths she now understood, and confused by her relationship with the Earl. And every time she looked at her son and watched him growing into his father, she remembered Rob with a stab and, snow or sun, she escaped into the garden to attack some part of it until she had driven him from her mind.

Thomas found her there one day before noon when the frost had finally melted under the weak winter sun. Moth raised her head and growled. Buena hissed a warning, and Isobel looked up from tying in stubborn stems John held back for her.

"What does 'e want?" John scowled in Thomas's direction. "Better 'e come wi' a spade than dressed like an' earl. Dog don't like 'im, and yer should always listen t'dogs."

"Shh." Isobel nudged him. "Go and prune something, and take Buena and Moth with you before either of them does something I won't regret. I will watch over Drew."

John trudged off, calling to his garden lads to join him and leaving Isobel to greet Thomas. He sidled past snagging stalks, sunlight making the dark green silk-velvet of his fur-lined mantle gleam like deep water, then bent to kiss her. She moved her head, and his lips found her cheek instead.

"You are looking very… er, splendid, Thomas; have you been to Hull?"

"I have, and I have much to tell you." He swept his cloak back in a self-important gesture, revealing a staggeringly short pleated doublet of garnet and gold that left little to the imagination.

Isobel tried not to wince and looked away. "What news is there?" A stem had escaped and nodded defiantly just behind his shoulder, distracting her.

"I sometimes think you only wish to see me because you want my report," he grumbled. There was an element of truth in his observation. Thomas brought fresh intelligence on the world beyond the manor's demesne, although Isobel considered that – as it was through the filter of his eyes – the veracity of his commentary might be suspect. "However, I do have something to tell you – if you'll hear it," he added as she tidied the wayward stem. She stopped and he continued. "I met with the Earl of Lincoln today, and he was minded to seek my counsel in certain matters." The King's young nephew, John de la Pole: that would explain the shaving cut, the extravagant hat, and the lashings of musk.

"Why?"

"Might my counsel not be thought worth seeking, Isobel? I am not the boy you knew. I hold offices from the King and have seen battle and commanded men. Some lords might not have thought my service worthy of their lordship, but the greatest did, and the Earl of Lincoln knows it."

Isobel said nothing in case she bit back at the slight against the Earl and wondered that the Earl of Lincoln would think Thomas a suitable source of guidance, given he had fought against the King not so long ago. "Anyway," he continued, "the earl has asked me to accept his lordship, and I said I would give it my consideration."

"That was good of you," Isobel murmured.

"Yes, well, it would be wrong to squander my service on someone unworthy of it. I said I would give him my answer before Yuletide."

"That is near a full moon hence; why so long?" She blew on her fingers to warm them, making the cuts sting.

"I have other matters to consider. My marriage, for instance."

"Oh." Bundled against the cold, Drew had managed to pull up the blanket protecting him from the damp ground and was now inspecting something beneath it with intense concentration. Isobel watched him closely.

"I see you wear my ribbon." Her hand went to the ribbon from which two items now swung, her calloused skin tagging the delicate silk. "And that ring next to your father's seal – was that the Earl's gift?" She didn't answer, and Thomas tried again. "I said to de la Pole that I wish to contract a marriage."

"Mmm." Drew picked something up.

"Isobel, are you listening to me?"

She kept one eye on her son. "Yes, you want to marry again." Drew's hand went to his mouth, and she intercepted just in time to prevent an empty snail shell from being consumed. She whisked him up and persuaded him to relinquish his latest acquisition.

Thomas's mouth shrivelled in disapproval. "If you had a decent nurse for him you would have no need to bring him outside."

Isobel took Andrew to the garden trough, where cold water flowed from the tank, and washed his hands. He beat the icy water, sending drops in a rainbow arc soaking them both. They laughed. "He likes being out here with me. I might keep ten nurses and I would still bring him into the garden." She dried his hands on her handkerchief and bopped his nose with the end, making him laugh again. "So, you intend to marry; who is it this time?" She sat down on the stone bench, balancing Drew on her knees.

"I thought that would be obvious." She looked up at him blankly. "Isobel, have you forgotten we were to be contracted to each other before your father died and the Earl forbade it?" He sat down next to her when she didn't respond. She shifted away. "We would still be married now if things had been different. This might be *my* son you hold." The cold, light breeze lifted her loosened hair, obscuring her expression. "Would your father not wish it if he were still alive? Your noble mother?"

Would Thomas really want to marry her if he knew the truth of her parents' bigamy? He was waiting for an answer, but she had none to give, or at least not one he wanted to hear. He frowned. "I might not yet be an earl, but I am rising in the King's favour and with the Earl of Lincoln's patronage, am like to rise further. You might even come to Court one day and meet the King. Perhaps, as my wife and if you please her, you might serve in the Queen's household."

"I have met His Grace and have no desire to serve the Queen. You need a wife who will further your ambition, Thomas. I only wish to stay at home with my son and protect my people."

"I can hardly believe *that*," he snorted. "You were the Earl's mistress. I know how he favoured you over the Countess, and now you are content with… *this*?" He encompassed her world with a dismissive wave of his hand. "I can offer you so much more."

"This is all I ever wanted," she said quietly.

Tight fists resting on his thighs, everything about him seemed terse and tense, as if her decision mattered more than she believed it did. "Isobel, I understand it must be awkward having known such a life as you have lived these last two years and now living here with your bastard child. You need a husband to give you standing and protect you. It must be difficult to procure supplies and make contacts with only the memory of your father's name on which to call." A solitary bee braved the cold, and Drew bounced up and down, babbling excitedly. "And your son needs a father to correct him."

"He has… had… a father," she said.

"I will give him my name and remove the slander of his birth. You need never be ashamed of him again and hide away."

"I am *not* ashamed of him," she flashed, "nor do we *hide away*."

"All right, all right," he interrupted, "I meant nothing by it. Think rather that I can promote his interests at Court, find a placement for him. No one will remember his parentage, only that he is my son and that is what will count. Is that not what you want for Andrew, a good position so he can make his way in the world and contract a beneficial match?"

"He will know his father because I will tell him when he is old enough to understand. I will not keep secrets from him, Thomas. My son will know his father even if his father is unable to acknowledge him."

He looked as if he were about to argue but instead formed a conciliatory smile. "Of course. Even if we had our differences, the Earl was a great lord, and the child should have the benefit of it. No doubt I can remind the King of his love for the Earl when the time comes to place the boy. But until then, we must ensure his safety, hmm?"

She looked at him swiftly. "Safety? Why should he not be safe?"

Thomas picked at the half-healed shaving scab on his neck, regarding the red stain of fresh blood on his fingers with detached interest. "No reason, but the Countess is a vengeful woman, I hear, or so the Earl of Warwick led me to believe. Still," he said, standing and aligning the run of his sleeves precisely and adjusting the cant of his silver-gilt belt just so, "I doubt you have anything to fear. Although—" he bent to retrieve his hat from the bench, "—there have been reports of brigands recently, lordless men – ungoverned and ravenous for spoil. Not that I wish to alarm you, of course, and you know that you can always call on my support should you need help." He flicked a dry leaf from his hat and read the sky. "My tenants say this sun will not last and predict a turn in the weather. Snow from the east, they say, travelling along the Humber. You know how the river causes malady in the young and the infirm. Have a care the child does not take the cold." He patted Drew's head as he would a dog. "Such a fine boy; I am passing fond of him already. I really would have thought the Earl would have made better provision for you. Still—" he placed his hat at an exact angle on his head, "—I can provide for you both. It has been a thin harvest, and times are lean. Think on my proposal, Isobel. I wish to inform Lincoln I have made the match before this month's end."

"Have you heard of bands of men crossing our land?" Isobel demanded as soon as Thomas had left and she had located Arthur.

His sandy brows rose in surprise. "No, my lady."

"You had better make the village aware and tell the miller to keep a watch out and sound his bell if he detects anything. Oh, and send someone to warn my tenants at Walcott and Winterton. Any mention of disturbance of any kind – people threatened, stock killed – anything, I wish to know immediately."

"Did Lord Lacey warn of trouble, my lady?"

Isobel handed the baby to Buena. "In a manner of speaking, yes, Arthur, he did." She turned to leave and then remembered something.

"And, Arthur, I think it prudent to bring our animals closer to the manor where we can keep an eye on them, and we should also account for our provisions, or what's left of them."

He shook his head. "There's not much; what stores we had are depleted. But we have wood, though, plenty of wood."

"Then at least we can keep warm while we starve," she smiled grimly.

Chapter 36

IN A MATTER of days, the raids began. The more remote parts of Fenton land felt the first prick, as if the small band of scavengers tested the boundaries and Isobel's resolve to defend them. It reminded her of not so very long ago, when her father had talked in hushed tones to her mother of the bands of Lancastrian renegades pilfering the cotts and farms. Then, he had dispatched George and their own armed men and sent a clear message to any who dared venture on his lands. But that was then, and both her father and her sergeant-at-arms were dead, and the total number of men she could winnow from the remains of the garrison the Earl had established to defend the manor amounted to three, and one of those was just a boy.

"Jack," she called from the door of the kitchens. He came running, tugging his shirt over his sweat-streaked skinny arms and emerging with his hair resembling a stook of hay. "Has your finger healed fully?"

He bowed and grinned. "Aye, m'lady, right straight an' all." He demonstrated by flexing it in front of her.

"Have you had any training in arms?"

"Aye, er, nay, m'lady,"

"Do you cut wood with an axe?"

"Yea, I do tha'." He grinned again, toothily.

"Good, then you can cleave heads."

She arranged for the sound in body and mind to spend part of each day under instruction from Arthur Moynes in the use of whatever weapons they could lay their hands to. Nor did she discount the value of the remaining women on the manor, nor those in Alkborough itself. Isobel sent word to as many women who would come to the great hall, and there addressed them. They were a mixed lot, and she had known most for much of her life: the miller's wife and their unwed daughter, the blacksmith's sister, the chandler's widow – now trading in her own right – and others. Strong women, independent-minded, curious, cautious.

"I am not saying the manor will be attacked, but if it is, the village will bear the brunt of it unless you are willing to defend it. Being wives and daughters, young or old, widows or maids will be no defence against brigands, and they will take what they want and kill the rest." Murmured responses rose from the women; exchanged glances but little support.

One woman, beef-armed and face reddened with broken veins, spoke up. "Our men 'ave spent 'nough time as it is practising arms without us takin' time out to join 'em. Who'll give recompense for our losses, eh? Our businesses'll suffer more'n they've already done this past year." A few of the women nodded agreement.

Another ventured, "Aye, in times past, the manor would've defended the village and Sir Geoffrey would never 'ave asked such o' us, my lady."

"Nor the Earl," another added. "He would 'ave seen us right."

Isobel's face reddened, but she stood her ground. "*I* am your lord, and my father and the Earl are dead. If you do not want to see your daughters spoiled and your homes burned, then do as I bid, because the manor cannot defend you anymore."

The raids escalated and grew bolder. One farm took the brunt on a Monday evening, the brigands taking the semi-inebriated young freeman off-guard and making off with several pigs, driving cattle before them and scattering sheep onto neighbours' land.

"To whom can we turn?" Isobel asked Arthur when the young man stood battered and visibly shaking before her. "Who is Justice of the Peace now?"

"That'd be George Bolle, my lady – Lord Lacey's man."

"And the sheriff?"

"Richard Welby. But that's like to change, and it's rumoured Leonard Thornburgh'll be the next sheriff."

"Does that matter?"

"Lord Lacey invites him to hunt on his land. He's also kin to Lady Lacey, God have mercy on her." He crossed himself.

"Are we so friendless? What of my father's allies?"

His hesitation said it all. "My lady, it is best we look to our own resources."

UNEXPECTED SNOW HAD settled on the trees in the orchard when Thomas made his next appearance. Isobel watched him dismount in the courtyard and toss the reins to his young esquire as he noted the man posted on the tower. His glance ran across the wall heads to the gatehouse behind him and then back to the tower windows, where his eyes caught hers. He raised a hand to her unsmiling face.

"I see you have a guard on watch; had trouble?" he asked casually, settling into her father's chair by the fire without being invited.

"No. I always have a watch. I am surprised you have not noticed."

"Very wise. You can never be too careful." He flicked his fingernails, watching as she sat in her own chair and folded her hands in front of her. "You are very quiet today."

"Am I?"

"Your son does not ail, does he?"

"No, he is well."

He flicked again, *flick*, *flick*, competing with the ticking of the burning wood. "You are looking a little thin. Are you not eating enough?"

His solicitude galled, given he was looking well-fed and complacent on it. "I eat well enough."

"I thought perhaps you were short of provisions; this season has been particularly harsh."

She looked directly at him for the first time. "If we find ourselves short of food it is because our stores were left that way, and that which remains has been impoverished by the vermin that frequent my tenants." She detected him twitch, but he quickly recovered.

"I will have some victuals sent to you, some wine also – to sweeten your humour." If he meant to lighten her mood, he failed. "Do you have an answer for me?"

Her hands squeezed a little tighter around something she held in them. "I have not had enough time to give it consideration."

"How much more time do you need?" he asked, a shade off caustic.

"As long as I want." And she gripped the sprig of dried rosemary left for her by Rob in her clenched hand.

He arrived unannounced a week later with a wagon of provisions and a cask of wine. A side of cured bacon scented the air. Isobel salivated and briefly wondered whether the animal had been one of her own hogs.

"You will be able to feast on the contents of this." Thomas slapped the side of the wagon. "I've brought wine – fresh spices as well. You can make me clarry now." He ran his eyes up and down the length of her body. Smiled. "I'd better be careful, or you'll fade away and that would be a waste. You!" he called to Arthur, who had hurried to join them and awaited instruction. "Have wine brought to my lady's solar, I have a thirst about me." He turned his back on Isobel's steward and missed their exchanged glances.

As soon as they reached the privacy of her solar, she turned on him. "Three cotts were burned yesterday this side of Appleby, Thomas, and one man killed. He leaves a wife and four children without husband and father to provide for them."

"I am shocked. You should have sent for me."

"Are you?"

"Of course. Isobel—" he attempted to take her hand but ended up holding the tips of her fingers as she tried to withdraw it, "—I cannot have anything happen to you. Do you know who is behind the attack?" She pulled her hand free and shook her head. "Is it the Countess?"

"I do not know." She put Drew on the floor, and he scuttled on all fours like a crab after Moth.

"This is exactly what I was afraid of – you and little Andrew alone and undefended. Tell me you have given consideration to my offer?"

"Will the attacks stop if I accept the match?"

"Why should they—?"

"Thomas – will the attacks stop if I marry you?"

His eyes slid from hers. "If you marry me, it will be known you have my protection, so, probably, yes."

"Then I accept your proposal. There is one condition."

His smile, tinged with smugness, stalled. "Which is?"

"We live here at Beaumancote, and it remains mine to leave to my son on my death."

His expression soured, but he remembered to govern his tone. "We will have other sons."

"Drew is to inherit Beaumancote. I stipulate nothing more."

"Of course, but you'll—"

"Good." She nodded curtly. "As you agree, I will have a contract drawn up to that effect and a copy sent to the King."

"The *King*, no less," he murmured, plucking at his lower lip and considering her through narrowed eyes.

"I think it wise so that we can avoid any future misunderstanding."

"Don't you trust me, Bel?"

She gritted her teeth, "Do not *ever* call me that again."

They remained staring at each other, and his eyes hardened. "You have grown so cold. I never remember this lack of feeling towards me before you went away."

"We have both changed. Circumstance has changed us."

"And yet here we are, brought together again by Fate. What God wills—"

"God does not harry my people, my tenants despairing for their livelihood, their livestock driven from the fields. He does not spoil wells with carcasses of sheep, nor break the dykes to waste the crops. Would God threaten the weak and feeble-minded as they lie cowering by their hearths? It is not by God's divine will, Thomas, but by Man's." She waited for her temper to abate before saying, "Look, I have agreed to marry you; that is what you want, is it not? To gain title to my lands and property. I am not so foolish to imagine you have any affection for me, nor will you believe that I hold the same for you. But I want these attacks to stop, and if marriage to you is the price I must pay then so be it."

He looked at her without blinking, pale eyes calculating. "Agreed."

"And Drew inherits Beaumancote. Say it, Thomas, swear to it. Andrew will never be disinherited."

He took longer to reply this time. "As you say—"

"*Swear* to it, may God strike you should you ever break your oath."

He looked at the child, then back at her. "I accept… all right, all right, I *vow*: Andrew will inherit this manor."

Satisfied, Isobel sat back, resting her hands on the arms of her chair. "You get what you want, Thomas, and live where you wish, but I stay at Beaumancote with my son. Do you understand?"

"Your *son*. His *bastard*." Without warning, he leaned from his chair and grabbed her wrist, holding her hand so that the Earl's ring she now wore burned orange in the light of the fire. "You wear his ring. When we marry, you will honour *me* as your husband in all ways, and you will not wear *this*." He shook her hand, making her bones crack. "*All* ways, Isobel, and I will make you forget him and raze his seed from your womb so no trace of him remains." Moth growled and, sensing tension, Drew began to fret. He rolled onto his knees and crawled towards Isobel. Thomas stared unblinking into her eyes. "Do *you* understand?"

She tried to pull her wrist away, but he held on. "I understand," she said, managing at last to dislodge his fingers and rubbing the reddened, pinched skin. Drew pulled himself to unsteady feet using her skirts. His lip trembled, turning down in a neat bow as he regarded Thomas with solemn eyes. He wobbled, tried to grasp the end of Thomas's gown to steady himself, but Thomas struck the furred fabric from the little hand and Drew fell back, bumping his head against Moth. He lay, startled. Isobel scooped him up, feeling the shock in his small body, angry beyond words.

"And as for your bastard brat, you will keep him from my sight."

Heat scalding her face, she snarled, "Get out!"

Thomas remained seated, arms draped over the sides of her father's chair. He waved an airy hand and in a bored voice said, "Sit down, Isobel. We have an agreement and a date to set."

"I said get. Out. Of. My. House."

He stood, slowly, looming, her eyes level with the brown furred neck of his gown. "If I leave now, my *Bel*, I will never return as your friend."

Isobel took a breath and spoke slowly and deliberately as she exhaled. "I overlooked your lies and the theft of my possessions. I tried to understand your treatment of my people, but the Earl was right all along: you are a traitor and a coward, and nothing you ever do or say can be trusted. I might have been willing to forgo my own happiness, but not my son's – *never* my son's."

"You will regret crossing me."

She looked up and held his gaze. "I regret ever imagining you might become the man my father hoped you would, or half the man the Earl proved to be."

He might have slain her with the look he now gave her had she cared. He shoved past her, knocking his cup to the floor and spilling the contents across the hearth. He crashed past Buena as she came hurrying into the room. Within moments, from the courtyard they heard shouted commands, Arthur's exclamation of surprise, hooves striking the cobbles as horses left at a canter.

Before the gates had closed on Thomas and his esquire, Arthur Moynes came running up the tower stairs and into the solar. "I'm not sorry to see the back of him, my lady," he said, when he had assessed the situation.

Isobel breathed out and nodded. "I only hope that I have not made it worse." She kissed Drew and handed him to Buena. "Arthur, have braziers set on our wall heads and gatehouse, and tell the priest to let a watch sit on the church tower to sound the alarm if he sees anything. That should give the village some warning of attack. As for the manor, we have three men who can handle the crossbows of two feet, and several women who can manage the one-foot crossbows, but none the great war bow. There are enough casks of quarrels, but very few sallets and breastplates and certainly not enough to go around. Did you say we have helmets of *cuir bouilli*? That's better than nothing. There are pikes and a number of billhooks – and we have a bucket of caltrops somewhere." Her mind raced. "And if the village is attacked, I want as many families behind these walls as possible. The menfolk can help man the walls, and the women can do what they can to support them." She ran her hands, tacky with perspiration, down the front of her skirt.

"My lady, we don't have food to make provision for them all."

"They can bring what they can, and we have more than we did thanks to Thomas's wagon load. Besides, they have a better chance of protecting themselves here than in the streets, and Thomas will think twice about attacking the manor if it looks well-defended." She gnawed her lip, thinking. "My fader's harness will be too heavy, his sword as well, but is there a short sword I can use, and a gambeson that will fit me?"

"My lady, you cannot *fight*!" Arthur said, his face forming deep ridges.

"I sat for months in the great tower of Tickhill waiting while Warwick and Montagu whittled away at our resolve, and in the end the tower was no defence against the malign intent of the Countess. Drew came this close—" and she held her fingers up with the merest gap between them, "—to being smothered, and I could do nothing – not one thing – to protect him. I will not let that happen, Arthur. I never want my son threatened by such casual death again."

"I'll see what can be found."

He bowed and turned, but Isobel added, "Arthur, if it comes to it, get Buena and Drew to safety. I care not how – just... just get them away."

"Where to?"

She knew of only one place where they would be safe. "Find Lord Langton."

Chapter 37

LIGHT GRAZED THE eastern sky, yet dense night clung to the parapet of the tower to which she had been summoned from sleep. Isobel screwed a knuckle into her eyes, attempting to focus. "Is it dawn?"

Arthur lowered his voice. "Can you not smell the smoke?"

There, the telltale acrid scent. Isobel searched the surrounding area. "The mill?" A sudden explosion split the air, illuminating Arthur's face and making his eyes dance with reflected flames.

"That'll be the flour," he said. The night seemed so eerily quiet apart from the popping of exploding pockets of flour. And then the bell from the church tower began to ring the alarm.

"We are under attack?" Isobel asked, bewildered. "Already? But we are not prepared." Shouts from the village houses closest to the mill confirmed it, as new, raw fire climbed skywards. "They are burning the houses," she said, stupefied.

"My lady, better get off the roof. I'll see to the defences." There were screams now, women shrieking, the clash of metal. "My lady!"

Isobel came to. "They're burning the village; we must get everyone we can inside."

"It's too late—"

But she wasn't listening. Leaning from the crenel, she had spotted scattered figures running from the village like hares towards them, silhouetted against the increasing glare of the burning houses and cotts. "Get the gate open," she yelled down to the gatehouse. "Let them in!"

"No, my lady! You don't know who's down there. This is what they want."

"I will not leave my people undefended." She craned to see the figures making their erratic way. They were nearly there. "Can you make them out?" she called again.

"Don't let them in!" Arthur barked down to the man on the gate, then in urgent tones, "My duty is to protect you before all else."

But Isobel had seen the fear in the way the figures ran dancing and dodging over pits and bumps, stumbling as they looked over their shoulders. She made out the bunched bodies of women carrying children. "And my duty is to my people." She picked up her skirts and ran to the stairs, bumping against the unlit wall in her haste and using the steep curve against her shoulder to guide her way. She flew out of the tower and across the courtyard. "In Jesu's name, let them in. *Now!*" She ran to the gate, struggling with the bar, scraping skin from the heels of her hands. Voices crying, pleading came from the other side. "Raise the portcullis. Do it!" The windlass ground above her, and the portcullis rose, rattling in its race. She heard laboured breathing behind her, and Arthur leaned his shoulder against the bar, shifting it into the deep wall socket. Wild-eyed, mouths gasping for air, the first of the villagers bled through the gates, soot-soaked and reeking of smoke.

Arthur steadied a man carrying a child little older than Drew, then grabbed a lad blood-smeared and half-naked. "How many more of you?" he demanded. The youth gaped, senseless, and Arthur let him go stumbling into the courtyard and instead slipped between the panicking bodies and out from the safety of the gatehouse to see for himself. He returned moments later.

"Lower the portcullis," he bellowed, heaving the gates shut with the help of one of the men and hauling the bar into place.

Isobel grabbed his arm. "What did you see?"

"Nothing I liked. There's enough of them out there and too many to fight. Adam…!" He hailed a lanky man wearing half-armour and a scant beard whom he had managed to retain to replace George.

"Did you see Thomas?" Isobel asked.

"I wasn't looking too hard. Adam, see how many of the villagers are capable of bearing arms of any sort and have them equipped." He turned back to Isobel. "My lady, please..." But she was now among the subdued inhabitants of her courtyard, checking wounds, burns – quelling fear, courting hope. She spotted John Appleyard's wife among the women and children.

"Mary, where is John?"

The sturdy young woman's lips were white in her smoke-smudged face. "He wen' back for our oldest boy. They're burning the village, my lady; why'd they be doin' tha'?" She clutched a child to her breast, another clung to her skirts. "Will they attack t'manor? Are we safe 'ere?"

"Mary, leave the children with old Joan Wintel – she'll mind them in the tower where they will be safe – and come and help me." Shouted warnings from the gatehouse sent several people cowering against the walls. "See who else among the women is able to lift and carry and bring any who might be able to hold a weapon. Mary, come *on*. Doing nothing will not keep John from harm. We have to defend the manor to keep you all safe."

Mary blinked and ran a nervous hand over her mouth, then nodded. "Aye, m'lady."

Isobel ran up the stairs to the solar two at a time, bursting through the door to be greeted by a ballock knife to her throat. Buena grunted an apology, and Isobel pushed her arm away. "I need that gambeson and the sallet. No, I am not debating it – get them *now*."

The buckles secured the leather quilted jacket over her kirtle, but the combination felt awkward and she wanted to rip the fabric from around her legs and walk freely like a man. The sallet was worse, balancing over the arming cap that barely contained her hair. In all the frenzy since she woke, Isobel had not stopped to consider what she really intended doing other than whatever she could to keep her son safe. He slept in the same crib she had occupied as a baby, oblivious of the mounting fear around him. "Buena, I want you to see to the people in the chamber below and dress their wounds. I wish... I wish I had my casket..." She ran through a checklist. "The children will need food and coverlets. I'll send Cissy Hatton to watch over Andrew; she's a sensible girl." Buena regarded her with dark, appraising eyes. Isobel turned to leave, then added, "If Thomas gets through, this tower will stand longer than any part, the floors are made of stone. But, *if* they get through..." Her words quavered and Buena, placing her hand on Isobel's arm, squeezed reassurance into it. Isobel swiftly kissed the woman's cheek and, with a quick glance at her sleeping son with the Earl's chaplet by his side, left the room.

"There're about two score, perhaps more; it's difficult to be sure in this light," Arthur said. "We'll have a better idea at cockcrow."

Isobel's skin ran cold. "That many."

"Aye, but not all will be trained men; some looked like vagabonds."

"But still more than we have." Isobel looked down at the ragged bunch of men in the courtyard below, only the tops of their heads visible. A few women had joined them, bristling with whatever improvised weapons they could lay their hands to. Adam was organising them. Braziers had been lit the length of the walls and on the tower where they stood. From the stable, the horses stamped restlessly, smelling fire and fear.

"These walls were built strong, and your fader and the Earl had the foresight to keep them so. Three men may hold a castle, my lady, just three men and determination. I'm no soldier, and Heaven knows I've not been acquainted with arms these last few years as well as I might, but these people will fight to protect what's theirs, and Adam's given what training he can."

To the east, flames ate the village houses, leaving the tower of the church standing proud of the surrounding smoke.

"But it's all gone," Isobel whispered. "What have they left to fight for?"

Arthur followed her line of sight. "They're not fighting for the village alone, my lady, they're fighting for Geoffrey Fenton's daughter. They are fighting for *you*."

The sky showed signs of dawn. Gradually, Isobel could distinguish between knobs of bare bushes and clusters of men, beyond the manor's walls and out of bowshot to the south. They seemed to be waiting. Everyone seemed to be waiting, suspense hanging in the air, tangible like the smoke that thickened it making them cough. "Why have they not yet attacked?"

Arthur shook his head. "I do not know." As he spoke, one of the besiegers shouted, waving his arm to the men directly in front of the gatehouse. Almost immediately, fire sprang from a number of points as braziers were lit. "It begins," Arthur muttered. From the direction of Walcott, brazen hooves competed with the ring of harness in the frozen air, and moments after, a dozen men, clad in full armour, rode into view.

Arthur grunted. "They were waiting for Lacey."

The strengthening dawn brought little comfort. Evident on his big grey horse, Thomas led his mounted men in a brisk reconnoitre of the ice-rutted ground, then gave a few curt commands.

"Get back!" Arthur jerked Isobel behind the protective merlon as a volley of arrows cut the air, glancing and rattling against the stonework like hail. A second volley followed and then a third. The fourth came spilling fire from hollow-headed arrows. Screams alerted them to a similar scene in the courtyard.

Arthur stamped out the burning rags closest to Isobel's skirts, grabbing a bucket of water standing by. "Soak your kirtle." She did so without arguing, the heavy fabric clinging cold to her legs.

"Why are we not firing back, Arthur? We must attack!"

"All they're doing is expending munitions. We have the advantage of height; let them tire themselves needlessly. Sooner or later they'll have to come within range, and there'll be plenty of opportunity to loose our own bolts. Until then, I've given orders to keep behind the walls so they can't gauge our strength – or lack of it." His downturned mouth lifted. "I learned much from your fader. If we're careful with our victuals, we can hold out." The arrows ceased as suddenly as they had started, leaving an unnerving silence in their wake. "What now?" Arthur peered around the edge of the merlon. "Ah, I spoke too soon. Stay there, my lady." He evaded the crenels and loped across the roof to the stairs, where he exchanged words with one of the men.

Isobel risked a look. Archers with longbows ranged in a staggered line two men deep across the entire front of the manor as before, but more men were appearing in a fast-moving column along the Walcott road. Thomas dispatched a mounted man, and the column split, one group jogging towards the burning village, the other staying put to the western end beyond the garden. Flanked on three sides, pinned against the edge of the river cliff on its fourth, Beaumancote could only answer the onslaught of arrows with the great war crossbow; but it was no match. At least there were no more fire arrows. *Doesn't want to burn the place down*, she thought. *He'll attack women and children, but not destroy the manor.* "Shame!" she yelled over the top of a crenel. "You bring shame on your family, Thomas Lacey!"

She fell back as an arm around her waist pulled her down. "Keep out of sight, my lady!" Arthur hissed. "There's nothing we can do." But Isobel scrambled to her feet and dashed to the door.

"He burned the village to prevent the villagers from attacking him from behind. I cannot stay up here just... just waiting."

The courtyard smelled of burning wool and singed hair. One of the fire arrows had lodged in the stable wall and was still smouldering, another pierced a first-floor window. Pitched roofs of the low buildings prickled with shafts. One of the cotters – propped in the shelter of the gatehouse wall – had an arrow through his calf, and Buena kneeled beside him trying to stem the blood. Keeping tight against the walls, Isobel skirted the courtyard and ran up the narrow steps to the crenellated parapet where Adam oversaw the defence of the wall head. "Give me something useful to do," she demanded.

He swung around. "My lady, this is no place—"

"... for a woman, yes, I know, but the wives of my villagers are prepared to fight, and so am I."

He took one look at the determined set of her jaw. "Can ye handle a crossbow?"

"I have used a bow."

He bent sideways and plucked a small crossbow from a rack by the merlon. "Like this," he said, showing her, then placed it in her hands. "You try."

It was heavier than it looked, but she wedged her foot in the stirrup and managed to slide the drawstring onto its hook. The first bolt went wild, but by the third she had gauged the distance accurately enough to surprise her target, if missing him by yards. "You'll do," he said curtly, "but the moment them handgonnes start their firing, you're off my walls."

"*My* walls," she said.

"Not if I don't defend 'em they won't be. You'll be in my way, and death's no respecter of women, lady or no. 'Til then, you do as I say or leave; that's what you pay me for. An' keep yer head down," he fired as a parting shot as he set off down the length of the wall, shouting instructions to the men at the farther end before she could respond.

She tried to disregard the reprimand of the hand-guns, which sent invisible missiles over her head or ricocheting from the stonework, and concentrated on loading the flesh-piercing bolts and firing one slow shot at a time, with little hope of hitting anything other than the softening earth. But it was better than doing nothing; better than considering their fate should the walls be breached and Beaumancote fall to Thomas Lacey.

Arthur joined Adam on the gatehouse roof, pointing towards Walcott, his movements agitated.

"What is it?" she asked, puffing and feeling the ache in the back of her knees from keeping squat as she scurried to meet them.

Arthur directed her gaze. "There, can you see them?"

Standing on tiptoes and peeping over the wall, she screwed her eyes and focused beyond the garden towards the farm at Walcott, where the rising sun glinted off sallets as men in twos and threes moved in a dappled dance around objects she couldn't make out.

"Gonnes," Adam said. "Eight-foot serpentines – two of 'em."

"They cannot fire this far," Isobel stated with a certainty she didn't feel.

"Oh, aye, they can at that. Six hundred yards and they'll peck away at these walls like cheese, an' nothin' to be done about it, not wi'out gonnes of our own."

"Fader said we had no need of great guns."

"With Tickhill less than a day's ride, we didn't, my lady," Arthur reminded her. "Lacey wouldn't have attempted an assault when the Earl was alive."

"What do we do?" she asked, her voice thin.

"Get yer to the cellar with the other lasses and wains," Adam said, grim-mouthed. "When them gonnes start, with two or three chambers – breech-loaded – they'll keep up a rate of fire that'll take out the windows you have up there." He jerked his head towards the fine tracery of the tower. "Accurate enough fer it, though it might take a day or more to do any real damage."

Isobel scanned the delicate stonework. "Drew's up there."

"Better get him to the cellar, my lady," Arthur urged. "As long as the gate holds, that's the safest place to be."

"How long do we have?"

Arthur looked at Adam, and the soldier shrugged. "If they start up afore noon, I'd give it two days – five at most – before they've done enough damage t'storm walls, but by then you'll be beggin' to surrender."

"I will *not* surrender."

"Aye, I reckon after a few hours of the gonnes, my lady, you'll be ready and willin' to give 'im anything he wants." He rapped steel knuckles on the crown of her sallet, and she shied from the noise.

"That's enough," Arthur intervened sharply. "My lady, if it please you, take the child to the cellar and show the other women you're not afraid."

Afraid? She was petrified, but her fear would achieve nothing. "We must send for help," she determined. "If what you say is true, we have no other option than to summon aid from whomever will grant it." The two men swapped doubtful glances. "Look," she pressed, "Thomas Lacey might have persuaded some of his loyalty, but not all are as convinced as the King chooses to be." She took a breath. "If we can get a message to the Duke of Gloucester…" Adam rolled his eyes, and Isobel threw him a cautionary frown. "His Grace knows the true nature of Thomas Lacey; he has said as much, and he values loyalty."

"If you say so."

"I do say. What is more, this is my manor, and you will do as I bid," she snapped. "Arthur, whom can we send?"

"It's not so much *who* as *how*, my lady. We can hardly send someone out of the gate, and Lacey has the postern covered. There's not a way in or out he doesn't know, and he has the measure of our defences well enough."

Welling fear slipped up her throat as all ways appeared shut, bottled up, and corked. She felt the urge to run and hide in the garden with her son, disappear among the apple trees and the sandy warren at the farthest end where her coneys dug their burrows.

"Rabbits." She looked up. "They have dug under the wall bordering the river cliff. John had to shore it up, but the rubble is still loose there. If it is removed, someone small could tunnel through easily enough." Her thoughts quickened. "Jack – from the kitchens – he is slight and sharp-witted. If he can get out unseen, he can work along the ridgeway above the river flats to Stather—"

"... and cross by ferry. Aye, that might work," Arthur agreed.

The rain of arrows came to an abrupt halt, but the following silence was made more ominous by the series of short, dull thuds from the direction of the guns. Isobel could clearly see Thomas riding between them. Adam hawked and spat. "They're loading the chambers."

"What does that mean?" Isobel asked.

"That I'll be tellin' you to leave the walls to me. They're getting ready to fire."

SLIPPING DOWN THE stone steps in her haste, Isobel called to the other women to get to the tower's cellar, then sprinted to the first floor solar with Buena to collect Drew and directed her to take him and round-eyed Cissy to the windowless stores and relative safety. "I will return as soon as I can," she said when Buena tried to stop her from leaving, then went to find Jack.

THE FIRST SHOT barked like thunder and they ducked, grimacing at the clear sky. The stone ball cleared the manor entirely, falling harmlessly somewhere on the marshy flats out of sight.

"Gettin' their range," Adam growled. The second fell short by only a few yards. "I'd best be going," he sniffed, and Isobel tugged Jack into the shelter of the tower wall.

"I am not commanding you to do this. It will be dangerous, and I only ask you to undertake the task because I trust you and think you can achieve it better than anyone. But you can refuse, and I will think none the worse of you."

At nearly fifteen, Jack had not yet grown into manhood and his skinny shoulders were narrower than her own, but he was strong and agile, reminding her of the Duke she bid him seek. He flashed a grin. "I'll do it, m'lady, but how'll His Grace know what I say i' the truth when I gets there?"

She fished inside her quilted gambeson, lifted the ribbon over her head and, placing it over Jack's, tucked her father's seal out of sight under his padded jack. "Give this to His Grace, and say I sent you. He'll ask you why, and you will tell him what is happening here. Do you understand?"

"Aye, m'lady."

"Nobody else, mind, Jack – only the Duke. You know where to go?" He nodded eagerly, and not for the first time she felt a wash of anxiety. "Good. Let's get you to the garden."

They ran through the cross passage and out onto the brick path to the crack of guns as the gunners found their range and shot thudded into the ground nearby, sending an earthy skirt of grass into the air. There was no respite inside the garden. Nowhere felt safe anymore, and the sun merely mocked the peace she had once found there, shattering it beyond redemption. Is this what men faced on the field of battle? This thrill of fear?

They passed under the vine-clad walls climbing into the blue heavens, their footfall scattering coneys when they pushed into the warren's enclosure.

Fresh hay had been laid as winter feed, and dried dark pellets scattered the sandy floor around the pock-mark burrows. John's attempt to block the rabbits' escape route with rubble marked out the breach hard up against the rear wall.

Throwing aside wood and stone, Isobel started to tear at the temporary repair with her bare hands. Arthur joined them, and together they cleared the area until it stood free of obstruction. Soil had fallen back into the collapsed labyrinth, but it ran freely, made friable with frost, and she began digging feverishly at the base of the wall.

"My lady!" Arthur picked her up bodily. "We'll get this done quicker." She bent over, catching her breath, soil caking her nose and nails, watching as Arthur and Jack cleared a hole large enough for the boy to wriggle under the foundations like an eel.

He was back moments later, his neck scratched. "It's fair scroggy with brambles, but I can get through, and it give cover right enough all way down t'flats."

"I wish we could wait until dark," Isobel began, looking at the eye of the early sun.

"There's no time," Arthur said as shot found its mark unnervingly close. "God be with you, lad," and he clasped the boy's thin shoulder as men do when words fail them on parting. Jack bobbed his head, grinned again, and dived back under the wall, kicking his way through until all Isobel could see were the soles of his boots. And then he was gone.

Bruised rosemary smelled bitter-sweet held to her nose, and Isobel rolled the crumbling stalk between her thumb and fingers, thinking, watching, listening. In the low, cross-vaulted cellar rank with humanity, those who were too young or too old, frail or ill to fight sat in huddles among barrels and casks, or propped against the well-head's wall, talking in hushed tones as if whispering would protect them from the disintegrating world above. Between them, she, Mary Appleyard, and Buena had dressed what wounds they could and now, hours after the initial bombardment, time folded and became lost in murmuring conversations. Next to her on a blanket, Drew played alongside the miller's boy sitting close by with his knees drawn under his chin, round-eyed and watchful, his night clothes singed ragged. He had last seen his father when the miller had thrown his infant daughter from the burning mill into the older boy's arms. Isobel gave him a smile of encouragement, but he stared back, blank. She rested her head against the wall and closed her eyes.

"My lady." Arthur stepped between outstretched legs to reach her.

She wrenched her eyes open. "What is it? Are we breached?"

He leaned down, keeping his voice low. "It's Lacey, he wishes to speak with you." Only then did she notice that the constant crack and thud of the guns – fainter through the thick walls – had ceased.

"I'm coming." She eased herself into an upright position and followed her steward from the crowded room. She emerged into half-light, the air in the courtyard thick with charred wood and saltpetre yet smelling fresh compared with the foetid cellar. Like a candle seen through a horn lantern, the low sun fought to give light.

"What hour is it?"

"About two before dusk. It's the smoke." He looked tired, and his shoulders sagged as he led her to the gatehouse roof where Adam stood with his few crossbowmen. They aimed at something below. Ranged along the walls and on the tower roof, Adam had placed armed men in a show of strength Isobel knew they didn't have. "They're casks with sacking stuffed with straw, my lady," Arthur said from the side of his mouth when he saw her looking. "The polearms are real enough, though."

Broken stone capping and lumps of brick strewed the floor of the courtyard and littered the parapet where broken-toothed merlons stood. Shot had destroyed the upper part of the tracery window, and the sharply defined corners of the tower were chewed.

They reached the roof, and she gathered her wits. She held out her hand. "Give me a crossbow."

"Don't give him a target, my lady, stay back," Arthur warned at her elbow, but she pressed forward between two merlons, fully exposed. Flanked by his dozen knights and men-at-arms on horseback, Thomas was easily within bowshot. Her fingers twitched.

"Mistress Fenton," he hailed, his visor raised, revealing his insincerity. "I come to offer you terms."

Not far from him and on either side of the horsemen, she noted two groups of men holding hand-guns, slow matches smouldering at the ready. If he was within range, so was she.

Isobel cleared her throat, damned if he thought her frightened into submission. "You have nothing to offer me. Leave my land, and take your guns with you." A ripple of laughter spread among his men.

"I expected nothing less of my *Bel*." He looked right and left, then back up at her. "I vouchsafe you and your people safe passage if you lay down your arms and open the gates. Safe passage, Isobel, and you are free to go wherever you wish unhindered. You have my word."

"Would that be the same oath you gave the King before you broke it, Thomas? Your promises are written in chalk to be washed away at the first sign of rain. Your words are dust."

"My lady, buy us time," Arthur urged beside her. "We need more time."

Thomas's grey mare tossed her head against the bit pulled rigid in her mouth. "You have until dusk." He brought his horse's head around, ready to ride.

"Thomas!" she called after him. He halted. "I want proof you will honour your bond."

"You are in no position to make demands."

"Find Walter Yorke, the miller. When I see him safe and unharmed, I will open my gates to you, but not before. Those are *my* terms."

Thomas leaned across his horse's neck and exchanged words with one of his men. Isobel thought she saw the man's shoulders lift briefly.

"Did Jack get away?" she whispered, barely moving her lips.

"There was no sign of him being given chase, but whether he's made it to Stather and across the Trent..." Arthur let her fill in the rest. One of the horsemen broke away, galloping east towards a thicket where sheep sheltered in foul weather.

"God help him if he is caught with my seal," Isobel breathed.

"God help us all if the message isn't delivered," Arthur concurred.

Thomas raised his voice. "You have until dawn. If the miller is not found by then you will surrender—"

"Or what, Thomas? You'll continue picking away at our walls with your playthings in the hope you will wear us down? We have plentiful supplies of food and water, more than we need and more than you have. How long will it be before you need seek provision? What source do you have after you so carelessly burned the village and its mill?"

"This," he said, raising his arm and pointing behind him with a swagger. No one had noticed the thicket had moved until that moment, revealing six men, a small cart piled with round stones, and a snub-nosed gun directly facing them.

Adam's voice grated as he spat out, "That's a quarter-curtow. It'll blow the gate to pieces at this range. They must've used the cover of dark to move it into position."

Thomas kneed his horse around. "Until dawn, Isobel; those are *my* terms."

Chapter 38

THE GUNNERS WAITED until Thomas and his men were beyond range and then opened up again with the serpentines, the heavy gun made more sinister by its silence.

"I should have pressed for more time," Isobel said, sitting on a cask as shot after shot pounded the tower walls above them. "And I should not have berated him. It only made him more angry."

Arthur accepted the ale she offered with a grateful nod. He drank before replying, "It wouldn't have made any difference either way, my lady. He is determined to it, and he giving you more time is because it suits his purpose, not yours."

She handed him bread and cheese. "It was always going to come to this the moment my father was granted Lacey land and manors."

Arthur bit into the bread, chewing thoughtfully. "I once asked your fader why the old Earl did that."

"What did he say?"

"He said it was a wedding gift." Arthur chuckled despite himself. "Such a handsome gift to a gentleman from his earl, and I said as much. He smiled in that way he had, you remember, my lady? And he said he had done his lord a service and had been rewarded with the greatest treasure any man could have." He looked around the vaulted ceiling, where shadows jumped. "Aye, Beaumancote is beyond worth. No wonder Lacey wants it back and the Earl was so keen to protect it."

So, Arthur didn't know. Isobel wondered what he would think if he knew the truth behind her parents' marriage, the price of this manor paid in return for her father's cooperation, his loyalty, his silence. Perhaps she judged her father too harshly but, sitting here, listening to stone balls finding their mark, she felt less inclined to think so. Beaumancote: a treasure indeed, but corruptible, like the rest. Her steward continued with his reminiscence.

"Still, I was a young man then and didn't know what I know now."

"What is that?"

"All men want something. What sets men apart is not what they are prepared to do to achieve it, but what it is that they desire. Your fader desired peace and justice – that's why he agreed a union between Lacey and you, my lady; it would heal the division."

"Then perhaps I shou—"

"And before you say it, your marrying Thomas Lacey would have rendered nothing but misery for us all. Your fader couldn't have known it, or he would never have accepted the proposal in the first place. Above all he valued honesty, and in that Lacey would sorely have tested him. Forgive me, my lady, but I'm glad your fader did not live to see this day." He crossed himself.

Buena tapped Isobel's shoulder, saving her from the need to comment. "Drew is hungry. I must feed him."

Arthur smiled his lugubrious smile. "Aye, well that is a comfort. Here." He undid his short cloak and, rising, swung it around her shoulders. "To preserve your dignity, my lady."

"Thank you, but I am not sure how much dignity I have left."

"Dignity is not what you have, my lady," he said soberly, "it is what you are." He bowed and left her to feed her son.

SHE FOUND NO respite in sleep. Restless dreams merged with waking nightmares until she couldn't be certain whether she slept or woke. And still the relentless guns pounded beyond curfew and into the watches of the night. She gave up and, wrapping Arthur's cloak around herself, followed the newel stair to her solar.

Ill-slept, unwashed, hunger vying with thirst, she drank the dark, cold air pouring through the smashed window. Dust-coated water slopped over the rim of her basin as she crouched to wash filth from her skin. She cleaned her teeth, wincing as the birch twigs cut her gums, dragged the comb through hair matted with ash and smoke, then found a clean smock and kirtle. Dressing in frosted light, she knew every nook of the room that had belonged to her parents: the bed they had shared, the lock on the door her father had fitted to protect their privacy and their secret – the Earl's secret – and now hers. In short, rough movements, she buckled the gambeson, anger growing with every tug. Slamming her feet into shoes, she stood. Moonlight fell in long beams across splintered glass and crushed masonry, and she almost tripped on an object that stubbed her toe. She bent to retrieve a stone ball. The moon illuminated the delicate oriel window of which her father had been so proud; but the Fenton heron that had once stood in its roundel of painted glass had been displaced by a single, snarling Lacey pike on their emboldened coat of arms. Hoisting the ball, Isobel hurled it two-handed at the window and, without a backward glance, left multicoloured remnants shimmering on the floor.

THERE COULD BE no mistaking the oncoming dawn. From the tower roof, Isobel identified the remains of the mill still smouldering, and here and there pockets of flame flared among the village houses. The serpentines had ceased firing, but ominous activity around the great gun presaged worse. Some yards in front of the curtow, but still outside bowshot, men worked at something it was yet too dark to see.

"They've been 'ammering away there some time since."

"Are they building a siege tower?"

"Eh, I don't know what for, not if his lordship intends using that thing." Adam thumbed in the direction of the lone gun. "One fair shot of that and he'll walk straight in. That is, if you don't open the gates to 'im straight off." He looked at her out of the corner of his eye. "I'd be gettin' them folk ready to leave, if I were you, unless ye want to live with the consequence of it."

"Watch your tongue," Arthur warned. "You're not paid to counsel my lady on her conscience."

Adam shrugged. "As you like, master, but I'll not be paid at all if m'lady here stirs his lordship to use that gonne. I've seen 'em in the field an' it'll take the legs off a man, in harness or no, and turn wood to splinters such as it'll carry away any that's near it."

"If they get through the portcullis and gate, how long do we have until they break into the tower?"

Adam used the tip of his rondel dagger to itch the back of his neck. "That'd depend."

"On what?"

"On how much damage his lordship wants to repair after. Either way, that door'll keep 'em out only so long. Then there's them who'll do the fighting inside for ye. After that..." And he lifted his shoulders again.

"So, you are saying if he wants to, there is little stopping Lord Lacey taking Beaumancote?"

"Aye, that's about it. The only difference is how many get killed in the meantime, and that's down to you."

Isobel waited until Adam had left the tower roof before she sank against the wall. Her steward squatted next to her. "Arthur, I want you to get Drew and Buena and the women and children ready to leave. Thomas promised them safe passage, and I have to believe he will not harm them; but in case... if he does attack, it will be against me. Dress Drew as one of the village children."

The concern on Arthur's face became clearer as the thin light strengthened, his breath mist. "You don't intend to leave with them, my lady?"

"I will stay for as long as we can resist them." She looked at him, a note of desperation creeping into her voice. "I cannot relinquish Beaumancote. I will give the men a choice to stay or to leave with the women, but *I* won't... I *can't*."

He nodded. "I understand. You are your father's daughter right enough." The hammering stopped. He poked his head over the nearest crenel. "I'd best get things organised; we haven't much time."

The night wind had dropped, and voices from the encampment carried on the still dawn air. Harness chinked, a brazier burned by the gun around which men gathered for warmth. Isobel became acutely aware of the gritty brick beneath her bare fingers, the damp penetrating the heels of her shoes, the smell of the sacking covering the improvised and immobile guard. She forgot her hunger as nausea lodged in her stomach and pushed herself to her feet.

Gathered in the courtyard, the women and children bunched mute and fearful. The miller's youngest child clung to her brother's neck.

"We're safer here, my lady," the mercer's wife said. "We've no place left to go."

"Get to Winteringham. Provision will be made for you there."

"But we've lost everything."

"Not everything," Isobel said, fatigue sharpening her tongue. "You have your lives."

With Drew bundled in her arms, Buena stood apart from the others. Isobel took him from her, her cheek pressed against his, absorbing him through her skin so she could carry the memory of him for as long as she breathed. "I cannot give you my fader's seal," she whispered into his hair, "but I can give you this," and she slipped a soft, thin, wool-wrapped package smelling of rosemary between his layers of clothes. "For remembrance." She kissed his chin, the tip of his nose, his forehead. He chortled, and she murmured her blessing then handed him back, hugging Buena briefly as she did so and turning away as tears burned her eyes.

From beyond the walls came a thin sound. Whistling. Carefully nonchalant, the tuneless melody grated.

"My lady!" Isobel looked up at the gatehouse. "Lord Lacey approaches."

She mounted the stairs, past the guard chamber where she had hidden as a child, and up onto the gatehouse roof. The sun had reached the horizon, but a pall of low cloud strangled its light. Thomas sat astride his horse surrounded by his men, squeezing out the thin, eerie sound from between his tight lips.

"Good morrow!" he called, as if offering a common pleasantry. "I trust you passed a diverting night?"

She let the derisive laughter of his men subside before she replied. "Safe passage, Thomas, that is what you promised my people. Safe passage without hurt or hindrance."

He waved a casual hand. "Of course."

That was too easy. The horses at the back of his retinue stamped uneasily, sending shivers among the rest. "Something's wrong," she said in an undertone to Arthur. Adam had sensed it also. He levelled the great war bow.

"Why do you hesitate?" Thomas asked. "Open the gates, and let your people go free. There is no need for bloodshed. Come out at their head, and I'll give you an escort to wherever you wish to go and let the rest of your garrison leave."

Adam muttered, "He's hidin' summet."

"Do not go," Arthur advised. "Escape under the garden wall with Drew and Buena. When he realises you are not among them, he'll think you are still inside, and by the time he finds you gone, you'll be in Stather and away. We can hold them off long enough, I'm certain of it."

Thomas had taken up his whistling again. Some of his men joined in, mocking. Isobel ground her teeth. "You are right, Arthur, it is time to go. Take Buena and my son, and leave now."

"Not without you, my lady."

"He will not do anything while I am standing here. I will win as much time as I can, but you must go. That is my last command to you, Arthur, and I expect to be obeyed."

"I am wai-ting, Isobel," Thomas called, voice curling like vipers into a sing-song taunt.

Arthur hesitated. "Go!" she said. He took her hand, held the Earl's ring to his lips, and left.

Thomas called out, "Did your noble mother not teach you that it is discourteous to keep someone waiting?" Isobel silently counted the steps Arthur would have to take to the courtyard, the number from the courtyard through the cross passage, and then along the path to the garden. Thomas slapped his gauntlets against the high-prowed saddle. "Or did running with that baseborn father of yours whelp a graceless tyke?"

Arthur must be in the warren by now. She closed her eyes and imagined him hurrying Buena, who would be holding Drew tight to her. A sound from among the mounted men drew her back to Thomas's growing irritation. "Perhaps this will help you decide." The men moved aside, and from their midst two soldiers dragged a youth, writhing and kicking.

"Jack!" The boy lifted his bloodied face at the sound of her voice.

"Ah, so this is one of *your* spies?" Thomas drawled. "He was caught imitating a coney, arse-up in a bush not far from here. Did you know you have a tunnel under your garden wall? How many other rabbits are you missing, Isobel?"

He knew about the tunnel. Isobel turned, hurling out, *"Stop them leaving!"* only to find Adam had already sprinted across the roof and was disappearing down the stairs after them.

Leaning towards Jack, Thomas prodded him with the tip of his sword. "You know what we do with spies, don't you, Isobel?"

"Leave him alone!"

"We make an example of them." Thomas waved his gauntlets and, at his signal, Jack was towed towards the strange device of wood brought to stand a stone's throw from the gatehouse and directly between the portcullis, gate, and the gaping mouth of the gun.

"You know he is not a spy; let him go!" she shouted as she watched the boy being strapped spread-eagled on the cross like St Andrew, facing her so she could see the terror in his eyes.

"A deserter, then, who should be punished. You can save him – if you really think he's worth it. Come out with your bastard, and all will be well."

Isobel opened her mouth to say something, anything, but Jack rolled his head to and fro violently, his eyes now fixed on hers. She frowned. His shirt had been torn, and little remained to cover his scrawny chest, bare except for streaked dirt and blood. No ribbon. No seal. Thomas would have said if he'd found it, used it in his vitriolic arsenal against her. "Let him go," she said, finding strength in her voice, "and I'll come out, but alone. My son stays here, unharmed."

"Why?" Thomas shook his head. "*Why* do you always think yourself in a position to barter with *me*? Your sense of superiority is misplaced. Look at you – orphaned and without protection – mistress of a dead man and mother to a bastard. Who do you think you *are*?"

Breath rasping, Arthur pushed past the watchmen to stand by her side, gasping out, "They're safe inside, my lady."

Adam picked up the great crossbow, aiming deliberately at Thomas's chest. Isobel lifted her chin and raised her voice so it would carry clearly across the heads of his retinue to the ears of the gunners beyond.

"I am Isobel Fenton, daughter of Sir Geoffrey Fenton and Lady Isobella Wray, and this is *my* land."

Thomas's expression froze. On their restless horses, several of his knights laughed, but more nervously this time. Pulling on his gauntlets, he led his men a safe distance away, leaving Jack strung up in the direct line of fire.

"There's nothing we can do." Arthur took her arm. "We must abandon the gatehouse and get everyone into the tower."

Isobel wrenched her arm free, stretching as far over the parapet as she could. "You are a coward, Thomas Lacey," she yelled at his retreating back. "You have no honour. I know what you did at Barnet. The Earl was right – you are a coward and a traitor. I wish he'd killed you."

"My lady, please—" But she picked up the small crossbow and, aiming wildly, fired it. She heard a yelp, and a report broke from one of the hand-gunners. A chunk of coping stone flew past her elbow. Dragging her from the roof, Arthur managed to get her into the shelter of the gatehouse, down the stairs, and out into the courtyard as haphazard shot struck brick. Then a loud crack, almost immediately followed by a thud, shook the ground beneath them. Loosened, damaged mortar rattled in a shower, scattering the gathered women and children. Adam came tumbling out of the gatehouse shouting orders to his men and herding the villagers back towards the tower. Isobel snatched up the miller's child, tugging the older boy behind her.

The tower's outer door rammed shut as a second stone ball careered into the manor wall. Adam turned the great lock and drew the bar, muffling the sound of falling rubble. He wiped sweat with his sleeve. "They're getting their aim all right; that were close."

"Jack," Isobel said in despair.

"Aye, well, it'll be a swift end for him and that's for sure, once they get the 'cullis and gate. And they will. Them gonners know their range." He hacked and would have spat but thought better of it. "If we don't want the same fate, we'd better get these scabby jacks dispersed." And he started a count of men and weapons, leaving Isobel shaking with a combination of grief and rage at the injustice of it all and at her resignation that there was nothing she could do to prevent it.

"Will he let any of us live?" she asked Arthur.

"The Duke of Norfolk allowed safe passage to the folk in Caister when he besieged the manor, and Lacey'll be unwise to kill women and children with so many witnesses…" Arthur faltered.

"But?"

"But Thomas Lacey isn't Mowbray. You've humiliated him, and he wants revenge." Another stone tore into the protecting wall, and groans of terror rose up the stairs from the cellar. "My lady, make haste."

"Thomas cannot let me live. One way or another, he will ensure my death today." Her brow smoothed. "I do not want to die in the dark, Arthur; I will go to the roof and take my chances." Arthur made to follow, but she stopped him. "Stay with Drew and Buena. Thomas has no need to kill you, and my son and servant need your protection." She slipped the Earl's ring from her thumb and pressed it into Arthur's palm, closing his fingers around it and holding it there. "Give this to Lord Robert when you take Drew to him. You promised me, Arthur," she said when it seemed likely he would debate it. "You promised me you would look after them. There is no one left to say prayers for my soul. Will you have masses sung for me?"

Swallowing, he looked away, then met her gaze. "I will, my lady."

She gave a quick, thin smile and bolted up the tight stairs to the roof.

All that remained of the shewel men guarding the wall heads were splinters of wood and cast-off sacking. Her tiny force of crossbowmen covered three faces of approach and, at the riverward side, Adam had several villagers heating cauldrons on braziers into which they had placed pieces of stone, brick, cannon shot, and nails. Two women squatted nearby filling jugs and small iron pots with an evil-smelling concoction that seared Isobel's throat. They glanced up at her, and one bobbed her head in deference. Is this what it had come to, she wondered, cowering on the top of her tower waiting at Thomas Lacey's pleasure for him to take what her father had spent so many years defending? And not just her father. Her thumb felt strangely naked without the Earl's ring. William Langton wouldn't have let her manor go without a fight.

The flagstaff on the lookout above the stairs had been shattered halfway down its length. Isobel cast about and found the broken spar leaning lopsidedly against a crenel. She picked it up, dragging it up the narrow steps where she used her man's belt to lash it to the broken stump. From the lidded box kept specifically for the purpose, she took the waxed linen bundle and lifted from it the folded pennant her father had taught her to raise, reminding her each time, with words brimming with pride, of the dignity of their house. Now she tied it using the limp lanyards. Without a breeze, the pennant lay slack and lacklustre in the shallow light. Yet it was hers and her son's, and the thought of it made her heart swell with poignancy and the pointless waste of it all. She flinched as she heard a noise like a wasp and something stung her ear.

"Git down!" Adam hauled her without ceremony from the lookout, bruising her knee against the stone as she half fell. He jerked her to her feet. "Here, take this." He thrust a rag at her. "For your ear." She put her hand to her left lobe and found her fingers stained with blood. "It'll heal," he said gruffly. "If ye live."

From the distant gunners came a shouted warning, then the riposte of the curtow with fire and smoke, followed almost instantaneously by a resounding complaint of wood and metal as the portcullis buckled under the impact.

"The lad's nowt to worry about now," Adam stated, swivelling to give orders to his men. "They have their mark, aright. Make ready." He hefted the war bow, placed his foot in the stirrup, and wound the two-handled crank until the string was taut on its notch. He checked the bolt, touched the lethal bodkin to his lips. "This one's for that whoreson," he grinned, slotting it on the bow. "I'd give a year in purgatory for a clear shot."

Behind the curtow the archers and serpentine gunners gathered, armed with polearms and axes, swords and mace. Thomas had remounted and now waited in the midst of his men. "Here it comes," Adam muttered as a gunner raised his arm. The gate disintegrated under the force of the blow, struck from its hinges and sending shards as thick as staves into the courtyard. A roar went up from the assailants, and they moved in a group, hooves beating time as the mounted men swept towards Beaumancote. Breathing slowly, Adam levelled his crossbow at the defenceless gatehouse mouth and Isobel followed suit, sweat prickling her neck and beneath her arms, conscious of the shaking that threatened to waste her aim.

"Ready..."

Sallet-lidded men were through the gate before she realised, and her finger jerked against the lever, letting loose a wayward bolt. She grabbed another from a cask, reloaded, fired, this time narrowly missing a man wielding a woodsman's axe. He looked up at the tower, saw her, made an obscene gesture. She shrank back, took a deep lungful of air to steady herself, loaded another bolt. Hollow thuds from below carried up the face of the tower. "They're going for the door!" Adam warned over his shoulder, cranking the windlass. Two village men hiked one of the cauldrons and between them emptied the contents over the crenel, accompanied by jugs of the stinking molten brew and a shower of flaming sticks. Screams bore witness to the effects, but within moments the attack on the door resumed with renewed ferocity. "Where is 'e?" Adam hissed through narrowed teeth, not taking his eyes from the gate. He ducked back as arrows cut the air from archers using the shelter of the gatehouse walls to target them. He raised his head, taking careful aim, and fired. An archer fell forward, but another replaced him. Hand-gunners still positioned outside the walls fired in rapid succession, forcing the defenders to take refuge behind the merlons. The second cauldron poured liquid metal and hot rocks on the men. The women risked arrows to lob flagons of scalding ale and piss and pots of rancid fats then returned to heat more without witnessing the effects of the first volley. A dance without music, wordless, grim.

The changing melody of blows warned that the door was giving way. "Show yerself!" Adam cursed, torn between the chance to take Thomas Lacey down and the imperative to defend the door.

"He's letting his men take the brunt of it," Isobel spat. "He will not show himself until the door's down and he can be handed his prize." Adam snorted his agreement, let loose a bolt at a hand-gunner, dropped his weapon, and sprinted to the stairs, drawing his sword as he ran.

The smell of sweat and the fumes of heated metal, fats and fear saturated the air. Thirst gripped her, the crusting lobe of her ear smarted, yet the sky seemed brighter, as if the sun were melting the high clouds. Raising her face, she listened for birdsong. There, from the thickets and rushes they sang, unconscious of the petty wars of men, and she wanted to lift her arms and embrace their song. Far, far away, it seemed, she heard the door splinter, the crash of horses on the cobbled yard, the ring of metal. From her purse she took her chaplet and drew it over her head, letting it lie against her breast: the jet cross and the acorn, the glass pilgrim token. She wanted to dissolve, find peace among the leaves and the birds. The air moved and above her head, licking the breeze, her pennant threw out its tongue. Isobel smiled.

She became aware of the changing song of battle, of fresh voices joining the chorus. The defenders on the tower roof – smeared in grease and with fingers scorched – had seen something and snatched chances to squinny south between merlons. Isobel pulled herself upright and drew the short sword from its scabbard. It shook in her hand. Some lord she made, a picture of chivalry and honour leading her people from the front to victory or defeat like Jeanne d'Arc. She laughed wearily and leaned over the battlements. Perhaps Thomas would become careless, and she could take one last shot at him before his men, like flies, stormed the tower. Bodies littered the courtyard, steel-coated men jerked like puppets in and out of her vision as they battled at the door. Adam would keep them back as long as he could, and then they would come for her. They would come for her.

A hubbub set up among the women. One of the men turned and pointed. "M'lady! There, by Coleby Wood…" Spent arrow shafts rolling under her feet, she shielded her eyes from the glare. It took a moment to focus and then… men. Men in harness riding hard from the direction of the demesne wood towards them. Her heart rattled unevenly, her mouth ashes. More men streamed behind them, a column snaking from the cover of the trees and spreading like glittering floodwater over the fields. Reinforcements. She could count the moments before the manor's defeat in the ticking of her pulse. Her end was sealed, but what of her son? A low moan escaped her lips.

But the great guns were being hauled to face the newcomers. A shot rang from one of the serpentines, then another, falling short and kicking up earth. Confused, Isobel watched as a group detached from the incoming swarm and bore down on the gunners, engulfing them before they could flee.

An assailant keeping watch from the gatehouse ran to the tower door shouting, and men broke away from the fight. Isobel spotted Thomas emerging into plain view, mounting his waiting horse and casting a look up at the tower. With newfound hope Isobel came to, aimed, but her bolt missed him by an arm's length, skimming the courtyard flags as his horse's shoes struck sparks from the stone. By now the newcomers had overrun the curtow, and the hand-gunners turned their weapons to their own defence. Another group broke away, heading directly for the shattered gate where Thomas had emerged beyond the manor walls and was riding as if the hellhound Barghest pursued him towards the smouldering village. "He's making for Barton!" Isobel exclaimed. Chaos broke out below as the remainder of his men, realising they had been abandoned, scrambled free of the melee and made a bid for the gate. Those not cut down from behind leaped onto their horses and attempted to follow Thomas along the only route not barred. Others made it as far as the church and could be seen begging sanctuary from the priest. He dithered, and the villagers who had taken shelter there made his mind up for him, bolting the door in their faces and leaving them to the mercy of the attacking horde.

"Who're they, m'lady?" a broad-hipped woman next to her asked. Searching for some identifying insignia, Isobel couldn't make out the smudge of the livery badge in the storm sweeping over those attempting to defend themselves. Adam appeared, battered but alive, from the base of the tower, making for the remains of the gatehouse. He materialised on the roof, scanning the scene and shouting something she couldn't hear as he pointed towards the village. Then she saw. Thomas came bolting back from the east, his helmet discarded, looking repeatedly over his shoulder as he galloped for the manor with only a handful of remaining men. He tore under the gatehouse arch and flung himself from his horse. With the other horsemen almost upon him, he would find no shelter in the defenceless manor, unless…

"Drew!" she screamed, racing across the roof and down the stairs and crashing into a soldier at the bottom. She lugged open the inner door. In the dim light pale faces turned towards her as children and the old clung in terror to each other. On the far side she made out Buena by the well head, hunched over a bundle, knife raised in defence. And there, searching among the faces, was Thomas. Isobel scrambled over bodies to get to her son before he could. She was too late.

Thomas spotted her. "Get over here!" he yelled, his hoarse voice breaking as he stumbled over rubble and legs towards Andrew and Buena, bloodied sword in hand. Isobel froze. He swept Buena's brandishing arm aside, reached down, and grabbed Drew by the scruff of his clothes. Swinging him around, Thomas dangled the whimpering child over the open mouth of the well. "*Now*, Isobel, or by God I'll kill the boy."

Heavy-legged, she lurched towards them. "Not my son! Thomas, whatever you do to me, spare him!"

She was within a few steps of him when Thomas said, "And why would I do that?" He loosened his grip slightly, and Drew jerked downwards. Thomas gave a satisfied grunt as horror swept over her. "The Earl's *brat* and his *whore*," he said, and released his grip.

"No!" Isobel screamed, launching herself towards them. She caught the hem of Drew's gown as it disappeared over the well edge. Feeling the fabric slip and tear, Isobel flung out her other hand and hauled him towards her, Drew's little legs fighting the empty space beneath him. An old woman grasped her waist and Isobel, grabbing fistfuls of linen, brought Drew into the safety of her arms.

Sobbing her relief as she clung to him, Isobel became conscious of other voices and shouted commands, and she swung around to find Thomas against the wall with Buena's knife to his throat. Someone said, "Back away, woman, leave him to us." Silhouetted figures crowded the doorway, blocking the light. One parted from the rest. Armoured and with sword in hand, he closed in on Buena. "Leave it!" he barked as she pressed the knife deeper, blood seeping around the point.

"Buena!" Isobel called, and the woman blinked at the sound of her voice and stepped back. Instantly, Thomas was surrounded and, one leg dragging, was towed to the door and out into the courtyard beyond.

From the vantage of his great bay horse, a visored knight dominated the clustered men around him. More men were in the process of dismounting and, from around the shattered buildings, the straggling remnants of Thomas's army were being driven into a knot. The mounted lord seemed to be searching the faces of those now gathering in the courtyard. Holding Drew tight to her, Isobel stepped from the shadow of the doorway. The man found what he sought, lifted his visor, and hooked it back. He looked down at her, and when she didn't speak said, "Do you not know me, Isobel?"

Isobel stared, her mouth opening although no sound came. Her senses numbed, she mumbled uncertainly, "Robert?"

He dropped from his saddle, landing solidly and tossing the reins to one of his men. "Is this all that remains of your people?" he asked.

"They… they are in the… the cellar," she stuttered, seeking the solidity of the wall at her back. He flashed a look at one of his men, who vanished inside the tower. "Why…? How…?"

"Later," he said. "There are matters we need to address without delay." Indicating the scraps of Thomas's retinue, he addressed his own. "I'll deal with them later. But you, my lord," he said, turning cold eyes on Thomas, "will be dealt with now."

Isobel watched as, hands bound behind him and without ceremony, Thomas was brought to the centre of the courtyard where all who had congregated could see him. "What are you going to do?" she asked.

"What should have been done a long time ago."

One pauldron hanging loose, his breastplate buckled, and his leg bleeding where Buena had attempted to sever his hamstring, Thomas looked shrunken but defiant.

Rob stood at the head of his knights, and it seemed to Isobel he had grown in himself and changed. His voice carried clearly to those listening. "Thomas Lacey—"

"*Lord* Lacey," Thomas corrected.

"Thomas Lacey, you stand accused of making grievous war on the King's subjects—"

"Accused by whom?" Thomas looked around until he found Isobel, sheet-white, staring back. "*Who* dares accuse me?"

"Isobel Fenton, daughter of Sir Geoffrey Fenton and lady of this manor, do you charge this man – Lord Thomas Lacey – of theft and destruction, and the raising of war against you and your property?"

Years slipped in her memory, and once again the gangly youth stood before her, hair the colour of yellow clay, skin reddened by the sun. A boy she had known her whole life, almost a brother. She pushed the memory aside. "Yes," she said, and heard herself condemn him in a single word.

Slowly, Thomas ran his eyes up and down her dishevelled form, and his lip writhed. "*That,*" he said, "has no authority."

Rob's mouth compressed into a rigid line. "Thereby, in making war on the King's subjects, you do so on the King's Grace, which is deemed treason—"

"By whose command?"

"… and punishable by death."

"None here is my equal," Thomas challenged. "I demand to be brought before a higher authority and judged by my peers."

"It is by your actions, Thomas Lacey, that you stand judged and condemned."

"By this rabble? By *you*? What makes you think *you* are *my* equal?" He spat at Robert's feet. Rob contemplated the pool of spittle glistening on the stone and then the man's face, distorted with contempt. They confronted each other eye to eye.

"By the power granted to me by our sovereign lord and King, and as Earl—" Thomas staggered as if struck, and Rob, grasping his arm, added in a low voice, "—and in memory of my brother, William Langton, may God give him eternal peace, and our noble father whom your kin slayed, I find you guilty." He let go of Thomas's arm and, stepping away, motioned to a sergeant standing nearby with his back to her. The man stamped up to Thomas, and only then did she identify him. With a stubby finger, Philip Taylor indicated Thomas should kneel among the fractured debris.

"You do this here – *now*?" Thomas looked around wildly to be met with uncompromising stares. "Isobel, would you have my death on your conscience?" he pleaded. "Remember your father; what would he do?"

Her mind spun back to the crack in the shutter through which she had spied Thomas kneeling at the Earl's feet – before she knew the Earl, before she had seen him eaten with grief and guilt – and she remembered the judgment passed by her father that allowed Thomas Lacey to live. She lifted her chaplet to her lips, kissed the cross and, silently asking forgiveness, said, "May God have mercy on your soul, Thomas."

His pale eyes widened, and then he nodded, slowly, as if it all made sense and, sinking to his knees, he dropped his chin to his chest. And it seemed to Isobel, as the head of Thomas Lacey rolled unevenly to a standstill, his blood filling the cracks between the rough stone flags, that in the moments before the sword fell, he smiled.

Chapter 39

ROBERT HERDED THE coloured glass into a small pile with the side of his boot. "The damage is not as bad as it looks. Lacey obviously wanted to spare himself the cost of repairs."

"He said he never wanted to live here – *it's not fit for a man of my degree*, or something, he said. I cannot remember." She used her sleeve to wipe her nose free of dust and tried not to sniff. Rob watched her from the corner of his eye.

"I think Lacey coveted you and Beaumancote and harboured the deep-seated rancour of his family, and in a shallow man, those are dangerous things."

"He wanted Beaumancote, perhaps, but not me." She rubbed her arm, stiff from unaccustomed use of the crossbow, releasing grit from her gambeson as she did so.

"Yes, he wanted *you*, Isobel." He saw her forehead crease. "When I heard you had agreed to marry him, I thought I had lost you, but then John Appleyard came bearing your seal saying Beaumancote was under attack, and I…" He shook his head, raising his face to the ceiling, the uneven light throwing shadows across his features. He exhaled. "The Duke sent me. I had few men at my command, but I would have come by myself if I had to. Those are mostly his men out there." He hesitated, then added, "His Grace holds you in high regard." He gave her a half-smile, which hurt her like knives because it was remote and without warmth. "Here, I have your father's matrix." He took it from his pouch and held it out to her, closer now than he had been since riding in that morning. "Isobel, why did you not come to me for help? Why wait until it was almost too late?"

She took the seal without answering and moved away from him on the pretext of washing her hands. "You are the Earl now," she stated, still coming to terms with it. "Then you must know about Felice, about... my mother?"

"I knew nothing of it until Sawcliffe handed me my brother's codicil entailing all land and properties to me. And this..." He held out a slim document, the three ribbons that once sealed it now dangling loose. Her brow corrugated. "You had no knowledge of it?"

"I saw it there; it was behind his son's toy horse and this..." Isobel held out the Earl's paternoster. "He wanted Andrew to have it."

Rob's eyes flicked to it and then to the chaplet around Isobel's neck. "I thought there was something familiar about your beads, but William had not used his for so long..." It was his turn to frown. "Anyway, his letter to me explained his pre-contract, asked forgiveness, and named me as his heir. I... could not accept it at first, but then I started to recall all the things he had said, the things he had done over the years, and it made sense. *You* made sense. He also named Andrew as his heir should I die without issue." He looked at her. "Isobel, even if Andrew were his son, he could not legitimately inherit the title."

"Oh." Isobel paused, thinking. "I think he considered we had made vows to one another; would that make Drew his legitimate heir if his marriage to Felice was void?"

Rob's expression froze. "And... did you?"

"I... no... well, yes, he did – and he wanted me to; but I didn't, I couldn't."

Ripples of tension flowed through him and lodged as a tic in his cheek. "Why not?"

Why did he think? He surely must know why not, but it irked her to say it, so she said instead, "Does it matter?"

Shoulders hunched, he swung away. "Yes, it matters. To me."

"Why?" She glared at his back. "Why does it matter whether we exchanged vows? What difference does it make now?"

"*Now?* What about the oath we made between *us*, Isobel? Did that mean nothing to you?"

Her temper, born of days of relentless anxiety, flared. "Of course it did, but then you… you broke it."

He swivelled to face her, hair in disarray, his eyes consumed with anger. "What are you talking about? I have *never* broken my promise to you!"

"How can you say that? You are *married!*"

He opened his mouth, changed his mind, and gradually straightened his back. "How is your wife?" Isobel enquired calmly when he failed to supply her with an answer.

"My *wife*? I have no wife." Then, "I spent some time abroad on the Duke's business. When I returned, the King pressed me to the match, but I made some excuse or other, and then William… died." He regarded her gravely. "I could not marry her, Isobel; I could not marry someone I do not love."

Later, when Isobel had seen Drew fed and together they bathed the filth from their skin and hair, Rob returned from the village smelling of smoke and ashes. Grime lined the creases of his face, making him look older and more like his brother. While water was being drawn and heated in which he might bathe, Isobel gave him what food they had. "It is not much."

He dipped stale bread in warm ale. "It is more than the villagers have."

"What little Thomas left us I have given my people. I could not let them starve; they have lost so much."

"Not all the houses have been destroyed. Those without means have been given shelter by their more fortunate neighbours. It is strange how such merciless acts by some can bring out the charity in others." He picked up another piece of bread, but it seemed almost too much effort to dunk it in the ale and he ended up crumbling it, too tired to eat. "I will suggest restitution is made from Lacey's estate before he is declared attainted. The Duke will be keen to see justice done and will choose his moment to broach the subject with the King." Isobel cut thin slivers of bacon and put them in front of him. "Some good news, though; the miller you asked about has been found alive. The clothes were burned from his back, but he took shelter in the church. He has spent the last two days thinking his children were dead. He was speechless when he saw them unharmed."

"And… Jack?"

"No, not Jack. His body has been taken to the church with those of other villagers who perished – not as many as you feared, thanks be to God – and treated with due dignity. He gave the seal to John Appleyard before being caught on the banks. John said Jack acted as decoy so he could get away. He was a brave lad and loyal. I am sorry, Isobel."

Balancing on her knee, Drew appeared none the worse for their ordeal. Clean and well-fed, he bashed his hands up and down on the cloth-covered table, blowing bubbles and babbling. Rob watched him for a few moments, unreadable, then looked away. He ate a piece of bacon. "The rest of the men who died will have to be buried in some haste. Animals will start scavenging, and the villagers will not allow the enemy to be laid out in the church with their kin." Drew had found a cube of bread and was trying to feed Isobel with it. He laughed, and she kissed his fingers. She caught Rob frowning at them, then he continued, "I will ensure you are also fully compensated and send masons from the castle to get started on repairs immediately. I do not expect there to be further trouble, but the manor must be protected."

Why was he talking like his brother? Where had this distance between them come from? There, that surreptitious glance at the baby. He had barely looked at Drew since returning from the village and had not once asked how he fared other than to ensure he was unharmed. Now Drew picked up a spoon and banged it enthusiastically on the table. Robert pushed his chair back and stood abruptly. "I will take my bath," he said.

Later still, Robert sat in her father's furred gown before the fire, absorbed in his own thoughts. Moth and Drew played their own peculiar game with a ball, and he watched them without expression. Isobel approached and kneeled next to the chair, as she had done so many times when her father sat in it, and placed her hand on his arm. He looked at it, then covered it with his own. With his thumb, he stroked the back of her hand rhythmically, but he was absent somehow, and silent.

Isobel followed the movement of his thumb before speaking. "The Earl never blamed you for leaving, Rob, nor for any dissension between you." She waited for a response, but he didn't reply. "He loved you to the end; he trusted you." She paused. "And he would want me to give you this." She removed her hand from beneath his, leaving him to find the Earl's ring she had retrieved from Arthur. "This is yours by right, now." He picked it up and turned it over so the lovers faced him. "Robert, the Earl loved me and treated me with great kindness, but I was never his; and he thought Andrew his own son, but he was not his father." She rose, leaned forward, and kissed his forehead.

At the door, she turned around. Rob had covered his face with one hand, the ring clutched in the other, and his whole body shook. As she deliberated whether to go back to comfort him, Drew crawled over to the chair and, pulling himself upright, patted Rob's knee with his chubby hand. Running his sleeve across his eyes, Rob looked down at the child. Drew chortled his rolling laugh, wrinkling his nose as he smiled up at his father. For a moment, Rob didn't respond, then he bent down and carefully picked him up. They regarded each other for a solemn moment in which Isobel held her breath. Then he brought Drew to his chest, buried his face in his son's neck, and made a small noise like the sigh of someone letting go.

Author Notes

'... in the ninth year of king Edward, being the year of our Lord 1469, there arose a great disagreement between the king and his kinsman, Richard, the most illustrious earl of Warwick; which was not allayed without the shedding of blood of many persons.'

Croyland Chronicle, Second Continuation, Part IV

FROM THE MIDDLE of the fifteenth century, England became drawn into an internecine struggle for control of crown and government. Over the previous hundred years, major conflict had been concentrated elsewhere as France and England battled for supremacy in Europe. With England's ultimate defeat and withdrawal from the continent, reduced incomes and sense of esteem focused the minds of the social elite on their political and economic situation on home turf.

England might have weathered the storm of defeat in France had its own ruler maintained a handle on his realm. As it was, Henry VI's grip on the fluid political situation slipped, along with his mental capacities, leaving the country without strong leadership at the highest level. As with any political vacuum, the resulting uncertainty led to a power struggle between the most senior members of the aristocracy and their kin: the Dukes of York and Somerset. In a period when land, offices and patronage were the foundation of wealth and power, any reduction in these could result in the destruction of individuals and their affinities. So, when York and Somerset vied for power they did so not merely for personal gain, but in response to threats to the security and future of their family and their wider affinities and, ultimately, their country.

Nor can the importance of blood lines and the right to rule, God's purpose, vendetta and personal characteristics be underestimated. There is no simple explanation of this highly complex situation and much has been written about the causes of the bitter struggle for power named the Wars of the Roses by a later generation. As with any civil conflict, memories run deep, with wounds and slights becoming embedded in the personal, regional and national psyche.

The history reflected in *The Tarnished Crown* series begins some years before the opening chapter. The Duke of York, his son and their kin were slain at the battle of Wakefield in December, 1460, his memory afterwards humiliated by the exhibition of his head, topped by a paper crown. It was left to his eldest son, Edward, Earl of March, to uphold family honour and power. There could be no half-measures – it was fight or die. Supported by his cousin, Richard Neville, Earl of Warwick, Edward went on to win the crown as Edward IV, the summation of his father's hope. But it left an embittered, factionalised, and defeated enemy, an anointed former king, his determined queen, and their heir, still at large. The crown of England might have been won by Edward of York, but the battle was far from over. The lives of Isobel Fenton and other fictional characters in *The Tarnished Crown* series are unique, but the situations in which they found themselves were not. Memories ran deep and past slights deeper still, and it is into this toxic mix that Isobel, the Earl and his family are thrown.

Historical Notes

NOT FAR FROM Doncaster, close to the Great North road leading up and down the spine of the country, is the small south Yorkshire town of Tickhill. Once dominated by its great multi-sided tower, the castle's motte and bailey would have been a spectacular reminder of local lordship. This is where I have placed the fictional Earl and the Langton family whose sphere of influence stretched across the land like fingers and felt the political pulse.

Standing on top of the near naked motte and looking out over the miles of land, it takes a short leap of the imagination to envisage a time when social and political influence depended on the personal relationships between king and lord, noble and knight, gentleman and yeoman. This interdependency affected all areas and levels of society from the earl in his castle, merchants in the towns, to the labourer in the field and no more so than in the second half of the fifteenth century. Social, economic and political wheels turned and turned about and who knew, when Lady Fortune spun the wheel, who would rise and who would fall?

While I have fictionalised the ownership and events at Tickhill castle for the sake of story, its very real history is no less tumultuous. Starting out as a motte and bailey earthwork in the eleventh century, its construction was instigated by Roger de Busli, a Norman magnate, and became the principal castle of the honour of Blyth. A stone curtain wall around the bailey was added in the early twelfth century, but it wasn't until the end of the century that Henry II and his successors built the stone keep in its polygonal form and further fortified the castle. Eleanor of Aquitaine had the bridge and chapel built, and their son, John, kept Tickhill as one of his main strongholds. It came into the ownership of the Duchy of Lancaster when it was granted to John of Gaunt by his father, Edward III. But it is perhaps as one of Richard of Gloucester's lordships that Tickhill holds most interest for those interested in the Wars of the Roses, and one of the reasons why I have taken the liberty to create a family whose Yorkist connections tie them firmly to the town.

Through *The Tarnished Crown* series I have returned to my historical roots and a lifelong and enduring passion for the second half of the fifteenth century – the years of upheaval we now refer to as the Wars of the Roses. I have drawn on contemporary sources and eye-witness accounts, manorial records, Court records, Pardon Rolls, letters and wills. I have scoured primary pictorial sources and artefacts, trodden the paths of our forefathers, walked ramparts and surveyed castle ruins. I have talked to other historians, archaeologists, military and weaponry experts, visited museum collections, and watched specialist reenactors. I have experimented with medieval recipes for spiced ales and scoured modern European cuisine to find the remnants of medieval fare. I grow native plants that would be recognised by our ancestors, have used Castile soap made to a medieval recipe as the nearest example of the hard soaps used by late fifteenth-century nobility. I have researched rabbit warrens and dovecots, wall fruit and exotic imported fare of the period. I grow and harvest the saffron so highly valued at the time. I have danced (badly) medieval dances and listened to its music played on authentic instruments. A lifetime of research and experience has fed my senses and imagination and yet I have merely skimmed the surface of what there is to know about this enigmatic period. The search continues.

Acknowledgements

In writing this book for over a decade I have incurred debts of gratitude to many people. There have been those right there from the beginning – my family and close friends – without whose support, enduring patience and infinite wisdom this book would not have been created. For my husband and friend, Richard, whose depth of historical knowledge is equalled by the breadth, and who readily, *joyously*, shares his expertise on all things military, architectural and naval. Our daughters, who have grown up with these books, and who continue to indulge their mother's obsession with great good humour as I write the series. My mother, who let me watch historical TV series when still a tot and who bought me the Ladybird *Warwick The Kingmaker* and a library of books. My father, for taking me to every medieval edifice I could find and who guided me through my first forays in fiction writing. Little did they know where it would all lead. My friend and grammar guru, author S.L. Russell, who unstintingly takes the time from her own writing projects to read mine, and Alison King, whose unique skills and specialist knowledge continues to substantiate my research.

I wish to thank those who so kindly read and endorsed *Sun Ascendant* – my friend and historical novelist Elizabeth Chadwick, on whose candid opinion I can always rely, and Matthew Lewis, writer, medieval historian and chair of The Richard III Society.

In addition, I thank the editors and proof-readers, the artists and all those involved in honing and polishing the manuscript, including professional proof-reader Julie Frederick, and especially my wonderful editor Liz Carter at Resolute Books.

I am indebted to the countless historians, reenactors, medieval specialists, archivists and museum curators, the enthusiastic attendants at heritage sites and knowledgeable church wardens, all of whom have indulged my quest for knowledge.

Nor can I neglect the many historians, writers, and academics whose research and analysis – condensed and attainable through their own books and papers - have saved me many years of work. It is impossible to represent the value they have collectively added to unearthing and understanding the complex historical record of the period. You are too numerous to mention here and, even if I did, there would be many more I have unjustly neglected.

Foremost and lastly, this book is dedicated to my mother, Mary, whose infectious passion for literature and art was the foundation upon which I built my own, and whose love and support never wavered, nor her light dimmed.

Glossary of Terms

Alaunt – a type of dog used for the hunt. Medium to large, fleet of foot, heavy-headed, and ferocious, it was used for larger game and baiting.

Allée – in garden design, a (usually) straight path lined either side with trees or large shrubs to create an avenue.

All-night – a call made or a bell rung to sound a sort of curfew in the evening (varying between 8 and 10pm). A light, all-night meal might be left for the lord's sustenance.

All Souls' Day – 2 November.

Arras – a woven hanging (tapestry) of very great value associated with Arras, a town in the Duchy of Burgundy, now northern France.

Aumbry (ambry) – a recessed wall cupboard.

Ave – the (often) smaller beads used in groups of ten – a decade – or five, when repeating the Ave Maria or similar prayers using a chaplet or paternoster. See *beads*.

Ballock dagger – a dagger with a pommel resembling male genitalia.

Bards – an ornament or armour for the neck, breast, or flank of a horse.

Barghest – a huge, ghostly black dog of Yorkshire and Northern folklore.

Barmkin – (north country and Scottish) a small, defendable enclosure.

Beads – a set of beads of varying number used for 'bidding' prayers and personal devotions. Beads could be made from anything and everything, be simple or extravagant, have markers dividing them (aves and gauds), be many or few, terminate in a tassel or cross, be in a single line or circular. Beads might be worn as a necklace, around the wrist or waist, or carried in a purse or pouch. They were an essential part of everyday devotional life as a Christian.

Bevor – armour; used with a sallet, a bevor protects the neck and chin.

Blanchet – very coarse woollen cloth.

Braies – (long, medium, and short) the medieval equivalent of men's boxer shorts.

Burgher – a town-dweller of standing, often a merchant, who holds land in a town and might be trusted with civic responsibilities.

Burgundian gown – very similar to the houppelande, both types might have deep cuffs and a folded back collar in a contrasting fur or fabric. Low v-necked, high-waisted with tightly fitting sleeves.

Buttery – an area used to store butts of alcohol (from which we get "butler"). Often associated with the pantry (overseen by the pantler).

Caltrop – a multi-spiked weapon designed to present a spike whichever way up it landed and used to impede or wound horses and people.

Caranets – highly decorative roundels or squares made of silver or gold and decorated with gemstones and/or enamels. Used singularly as jewellery and in linked groups on collars of estate by men and women.

Chaperon – elaborate headgear worn by men, often with long 'tails' that could be draped around the neck and shoulders. Gradually lost favour towards the end of the century.

Chaplet – a short set of beads of varying number for saying personal devotional prayers (chaplets).

Chewit/chewette – little sweet, savoury, or mixed pies filled with meat, cheese, peas, or fruits and probably similar to the mince pies we know today.

Chouchou – French for cabbage.

Clarry – a sweetened, spiced wine.

Cockeburr – agrimony (botanical name) widely used in medieval medicine for healing and as a sedative.

Cog – a broad-bottomed ship used extensively for transport and cargo.

Coif – a close-fitting cap, used by men and women, made of linen (or similar) and worn by itself or under other headgear.

Constable – in terms of a castle, the constable was responsible for the maintenance of order and the soldiery retained for its protection.

Cott (cot) – a small house for agricultural workers (cotter/cottager) with an enclosed area for livestock and possibly a barn.

Counterpoint – former name for a counterpane.

Court Baron – a manorial court held to, among other things, resolve disputes between a lord's free tenants.

Cranage – a levy on the use of cranes for loading and unloading goods.

Crenel – the low sections on battlements between merlons.

Cresset – a metal basket or container, filled with flammable material, suspended from a ceiling or mounted on a pole to provide light.

Cuir bouilli – leather which has been rendered tough and very resilient through a process of soaking and heating.

Cuisse – armour; plate of metal, leather, or quilted material to protect the thigh.

Dagged – a toothed decorative edge used with hangings.

Demesne – in feudal terms, the land retained by a lord for his own use rather than that rented to tenants.

Didder – (dialect) to shake, shiver, be jumpy.

Doublet – worn over a shirt by men, a sleeved or sleeveless garment of varying quality, decoration, and fabric, belted at the waist to give the appearance of a short skirt of fabric. Doublets became increasingly short throughout the period, especially for young men.

Douce powder – a (sweet) powder made up of different spices according to personal taste for flavouring drinks and food.

Dun brown – sandy light brown.

Dwale – a medieval medicinal drink for pain relief and for inducing deep sleep. Made to recipes handed down from mother to daughter, master physician to apprentice, it might contain (among other things) lettuce, henbane, opium, belladonna, bile (gall), and various other herbs. It was understood that dwale-induced sleep might result in death if the patient could not be roused.

Ell – a measurement of length roughly from the fingertip to the shoulder of a stretched arm. Mostly used to measure cloth.

Embrasure – a splayed opening in a parapet or wall; an arrow loop in a merlon.

Espiouress – a female spy.

Fardel – a small pack or parcel.

Feoffee – a person entrusted with freehold property (a fief) held for the benefit of the owner.

Fewterers – a keeper of dogs (especially greyhounds) for the hunt.

Fleam – a knife-like tool used in bloodletting.

Gambeson – a quilted, padded jack(et) used as an additional (or the only) defensive layer in combat and for warmth. It could be made of fabric, boiled leather (cuir bouilli), or a combination of materials.

Gaud – a marker bead in sets of beads making up a chaplet or paternoster. Often larger, decorated (as in "gaudy"), or a different colour or texture from the groups of aves.

Glaikit – (dialect) stupid, senseless.

Gleet – a sexually transmitted disease.

Gong-farmer – a highly profitable occupation of gathering human and animal excrement for fertilising fields.

Gonne/gonners – a gun/gunners.

Grains of paradise – a small, brown, popcorn-shaped spice native to West Africa valued for its peppery, gingery, citrusy flavour when ground and added to sweet or savoury dishes and drinks.

Grayne – fine woollen cloth, often dyed red.

Green cheese – freshly made cheese a bit like cottage cheese.

Groat – money, a coin equivalent to four pence.

Guising – dressing up in masks and/or costumes.

Hennin – women's headgear in a short and blunt or long cone shape. Worn over a fabric under-cap and covered in a rich material. It hid the hair entirely and might be worn with or without a veil. Later versions might be split into horns and known as a butterfly hennin. These might be heavily jewelled or decorated.

Hood – worn by all classes and both sexes depending on the weather and the situation.

Hose – single leg or joined with a gusset, men and women's stockings/tights. Some were footed, that is, had a shaped foot, whereas some were more like leggings.

Houppelande – a very fashionable loose-fitting gown, belted at the waist (for men) or underneath the bust (for women). The sleeves were fitted at the shoulder but voluminous lower down. A gown perfectly suited to display the wealth of the wearer in the sheer quantity as well as quality of the cloth used.

Hurdy-gurdy – looking a bit like a violin on its side, a hurdy-gurdy is played using a hand-cranked wheel that rubs against the strings as they are depressed.

Hypocras – a fragrant spiced wine often accompanied by wafers, sweetmeats, and 'banqueting stuffes'.

Jetty – the upper floor/s of a building built out over, and overhanging, the lower.

Jongleurs – entertainers, often travelling groups but sometimes attached to noble or royal courts. Musicians, jugglers, actors, acrobats.

Kendal – a coarse woollen cloth, often dyed green, associated with Kendal, Cumbria.

Ket – (northern colloquial) rotten meat.

Kirtle – the undergarment or kirtle was usually made of a contrasting colour and fabric and was meant to be seen beneath the outer gown.

Lady Day – 25 March.

Lent – an extremely important period in the Christian calendar lasting from Ash Wednesday to Easter Sunday (40 days) in which prayer and a restricted diet played a central role in the preparation for Easter itself.

Luce – a pike (fish).

Manchet – fine, white wheat bread.

Marcher lords – lords with landholdings and responsibilities on the English-Welsh or English-Scottish borders, ostensibly to represent the English Crown and maintain peace along troubled borders.

Maslin – a coarse bread made from mixed cereal grains, ground peas, or similar.

Melee – a confused group of people, or a free-for-all in battle with little overall control.

Merlon – the 'teeth' seen on castle battlements.

Michaelmas – feast of St Michael celebrated on 29 September. It was common practice to mark important events such as marriages or the exchange of contracts, tenancies, etc., on, or with reference to, feast days in the Christian calendar.

Midden – a dump for everyday kitchen, domestic, and garden rubbish. An invaluable source of primary evidence for archaeologists!

Mignon – (French) delicate, pretty.

Misericorde – a long, thin-bladed knife used to kill a downed man on the battlefield. From the French word miséricorde (mercy) the narrow blade could penetrate the narrowest gap in armour. Not to be confused with a misericord, which was a ledged, hinged seat in a church choir stall for support when sitting or standing and often highly decorated. Think in terms of 'mercy' for those standing for long periods of prayer.

Mullion – the vertical stone, brick, or wood element between panes of a window or lancets.

Mural hall/passage – a passage built within the wall of a castle or fortified building.

Murder hole (meurtrière) – an opening in the ceiling of a gatehouse or similar structure of control through which missiles could be fired at attackers.

Murrey – a burgundy colour. Murrey and blue were the colours adopted by the House of York.

Numbles – properly, the edible viscera of animals, but could be used as an archaic reference to men's genitalia.

Nuncheons – a light meal taken around noon.

Palfrey – a lighter-weight horse, smooth of gait, used for riding by high-status women and children as well as men.

Pantler – the person in charge of the pantry where bread and similar foodstuffs were kept.

Pated hanging – a fabric hanging with a decorative edge.

Paternoster – from the Lord's Prayer (Pater Noster), using a set of beads of varying number but often 10, 50, or 150 beads, with gauds or dividing markers, for saying prayers.

Pattens – an overshoe of wood or leather to raise feet out of the mud. Clogs are an example of this.

Pauldron – plate armour covering the shoulder.

Peter's Pence – the plant we now call honesty.

Pleached – tree branches (often lime/linden) grown together to form an avenue.

Pleasance – a formal, fair garden.

Points (point) – the (often) metal pointed end of a tie or lace used to make the threading or the lacing of a garment easier. We use them now on the end of shoelaces.

Pole – (also perch and rod) a unit of measurement equivalent to five and a half yards.

Poleyn – armour, shaped to protect the knee.

Posset – a nourishing, warming, comforting drink made by combining cream or milk with ale or wine, adding sugar or honey, often egg, and flavouring with spices (think of eggnog). Now made as a thicker version and served as a dessert.

Pricker/scout/stalker – someone sent to gain information, especially in covert terms, of battle lines and enemy whereabouts.

Pricket – a stemmed candle holder, more often with a spike with which to secure the candle.

Prie-dieu – (furniture) a kneeling surface used in personal devotions with an upright on which to rest hands or a book.

Quarrel – a crossbow bolt (a short, thick arrow).

Quarter-curtow – a type of field cannon.

Rapere – rape – from to seize, carry off

Reeve – a manorial office. A reeve oversaw the work undertaken on manorial land.

Rondel dagger – a well-balanced weapon commonly carried by soldiers of middling status, knights, and merchants.

Rosary – prayers of a number of forms said using a string of beads of varying number.

Rouncey – an everyday horse used for riding, occasionally as a pack animal, or as a war horse.

Sallet – armour; a helmet with a fixed visor (used with a bevor) that covers the entire head.

Sard – an orange-coloured semi-precious stone often used in the making of intaglios from antiquity onwards.

Scot's pint/joug – three pints (of ale or beer).

Serpentine – an early type of long-bore cannon used in the field, as a siege weapon, and in defence.

Shawms – a loud, rather penetrating oboe-like instrument. Useful in crowded great halls or in street processions.

Shewel men – scarecrows.

Shift/smock – a linen, silk, or later cotton undergarment worn next to the skin to protect the kirtle and outer gown from sweat.

Smatter/jangle – gossip.

Solar – a private (bed) chamber for the lord and his family.

Squinny – to squint at, to spy.

St Andrew, feast of – 30 November.

Steward – a manorial office; the senior officer retained to manage the manor and estates and to represent the lord in his absence. Often drawn from gentry, the position required a good degree of education and management skills and was endowed with a great deal of trust by the lord.

Stooks – sheaves of grain stood on end together to keep the heads dry prior to gathering.

Surcoat – a loose, sleeveless outer garment worn by both sexes, later by men to cover armour, often bearing the colours and insignia of the wearer or their lord.

Sweetmeats – delicacies made with honey or sugar such as small cakes, wafers, or preserved and embellished fruits.

Syncope – an illness defined by fainting or loss of consciousness; 'failure of the heart's action'.

Table dormant – a table made for permanent use (i.e. not disassembled like a trestle table), most often reserved for the use of the lord.

Tables – another form of backgammon.

Tawny – an orange colour; think of tawny marmalade.

Trenail (treenail, trennel) – a wooden peg used in building to secure pieces of wood together.

Trencher – a flat object on which food is served. Often made of bread or wood. Bread trenchers could be eaten at the end of the meal or given to the servants or as alms to the poor.

Van/vanguard – the leading part of a battle formation, ahead of the main (middle) and rear (back).

Villein – a feudal tenant subject to a manor or lord to whom he paid dues or gave service in return for land.

Wagtail – euphemism for a woman of loose morals.

Waites (waits) – a band of town musicians employed for civic entertainment. Thought to have had watchmen duties in earlier periods, this aspect became secondary to their role as musicians.

Weld – bright yellow from the plant *reseda luteola*.

About Resolute Books

We are an independent press representing a consortium of experienced authors, professional editors and talented designers producing engaging and inspiring books of the highest quality for readers everywhere. We produce books in a number of genres including historical fiction, crime suspense, young adult dystopia, memoir, Cold War thrillers, and even Jane Austen fan fiction!

Find out more at resolutebooks.co.uk

for the joy of reading

Printed in Great Britain
by Amazon